STING OF THE SCORPION

STING OF THE SCORPION

A NOVEL BY
ROBERT MARCUM

Bookcraft
Salt Lake City, Utah

Library of Congress Catalog Card Number: 93-72100
ISBN 0-88494-889-7

First Printing, 1993

Printed in the United States of America

With the completion of Scorpion I dedicate the entire Daniels trilogy to the men and women of today willing to do the right thing in morally challenging times. From the housewife who fights against drinking and driving, to the "whistleblower" who calls his company to account for their internal corruption and greed; from the state or national leader who is often forced to swim in politically rancid waters but refuses to drink, to the soldier who fights, and often dies, in faraway places defending the rights and freedoms of others.

And last but not least, I dedicate the story of Scorpion to the hundreds, even thousands, who have given their lives in the fight against the international drug trade Scorpion attests to. From the growing fields of South America and Asia to the cities and small towns around the world the battle against the kingpins and overlords of the drug world goes on daily. Scorpion is intended to recognize the sacrifices of those who actively oppose this evil. May God bless them in their continuing fight.

*And their torment was as the torment
of a scorpion, when he striketh a man.*

*And in those days shall men seek death,
and shall not find it; and shall desire
to die, and death shall flee from them. . . .*

*For their power is in their mouth, and in
their tails: for their tails were like
unto serpents . . . and with them they do
hurt.*

*And the rest of the men which were not killed
by these plagues yet repented not of the
works of their hands, that they should not
worship devils, and idols of gold, and
silver . . .*

*Neither repented they of their murders, nor
of their sorceries, nor of their fornication,
nor of their thefts.*

(Revelation 9:5,6, 19–21.)

*"The power of Cosa Nostra has four components: human
resources—literally, man power; the power of violence; political power; and financial power. Whether employed singly or in
conjunction, the manipulation of such variegated power makes
it not only anti-state—able to put its own authority against
that of a democratic society; state within a state—complete
with government, army, financial resources and territorial
competence in which it operates with relative impunity; but
even to be the state: Cosa Nostra has been represented in
local and national government, in the judiciary, the police
forces, in public corporations, on the directorial boards of
banks, hospitals, and business enterprises."*

*(Alison Jamieson, "The Modern Mafia: Its Role
and Record,"* Journal of the Center for Security
and Conflict Studies, *September 1989, p. 2.)*

Day One
November 13, 1997

CHAPTER 1

2:00 A.M.—Las Vegas, Nevada

Kentucky Trayco hit the button on the two-way radio and spoke quietly, checking with each of his men, making sure that voice contact was clear. Caesar's was a big place, and watching all the exits wasn't going to be easy. They had worked too long and hard for this day and he wasn't about to have it screwed up by something as small as a fuzzy transmission.

After completing the checks, he relaxed a little, letting his large frame settle into the white leather seat of the limo. The stretch Mercedes was loaded with extra-special goodies beyond the telephone, fax, and high quality sound system that his other limos had. They were for clients; this one was Kenny Trayco's office, often his home. In front of him was a bank of three television monitors by which he could keep an eye on his work—the protection of the world's elite rich who came to Vegas to spend their millions without the worry of being bothered by fans, enemies, or other parasites who looked to hang on them like old clothing. Kentucky Trayco was a bodyguard. A highly paid, very professional bodyguard who owned his own protection agency.

Trayco watched one of the monitors in the console in front of him. One of the beauties of the system was that he could receive signals from a hotel's own surveillance units, giving him an eye to areas of the Palace he otherwise might not be able to keep tabs on. Through a series of negotiations with the major hotels on the strip, who perceived that the protection of high rollers such as Trayco represented was good for business, Kenny had received permission to place his own system's transmitters inside the hotels' surveillance consoles. The one at Caesar's was sending a clear, distinct picture of the halls outside the hotel's executive suites, private gambling rooms, and the very private conference room his target was using. Unfortunately there were no surveillance cameras beyond the conference room door, so Kenny had found it necessary to make special arrangements to see and hear the target's conversation.

Trayco was on a different assignment from those he was used to, but it was one he had accepted with relish.

Trayco had come to know a man named Daniels, Jeremiah Daniels. In Vietnam, Daniels had been a transport chopper pilot, a very good one, but he had been shot down behind enemy lines. Trayco, a leader of a marine special operations group, had just finished knocking out an enemy ammunitions dump with high explosives and was in the vicinity when he got the message to check out the downed chopper for survivors. He ran headlong into Daniels just after he and his copilot had tripped a mine and nearly blown themselves into the next world. Trayco and his men carried them through treacherous country to a pickup point from which they were flown to a field medical unit. Daniels lost an eye, his buddy lost the use of his legs. Both of them were lucky to be alive at all.

Two years later Trayco left the service under pressure. His commanding officer, a young hero with a hunger for glory and a commission bought by his wealthy father, was getting too many under his command killed as a result of his bad decisions. He had ordered Trayco and his men into a suicide mission. Trayco obeyed, but he forced the young lieutenant to go along. The kid had never really seen combat—not up close and natural, as the men had whom he was driving like cattle. He froze at the first sign of danger, and Trayco had to beat him to make him move and keep him alive. By the time they got back the young lieutenant had been humiliated in front of his troops and had sworn vengeance. His last words as Trayco dumped him in his quarters questioned Kentucky's parentage, at which Trayco broke the lieutenant's nose.

Kentucky Trayco was the most decorated man in the marines elite special operations forces. The corps couldn't boot him out, so they forced him into "early" retirement. The lieutenant had his revenge, but he didn't enjoy it long. Another of his decisions brought enemy fire on his own position and he was pushing up daisies the day Trayco left Saigon for the States. Unfortunately so were ten of his men.

A return to civilian life was difficult for Kentucky. He had been forced into the army by a judge who told him he had two choices: prison or the service. Knowing what had happened to some of his friends who opted for jail time, he took the service. The marines trained him to kill people. It was all the training he had. When he found himself on the streets again he gravitated toward that which he knew. The result was a fight in which he nearly killed a man, for which he ended up in front of another judge. There was only one person he knew he could call on for help: Jeremiah Daniels.

Daniels had been sent home after the loss of his eye, but he hadn't forgotten Kenny. Other than the weekly letter Trayco received from his mother, letters from Jeremiah Daniels were the only mail Trayco ever received with any regularity. Although he appreciated it, Kentucky never wrote back. His writing wasn't too good and penning a letter took him a long time. Too long.

But he hadn't forgotten Daniels's promise of help if it should ever be needed. When Trayco was thrown in jail, he phoned Jeremiah Daniels. Daniels took the next plane to L.A. from Las Vegas, where he had set up shop as a broker for an international firm, and went before the judge, asking that Trayco be released into his custody. They returned to Vegas on the next flight.

Through one of his wealthy clients, Daniels got Trayco a job at one of the hotels. Trayco got his act together and began building a reputation as a man who knew how to ensure people's safety. Five years later he had his own thriving business. He owed it all to Jeremiah.

Now Daniels was the one in need of help.

Trayco and Jerry Daniels had been through a lot together, good and bad. Through a strange set of circumstances over the last fifteen years Daniels had ended up as the nation's drug czar. He wasn't a politician. In fact, he had no desire for public life. But after the death of his first wife from cancer, he had met a brilliant and beautiful attorney with the Securities and Exchange Commission who was out to nail his hide to the wall for allegedly defrauding his clients by embezzling money from their accounts. In showing he was innocent, he and the attorney had uncovered a much bigger fraud: one in which terrorist drug money was being laundered through Daniels's firm. They had both nearly lost their lives fighting that one before digging up the evidence necessary to put the terrorists out of business.

As a sidelight, they fell in love and got married.

Michaelene Freeman, the beautiful attorney, was the daughter of one of the few honest politicians left in Washington in 1989. As senator from Wyoming, James Freeman was head of the powerful Senate Intelligence Committee and a potential candidate for the presidency, but in 1994 he opted for drug czar.

After the fight against communism was won and he became disillusioned with Congress and their inept handling of the national debt, James Freeman decided to change venues and take on the next enemy—the national crisis in drug use and its proliferation.

Freeman felt that drugs were the country's number one enemy, and that if something were not done soon they would destroy the next generation. To him it didn't matter how big the deficit, how bad the economy. Drugs were killing people. Drugs were becoming big business, and this threatened to destroy the very fiber of ethical and moral values in the country. The illicit drug trade had to be eliminated. In his last year in the Senate he was able to get the Democratic president to reinstate the position of drug czar; then he promptly retired to fill that position.

James Freeman did his job well. In the process he stepped on a lot of toes. Using his influence, he was able to get several new laws passed that gave drug enforcement agencies more powers. Now there were greater penalties connected with drug-related crimes, including life in prison without opportunity for parole in cases in which one person caused the death of another while involved in the sale or distribution of drugs on the street.

In addition the czar was given power to authorize investigation into the sources of income and the tax situation of anyone suspected of drug-related activities, and could request such information from any public administration office, as well as from a public or private banking or credit institution. Unless the suspected person could prove the legitimate source of his assets they could be impounded and subsequently confiscated. If illegal activities were proven, the guilty party for the rest of his life lost all rights to hold public office or serve in a civil service capacity. All rights to work in the banking, brokerage, and other credit institutions were also denied. If the institution for which the guilty party worked was also proven guilty, immediate loss of license and certification was directed.

Finally the czar was given broad powers to work with and use the military for interdiction purposes. Freeman felt that the nation was at war and the military was needed to stop her enemies from sending their product into the country. He equated it with allowing Hitler to sell his automobiles and other goods in the United States so that he could amass the wealth necessary to buy tanks to kill U.S. soldiers. To win the war you had to crush the financial foundation on which the enemy was building the war machine.

Half a dozen banks were put out of business for laundering money. He used military resources to stop flights and shipments, severely curtailing production and sales in the United States. He worked feverishly for international cooperation and was instrumental in involving the United States in an international task force for the discovery and destruction of all elements of the drug trade.

What the task force discovered was the involvement of the world's oldest and strongest secret combination—the Cosa Nostra. Freeman had come to believe that there was one head, one organized body controlling drugs internationally. That head was a financial kingdom that used its money and power to bring the world drug trade under its general control. Through consolidation of a network of national and international contacts, the Sicilian Mafia had organized to recycle their money from all forms of illicit operations into the even more lucrative drug trade. They had infiltrated and used the international banking system so that they could, without consequence, transfer illegal capital to any bank in the world. In doing so they could pour dirty money into the faceless currency market while avoiding the risky and cumbersome physical transportation of cash and thus could put their money to work internationally, with little or no danger.

To destroy the cartels of Colombia was to hack off only one of Cosa Nostra's far-reaching tentacles. You had to go for the head. When you cut that off—and not until then—you could destroy the entire menace. Secretly Jim Freeman had helped organize the world's anti-drug forces to focus on the financial empire and power structure of the Cosa Nostra, working closely with authorities in Sicily, where that organization's power was based. Then eradication began.

Freeman dropped the bombshell on Cosa Nostra when he called a surprise news conference in which he disclosed the reach of the Sicilian Mafia in world politics. Without naming individuals, Freeman showed that Cosa Nostra had "associates" in every major government, intelligence organization, and military establishment on the globe. He gave evidence of how the beast had set itself up to control every facet of the drug business through the use of financial manipulation, intimidation, fear, blackmail, and murder. He read, again without giving names, the signed affidavits of five people in high places, three of them in the United States, who had been approached and blackmailed by the Cosa Nostra in order to achieve protection for its drug smuggling and money laundering activities. The next day, a federal grand jury indicted numerous individuals and credit institutions on federal racketeering charges, and they were brought to trial.

Cosa Nostra retaliated. Kentucky Trayco had been amazed at how many people tried to defame Freeman, discredit his suppositions, and force him to reveal his sources. To Kenny these were a discomfiting but viable indication of how far the Cosa Nostra tentacles reached. They were calling their associates to battle.

But Freeman and members of the task force from other countries withstood the political onslaught and continued making arrests. Then they began arresting Cosa Nostra capi (chiefs).

That was when the killing started. Although task-force members had round-the-clock protection, three of them were assassinated within a twenty-four hour period. Two days later two more were killed. The world was outraged, but fearful. The task-force coalition began to struggle. The British member disappeared from public life along with his family. The Colombian, Brazilian, and Peruvian members made statements contradicting Freeman's original hypothesis, then denied they had ever supported it. People were running scared.

But in the United States Freeman held it together. More arrests came. More imprisonments. The biggest catch was a Sicilian who had been at large for more than twenty years, a major force in the leadership of the Cosa Nostra. But before he could be brought to trial four more members of the task force were killed. The most notable was James Freeman himself.

The message was clear and frightful: the Sicilian Mafia would tolerate no interference. They could reach even those who were most protected. No one was safe.

A heavy shadow fell over what Freeman had accomplished. Judges and juries were afraid to convict. Attorneys wouldn't prosecute. Evidence disappeared. In six months no one took up the gauntlet. The task force fell apart, international cooperation came to a standstill. Governments found new directions, new problems that were more pressing.

The drug world was back to business as usual.

It was then that Jeremiah Daniels volunteered. Trayco had watched it on TV: a presidential news conference. Jeremiah picked up his father-in-law's torch. At that moment Kentucky Trayco knew he would be getting involved.

It had taken a year to put everything together. They had met secretly, going over Jim Freeman's records and notes, planning their strategy, making their decisions. There would be no press coverage, no announcements of their intentions, and (outside of their immediate team) no international cooperation. Operation BOOMERANG would start with the Sicilian Mafia's biggest market, the United States. By attacking its largest tentacle the new drug czar and his team were hopeful of paralyzing the entire octopus.

That would be no small task. The American drug trade was much more organized than would appear on the surface. The Cosa Nostra ran things from abroad and had absolute control, the American branches of their business being a series of tentacles running into every section of the country. From production to sales on the street the operation seemed loosely organized, but as the new task force dug deeper they discovered just the opposite. The country was broken down into sections each having a particular "family" responsible, with a capo in charge. The capo represented the family on the "Capo Commission," which consisted of the chiefs from each section of the country. The commission was responsible for ensuring that production and distribution networks nationwide functioned effectively between families; they also made decisions about whose goods would be used in one section of the country versus another, thereby reducing unnecessary competition among families for product and keeping prices under their control.

At first glance the Capo Commission seemed to be the ultimate authority, but Jim Freeman had discovered otherwise. One member of the commission was designated to report to a selected member of the Sicilian Super Commission of the Cosa Nostra—a capo responsible for all facets of the American drug trade. The Super Commission was headed by the capo dei capi, or chief of chiefs, the ultimate decision-maker in the system.

Absolutely essential to the success of the Cosa Nostra in the United States had been the "soldati" or soldiers. The soldati were the grass roots of the system—the manpower. They were of proven courage, ruthless, and decisive. A proven "man of honor" earned the title by murder. It was the soldati who, over the last twenty years, had infiltrated the American Mafia and worked their way into positions of importance so that when the Cosa Nostra was ready for a takeover things would be much easier. By their murder and intimidation they were able to "prepare" the American Mafia for "greater" leadership.

The American Mafia fought the takeover, but most Americans saw the Mafia wars and murders as simply family infighting that didn't concern them much. Some of the American mafiosi saw early on what was happening and were able to keep the Sicilians out of their families. One of these was Paulo DeGuillio, head of the Las Vegas mob and godfather of the American Mafia for the West Coast. Most of the others, however, were controlled by Sicily as early as 1970 and were prepared for the Cosa Nostra's greater plans. What most of these men didn't realize was the extent of control planned by Sicily—something to come just around the corner.

It was this control that Jeremiah Daniels and his team intended to prevent. To do so they had to reach the top, the capo dei capi. The man protected by layers of soldati and capi, including the man responsible for the Cosa Nostra's business in the United States—the man in Sicily who reported directly to the capo dei capi and the Super Commission.

Trayco knew what it had been like on the streets before. He had lived there. It was dangerous; people killing other people for territory in which to sell their drugs and steal from their neighbors. The money drew normal people into crime and murder like lead filings to a magnet. He had seen the violence the American Mafia had inflicted on people. In those days it was prostitution and gambling. When drugs hit the inner city every rat in the woodwork tried to get a piece of the pie. The family had used its soldiers to eliminate opposition until its challenge was met by opposing forces just as willing to kill and intimidate—the gangs. Now the Sicilian Cosa Nostra was moving to control both.

When Jeremiah Daniels had asked him to help, Trayco had gone back to L.A. and visited his old haunts. He saw the drug wars firsthand and it made his skin crawl. The neighborhood was turning into a bad movie. That was all he needed to be fully committed.

Trayco looked at the middle monitor: the private conference room. That was where Anthony DeGuillio was.

Tony D was a capo of the Cosa Nostra. A convert. He didn't often come out of his fortified compound in one of the more prominent neighborhoods of Las Vegas—in fact, he'd done it only once in the last fourteen months. He had too many enemies who considered him a traitor.

The DeGuillio family controlled mob activities west of Denver, with Paulo DeGuillio as godfather. He was also the only one Sicily hadn't been able to get to. Rumor had it that they made a deal with Tony: get rid of your father, and we promise you a bright future. Paulo died in a car bombing. Tony went to the funeral on a Tuesday. By Friday there were four more deaths, all done by professional assassins, all relatives who stood in the way of Tony gaining control.

According to informants the Cosa Nostra was responsible but had acted in concert with Tony. The FBI had tried to prove it but came up empty-handed.

Members of DeGuillio's family weren't happy, and several swore vengeance. A week after Tony was acquitted an attempt was made on his life. Since then, while the first Mafia wars in Las Vegas in more than forty years took place, he had been careful. When the wars were over, Tony was in charge and the opposition was gone. At least most of it. The FBI investigated again but could make no connections to Tony. The hit men were outsiders—a recent Cosa Nostra change—and were never caught. Tony was home free. But still cautious.

For his efforts DeGuillio was given charge of the Cosa Nostra's West Coast operations. He was making a seven-figure monthly income from business and was head of the American Capi Commission, directly responsible to Sicily. By murder and mayhem Tony D had reached the top of American Mafia operations.

It was going to be a pleasure nailing Tony. A real pleasure.

"Nest, this is Birdwatcher."

Trayco sat forward and lifted the two-way radio to his mouth. Birdwatcher was Jack Canyon, Kentucky's business partner and best friend. He was in a hotel room of the Mirage several blocks away with a high-powered telescope and a highly sensitive directional listening device honed in on Caesar's very private conference room.

"Go ahead, Watcher. What's our little yellow-breasted sapsucker up to?"

There was a slight chuckle. "I hate to enjoy someone else's discomfort, but Tony D is within inches of having his accountant for dinner. The poor little weasel is . . . Oh, oh . . ."

"What is it, Watcher? What—"

"Move in, Nest! Gunshots!" A pause. "He's killed him! He killed the accountant!" Jack said in an unbelieving tone.

Trayco watched the monitor as half a dozen goons burst into the view of one of the cameras as they hustled Tony D out of the conference room and toward an exit. Trayco's stomach lurched into his throat. Tony had killed the accountant and was now on his way back to the safety of his compound. He had to stop him!

"All units! The prey is leaving by the rear tunnel. Get him! But keep your heads down! He has half a dozen well-armed thugs with him! Move it!"

Trayco grabbed the car phone and punched in 911. "A man has been shot in a conference room at Caesar's Palace," he shouted, then threw the phone on the soft leather as he lurched from the rear seat, opened the driver's door, and planted his 6'4" 220-pound frame behind the wheel. He laid twenty feet of fresh rubber on the asphalt as the huge engine responded to his heavily placed foot. As the limousine accelerated through the parking lot he heard the sharp report of gunshots through the open two-way. The battle had begun. He had only minutes to have it stopped and get his men far away from Caesar's before official blue arrived on the scene.

His instructions were no police, no FBI; not yet, maybe never. Although the task force had special powers granted by the government, nothing was going through regular channels. They had learned in the past how far-reaching the arm of the Cosa Nostra was. Using channels was too dangerous.

As he slammed on the brakes, bringing the limo to a screeching stop in the shadows of the building, Trayco spotted Tony hunched down behind a large garbage receptacle. Two of his thugs were firing automatic weapons at several spots but were pinned by Trayco's men. DeGuillio looked scared, panicked. It gave Trayco an idea.

He stepped on the pedal, bringing the long stretch limo into the direct line of fire between his own men and Tony's. As he pushed a button the rear door jolted open, giving Tony D a clear run at it. Trayco could see him hesitate, squinting, trying to see who his savior was, unsure. Then he bolted, yelling for his thugs to follow, their guns on full fire. One was out of ammo before he ran three steps, was immediately downed by incoming bullets, and crawled to cover. As Tony leaped through the door onto the seat, Trayco pushed the button again, slamming and locking the door before anyone else could get in. Trayco gunned the vehicle and watched in his rearview mirror as the muscle-bound bodyguard who had been with Tony realized his vulnerability, dropped his gun like a hot iron, and flung his arms in the air.

Trayco picked up the two-way and gave the command. "Turn Tony's men over to local authorities and lead them to the accountant in the conference room. Tell Captain Trackis in homicide we'll be in touch." Kenny paused. "Tell him if he has any questions to call Washington. You know the number."

A dark, bullet-proof window separated Trayco and Tony DeGuillio, Kenny pushed the button that opened communications between the two compartments and spoke.

"Where to, sir?"

"My . . . my com . . . my compound!" came the answer from the breathless, overweight killer.

As Trayco turned right off the strip and toward the freeway he pushed another button, allowing the darkened screen to turn crystal clear. Watching his sweating captive through the rearview mirror he could see that he was unarmed. Trayco spoke in a mocking tone.

"How ya doin', Mr. D?" He chuckled at the sudden recognition that crossed the mobster's face.

"*You!* How—"

"In the flesh, Tony!" Trayco smiled.

DeGuillio grabbed the handle of the door, jerking on it. Nothing happened. He jerked again, harder.

"No chance, fat boy," Trayco said. "You're mine now!"

"But you can't! This . . . this is against the law! I have rights! I . . ."

Trayco took the warrant from his pocket and waved it. "You've been indicted, Tony. Federal charges. And . . . we could go back to Caesar's. The conference room."

Tony went pale. "You saw—"

"Same as." Trayco paused. "Did you kill him, Tony?"

DeGuillio sneered. "Me? Not me!" He waited for effect. "But he *is* dead! Just like you're—"

Trayco's laugh interrupted Tony. "Save the threats. You won't be seeing the light of day for some time to come. Not at all if I have my way about it."

"I demand to see my attorney," Tony said, indignant.

"Soon, Tony." Trayco turned off the mike as Tony launched into a tirade of bad language and a denunciation of Trayco's parentage. The latter glanced at his watch, his mind turning to another place. One in Colombia.

3:00 A.M.—*East of Miraflores, Colombia*

Colonel Thomas Macklin held tight to the chopper's seat as it lurched so close to the jungle ceiling that he could reach out and touch its trees. He had twelve men; the other three choppers carried similar loads. Their support included four AH 64 Apache attack choppers, two F117A Stealth fighters carrying surgical-smart bombs, and two F111 Ravens. The Raven was a radar-jamming platform and would keep the target from recognizing their position and strength until it was too late. The Apaches would institute attack and cover for transports disgorging troops. The Stealth fighters would come into play, destroying specified targets, after the ground troops and the Apaches had accomplished their missions.

Operation SHOCK was covert, sanctioned by the president of the United States but without clearance by Congress or even the president's cabinet, simply because of the danger of leaks—something that had become too real in the U.S. halls of government when the Cosa Nostra and the world drug trade were concerned. At precisely the time the battle began, the Colombian government would be notified and told where they could go to pick up prisoners. They would also be told which accounts in their banks should be closed and what information should be forwarded to the United States to help in the prosecution. A formality—permission from the Colombian government had been received sixteen hours ago.

Juan Portillo Alvarez was a drug lord. The SHOCK team under Macklin's command would destroy the Colombian's operation: factories, warehouses, planes and boats used for transportation, everything. In effect, when they were finished the multi-billion dollar drug operation would disappear, hopefully forever. Alvarez's associates who survived the SHOCK attack would be confined for life to Colombia's unpleasant prisons. Only innocents, particularly women and children not involved, would not be taken captive, becoming wards of the Colombian government. Macklin would escort Alvarez back to Miami, where the drug kingpin would be arraigned and imprisoned to await trial for criminal acts against the United States.

"Five minutes, Colonel," said the pilot.

"I copy, Captain," Macklin responded. That meant the F111 jammer was rendering Alvarez's radar system ineffective. In a few minutes the real battle would begin.

Thomas Macklin was the marines' veteran special operations leader and a friend of Jerry Daniels. They had worked together on two other occasions when national security was involved, and were good friends.

Macklin was a career marine, a man who at the relatively young age of thirty-nine had refused to be busted up the ladder through promotions, preferring to stay in the trenches. He hated desk jockeys and pencil pushers, and the thought of becoming one gave him nightmares.

Macklin was top-notch, a veteran of anti-terrorist operations in Kuwait and Israel during the Iraq war and of other covert operations in Colombia, Peru, and Mexico set up to help those governments destroy drug factories and bring back evidence against lords the government was trying to prosecute. On two occasions they decided the best evidence was the man himself. One had come back and was tried in the U.S. courts, found guilty, and was now serving time. The other tried to stay where he was. He died from an overdose of self-confidence.

It was in Israel that Thomas Macklin's life had changed to a more tranquil style. While working with the Israeli government to blow up a terrorist chemical warhead factory in Syria he met Ruth Levona, a tough colonel in the Aman (Army Intelligence). Smart, competent, and beautiful, Ruth Levona had turned Macklin's head in spite of the fact that she was also hardheaded, stubborn, and Zionist. After surviving the successful mission that nearly killed both of them, they decided they were made for each other and got married. Macklin asked to stay in Israel as military attaché at the American embassy.

Until, that is, the call came from Jeremiah Daniels at the behest of the president. The tranquillity had come to an end—something for which Tom Macklin was silently grateful.

It was time. Macklin stood, dispelling thoughts of the past and concentrating on the task at hand. "All right, you eggheads! Let's get ready." His men stood, taking a position facing the rear.

He went over the plan of attack in his mind. The Apaches would soften up the enemy with their Stinger missiles as his men unloaded from troop transports into the jungle surrounding the Alvarez compound. Using hand-held TOW missiles, the troops would then breech the compound's walls and secure the inner courtyard. An elite attack group from Israel, under the command of a good friend of Macklin's, would take the house.

He felt the bottom drop out from under the chopper as it swooped down into a predetermined landing site. He heard the first explosions and the chatter on his headset as the Apache units talked to each other. They were instructed not to hit the house directly but to dismantle the opposition's firing positions in the surrounding hills and along the compound walls. The positions at the house would have to be stormed by ground troops in order to ensure that prisoners were taken alive.

The chopper landed with a hard thud, its back gate already open. The troops it disgorged were quickly moving through thick jungle toward the compound wall. Now the work began.

———————

Lieutenant David Gad was the last to leave chopper number two. As commander of his Israeli special forces group he gave instructions that moved his men into position for an assault on the compound's north wall and the house beyond. As he and his men disappeared into the jungle, the transport lifted from the ground and flew off into the darkness.

"Shock One, this is Shock Two." Gad spoke into the small mike suspended in front of his chin. "We are in position."

"Understood, Shock Two," came Macklin's reply. "Choppers three and four are unloading. Let's move it."

The sky was alight with the orange hue of flames as the Apaches fired their Stinger missiles on the compound's perimeter defenses, then swooped over the compound, wreaking havoc with their fifty-caliber cannons. As a Stinger decapitated a nearby enemy position, Gad's team used their hand-held TOW missiles to blow large holes in the compound walls.

Moving quickly through a smoking, jagged-edged hole of concrete Gad remembered reading Alvarez's challenge to the United States and its allies. "We are impregnable. You cannot touch us." Considering this arrogant posture, the drug lord was embarrassingly unprepared.

Gad's team was halfway across the inner courtyard before they encountered opposition from a gun emplacement near the compound's ten-car garage. That opposition was quickly dispatched with another TOW missile. Five minutes later they were firing directly at a gun emplacement near the patio of the main house. Two minutes later they were knocking down the door with plastic explosives, Shock One at their side.

Alvarez was found under his bed, his wife and children at his side. He was pale, but vocal. Gad didn't understand much Spanish, but he surmised that everything from his heritage to his parentage was being cursed by the plump, moustached Colombian.

The troops went through the house, taking all the files, records, and papers they could find. The safe lock was quickly breached and its contents loaded in strong cloth sacks brought along for just such use. Gad figured there were several million dollars, half a dozen kilos of cocaine, and enough paperwork to put Alvarez away for the rest of his life.

"Records of his own organization, but not his connections to the others," one of the men said. "Nothing about his bosses."

Gad looked at Macklin, who was going through a handful of papers. Macklin shrugged. "Not surprising. According to BOOMERANG there won't be a paper trail to the top." He looked at his watch. "Let's go. Choppers will be arriving in two minutes. I'll take Alvarez and head for the rendezvous. Shock Three will drop off the women and children at the village over the hill, while Four takes the remaining men to the Colombian army waiting in the next valley over. You finish up here with the explosives. Any casualties on our side?"

"None."

Macklin smiled. "I don't think these guys down here are really ready for the war they keep asking for, do you?" Both men laughed. "Don't lag," Macklin said to Gad as he grabbed Alvarez by the arm and pulled him toward the door.

An hour later nothing but smoke, fire, and rubble remained of the Alvarez compound. To the north, further in the jungle, a large production factory was eliminated with three carefully placed smart bombs from an F117A. On their way out the Apaches destroyed an airfield containing six planes—two Lear jets and four Pipers. At the port city of Cartagena the first F117A teamed up with the second and eliminated four boats, two hundred-foot yachts, and two larger transport ships with surgical precision. All were registered to half a dozen companies, all traceable to Alvarez.

A small group of government accountants were waiting for the Alvarez papers at the rendezvous point in Grenada. Their well-equipped Boeing E-3 Sentry flew them back toward the United States, across Mexico, as they used sophisticated optical scanners to download the drug runners' paperwork, account numbers, and access codes into their computers. Then, by using a satellite communication system and a new-found cooperation from banks (after James Freeman hadn't gotten tough with the industry) they were able to tap into bank records and transfer Juan Portillo Alvarez's millions from bank accounts in Switzerland, the United States, Britain, Australia, Germany, and Japan (among others) into government accounts in Washington, D.C. They were finished by the time they landed at Tinker Air Force Base, Oklahoma, in time for breakfast.

That same morning the Colombian government seized all bank records and accounts belonging to Alvarez and his organization within their own country. They used account numbers and access codes that they found safely tucked away in their computer when they arrived at work that morning: a gift from the 965th Warning and Control Squadron at Tinker.

In all, property and money seized amounted to nearly two and a half billion U.S. dollars.

Juan Portillo Alvarez was out of business.

Bekaa Valley, Syria

Nabril Al Razd knew the Bekaa. He had escaped to it when he was forced to leave Lebanon by the Israelis in 1988. He shook his head. Now he was working with them. His father would turn over in his grave.

Nabril had been with Ruth Levona and Thomas Macklin when the group destroyed a chemical warhead plant in Syria, preventing the wanton firing of chemically loaded missiles into Israel and the West Bank by terrorists who wanted to take control of Palestine over the dead bodies of Jew and Arab alike. Nabril's best and most honored friend, Mohammad Faisal, had been working on the West Bank to bring peace to their homeland by protecting people from the Arab PLO terrorists sent there to assassinate anyone who refused to follow PLO guidelines. It was then they discovered the terrorist plot and worked with Macklin and Levona to stop it. Faisal had been killed. Nabril had lived.

Now Nabril worked with a new segment of Israeli/Arab society, a segment which fought common enemies instead of each other. Of course, he still had political differences with Israel. He still didn't have a free homeland, but they were getting closer. More and more Israelis and people worldwide were putting down their weapons and working for peace. More and more people recognized who the world's real enemies were. Enemies like Nafez Boudia, Syrian-born drug runner.

Few realized the amount of drugs shipped worldwide by way of the Middle East. Few understood that Boudia was one of the main suppliers of pure-grade opium products to the United States. Boudia controlled what had become known as the Golden Crescent, which started at Turkey's eastern border and embraced Iran, Pakistan, and Afghanistan—the largest opium and heroin producing region on earth. Jim Freeman and the international task force had discovered Boudia's only customer: Cosa Nostra. The Sicilians paid the Syrian well and shipped his product to their organization's members worldwide—especially the United States, the largest market for heroine—and made Boudia a rich man.

After tonight, few would need to know of the Syrian's infamy. Nafez Boudia, Allah willing, would be out of business.

Nabril and Ruth Macklin had received word of the successes so far obtained in South America and the United States. Their preliminary goal of shutting off three of the Cosa Nostra's largest supply lines for illicit drugs was nearly accomplished. Boudia was all that remained. The act was meant to send a message to Sicily: It was time they retired.

He watched Ruth sitting on the other side of the chopper. He had attended the wedding of her and Colonel Thomas Macklin a few months after first meeting them and working together to keep fanatic terrorists from blowing up the Middle East. He had come to know their hearts and their dedication to both Israelis and Arabs. Working together to bring terrorism to an end and peace to reality, Nabril and the Macklins had become the closest of friends. Nabril was dedicated to both of them because they were dedicated to peace. A peace everyone could live with.

Ruth Levona Macklin was an amazing woman. She knew Arabic as if it were her own language. She even looked Arabic now that her hair was changed from its usual dark brown to black with streaks of auburn. But was it enough to fool Nafez Boudia's people? The thought still gave Nabril goose bumps.

The plan was a simple one: to prosecute the Syrian and showcase him to the world so that everyone would understand how such business would be dealt with. To accomplish this they needed Boudia alive and his files intact. The chance of their getting either with a frontal attack was one in a thousand. They needed something more subtle.

The LION, Israel's elite chopper with her frightening weapons and her stealth capability, wasn't the answer. Even if they were able to get the deadly bird within feet of Boudia's house they would not get inside in time to keep Boudia from destroying the most critical portion of his records. The LION's abilities would be used all right, but only after Ruth Macklin was inside to prevent Boudia's panic from destroying what they had come for.

And it was that part of the plan that, as he now considered it, made Nabril's stomach churn and his dark face turn a pale white.

"Five minutes to rendezvous," said the pilot. Rendezvous was a point several kilometers from Boudia's fortress. The chopper would take Ruth within driving distance, where a car of sorts awaited her; then she would be on her own. The LION's radar system would keep track of her through the small tracing chip placed in the heel of one shoe, but it couldn't prevent her death, nor could it read her mind. After arriving at the compound she would have twenty minutes to enter the house in the disguise of Arab house help, dismantle the alarm system, and find Boudia, putting a gun to his head to keep him immobile and quiet. Nabril and five others would do the rest.

"Do you want to go over it one more time?" Ruth asked.

He smiled. "You know that the alarm system can kill us? If it isn't off and we trip it . . ."

"Yes, I know. Land mines and booby traps are not a pleasant thought, are they?"

"If Thomas knew what you were doing . . ."

She smiled. "I know. He has tried to keep me out of the line of fire before."

The LION dropped to the ground abruptly. Nabril watched as Ruth jumped to the ground; he waved as the chopper lifted him away into the early morning light, speaking lightly to himself. "May Allah go with you, Ruth Macklin. You are in his hands now."

The vehicle stood in a thicket of scrub brush. A beat-up German Volkswagen bug with the top sawn off just behind the windshield. Dusty, the seats shredded from heat, it looked abandoned.

Ruth eased herself into the driver's seat and turned the key. The engine immediately came to life, bringing a smile to her face. One should never judge a book by its cover.

She flipped a toggle switch hanging by wires under the left side of the dash and the lights came on, illuminating the ground in front of her.

She glanced at her watch: forty-one minutes. Taking a deep breath she jammed her foot to the pedal, spewing dust as the doorless old car lurched out of the brush and onto the road.

Ruth Macklin was a fighter. She had been a fighter for Israel since her birth. Both of her parents and two brothers had died fighting for Israel, leaving her alone. The army was her only remaining family. From that point on, most of her life had been focused on vengeance—finding ways to kill Israel's enemies, their blood atoning for the spilt blood of her family.

She had met Thomas Macklin about the same time that the hate had reached the boiling point. Their work together had saved Israel from a horrible catastrophe, and Thomas Macklin had saved Ruth, replacing the hate and emptiness in her heart with a hope and love she had forgotten she could feel.

She continued to be a fighter, but now it was for the right reasons and against the right people.

As she shifted into a lower gear to climb a small hill, her mind turned to Nabril. He had been a terrorist with Mohammad Faisal, both enemies of Israel. They had been Ruth's sworn foes at one time. Now she trusted only Thomas more than she trusted Nabril.

Sight of the compound brought Ruth's thoughts back to the present. Unusually high walls and armed guards surrounded the palace; an evil man's way of easing his mind enough to sleep at nights.

From intelligence reports Ruth knew that Boudia's house was nothing more than a bunker; that Boudia slept and worked below ground in a suite of rooms surrounded by walls three feet thick, with a door more like that of a safe vault than anything else. She also knew that door slammed shut if the alarms went off. That was something she must prevent, or they would never get their hands on the Syrian drug lord and the papers inside his file cabinets.

She pictured in her mind the bird's-eye view of the compound itself. There were actually two fences, two feet thick and eight feet high with a gate in each wall. The fences were separated by bare ground, mined for intruders. The inner compound was a large twenty-acre park containing numerous trees, fountains, and gardens. Guards with attack dogs roamed, while surveillance cameras watched from hidden locations. Ruth didn't know what other surprises awaited uninvited guests to Boudia's residence, but she was sure there were some.

The car approached the huge steel gates, the guardhouse looming to her left at the corner of the main road and the entrance. A fifty-caliber machine gun rested on top beneath a shelter, and the barrel seemed to float with the movement of her vehicle. Was it manned or computer controlled? It didn't matter. Either way it could kill her before she could blink.

She removed the ID card from her shoe, flashing her brightest smile. She was a replacement for one of the regular house help, her identity cleared several days in advance of this visit. In trying to find a way to get at Boudia, Ruth had investigated the background of anyone working for the Syrian. Hamid Farouk, a Lebanese businessman and provider of Boudia's maintenance, grounds, and house personnel, was caught with his hand in Boudia's bank account. The amount was not great, and Ruth knew Boudia may have even known about it, but Farouk did not know that. When approached in the dark of night about his activities and threatened with disclosure to Boudia, he became cooperative.

The car stopped leaving the guard amazed that such a clunker had survived the journey from Zahlah, some twenty miles away. Then he saw Ruth.

"You are new." He smiled, speaking in Arabic.

"Yes, and happy to be working." Ruth answered in the same language but added an eastern Lebanese accent.

"Your identity card?"

She handed it to him. "I replace someone. Hamid . . . I mean Mr. Farouk," she said shyly, "said a letter would be sent to identify me."

He looked at the guardhouse. Another man stood in the door, admiring the new help. "You heard her!" the first said sharply. "Check the file."

He smiled at Ruth. "I am sure everything is in order. We get replacements quite often. But none so—"

"Here it is," the other said interrupting and vying for attention. "She is cleared."

The first became suddenly businesslike as a third man appeared in the door. "We must search the vehicle. Will you step out, please?"

She gave the soldier a wry grin as she stepped from the doorless vehicle, sending a sheepish glow of red across his face. Standing to the side with her arms folded she waited, feeling the eyes of the officer at the door trying to see into her soul, force a negative reaction. It seemed like forever before the men finished, glanced at their superior with a shrug, and waved her back to her seat. As the officer disappeared from the doorway, his face bland and unreadable, the gate started to open. Ruth wanted to sigh with relief, but forced the tell-tale pleasure aside.

"When you enter the compound through the second gate, stay left. It will take you to the back of the house. And do not walk on the lawn." The young soldier smiled. "It isn't safe. Boom!" He grinned, gesturing with his hands. "At the rear of the house you will be let in and given instructions for your house duties. It is most dangerous to be wandering about the grounds." He pulled away from the side of the car. "When you finish work . . ."

She waved as the VW moved within the compound's now sun-brightened walls. She looked at her watch. Nearly 7:00 A.M. She had fifteen minutes in which to get Boudia in her gunsights. And to do that she must first find a gun.

When Ruth passed the guard at the back door of the house and entered through the kitchen she found only a cook preparing breakfast. The woman's back was turned, and Ruth slipped down a hall and into a large storage area where tools and linens were kept. She saw the camera, cognizant that she had been watched since entering the back door. While picking out linen, towels, dust mop, brush and chemical cleaners, and putting them aboard a small cart for carrying, her mind went over the layout that the intelligence reports had given them by way of a Russian contractor.

Glasnost had produced some immediate benefits for Israel. Since 1992 Ruth's country had been able to buy numerous amounts of data, equipment, and intelligence material from the former Soviet Union, which gave Israel additional information about the capability of her enemies.

Ruth knew she was early. She had intended to be. She

didn't want the rest of the help getting in the way, watching her movements. She knew there was a weapons room in the right wing, but there was no way to get to it without being seen. Her domestic chores would take her only to the left wing—the bedroom and living areas of the house—without suspicion. That was where she needed to be, but it meant taking a gun from one of Boudia's personal bodyguards. The question was, how could a woman of less than one hundred and twenty pounds overpower a man who probably would top two hundred?

Then she saw the can. Spray wax. A plan formed in her mind. With the wax, a broom, and quick hands . . .

The door flew open as she stuffed the spray can inside the carrier.

"You take too long in here," said the cook. "Get to your duties."

Ruth thought the woman hadn't noticed her arrival, but she was glad it was her and not one of the guards. Her heart returned to her chest as she slipped past the hardened body of the nearly six-foot-four-inch frame. One thing was sure: she wouldn't want to get into a wrestling match with that!

She checked her watch as she pushed the cart down the hall. Seven minutes and thirty seconds had come and gone. Time was running out. She turned left into another hall. Another right and she came to the elevator. She went to push the button but found only a keyhole. She had no key! Where would the key be kept? Then she remembered Farouk's instructions. "Pick up your keys from the cabinet in the linen room."

She hesitated. It would take at least another two minutes but she had no choice. Turning, she ran back down the hall. As she made the second corner she ran into the hard muscles of the cook and was instantly knocked to the floor. As she looked up from her fallen position the cook jangled the keys and leaned down.

"Forget something?" she said in cold Arabic.

Ruth grabbed them and jumped to her feet, the anger showing in her face. She bit her tongue and turned, moving back the way she had come. In seconds she had the key in the hole and the elevator doors open. Entering she found no button, only a speaker phone.

"Code?" said a computerized woman's voice.

Code! She had to say the word for the elevator to move.

Farouk had given it to them, but what was it? . . . how could she forget? . . .

"Code?" said the voice again. "Thirty seconds and counting."

She looked at the camera in the corner and the automatic weapon next to it. Both seemed to get larger and move toward her as her mind struggled to find the word.

"Sultan," she said in Arabic, the word suddenly exploding from a locked corner of her memory. The elevator started to move and the small enclosure stopped whirling around her.

"That is correct," said the computer in perfect Arabic.

As the doors opened she checked her watch again and took a deep breath. Seven more minutes.

Boudia's suite was down the hall to the left, as were the guest rooms and baths. She knew it was fifty yards to Boudia's door, but only twenty to where she should stop to do her duties. How to cover that last thirty yards, get a weapon, and . . . ?

She saw the guard at the end of the corridor. He had a curious look on his face as he spoke into a hand-held radio then moved toward her. She came to the first door and knocked, ignoring him while she took out her pass key and opened the door. As nonchalantly as possible she removed the spray can and broom from the cart and entered the large guest room. The bathroom was to the right, the closet to the left; a large bed, a couch, table and chairs, along with a well-stocked wet bar filled the main room. There were no surveillance cameras, no windows, no exits at all.

She flipped on the bathroom light and began checking the sink, turning on the hot water and soaking the rag. The place was clean, and apparently it hadn't been used since it was last cleaned, but she had to delay until the guard came to her.

She hummed lightly, sensing his presence at the door. As his head came into view she pushed the valve on the wax can and sprayed him in the eyes. He dropped the radio and went for his gun with one hand while trying to clear his vision with the other.

Ruth used the broom effectively. Jamming its hard handle under his rib cage she knocked the air out of the man's lungs. As he bent over gasping, she cracked it in halves across his skull, sending his face into the pile of the white carpet. Her hand found the gun and she used the butt to render him unconscious.

Taking deep breaths she quickly entered the hallway,

speaking over her shoulder as if saying something to a guard still healthy and standing just out of camera range in the room.

"In a moment. First I must check the other rooms." She used the key to open each door, check briefly inside, then move to the next one. As she approached the last room, some twenty feet from the end of the corridor, she bolted. Withdrawing the gun from her apron she rounded the corner and faced the door: no guard—the heavy door half open.

Ruth had taken only one step toward the door when suddenly the alarm went off and the door started to close. She sprinted through it and into the room, gun at the ready. She watched the big door swing silently closed, shutting off the world outside.

Sweat rolled down her face as her eyes swept over the outer office. No one! Dashing to the bedroom door, she heard water running in the bathroom. Her first inclination was to enter, but something held her back. Something isn't right, her mind screamed. The next second she realized what it was: there were wet footprints on the carpet. They moved out of sight to her right. Boudia was waiting for her to come in the room.

Placing herself against the wall, she glanced at her watch. In two minutes Nabril and the others would be ready to breach the compound's defenses, and the LION would move into position. Her mind went over the layout of the room. The control panel was to the left. She had to get to it! But how? If she even stuck a toe inside the door, Boudia would blow it off!

Sweat poured down her face. It was hot. She took off the cloth that covered her head and used it to wipe her face. She checked the outer office for surveillance cameras. Could he see her? She heard a clicking noise behind her and saw the door move slightly on spring-loaded hinges. She must act quickly—only a minute and thirty seconds left.

Her eyes focused on the ceiling tiles. The wires from the main power source to the panel were in the space between concrete and a false ceiling. The space also contained air conditioning vents, wiring for lights, and other paraphernalia. She moved to the desk, put a straight-back chair on it, and quickly climbed to the top.

With one eye on the slightly opening door, Ruth shoved on one of the two-by-four-foot tiles, pushing upward. It gave. She poked her head into the opening and peered into the dusty maze. Only arm's length away she saw the cable. She raised the gun and fired, sparks flying in all directions as the high voltage cable was compromised. She fired again, completely severing the two lines and putting the lights out as the main breaker shut the entire system down.

She leaned down and looked in the direction of the door. It had stopped moving. There wasn't enough room for Boudia to get through the doorway, but a gun might—

Acting on the thought before it was even finished, Ruth jumped down and landed behind the desk as she heard the plink of metal on metal. An automatic weapon lit up the room, the bullets careening violently off the concrete inner walls. Glass mirrors exploded around her, expensive artwork was ripped to shreds, and Ruth shrank into a tiny ball, trying to make herself a smaller target.

It stopped as suddenly as it had begun. She looked at the night dial of her watch. Nabril and the others were in the compound. Hopefully their presence had drawn the guards out of the complex.

If she could stay alive and keep Boudia penned up in the bedroom . . .

In the pitch-black darkness of the room she couldn't see a thing. Where *was* Boudia? The situation reminded her of a show she had seen long ago. An American movie about a blind woman who was being stalked by a murderer. The murderer had used the light of an opened refrigerator to find her, and only by a miracle had she been able to stab him and then get away from him, leaving him to die.

She moved to the far side of the desk, taking a chance that the gunmen at the door were really gone. From there she felt her way through the darkness to where she had seen the heavy leather couch. As she did so her feet crunched on broken glass. She heard the click and felt the beam of light behind her as she flung herself through the air. The bullets thudded against the floor and wall where she had been, then embedded themselves in the couch as she landed on the floor behind it.

The light went out.

"Ah, the enemy is a woman," came Boudia's voice through the blackness, cold and confident. "You have intruded on my privacy. Not a nice thing. There is no excuse for such behavior . . ."

The voice was moving to her left. Ruth grasped the gun

tightly. How many bullets had she used? Two! Only two! He was trying to get to the door. No! To where he could fire behind the couch.

"You will have to pay."

Ruth felt panic in her stomach as her hand groped for something, anything!

Her fingers hit the hard, cold steel of something round and flat. She hurled it toward the far corner where she had seen a lamp, then got to her feet and raised the gun. As the ashtray crashed into the expensive glass, Boudia's flashlight came on. She fired, emptying the Makarov pistol without realizing it.

The darkness was stifling, the quiet overwhelming. She could hear heavy breathing and sobs. Someone was crying. It was a full minute before she realized the sobs were coming from her own mouth.

———————

Cold liquid crossed her lips and Ruth gulped the sweet water into her system, blinking in the bright light of the day and relishing the fresh air of the garden that surrounded her. Nabril approached, "You were lucky, Ruth."

She forced a smile. "Is Boudia dead?"

"Not quite, but close. The LION took him to Israel. We'll catch up with him there."

"Did we get the files?"

"Yes. We're ready to leave here. The explosives have been planted. Are you ready?" There was genuine concern in Nabril's voice.

"More than ready," Ruth replied. "Let's get out of here."

"The factory and warehouse were destroyed by the LION," Nabril explained. "The airfield and its planes were destroyed by the Israeli air force. We have his bank account numbers and can close them as soon as we get back."

"Then there were account numbers and access codes; all we were told?"

"Yes," Nabril confirmed. "Everything."

Ruth climbed into the helicopter, collapsed into a seat, and buckled the harness, her hands shaking from the fear and the adrenaline still running rampant in her system. The war was on, the message sent.

It was time to go to Yellowstone.

Day Two
November 14, 1997

CHAPTER 2

9:00 A.M.—Yellowstone Lake

Jerry untied the knot and threw the rope into the front of the boat. Hopping aboard, he turned the key and fired up the inboard's powerful eight-cylinder engine. Reversing the rumbling motor of the Glastron, he moved away from the dock quickly and swung the nose toward deep water. He pushed the gear shift forward and throttled the big engine. It leapt to life with a roar and lurched forward atop the dark blue water of Yellowstone Lake. Picking up the radio's mike Jerry said, "Skipper, this is Yellowlake One. Do you read?"

"Yellowlake One, this is Skipper. I have you on radar."

"Everything okay?" Jeremiah asked.

"Roger. See you onboard."

Jeremiah hung up the mike.

The flight to Jackson Hole from Washington, D.C., by way of Calgary, Canada, had been uneventful, allowing him to catch up on some much-needed sleep. But from the Jackson airport to the private heliport on the promontory of Yellowstone Lake the weather had grown progressively worse. Now the waves pummeled the bottom of the Glastron, making it airborne a good portion of the time as it jumped from wave to wave, the thirty-five-mile-an-hour cold wind freezing the lake water where it sprayed against the windshield. Snow pellets hit the Glastron like BBs, further blurring his visibility and reducing it to a hundred yards. Jerry didn't mind. The storm offered a degree of security. If anyone had been able to follow him it would hinder their ability to see his actual destination.

Hiding created paranoia. Everything that could be done to keep this place from the knowledge of Cosa Nostra had been done. He knew that, and yet he knew the Sicilians. Over the past year he had discovered just how deep the enemy's tentacles could go and it was frightening. He found himself constantly looking over his shoulder.

But Sicily didn't know about Yellowstone—not yet, anyway. It was too early. There was no reason. To the world, operation BOOMERANG was unknown; Jerry had seen to that. With the first action against the enemy only a few hours past, it was too early for them to know he and his team were involved. The real danger lay in the future. Jerry had no false illusions. He was trying to finish what James Freeman and others had started and the Cosa Nostra wasn't about to let him get away with it. Not if they could find him or his family.

Jeremiah had completely accepted the dangers to himself. There was no way around them. Deep in his heart he figured his chances of survival were about one in twenty, but he wasn't willing to accept that for his wife and children. Yellowstone and other contingency safeguards were set up to protect them while giving the team safe places to hide, ride out the storm, or keep one step ahead of sure death. He could only hope that such precautions truly worked.

When he knew he was within a mile of his destination he flipped a switch on the Glastron's panel. A foot-square radar screen on his right flicked on, its multi-colors of yellow, red, black, and purple on a blue field detailing his approach.

Jerry took his glasses out of his pocket and put them on as he sat down and throttled back. He could probably find the yacht without using the Glastron's small but sophisticated radar, but this was a good time to make sure it worked well. If a time came when they really needed it he wanted no glitches.

The Glastron's radar showed Jerry everything in front of him. The lake's bottom was shown in black; its jagged canyons jutting upward toward the Glastron were shown on the screen in purple. The shore of the lake could be seen as a low black line on the screen's horizon, and the sky above was a blue field. The yacht was a yellow dot of light framed in a red circle.

The brains of the system was a computer housed below

decks in the Glastron. Once the radar was turned on, it used its situation assessment module, linked to infrared search-and-track equipment, to detect all vessels below, on, and above the water. Using a laser range finder it could calculate the range, heading, and speed of all vessels, planes, or sub-mersibles, give a description of each and its weaponry, then evaluate and offer the best possible route of avoidance.

The Glastron housed no missiles or torpedoes, although it did have several automatic rifles and two hand-held TOW missiles along with a few other goodies hidden in a water-proof compartment under the floor.

As Jeremiah watched the screen, only one target showed: the series of three-sided red boxes snaking toward it, outlin-ing the Glastron's route of interception.

"Target *ISSA*. Do you wish to approach?" The computer's voice synthesizer asked.

Jeremiah knew that the computer had been programmed to read the *ISSA* as friendly and would not calculate avoid-ance parameters.

"Are there any other targets?" he asked the computer.

"Negative."

"Take us in, please," Jerry responded, letting go of the wheel as the computer's systems took control. The Glastron veered slightly left and slowed its pace. Moments later the *ISSA* loomed through the thickening snowstorm in front of him.

The *ISSA* was a modified cabin cruiser named after Jere-miah's oldest daughter and, like the Glastron, was special. With the latest in radar and communications equipment she was able to watch anything approaching from a little more than a hundred miles, and her sonar covered every inch of the lake's bottom from shore to shore.

Jerry switched off the radar with a verbal thank you, then pulled the speedboat alongside and tied her securely before climbing the stairs to the *ISSA*'s deck.

The ice gathering on the rope ladder was slippery and made Jerry's ascent difficult, the cold wind blowing off the water chilling him clear to the bone. By the time he reached the top rung his ears and nose were a rosy red and his hands and feet were cold. The wool topcoat and fur-lined gloves of the businessman would need to be exchanged for something warmer. Winter had set in at Yellowstone with a vengeance.

"Welcome aboard."

His eyes greeted the beautiful face of his wife, Michael-ene, as he welcomed her into his arms. Their lips met and he felt the weather-induced chill dissipate. "Hi," he said, as he pulled his head away enough to look into her dark eyes. "Everything okay here?"

She nodded as they moved toward the door and the warmth of the cabin. "You've been out of touch."

"Necessary under the circumstances. We aren't taking any chance of the enemy finding this place."

Michaelene Freeman was a Wyoming-raised lady who was as comfortable in a saddle chasing cows out of the hills as she was in an expensive law office putting people in jail. The daughter of a rich cattle and oil man turned U.S. senator, she had half a dozen proposals before she was twenty-one and many more before she met Jerry at the ripe old age of thirty. Her only explanation for never accepting one of those propos-als was that she hadn't taken the time. When Jerry had won-dered about that, she told him: "Love takes time. Until I met you I hadn't fallen in love, so I never took the time."

Michaelene Freeman was also fiercely patriotic. Like her father, she hated dishonesty in government and despised people who used American laws to hide their greed, dishon-esty, and larceny while protecting themselves from prosecu-tion. It had galled her to see the scandals in Washington, and during the years 1992 and 1993 she had worked hard helping her father and other honest congressmen bring down members of their establishment involved in the House bank-ing scandal. After that, she retired to the ranch to raise kids and cattle. Something she did with the same devotion and tenacity as putting away crooks, and which left Jeremiah Daniels exhausted at the end of a day.

"Fill me in," Jerry said. "What's been happening since I left Washington?" He hated being out of touch, but felt it necessary in order to protect his family. They couldn't afford to take the chance of communication interception if he was being watched.

"Everyone's here. Ruth's sleeping. She's pretty shaken up."

"I'll bet!" Jerry said tightly. "What got into her, endangering herself like that?"

"Settle down, dearest," Mike said, snuggling under his arm and next to his side. "What's done is done. You gave her a responsibility and she did what she thought needed doing. You would have done—"

"The same thing," he said with an exasperated grin. "It's just that when *she* does it—"

Mike slugged him playfully. "Chauvinist!"

He smiled. "Yeah. So sue me."

Mike's face grew serious. "Don't push it with her, Jerry. The nightmares she'll have for some time to come are enough."

"Pretty bad?"

"She's lucky to be with us, and she knows it. We don't have to remind her."

Jerry smiled. "I'll bet Macklin was livid."

Mike laughed. "He sure was. But, controlled. He knows it won't do any good to lecture Ruth. It's never worked yet." She paused. "He and Trayco are interrogating our Tony DeGuillio in his specially built quarters."

"Alvarez has been turned over to authorities in Miami?"

"Yes. It will hit the press this morning."

"You're sure about the federal prosecutor? He's clean?"

"I left two of our people to make sure he stays that way." Mike said. "His family has already been moved into seclusion. We have twenty-four-hour protection for everyone involved. Gad and his team will live with Alvarez until the trial is over. We should be all right."

"But one never knows when the rats will come out of the woodwork, does one?"

"There is always that chance."

"What about Boudia?" Jerry asked.

"Ruth left him with Nabril. When he is stabilized he'll be flown to Washington by Nabril's team. A private hospital there is preparing for his arrival. He'll be arraigned in federal court in New York. Judge Widdison."

"What happened to Judge Longer?"

"He disqualified himself. He'll be retiring from the bench." She smiled. "Poor health."

"Whose payroll was he on?"

"Alvarez's. Two of the Colombian's delivery boys were caught in New York City in a sting operation by some honest cops. Longer was paid fifty thousand to slap their hands and let them go."

"Well, the files are giving some immediate value."

"You'd be surprised who Alvarez wrote about. He must have felt a real need to keep accurate records."

"Future blackmail," Jerry said. "Get 'em once and you've got 'em for a lifetime."

"You've won round one," Mike interjected, "How does it feel?"

"Precarious, my love," he said, as he opened the outside door for her. "Very precarious. How are the kids?"

She smiled. "Safe. Raoul has left for the Wind Rivers."

Jerry tried to hide his concern with words. "I've never seen anyone as good as he is at living off the land. He knows what to do? Where to go if . . ."

"He knows." She smiled. "Rashid? Did you take him to the university on your way to Washington?"

"As planned," Jerry replied. "Under an assumed name, of course, and the new identity papers we got for him. He's living in the Towers and trying to act like he's enjoying himself." He paused. "And the girls?"

"Inside."

"Good. The baby over her cold?"

"Shai isn't a baby anymore, dearest. She's nearly six." Mike reminded him.

"I forget. Another thing for which you can sue me."

Mike spoke as Jerry opened the door for her. "I'm glad they're here rather than in some safe house halfway round the world as we originally planned. It will be hard enough worrying about the boys."

"It's not safe anywhere now, Mike. We both know it. If they find this place . . ." Jerry shook out his coat, afraid of finishing the sentence.

"I know, I know," she said tightly. Jerry took her in his arms and held her close. There had been many sleepless nights while they were deciding how best to protect their family from what they knew would come if they went after the Cosa Nostra. They had taken it to their three oldest children for discussion. There hadn't been total agreement.

Raoul, Rashid, and Issa had all been adopted, and all were veterans of survival on the streets of East Jerusalem. Raoul had lived with his grandfather since childhood because his mother had died in childbirth and no one knew who his father was, not for sure. When his grandfather went blind the boy had gone to the streets to earn enough to keep both of them alive. He had done so successfully for two years before his grandfather passed away.

Rashid and Issa were real brother and sister. Their father had gone to Lebanon to fight with the PLO and was killed there. When Issa was only four their mother died from pneumonia. Rashid knew that if they were found by authorities and sent to an orphanage they would be separated. Instead he provided for them in the streets. He had been doing it for four years when a strange set of circumstances brought them into the lives of Jeremiah and Michaelene Daniels.

In 1992 when Jerry and Mike had been in Israel with the advance peace team, there had been an attempt on their lives by terrorists trying to discredit the American aims in peace talks. The children had been instrumental in saving their lives. And Mike and Jerry found themselves firmly attached to three young Arab children.

The Israeli government had cleared the red tape away in the adoption process so that the children could leave the country with their newly found parents. The five had been a family ever since.

There had been good times and bad times after their arrival in America. It was hard for the children to adjust to their new environment and new lives on a ranch in Jackson Hole, Wyoming. Issa never looked back, but when the boys were confronted with new rules, school, and some old-fashioned American prejudice, they had a hard time despite their love for their new parents.

Then Shai had come.

Shai was born a few months after their return from Israel. She came at just the right time. Issa needed a little sister, and the boys' minds were diverted by her soft little body and beautiful smile. Jerry and Mike were amazed at the change as the kids focused all their attentions on their new little sister. The problems that seemed to be mounting soon disappeared as the boys became more willing to make adjustments. Of course, there were still prejudices that had to be dealt with, things to be taught and learned, but the change Shai engendered gave them the incentive.

Even Mike changed.

Mike had loved the children from the first, as she loved her twin nephews, but the sudden thrust into parenthood had needed more than that. Issa had been the easiest for Mike. She was young, willing, and very loving, and they had drawn close, but still something had been missing. The boys had been more difficult for Mike to adjust to, and she found herself gritting her teeth against their obstinacy at times and wanting to shake them at others.

She did love them, but not enough. A moment in the hospital, however, changed all those things for her.

The nurse had just delivered Shai to her for feeding when Jeremiah and the three kids showed up, sneaking into her room through a back entrance. They all beamed at the sight of their new little sister, cuddled her, kissed her gently, and held her close, the love for her shining from their eyes like sparkling stars. It was at that moment that Mike stopped thinking of Issa and the boys as something other than her own flesh and blood. It was as if she had given birth to all of them.

The boys hadn't converted to the Church easily. Islamic traditions and beliefs were a far cry from the structured worship of the gospel of Christ, and they had a difficult time adjusting. Issa, on the other hand, loved Primary with all the activity and the lessons; and being young, she embraced the new life of a Latter-day Saint, and her testimony of the things she was taught came as a natural part of her growing up. Jerry had baptized her a year after they came from Jerusalem.

But Raoul and Rashid had taken longer. Raoul had always relied on Rashid for spiritual guidance, and this time was no different. He waited for Rashid to begin reading the Book of Mormon, then they read it together. He listened as Rashid explained the doctrines to him—at least the ones Rashid understood—and was there when Rashid asked Jerry question upon endless question. But it was Raoul who finally got them both off dead center and into the water.

They were in the mountains rounding up cattle when a rainstorm blew in and forced them to take temporary cover.

They talked about what they had learned and, as with so many times before, Rashid had rationalized waiting. This time Raoul forced the issue.

"It's true, Rashid," he had said adamantly. "And it's time we stopped dragging our feet and did something about it. I'm going to ask Jerry to baptize me next Saturday. I've only got three years until I'm old enough to go on a mission and I want to be ready. I'm going to be baptized."

Rashid later told Mike that he thought he hadn't heard properly at first, but after a few minutes of wonder and questioning he, too, had decided that all he was trying to do was put off the inevitable. He knew the Book of Mormon was true—had known it since the first time he read it—but had rationalized putting off baptism in a Christian faith. He was Arabic and Arabic was Islamic. It was hard to shake the old to put on the new.

But they had done it. On a beautiful summer day the boys had been baptized in the cold waters of the Hoback River by Jerry, then confirmed by their good friend, Bishop Hansen.

A month later the children had told Jerry and Mike that they wanted to go to the temple to be sealed as a family. It had been a beautiful moment. After that experience they had become true followers of Jesus Christ and never looked back. Raoul eventually went on his mission, serving honorably among the Islamic people living in southern Ukraine. He had only been home six months.

After the sealing in the temple feelings changed in the Daniels family. Previously there had been mutual respect and honor between the kids, Mike, and Jerry. Afterward they had love. How deeply their love was shown in their response to the challenge of Cosa Nostra.

Jeremiah had told them the whole story and what the consequences might be if they took up the torch their grandfather had been killed for carrying. Jerry made it very clear what the dangers would be and how serious the enemy would take their opposition.

The children could see the inner conflict in their father. They sensed his reluctance to get involved because he feared for his family. They tried to put his mind at ease with overwhelming support, until he told them he was sending them back to Israel.

Jeremiah had made arrangements to hide them with

friends in their old country. He told them why it was best and tried to convince them that they should go without a fuss. They balked.

"They're going to find us no matter where we go," Raoul had said.

"You said yourself no one can escape," Rashid chimed in. "So why run? That just makes it harder. We won't run!"

"I want to be on my own turf—the mountains," Raoul said. Since the first year Raoul had been in Jackson Hole he had loved the Wind River and Gros Ventre ranges. He had spent every minute he could exploring them, learning to live in them. By the time he was a senior in high school he was an expert on survival, and Jerry and Mike had become somewhat jealous. He seemed to love his bay mare, mule, and the Wind Rivers more than he did them.

"I'll be safe in the mountains, Dad," Raoul said. "You take Rashid and the girls to Israel."

"Not a chance," Rashid said, with a smile on his carefree face. "I go on with life as usual. Just get me a new identity, Dad. Nobody can find students at BYU! Not even the professors." Then the smile left. "I'm not going to Israel. I'm not going into hiding."

Then there was silence. Jerry was flustered. The boys had always been headstrong, always able to express themselves and talk to him, and he had always listened. This was different. This was their lives.

"I'm sorry," he said, "but you go."

The boys were about to erupt when quiet little Issa, who said very little most of the time, and never disagreed with her father, spoke firmly. "We're not going, Dad. If they came after Shai and me in Israel, what would you do? I'll tell you what you'd do! You'd endanger yourself coming to our rescue! It's better that we stay together."

So, with their family in total rebellion, Jerry and Michaelene Daniels rethought their plans. They decided Issa was right. If the kids were too far away and got into trouble they would never be able to get to them in time. They would be better off close by. Raoul *was* better off in the mountains, with thousands of acres in which to hide and friends and family to whom he could run if needed. Jerry and Mike *would* feel more comfortable with the girls close by, under their own watchful eye and those of their friends, instead of thousands of miles away in the arms of relative strangers.

Rashid was Jerry's biggest worry. The boy didn't take life very seriously; he never had. Jerry understood why. Rashid had been raised a street-smart Arab kid in Jerusalem's volatile atmosphere, where he survived day to day by his wits, fast thinking and daring. He had seen and dealt with enough crises in his young life that it was hard to take this one any more seriously. It was far more serious, however, than anything he had encountered in the past.

But Jeremiah Daniels's second oldest son was smart—a survivor—and Jerry trusted him more than he could explain. Rashid would be all right at the University. He would be all right anywhere.

Just in case, however, Jeremiah and Mike had planned carefully for the unseen, giving both boys numbers to call, setting up escape routes, making sure someone who could help would be close by.

———

Jerry put his arm around Mike's shoulder and moved to the door on the far side of the living area. It let them into a small hallway with several doors, and a set of stairs going up to the captain's deck and down to the cabins and engine room, computer room, and weapons storage.

"I want to go with you to L.A. when you take DeGuillio before the judge for arraignment," Mike said.

Jerry frowned. "Too dangerous!"

"I want to," Mike said firmly. "The judge there—"

"We'll see."

Mike gave him the look that said, "I'm going," but didn't say any more.

"I assume the kids are in the playroom. Tell them I'll be in shortly. I'd better check with Stockman, then with Trayco and Macklin."

They kissed, then moved off in separate directions. Jerry went down a level and entered the communications room from which the yacht was operated.

———

Ruth stood at the counter filling her glass with orange juice and occasionally glancing out the window. The sky was a white gray, the wind slapping snow against the rectangular triple pane window. It matched her mood.

She heard a slight noise behind her and turned to find Tom staring at her from the door of the galley, a worried look on his face.

"What?" she asked, raising the glass to her lips.

"Nothing," he said. "Any of that left?"

She reached for the pitcher of juice and handed it to him. Pulling a glass from the cupboard, he filled it while she took bread from the plastic bag and shoved a couple of slices in the toaster. "American breakfasts aren't really very appealing," she said. "No fish, no olives, no tomatoes, just toast. Boring."

He smiled. "There're always waffles."

"Fix me some?"

"Sure. Do you want blueberry or strawberry topping with your whipped cream?" He smiled, remembering their second breakfast together. It seemed so long ago since that military assignment that had brought them together. So much had happened since then. So many good things. So many things he didn't want to lose.

"Strawberry. What happened while I was asleep?"

He shrugged. "Not much. Jerry's here. I imagine we'll have a briefing soon. We'll see."

"Did you get anything out of DeGuillio?"

"What we did get you wouldn't want to hear." He sat the empty cup down and pulled a bowl from the cupboard. "Do you know where they keep the pancake batter?"

Ruth pointed toward a door. "In the pantry."

When he had retrieved the sack of Krustaez and poured two cups in the bowl he spoke again. "Are you all right?"

Ruth shrugged, but didn't respond.

Macklin's stomach was a knot. He had slept very little. Ever since she had lost the baby, Ruth had been down and depressed. He couldn't help but think she had put herself at risk needlessly in Syria—without thinking or caring about the possible consequences.

They had gone through this once before. When they first met, Ruth had suffered through so much death and loss that she was empty of anything but hate. Her parents, her brothers, her first husband—all killed for the sake of Israel; all driving her a little closer to the edge of sanity.

But she had gotten over it. He had watched the sadness leave her eyes, the emptiness fill up. Hadn't he?

Macklin shook off the thought. Of course he had. This wasn't the same. There *was* sadness. Losing the baby was hard on both of them. Of course, it was hardest on Ruth, but that didn't mean all the rest had to come back.

He stirred in the water, using a spatula. "You slept for nearly fourteen hours, Mrs. Macklin," he said while adding more water.

She sipped from her cup. "Umm, it felt very good," Ruth responded flatly. She forced a smile. "Hurry up, will you? I'm hungry." She went to the table, pulled out a chair, and sat, watching Tom at the counter and stove.

Thomas Macklin had changed her life. After all the emptiness, she had finally felt love and caring again. The hate and anger had fled like startled birds and she had wanted to live again. Then when she had become pregnant— oh, what a glorious thing it had been!

But like the rest of her life her beautiful world had collapsed again. Losing the baby, losing the chance for any babies! How could life be so cruel? Couldn't God see her need to have that child, to have more children? Hadn't she given enough? Hadn't she lost enough?

She gripped the cup tightly, squeezing it until her fingers turned pale white. She took a deep breath, running her free hand through her dark hair. It was all coming back. The anger! The emptiness!

But at Boudia's she had wanted to live. Before she had fallen in love with Thomas, she hadn't cared. He had been her salvation.

She glanced at him as he poured a package of berries into the batter and began stirring. A slight smile creased her lips. He was still her salvation, her deepest reason for living. Oh, how she had wanted to give him children!

Tears sprang to her eyes and she quickly rubbed them away, afraid Tom would turn around and see them. Her sadness hurt him and she knew it. She'd hurt him enough.

"Good morning, you two," said Mike, coming into the galley.

"Morning," replied Macklin, half turning from his chore.

"Hi," Ruth said with half a smile.

"Jerry's with Dolph," Mike said to Macklin. "He'll want you and Trayco in with DeGuillio in a few minutes."

"I've started some pancakes. If you'll finish . . . ?" he looked questioningly at Mike.

"Got it." She took the spatula. Macklin ran his fingers through Ruth's hair and kissed her forehead, then headed for the hallway and stairs beyond.

Mike finished stirring the batter, removed the grill from a cupboard, and plugged it in. "How are you doing?" she asked.

Ruth's brow wrinkled. "Better. Thanks for the sleeping pills. I was so tired and yet my mind couldn't seem to shut down."

"You were ready for a nervous breakdown, Ruth. You need to tell Tom."

"I'm fine, really. It's over. My body is rested now."

Mike looked at Ruth wanting to say more but deciding against it. She had told Jerry about Ruth, and he had promised she was out of the picture from here on out. Given time to pull things together, Ruth would probably be all right. Since coming to know her, Mike had been awed by her amazing strength and ability. But she knew what was happening inside Ruth's head as well. They had talked about the loss of the baby and the fact that the doctors had removed most of Ruth's reproductive organs because of a growth discovered there. That part Ruth had hidden from her husband. Why, Mike would never be able to understand. She sighed as she poured the first row of pancakes on the grill. At least the tumor had been benign.

"What happens now?" Ruth asked.

"We hide, and wait. Tony D will be arraigned in the morning, and Alvarez is in maximum security awaiting his trial; Gad is with him. Boudia is under Nabril's able protection. If he lives he'll be brought to the United States and arraigned as well. They go after Lima tomorrow or the next day. All of it will force someone's hand."

They both heard little feet coming down the hall and turned to see Shai running into the galley. It was time for breakfast. A knot formed in Mike's stomach as she remembered the two boys wouldn't be at the table this morning. She missed them.

And she prayed they would be careful.

Four men occupied the communications room, and all smiled and greeted Jerry as he entered. Everything was operated from here, including steering the ship which was all done by computer. The chief officer shook his hand. "Welcome back, Jeremiah. Everything okay in Washington?"

"Yup. The war is made. Is everything all right here?" Jerry asked.

"Fine," said the chief officer, pointing toward a bank of computers and radar screens. "Nothing within a hundred miles. This storm is growing, and it's supposed to get worse over the next few days. It will probably force the evacuation of tourist facilities in the park. Shut it down." He smiled. "Wouldn't hurt my feelings."

"Will the cloud cover hide us from satellite detection?" Jerry asked.

"Mostly. The high resolution systems they have now can see through some of the lighter stuff."

"Well, let's hope our pretty little yacht escapes their scrutiny," Jerry said. "We need a few days before we start worrying about running for our lives."

The chief officer pointed to a pile of papers on his console desk top. "A stack of stuff you need to look through when you have some time, but nothing critical. Everything seems to be falling the way we intended. The press has just picked up the story of Tony's disappearance and the murder at the hotel. Everyone is trying to put the two together and come up with a mafioso reprisal of some kind. That'll keep the media kids busy and away from us. I expect Alvarez and Boudia will hit the international press tomorrow, but I don't think anyone will make the connection to Tony."

"They shouldn't," Jerry assured them. "Nobody had the slightest idea. Anything from LOGOS?"

LOGOS was the code name for a pair of computer specialists housed in Washington, D.C., who had access to the world's intelligence information through TITAN, the United States information gathering network. LOGOS gleaned, evaluated, and assimilated all intelligence information they could access and watched for tidbits that could bring down the Cosa Nostra. It fed all the information into the command center computers in the *ISSA*.

"Nothing," said the chief officer. "LOGOS has her ear to the ground, but it's still too early. The enemy is probably scrambling. We should start to see something happening in Tony's organization tomorrow."

"Are we still plugged into his office?"

"Loud and clear."

"And Lima?"

"Our sources say he's heard and has doubled his security. But he'll be where we want him when we want him."

Jerry smiled. "A year of work is paying off."

"More than that. Your dad-in-law—"

"Yeah, I forget sometimes. Four years of work. Thank goodness he had you guys well enough organized to keep me afloat when I took on this job. Without you, and the others left from the task force, and his notes . . ."

"Umm . . . You'd better get upstairs," the officer suggested. "I'll let you know if anything new comes through."

Jerry turned and went back the way he had come. Adolph Stockman, chief officer of the *ISSA* command center, had been Jim Freeman's assistant. When it was decided to go after the Cosa Nostra, Jerry gave him direct responsibility to oversee field operations. A more qualified man for the job didn't exist. A veteran of both the Korean and Vietnam conflicts he had moved up through the ranks of army intelligence. More times than the generals wanted to admit, Dolph Stockman had saved their skins—and several thousands of lives.

But Dolph had quit; he took out early retirement. Nam had sickened him and he refused to continue working with a corrupt hierarchy. He returned to the private sector, becoming the heart and soul behind one of Washington's most prominent war-game think tanks. He was so good that he caught the eye of the president and was brought on board as a special consultant to the White House on intelligence matters. That was where he had started palling around with James Freeman, head of the Senate Select Committee on Intelligence. When Jim retired from the Senate to become drug czar and needed an intelligence savvy individual to help find the roots of the evil, he found Dolph Stockman was the natural choice.

Jerry opened the door and entered the small room used as a lockup. A belligerent but tired Anthony DeGuillio sat on a straight-backed chair against the wall, the two front legs off the floor. Trayco was leaning against a sink vanity built against the far wall, and Macklin was behind a desk with a series of papers in front of him. He seemed engrossed.

"Morning, gentlemen," Jerry said.

"Jeremiah," Trayco said tightly.

"Jerry." Macklin looked over the top of his reading glasses, then back to the report. "About time you showed up. The whole world is falling apart and you're off for a sunny holiday."

"It's cold in Washington and I haven't had a vacation in years. Mr. DeGuillio, I presume?"

Tony got to his feet. "You the big boss around here? Well, I want outa this prison. I want my attorney!" He walked toward Jerry, but Trayco grabbed his arm and slapped his chubby frame back onto the chair. Jerry eyed his big friend.

"You seem to have upset Mr. Trayco, Tony."

"This pig?" he said, leaning the chair again. Trayco kicked the legs out from under it, sending Tony sprawling on the floor with a plop. He screamed a line of obscenities while scrambling away from Kenny.

Jerry walked to where Tony cowered against the wall and took him by the arm, helping him to his feet, and mockingly dusted him off.

"Tch, tch, Mr. DeGuillio. You'd best watch your language. I can't be here every minute to watch out for you, and Mr. Trayco doesn't take kindly to name-calling."

Jeremiah jerked Tony toward the table and chairs near the center of the room and shoved him in their direction with a motion to sit.

"Please. We have things to discuss." Jerry gathered another chair and placed it across from Tony D, who was trying to stare Trayco down. It wasn't working and his eyes finally moved to the table in front of him. Most men felt intimidated by Kentucky Trayco, especially if they knew his reputation. Tony knew.

"First of all, we have you, Mr. DeGuillio, for two murders. One that Mr. Trayco's team watched you perform and which one of your thugs screamed to the cops about. His testimony has you cold."

Tony scoffed. "It was self-defense. There were other witnesses—"

"Please, don't interrupt me," Jerry said, a fake smile crossing his lips. "Second, we are charging you with the murder of James Freeman." Jerry held out his hand and Macklin placed a paper in it. "That is a sworn statement. You were the one who gave the orders." He placed it in front of Tony and pointed at one sentence. "You will note that it says you even selected the killer to be used, the amount to be paid, and made the call."

Tony began to sweat, his eyes moving quickly down the page. The signature at the bottom was blacked out. He grabbed the paper with both hands and ripped it into shreds, throwing it in Jerry's direction.

"A photocopy. The original has been presented to a federal grand jury. You've been indicted for first degree murder." Jerry stood. It felt good to pronounce the man's future so boldly. "You'll never see the light of day again, Mr. DeGuillio. You will receive no bail, and you will remain with us until the day of your trial." He leaned across the table, putting his face near the sweating man's fat jowls. "Asking for the death penalty is going to be a pleasure."

"I . . . I want . . . my attorney. You can't hold . . ."

Jerry pointed at the monitor and camera attached to the far wall. "Your attorney will be contacted and a similar setup as that one will be placed in his office. You will see him and he will see you by television camera."

"But that's not the law. You can't keep me a prisoner . . . I mean, I have to *see* my attorney."

"You will *see* him. See is not touch, Mr. DeGuillio. Besides, it's for your own safety."

Tony took the bait.

"My safety?"

"You are a wanted man. Your West Coast organization has fallen apart and you have become a liability. Sicily will eliminate you."

Tony D smiled. "I don't know what you're talking about."

Jerry glanced at Macklin, now leaning back in the desk chair and enjoying the action. "Hear that, Macklin?"

Macklin stood and came around to the table, placing a sheath of papers on it. "Read those over during the next few hours, Tony. It will explain just how much of a liability you have become. We have your financial records. We have Alvarez and his records, and Boudia and his. All of it ties the three of you together in a tight little package that the prosecuting attorney will have a heyday with. As my friend here says, you'll never see the light of day again. *That* makes you a liability. They won't take the chance of you making a deal to save your own hide. You know how they operate. They don't trust people anymore, Tony. It's easy to get someone else." Macklin put his finger to his head and bent his thumb. "Bang."

Tony blinked, then shook his head. "I have nothing to say. I don't know any Alvarez or Boudia."

"Read the report, Tony," said Macklin. "You'll see your future as in a crystal ball. That's why we're going to keep you here. It isn't safe for you out *there*. They'll come after you. We know you're a capo. You know names, places, and things that can hurt them. If we don't protect you, they'll kill you."

"And we don't want that to happen," Jerry added. "We want to make our own example of you. We'll go after Lima next, then anyone else we can get our hands on. We intend to make sure Sicily gets a message. We want them out of this country and then we're coming after them, too."

Tony laughed loudly. "You think you can beat *them*?" He slapped his hand against the table and leaned across it, his red eyes wide, the hate in the hardness of his taut muscles. *"You fool!"* he spat toward Jerry. "They will break you like a twig!"

Tony got to his feet and paced to the wall, pounding it with his hand. "Lima is nothing. Replaceable in hours. All of us are replaceable. You think you are up against some small-time mafioso?" He turned back to Jerry. "I and my family, all of us, work for them. We do not do it because we want to! They control the drug trade! The rest of us do what we are told." He paused. "Or we are buried." He walked back to the table.

"My father was one of the strongest of the American Mafia. He was untouchable, always keeping a small army around him. People ate his food before he touched it, checked every building and room before he entered it. No one knew where he would be from one minute to the next minute, not even me. They got to him, Mr. Czar. They blew him into small pieces."

"With your cooperation."

"A rumor. I had nothing to do with it. But if I had, it would have been out of a desire to preserve my family. They would have killed all of us." He leaned across the table again, his voice full of rigid fear that made the hair on the back of Jerry's head stand on end. "You, *Mr. Czar,* are as dead as I am." He paused, a hateful grin spreading across his face. "Do not let your family out of your sight. They are dead as well!"

The room was silent for a moment. Tony returned to the

wall, thinking, letting his words have their intended impact before speaking again. "Sicily, Mr. Daniels, is Satan incarnate." He walked back to the table and sat, fixing his eyes on Jerry. He leaned forward again. "They will not allow *anyone* to challenge them. That is why James Freeman was killed and that is why you will be killed as well."

Jerry licked his dry lips and tried to swallow, before speaking as calmly as he could. "We know about the purges, the violence. In the last three years nearly four thousand known drug and Mafia people have been brutally murdered. We know—"

Tony slammed his open palm onto the desk again. *"You know nothing!* You have no idea what you are up against. By your interference you have signed the death warrants of everyone in this room, and many others who will get caught in the cross fire of transition. You, Mr. Daniels, have as good as murdered them, and for what? You think you can really stop *them*?" He laughed and Jerry's hair stood on end again. "No one, not even God, can stop them!"

He looked around the room. "You think you are well hidden in this place." His hand swept above his head in a wave of dismissal. "They may already know where you are." He leaned forward again. "They do not control the nation's drug businesses just with bullets. They control them through controlling everything around them. Everything! Everyone! If they haven't done so already they will find someone who will tell them where you are and they will buy him. Few men can resist speaking a few words for a million dollars of tax-free money." He leaned forward again. "Once they know where you are, they will come for you. We are all dead men."

Jeremiah worked up some saliva before speaking. "We know the dangers, Tony. We also know the only way for any of us to survive is by getting to them first. We need your help."

Tony smiled. "Not a chance."

"You're a dead man, Tony, unless we protect you."

"It is my family I'm trying to save now."

All were silent. Tony was cutting his losses.

"Be warned, Mr. Daniels. By fighting you, I show them I want my family to live. I will kill you, if you give me the chance. All of you. It is what they expect. If I do not try, my sons and daughters will never live to see children of their own." Tony's eyes were cold gray, his voice filled with an icy determination that made Jerry shudder.

Tony turned and walked through the door leading to the small commode, closing the door behind him.

Jerry glanced at the other two, then motioned toward the door while rubbing at the goose bumps on his arms. After they had climbed the stairs and entered the living room, he went to the wet bar and poured himself a glass of ice water, downing it in one motion.

Trayco spoke. "Makes your skin crawl, don't it?"

"Scares the heck out of me," Macklin said, joining Jerry at the bar.

Jerry poured another glass of water and downed it, the faces of his own kids filling his mind. He spoke. "I told you in the beginning what they have accomplished. Tony only gave testimony to that." He paused. "Did he change your minds?"

"Nope," Trayco said as Macklin shook his head in the negative. "But he should have changed yours."

The room was silent, each one deep in his own thoughts. Then Macklin spoke. "How'd things go in Washington?"

"Good. Support is strong, but the word really isn't out yet. I suspect that the enemy will start using their political connections today."

"Is the president still with us?"

"Don't worry about Seth Adams. He wants this worse than we do."

"I've always said odds in Las Vegas would put us down ten to one," Trayco said.

"Yeah." Jerry chuckled. "But we've made a start. Odds makers to the contrary."

Stockman came down the hall and handed Jerry some papers. "We just got these. We're tapped into Lima's office." Jerry handed it to Tom.

Macklin looked at the computer printout of the conversation. "Who was Lima talking to? Was it by phone? Did we trace it?"

"His computer operator. No, it wasn't by phone. Same method as always—encrypted computer message—and no, we couldn't trace it," Stockman said. "Their system encrypts using an interface message processor and sends it out in packets that are all jumbled up. Part of the words of the first part of the message could be in half a dozen packets. Then they send them out in bursts. If we're lucky enough to intercept, say, the first burst, the fifth burst, and the twentieth burst, we still don't have anything but a jumbled bunch of nothing."

Stockman paused, wondering if they understood what he was telling them. When there were no questions he went on. "What you have in your hands is all we have, and we only have that because Lima was careless and verbally dictated a return message to his computer operator. Our listening device picked it up."

Trayco took the printout and read it. "He's been told to get rid of Alvarez."

Macklin stood and walked to the window. The snow had stopped but the clouds were thick and white, and he could feel the cold coming off the thick window pane. It made him shiver.

"Tell Gad to get Alvarez under heavy guard as quickly as he can," Jerry said. "Which brings me to our next matter. DeGuillio's arraignment is tomorrow at 8:00 A.M."

"Shouldn't be a problem," Trayco said. "The judge is clean, isn't he?"

"Very, and we have his family under our protection, but there is, or at least could be, one problem. Jack Canyon called."

Macklin walked quickly back to the couch. "Rolf Koln."

"Exactly. He's in L.A. Arrived last night. Jack is keeping an eye on him, but I think you should give him a hand, Kenny, and I want you to join him as soon as you can. I want Koln watched. If he tries to pull this one himself, I want him caught in the act. He's closer to the Cosa Nostra than any outsiders we know of, and killers like him are survivors. He might make a deal with us, give us names and testimony."

When Carmen DeGuillio's son had come to the government for vengeance, he had given Rolf Koln's name as his first show of sincerity. Koln was Jim Freeman's killer, he said. Jerry had decided to keep an eye on the gunman. Although it had been difficult, and they knew where he wasn't more than they knew where he was, it had finally paid off.

Macklin remembered reading Koln's file, what little there was of it. German. Nearly six feet tall, blond, high cheekbones, blue eyes. Weight at about one hundred and seventy-five. Age, around forty. Served in the German Army special forces. One of their best. Member of their anti-terrorist squad for fifteen years, responsible for putting to rest some big names in that world. A national hero, so the file said.

Koln had quit the German military in 1986 then disappeared, emerging again in 1987 looking a little older, a little heavier, and a whole lot richer. With apartments in half a dozen countries, an estate in Switzerland, and a number of bank accounts in questionable places, Koln had a propensity for being in places where belligerent Cosa Nostra employees ended up dead. Always he had alibis and legitimate business reasons for being there, but he *was* there.

No one could figure out why the hero had gone bad, unless it was money—but Macklin had another suspicion. He just couldn't prove it. He didn't think Rolf Koln was really who he said he was. He thought that the real Koln was lying dead in a deep grave somewhere and that the new Rolf Koln had used his identity and a good plastic surgeon for his own purposes. But then Thomas Macklin had an over-active imagination.

"When Koln discovers he can't reach the judge, he'll make other arrangements," Jerry said. "I want you on his tail, Kenny. I want you to be there to take the gun out of his hand."

CHAPTER 3

11:00 A.M.—*Provo, Utah*

Rashid Daniels looked at the ID card and frowned. The picture was him but the name wasn't, and it made him nervous. He didn't like deception, playing games, or lies. He wasn't Ahmad Tabriz from Turkey. He hardly had an accent anymore, and had never been to Turkey!

He sighed, looking at the dwindling line in front of him. The deception had to be, for his own protection and for his parents' peace of mind. But he didn't have to like it.

He noticed the girl at the counter. Pretty. Her hair was dark, her skin olive in color, and she had dark brown eyes shaped like almonds. Arabic for sure. What if she was Turkish?

He gulped. She would speak with the Turkish dialect of Arabic, and would immediately know he was a fake! He quickly looked at the other lines and thought of switching.

No. That would look strange, too obvious. He stepped forward.

"May I help you?" the girl asked, only a slight accent to her voice.

Rashid looked up and found himself at the counter. Taken off guard, he opened his mouth but couldn't speak.

"May I help you?" she asked again, a curious smile creasing her well-formed lips. She was beautiful.

Rashid put his ID on the counter, then the paper stating his tuition had been paid, but that he needed to pay an additional sixty dollars in fees. "I . . . I . . . ."

She took the paper and glanced at it. "Mr. Tabriz, from Turkey, you owe the University sixty dollars for fees."

He removed his wallet, promptly dropping it on the floor. Flushing, he glanced at her then reached down for the wallet. She leaned forward, her eyes following his movements.

"Sorry," he said, his English almost too perfect.

She smiled, taking the hundred-dollar bill he handed her.

"Is this your first time to this country?"

Rashid quickly remembered the cover story his father told him to use. "No . . . no. I . . . ah . . . have been here several years. With an . . . aunt . . . aunt and uncle."

She smiled again. "There is an Arab club on campus. Are you interested?"

The question startled Rashid. "Club?"

"Yeah. We who are of Arab descent meet, talk about our countries, the old ways, that sort of thing. Would you like to come?"

Rashid felt the pressure of other students' impatience behind him while trying to deal with the girl's good looks and her invitation. Without thinking it through properly he said yes.

"Good." She wrote something on a piece of paper and shoved it his way. "That's the time and place for the first meeting. I'm Seriza. Seriza Maxwell." She saw the quizzical but somewhat relieved look on his face. "Arab descent through my mother. My father was American and was working for an American firm in Kuwait when they met. My home is in California now." She smiled. "See you at the meeting?"

He returned the smile. "Sure. Glad to meet you." He stepped from the line and turned away. His palms were sweating and his heart thumped against the inside of his

51

chest. Seriza. It was almost as pretty as the woman who owned it.

As his steps took him out the south door of the administration building, he came to his senses and stopped in his tracks, slapping his palm against his forehead. What had he done?

His heart sank. He just wouldn't attend, that's all. There would probably be students from Turkey, and they would expect him to know something of the country. As he went down the few stairs and passed the fountain he glanced back at the building, regretting the end of what might have been.

Raoul Daniels hitched the last rope over the mule's packs and cinched it tight. The snow was starting to fall again, and he pulled his wool-lined coat up around his neck to where it came in contact with his Stetson. The tips of his ears remained partly uncovered but had grown used to cold weather.

Looking over the campsite, he made sure he left nothing undone. The wilderness was beautiful. If man used it he should leave it no worse for wear and tear; a concept many tourist types couldn't seem to get through their thick skulls.

Raoul had been fascinated with the mountains since the first time he looked at them from the window of the Delta airline jet. He loved the beauty, majesty, and solitude they offered him. His adopted father, Jeremiah Daniels, had told him stories of the mountains and his mountain-man/Indian heritage. Those had intrigued Raoul, drawing him even deeper into the mountain's spell. Every chance he got he spent camped out, exploring the hills around the ranch. In the summers he spent all his time checking their cattle grazing deep in the Gros Ventre Range. He loved the wilderness and learned to live as a part of it.

He mounted the bay mare and spurred her out of the leafless trees and across a creek before reining her into the trail along Bacon Ridge. After a mile's journey he pulled over, dismounted, and tied the horse and mule. Taking a pair of binoculars, he moved quietly between trees and underbrush to an outcrop of rocks overlooking the snow-covered valley and hills below. Raoul put the glasses to his eyes and began checking his back trail foot by foot through increasingly heavy snow. His father had been explicit. The enemies of Jeremiah Daniels would come after his family and try to use them as leverage. He must be watchful—and ready.

For Rashid it had been a horrible day. Every class, and there were four of them on Tuesdays and Thursdays, had piled on the work. He was beginning to feel like Raoul's mule. The job of working at the university's computer center that he had wanted so badly had fallen through, going to some egghead senior who looked like the scientist father in *Honey, I Shrunk the Kids*. Then there had been the decision not to attend the Arab club meeting. The thought of Seriza excited him, and deciding not to go where he could see her again had added to his depression. He hated being Ahmad Tabriz!

The walk up the hill to Deseret Towers and his room seemed steeper than usual, and the air had cooled considerably, making him wish he lived below campus instead of above it—or that he had brought a coat that morning.

As he stepped into the crosswalk the honk of a horn startled him and he quickly glanced at the traffic light. It was red and he was in the right. He gave a hard stare at the driver, his coal black eyes boring a hole through the windshield. He was in no mood for some high and mighty idiot . . .

"Hi!"

His mouth dropped open as Seriza's head dipped out of the driver's side window. "Want a ride?"

Rashid gulped, then stammered, his hot breath filling the air with puffs of smoke. "Uh . . . I . . ." He pointed toward the Towers. "I just live there. It isn't far enough . . ."

"Come on, get in. It's cold, and you look like you've had it for one day. The Towers are on my way."

Another car turned the corner and swerved a little to miss the backend of Seriza's jade green Pontiac Grand Am. "Come on! Before somebody ruins my paint job!"

Rashid moved quickly to the door, opened it, and slid into the passenger seat. He buckled the safety belt as Seriza checked traffic then pulled away from the curb.

"Are you coming to the meeting tonight?" she asked, smiling.

"I . . . ah . . ." He wished he could quit stuttering. All he had done since meeting this girl was stutter. "I . . . no, I don't think so."

She looked surprised. "Why not?"

"I . . . ah . . . my teachers loaded me down like an indentured servant. I have to study."

She smiled. "Do you need some help?"

He looked at her quizzically. "You don't even know me."

"You're Ahmad Tabriz; you're a freshman at BYU; you're Arabic. I also am of Arabic descent, a sophomore who knows something about how things are done around here, and I'm glad to help. Besides, you're cute." She grinned. He flushed.

"Here we are," she said, pulling to the curb in front of the Morris Center. "I'll pick you up at five o'clock. We'll study together, then go to the meeting. How's that?"

Rashid was backing out of the car, pulling his books after him. A pencil fell out of his shirt pocket and he grabbed for it, dropping it again. He felt like such a klutz.

"See you then," she said as he closed the door. "Right here." The Pontiac moved down the street as Rashid stood on the pavement, numb but not feeling the cold.

CHAPTER 4

5:00 P.M.—Miami, Florida

Gad pushed the button on the remote and the end of the movie credits blipped off the screen. Standing, he stretched, then checked his watch. It was time.

Gad didn't like staying in one place too long. It gave the opposition time to plan. By moving Alvarez periodically and without warning he felt he could outwit the people, who might want the Colombian dead, keep them off balance. With Jeremiah's warning he had decided to move him yet again.

There were three other men on his team—all Israelis, all

trusted. But he had to deal with the American police system as well, and that made him nervous. Too many people dramatically increased the chance of leaks. Considering the kind of people they were up against and the money that could be offered, anyone's head could be turned. He had taken all the precautions possible; now he simply had to play the game handed him.

Gad picked up the two-way radio and spoke. "This is Diamond One, where are you, Diamond Two?" Gad said in Hebrew.

Diamond Two was made up of old friends. Daniel Irbev, Adam Akitsa, and Chaim Mizrah, all graduates of ATLIT, the top security commando base in Israel.

"Diamond One, this is Diamond Two." The response was in Hebrew as well. It was the only language they used in communicating with one another. If anyone was listening, they wouldn't have the slightest idea of what was going on unless they had some way of understanding Hebrew. "We are approaching the prison gates. Five minutes to pickup."

Gad walked to the cell block entrance. The guard opened it and let Gad in. Alvarez's cell was two doors down.

Four minutes later Gad had left the inner cell block and was walking toward the exit with Alvarez in tow, his wrists handcuffed behind his back. Three minutes later the van and its passengers were back on the main road. Now it got hairy.

Mizrah was driving and quickly got on the freeway, moving north toward the center of Miami. Gad relaxed a bit while putting on the chest armor all of them wore.

"Anything from Diamond Three?" he asked.

"In place if we need them," Mizrah responded.

Alvarez was trying to be nonchalant, but Gad sensed tension. The Colombian kept glancing out the front window. Gad didn't like it. The man had been in consultation with his attorney less than an hour ago and had been uptight ever since.

"Diamond Three, this is Diamond One. Move in tight." Akitsa shot Gad a quick glance from the front passenger seat, then injected a shell into the riot gun he carried. Irbev pulled the lever back on his Uzi and positioned himself near the windowless rear doors.

"Roger, Diamond One." Seconds later the Cobra combat chopper was above the van and keeping pace, its TOW missile pods menacing in the afternoon sun. The chopper was on loan from the army and held a trusted friend of Kentucky Trayco's from Vietnam days.

Ten minutes later the van turned off the freeway, and the chopper was forced to go higher. This was the part of the journey they had come to call the "Gauntlet." There was little protection here. The street was narrow, tall buildings looming on both sides, the two-lane road narrow and menacing.

Mizrah looked in the rearview mirror. No vehicle followed them off the freeway. That was the reason they chose this exit. It might be narrow but it made it easy to identify anyone following. The only way the Gauntlet could be a factor was if someone knew their plans ahead of time. Only the team knew where they were going, when, and by what route. He breathed easier.

Then he heard the explosion!

Gad rammed his rifle butt against what looked like a lid on the ventilation unit affixed to the top of the van and it broke away. He hit a lever, and a fifty-caliber machine gun sprang through the hole and positioned itself for use. Gad put his shoulders through the opening and did a quick once around of the landscape.

In the distance he saw the rubble of the Cobra dropping from the sky, a large ball of fire shooting skyward. Mizrah jammed the van into low gear and skidded around a corner. It was time for evasive action.

Irbev had already knocked out the breakaway panel in the rear door and was positioning himself with a hand-held TOW missile.

Alvarez sat in the corner his mouth hanging open in awe.

"Get your head down!" Irbev yelled in Spanish. "Your friends won't be particular about who they hit."

Alvarez noticed Akitsa had pushed on a button on the dashboard and a panel had flipped open, revealing a small screen and two handles like those that came with some computer games. What Alvarez couldn't see was that the handles controlled two thirty-caliber machine guns built into the lower front section of the van.

"We have contact," Mizrah said, as two vehicles jumped away from the curb and slammed themselves sideways, blocking the road ahead.

Akitsa pushed a button and the covers over his weapons exploded away. He fired both 30mm cannons, honing in on the vehicles' gas tanks while still a hundred yards away. The cars exploded into flames, their passengers running for their lives into doorways and behind garbage receptacles. Mizrah punched the gas pedal and rammed into what was left of the vehicle on his right, knocking it aside like a toy.

"Glad we had this thing reinforced," he said in English.

Gad saw the man step out of the alley, the long tube on his shoulder. "Missile coming from behind," he said as he fired, forcing the assailant to jump for cover, but not before the TOW had been launched.

The TOW was an old model, wire-directed. As long as the man handling the tube kept his direction steady he could guide the missile home. When the man fell, the missile veered left and exploded into a boarded-up warehouse, disintegrating the two-story wall.

Mizrah turned sharply right and punched it again. Moments later they were two blocks away and breathing easier.

Gad pulled the lever down, and the fifty-caliber gun sprang back into its resting place. Akitsa closed the weapons panel and Irbev leaned against the side wall, his eyes still watching their backside.

"Someone knew the route," Akitsa said in Hebrew, his eyes still scanning the road ahead.

Gad didn't respond, his mind already working on the problem.

Irbev looked at Alvarez and spoke in well-pronounced Spanish. "Don't misunderstand. They were not trying to free you. They were trying to kill you. They were trying to kill all of us."

Alvarez had already turned pale, his lower lip between his teeth. He had no response.

"Pull over!" Gad said in Hebrew. "Find a safe place and pull over." Mizrah flashed a puzzled glance at him, then pulled the van to a stop. Gad removed his revolver and pointed it at Alvarez. "Out. Now!" Alvarez looked bewildered as Gad shoved open the door. "Come on," he said to the others. "This vehicle has to be bugged. A homing device or something. If I don't miss my guess, they'll have more forces coming in here soon. Move it!"

Each grabbed his automatic weapon and extra ammo and jumped from the van. Mizrah pushed a button arming the vehicle's self-destruct system. "Two minutes. Let's go!"

Gad checked both ways. They were among warehouses

on a deserted street. Another reason for taking this route. Any other route would have endangered lives unnecessarily.

They were half a block away when the van exploded several times and became a flaming heap of rubble. Irbev glanced over his shoulder. "I sure hope you're right about this. That's a lot of money that just went up in smoke."

Gad stepped into a boarded-up doorway and rammed his rifle butt against the old lock. The double doors jumped open. "In here," he said. "We'll find out very soon." He scanned the large room. There was a small office nearby, its windows busted out. "Put Alvarez in there. Stuff his mouth with something and tie him down. I don't want interference from him." Akitsa shoved the Colombian in that direction.

Gad went to the window and rubbed away the smudge. The van was burning down, filling the air with smoke. That should bring friends as well as foes. The question was, who would get here first.

"Irbev, find your way to the roof," Gad instructed. "Akitsa will work his way through the back. See if you can get downside of the wreck without being seen. Mizrah and I will cross the street and do the same. Watch the airways, and remember, just because they're dressed in blue uniforms doesn't make them friends. Keep your guard up. We'll use the old hand signs for signaling." Akitsa returned and Gad told him what to do. "If the enemy does show up, I want at least one of them alive. All right, let's move it."

Five minutes later they were all in position. Gad was on the roof opposite Irbev. He watched the street as a black Dodge approached: unmarked, blackwalls, plain. It looked like a government vehicle but came in fast.

Gad recognized the man who stepped from the vehicle: Roger Match, narcotics section. Match was Jeremiah's contact in Florida and the only other man who knew much about what Gad was doing. If he was on the wrong side, it would make Gad's job more difficult.

Match lifted a two-way radio to his mouth and spoke something Gad was unable to hear. Two things could happen. If Match was on the right side, other troops would descend on the spot like vultures. If he wasn't, Gad was on his own.

He signaled to Irbev, who passed it on to Akitsa, unseen to Gad from his angle although on the same side of the street. He watched for Mizrah to appear at the window of the building nearly a block away and opposite him, then gave him the same signal. They were to wait.

Five minutes passed. Match was trying to get close to the vehicle, but it was too hot. He checked his watch and looked up the street. He was waiting for someone. Who?

Gad heard a siren. It came within several blocks then dimmed and went away. A moment later another vehicle appeared. A limousine.

As it pulled up, Match opened the door and a well-dressed man stepped out. They seemed to be arguing. Gad knew the enemy when he saw it. He gave the signal, and placed his weapon on the edge of the roof. It was an easy shot from this distance and Gad pulled the trigger. The sharp cracks of the automatics startled the two men, but the bullets struck the front of the Lincoln and riddled its radiator. Irbev took out the tires on the left, Mizrah the ones on the right. In seconds they had both vehicles handicapped and the men around them ducking for cover.

Gad placed a shot to the left of Match's foot where it stuck out from behind the side of the Lincoln. The foot jerked back. Match's partner started to move toward the Dodge, but Irbev placed a bullet in its windshield and the man ducked down again. Gad showed himself and spoke loud enough to be heard.

"Put your hands on top of your heads and stand up! Now! I have gunmen who can see you very clearly from their positions and I will not hesitate to shoot you and ask questions later."

Match stood, his face pale, but nothing compared to that of the owner of the Lincoln. The chauffeur slid from the vehicle and Match's partner stood clear of the Dodge. Mizrah and Akitsa were in the street and signaled for Gad to join them. Irbev removed Alvarez from the office and joined them as Gad finished his search of the men and threw their weapons in the back seat of the Dodge.

"Well, Mr. Match," Gad said tightly, "it seems you have changed sides. Who is your friend?"

Match cleared his throat but didn't speak.

"Who are you?" Gad asked the owner of the Lincoln. No answer. Gad reached inside the man's suit pocket and removed his wallet. It contained twenty thousand-dollar bills, credit cards, a couple of pictures, and a driver's license. He smiled. "Mr. Lima. This is a surprise. A man of your stature doesn't usually make his own deliveries." He took the twenty thousand-dollar bills from the wallet and threw them toward Match. "I think this is your blood money." Match grabbed at them, then let them blow away, his eyes cold and hard.

"Use the radio in the Dodge, Mizrah," Gad instructed. "Get an *honest* policeman in here. Charlie Buckles over at Central precinct seems like a man who wouldn't sell out. At least not this cheap."

Gad knew Buckles. The man was a sergeant in the anti-terrorist division. He was rough, hard-nosed, and a pro. They had met when Gad first entered the country with Alvarez. Gad had immediately liked Buckles, who had a boxer's face and fists like twenty-pound sledgehammers, thick and hard. Who wouldn't like him?

He needed Buckles. Match had compromised Jerry's group in Florida. They needed to move, and move quickly.

5:00 A.M. (Israel time), Jerusalem

Nabril Al Razd took the last swig of grapefruit drink in the can, crushed it with one hand, and tossed it. The aluminum hit the receptacle's plastic bottom with a dull thud. Standing, he stretched, the muscles of his chest rippling against the tight turtleneck he wore under a tweed sports coat. The handle of the American-made, nickel-plated Colt .45, given him by Jeremiah Daniels for services rendered years earlier, stuck above the belt of his black slacks. He checked his watch.

Boudia had regained semi-consciousness twelve hours ago. Two hours ago he had been removed from the critical care unit and placed in a well-guarded room nearby. It was time to check on things.

Nabril hadn't been home since the night Boudia was captured. He, his wife, and two small children lived on the West Bank in Ramala. Since 1992, when the peace talks started that he, Ruth and Tom Macklin, and the Danielses had nearly died for, things had become progressively better for Palestinians in Israel, especially since 1994. But even though Palestinians now lived with many of the same opportunities as Jews, moving about freely, working together in many of the same factories, and shopping in the same stores, there was still violence, still prejudice, and much yet to be done.

Nabril stepped into the hall. It was nearly midnight and the hospital was quiet except for the sounds of machinery, a few quiet voices, and the occasional moan from behind closed doors. Nabril hated hospitals. Not only because people died here (he was used to death), but also because they died so miserably. To him, dying slowly, relying on others to help you take care of even the most common bodily functions—it was humiliating. Given the choice he would much rather die quickly, without a lot of fuss.

The guards at the door were a mixed lot. One was Jewish, Ruth's choice from her branch of the Israeli Defense Forces (IDF). The other was Palestinian. Nabril had selected him from among the new Palestinian police force now keeping the peace alongside the Israeli army. He hadn't selected him for his size or his beauty—the man was only 5'8" tall and weighed less than 135 pounds, with a squirrely, pock-marked, hard face. He had been chosen because of his ability to work with the Jews. Raised on the West Bank during the days of Intifada, the man had never stooped to destructive violence and hate, preferring to fight for his people by talking out their troubles. Of course, his mouth had gotten him in trouble enough times, but both Jew and Palestinian respected him, and he was instrumental in getting the younger Palestinians to stop throwing rocks and work for the peace process. Dabib Jilani had worked hard to ferret out Palestinian hit squads, who were killing their own kind, so that the killers could be dealt with. He was a brave and intelligent young man who knew and loved his people, and Nabril saw him as the most worthy of the legacy the Nabrils of Palestine had fought for.

"Dabib, how is our patient?" Nabril asked, as he approached Jilani's position outside the door.

"Even stronger," Dabib responded. "Another few days and we should be able to take him to the United States." He looked at the other guard. "Amiram checked on him last."

Amiram gave Nabril the latest update. "He is sleeping, but without the labored breathing." He blushed a little. "The nurse says he is doing very well."

Dabib laughed lightly. "Ami tries to find himself a wife while he is here."

Nabril smiled. "A man his age. It is about time." Ami blushed an even brighter red.

"I will take the place of one of you if you wish to get coffee or sandwiches," Nabril said.

Amiram and Dabib looked at one another, then Ami

spoke. "I will go. I know a place close by." He started toward the elevators just down the hall.

Nabril watched as Amiram pushed the buttons, then glanced their way with a smile as the doors started to slide open. Nabril was just turning away when he saw a look of shock come over the Israeli's face; then he heard the familiar *phfft, phfft* of silenced weapons. As Ami was thrown against the wall, Nabril grabbed Dabib by the shirt collar and flung him toward Boudia's room, drawing his .45 and firing in the same movement. The bullets slammed into the two men with automatics who had appeared in the doorway of the elevator. As the second man fell to the floor he pulled the trigger of his automatic, placing three 9mm slugs in Nabril's body and sending him to the floor.

Dabib, recovering from Nabril's shove, fired at the downed assailant, silencing the weapon that had continued to spray the hallway with bullets.

Dabib saw Nabril's motionless, bleeding body and rage filled his heart. Holding the gun in both hands, he flung his back against the door and aimed the gun in the direction of the elevator. The first assailant had slid to the floor, his eyes still open, a twitch in his neck and cheek.

Dabib saw movement down the hall and his gun came up. Recognizing the nurse, he released the pressure on the trigger.

"Get help!" he yelled. "The alarm!" As she disappeared, Dabib moved toward Ami and the two assailants. He kicked the weapons clear, then knelt to feel Ami's neck for a pulse. Nothing.

A gun fired behind him and he heard the sound of breaking glass. Reacting instantly, he flung himself to the floor and flipped over, facing the door of Boudia's room. Nabril sat with his back against the door frame, his pistol pointed to the interior of the room. Dabib jumped to his feet as Nabril's head lowered to his chest and his hand fell, the gun clattering onto the tile floor.

Peering cautiously into the room, Dabib suddenly became aware of the alarms and chaos. A door near the elevator was flung open and the IDF launched themselves into the hall, automatic rifles at the ready.

"Get a doctor!" Dabib yelled, as they saw and recognized him. "Now!" He knelt by Nabril and checked his pulse. It was faint.

Dabib suddenly realized that another body was in the room—actually, it was half in the room. It appeared that Nabril had killed a third assailant, who had been standing outside the window on the ledge. The body had crashed into the glass and now rested over the windowsill.

A doctor appeared at Nabril's side and began giving orders. Nurses reacted quickly and he was placed on a gurney while an oxygen mask was put over his face. In an instant the emergency team had disappeared through the emergency operating room door.

Dabib checked the third assassin for a pulse and found none. Sweat poured from his face as he slowly holstered his pistol. He glanced toward Boudia.

Boudia was sleeping like a baby.

Day Three
November 15, 1997

CHAPTER 5

5:00 A.M.—*Los Angeles, California*

Koln watched the broadcast of the early news. He was feeling pleased. Things were progressing well. He should have Tony taken care of by noon tomorrow.

The stories about Tony, Alvarez, and Boudia were all on the news. Three drug-related incidents from three different parts of the world. No connection made. The average man on the street had no idea of the Cosa Nostra or how big it really was. Why should they? SCORPION moved in a different world, a world the everyday American wouldn't believe existed even if he saw it. Koln *had* seen it, and he understood it. He was made from the same cloth. After watching the news, he had a better idea of the damage Jeremiah Daniels was doing and was sure a contract on the czar's life would be forthcoming. SCORPION could do little else.

The Colombian government was disavowing any knowledge of the Alvarez kidnapping, blaming it on the United States; but they didn't condemn it. That was foolish. SCORPION would consider it an admission of guilt and order a few more political assassinations to teach them a lesson. Would that country never learn?

The report on Boudia was filled with the usual Jews-beating-up-Arabs slant. The Arabs were always looking for something to make the Jews look bad in the eyes of the world. Forget that Boudia was being protected by Arabs. Forget that he was the largest producer and seller of heroin in that part of the world. Forget that the man killed Arabs as some people kill rats. Forget all that and make it look like a Jewish-Arab problem. Koln laughed lightly. One of the reasons why the Cosa Nostra did so well was the world's propensity to muddy up the waters with nothing. People focused on the mud while the real problems swam about hardly noticed.

Koln remembered when the Iron Curtain fell. The world focused on the troubles between Russian politics while SCORPION was organizing the Russian drug trade, eliminating opposition, and putting itself in a position to control the black markets in food, gasoline, counterfeiting and clandestine arms sales. By 1994 the Cosa Nostra was firmly entrenched, with no one the wiser.

With Russia's extensive and unprotected borders, her struggle economically, and her propensity for corruption in the highest halls of government, she was a fully ripe and ready orchard waiting to be picked. The Cosa Nostra was more than willing to offer its services.

He watched as the pretty newscaster reported more events of the past eight hours: a few skirmishes, a political scandal or two, another possible coup in South America, a tornado that killed ten, and the usual reports on crime, which was soaring. Koln smiled. It wasn't safe to walk the streets anymore.

He pushed a button on the television's remote and the screen went dark. Turning in his chair, he faced a console that had several computer screens and began reviewing the bits and pieces of intelligence information that had come in during the night.

Kentucky Trayco's private jet had left the North Las Vegas Airport and headed west. The filed flight plan that was required by law said the Lear was headed for San Francisco. A few minutes into its flight, however, the pilot had declared the need for an emergency landing at a small military airfield on the edges of the government testing grounds north of Vegas. At that point the two men had disappeared.

Daniels's plane had flown north from Washington, D.C., into Canada, then went west. Refueling at Winnipeg, it flew to Calgary. After a stopover of several hours, the Cessna Citation had gone to Juneau, Alaska, where it was put in a hangar and remained there under lock and key. As near as Koln could tell, Daniels hadn't left Calgary.

Koln had asked SCORPION to have its people look in

Calgary, checking all commercial and private flights headed south into the United States via the major airports surrounding Jeremiah Daniels's stomping grounds of Jackson Hole, Wyoming. The hunted always hid where they felt the odds were best. Always.

SCORPION's report had confirmed his gut feeling. A man fitting Daniels's description had purchased a ticket on a Delta 727 to Helena, Montana. From there another Delta flight had taken him to Jackson by way of Idaho Falls, Idaho.

It was then that Koln found Trayco and Tony DeGuillio. Airport records showed a government-sponsored jet had landed in Jackson just hours before Daniels had arrived aboard the Delta flight.

Research on Daniels said the czar owned a ranch near Jackson. His former father-in-law had owned a place there as well, in partnership with his son, Bob Freeman. Freeman still ran it with his wife and two kids. Koln doubted that Daniels would make his job easy by using his own ranch or the ranch of his brother-in-law. It was apparent, however, that the czar was using the Hole as his base of operations. They were there—somewhere. And a man in hiding had to have food and other supplies. That meant contacts, people he trusted. People like Bob Freeman.

Unlike many assassins, Koln didn't work alone. He did most of the killing, but he had teams of advance people whom he would send in beforehand to find the target, watch him, and make notes of the patterns and places he went so that the hit could be carried out with the least possible amount of risk. They would also make preparations for weapons and escape routes. Koln would be on-site for less than a few hours, a day or two at the most. He was the trigger-man, his expertise the culmination of weeks, sometimes months, of hard work and detailed preparations.

Ten hours earlier an eight-member team out of Los Angeles had been dispatched to Jackson Hole. Their private Lear jet 31 had landed three hours later in Jackson during a heavy storm. Since then the storm had slowed them down.

Late last evening the team had split up into two groups, one to check out Daniels's ranch up Hoback Canyon, and the other trying to get into the Freeman place east of Kelly in the canyon that housed the Gros Ventre River.

Daniels's access road was completely drifted in and it didn't look as if any traffic had been that way, at least not since the start of the storm. The team had gone to a neighboring ranch and passed themselves off as friends of the Danielses from Washington, D.C. They were told that Daniels had cleared out all the livestock earlier in the spring and that the neighbors hadn't seen hide nor hair of anyone but the oldest boy since. In response to where they could find Raoul, the old rancher had laughed. "Unless you've got wings, you won't find him," he said. "He came here and got his mule's packsaddle my son borrowed a few weeks ago for elk hunting. Said he was going into the Wind Rivers."

"In a storm like this?" one of the team asked.

"Ain't near as bad south of us," the rancher replied. "Besides, weather don't mean nothing to Raoul. He practically lives in them mountains."

Accepting the old rancher's invitation for an early-morning cup of coffee, the team had found out where Raoul Daniels liked to hunt, then returned to the road and traveled to the place the old rancher said the young man would enter the mountains. They had found a trailer and a pickup registered to Daniels.

The other team hadn't been as lucky. The road to Slide Lake up Gros Ventre Canyon was drifted, and in their attempt to break through they had become badly stuck. After an hour of digging and pushing, they abandoned the vehicle and returned to Kelly on foot, nearly frozen. A local citizen had returned them to the airport, where they rented another vehicle and drove to Jackson. They were now thawing out in a local motel.

Koln picked up the scrambled telephone on his desk and dialed the Antler Motel. It was answered on the first ring.

"Yeah."

"Koln. I want four of you to get to Pinedale, Wyoming. Contact a man by the name of Madigan. He's a hunting guide. Tell him you're with the federal marshals, that you're after a fugitive, and you need his help. I'll have some false reports and arrest papers sent to the sheriff's office there to make your story plausible. Have him arrange for supplies, horses, whatever you need."

"What if Madigan . . ."

"Once you've got the kid, kill Madigan," Koln said. "The rest of you stay in Jackson. Get a condo or a house that's out of the way. Buy a good quality fax machine. As soon as you do I'll send you pictures of the people I want you looking for."

"Are we to terminate the kid?"

"Not yet. If Daniels persists in hiding, we'll use his family as leverage." He hung up.

After a moment of shifting mental gears, Koln started typing. Earlier he had used an associate's expertise as a hacker to break into the mainframe computer of one of the country's largest private universities. The task had been accomplished relatively easily because the hacker knew how to get into the computers belonging to the National University Admissions and Records Board, created in 1993 by the Clinton administration to make the transfer of student records from university to university quick, safe, and effective. Seconds later Koln had accessed registration files for nearly twenty-eight thousand students at Brigham Young University. It seemed that Daniels's talkative neighbors in Wyoming thought that's where the boy planned to be for the year.

He began his search. First he typed in Rashid Daniels's name, birthdate, and social security number, then waited.

"Rashid Daniels: withdrew, 10 Sept 1997," appeared on the screen.

Koln typed in, "10 Sept 1997," then added: "Search for students accepted on this date." A moment later Koln had a list of thirteen students. He pulled up each of their files on the computer.

Most were eliminated by obvious differences such as race, sex, age, and marital status. He was left with two students. The first one was Arabic, male, eighteen years old, unmarried, but a paraplegic. He discarded that file. The other student was from Turkey, Arabic, same age, same everything as Rashid Daniels, including blood type and medical history. His name was Ahmad Tabriz. Koln printed a hard copy of the file, then pushed several keys, and logged out of the university computer. He had what he wanted.

Koln checked his watch; nearly 5:30 A.M. He picked up the phone and dialed a Utah number from memory.

"Hello," came the sleeply reply.

"Hello, Princess."

"Dad? Where are you?"

"In L.A. Is everything okay at school?"

"Yes, wonderful. Are you coming this way?"

"As a matter of fact, I am. I have to see someone. The son of a friend." Koln looked at the printed matter, smiling. "Ahmad Tabriz. His father—"

"Ahmad? Are you sure?"

Koln's expression became quizzical. "Yes, but why . . ."

"I met him yesterday. We studied together last night, then went to the Arab club meeting." Her voice trailed off at the end as she realized he wouldn't like what she had said.

"Seriza," he started to say firmly, then stopped himself, breathing deeply, checking his words. "Can you introduce us? His father has given me a very important message for him."

"Sure. Do you want me to give it to him? And who *is* his father?" she said, giggling lightly. "I haven't been able to get a thing out of him about his family!"

"Jeremiah Daniels."

"The president's drug czar? You're kidding!"

"No, dear girl, but keep it to yourself. The young man's life is in danger."

"A phony name. I thought there was something funny—"

"Don't say anything to him until I'm in Provo, all right?"

Seriza hesitated. "Why?"

"You shouldn't know any of this, Seriza. He might run if I don't give him the proper message, and that could be very dangerous for him."

Seriza hesitated again, then agreed.

"About the Arab club," Koln said.

"Dad, you don't have the right to dictate."

"Yes, yes, of course I don't. All right. I'll see you later today. Are you still living in the same place?"

"Yes. What time?"

"I'm not sure, but after noon."

"All right. If I'm not at home, come to the administration building. I work in the financial office in the afternoon."

"You work? But I send—"

"It's still in the bank, Dad. You know I don't want your money."

"Okay, let's not argue. Good-bye, Princess."

Koln hung up, then swore, his brow furrowed deeply. A careless slip of the tongue. An unavoidable coincidence. He swore again. He shouldn't have mentioned the boy's name. Now if something happened to Rashid, Seriza might . . . His situation was so tentative with her as it was.

He leaned back in the swivel chair, placing his hands behind his head. Even though she was his daughter, Seriza knew nothing about what he did or who he was. She still believed he was simply Joseph Maxwell, a high-strung, world-traveled businessman who had never been home and never would be. They saw each other at least once a year, and both felt comfortable with the arrangement. If handled properly, Rashid Daniels wouldn't change that.

His face had a pleasant look as he thought about his daughter and her classical Arab beauty. The almond eyes, dark hair, olive skin, and clear complexion—so much like her mother.

And so little like him. His brow furrowed again, the unpleasant memories of his troubled marriage bouncing off the walls of his mind like a rubber ball. He shook his head against the nuisance of past history. A history that went back to a time before he had taken a second identity. Most of his work then had been done for the CIA, and they had trained him well. Most of what he knew about assassination had come from his CIA training. He had been their best deep-cover assassin and still did an occasional piece of work for them under his old name. He found his CIA connections still valuable. In fact, it would be those connections who would be used to send a packet to Madigan via the Pinedale sheriff's office.

Koln stood and stretched; that was another life. He checked his watch. Time for a shower. He'd need to fly the Lear out of LAX by noon.

The security console to his left beeped. He hit a key and the screen flashed on. He read the report, then smiled. It seemed the hunter was also the hunted. He typed in a response, flipped the screen off, and moved acros the room to the door from his workplace into his apartment. As the door closed behind him, the office lights dimmed, then went out, the computer console's colored lights giving an eerie feel to the darkened room.

5:31 A.M.—Los Angeles, California

Across the street from Rolf Koln's resident apartment stood a tall, half-finished bank building now in the final stages of foreclosure, another statistic in the savings and loan scandals of the early nineties. If Koln had been looking carefully through the darkness at the windowless opening a little over two hundred feet away, he would have seen another man shut down his equipment, put away his directional listening device and camera, and close a case containing a notebook and tape recorder. But Koln wasn't looking; he was showering and watching the news on the TV that he could see over the top of the chest-high door to the elegant ceramic enclosure in which he stood. Even then, a glance out of the bathroom window would have given him a view of the same man loading his equipment into the back of a black 1965 fastback Mustang that was built for speed.

Koln didn't look then, either.

But the driver of the Mustang wasn't happy with the results of the day's surveillance. Koln's apartment windows were made of some kind of material that prevented the listening device from picking up much more than garbled talk, with a clear word coming through only now and then. He did, however, have some good photographs. The close-ups of the computer monitor on Koln's left would be especially good, and would hopefully give them some idea of what Koln's next move would be.

Jack Canyon had set up his listening post earlier that day. He was tired, cold, and hungry, but he was anxious, too. Anxious to see if his film really showed anything.

Canyon started the engine as quietly as its souped-up engine would allow and gently urged it away from the curb. Ten minutes later he pulled into a safe house parking garage, armed the car's triple alarm system, gathered his gear, and walked the short distance to the elevator. He glanced over his shoulder as a man half stumbled, half walked through the darkness toward him. Jack let his hand slip to the .45 in his belt. Then the elevator doors opened. He stepped inside as the drunk collapsed to the floor near another tenant's car. Jack's hand eased off the pistol's grip. He glanced up at the camera in the corner of the elevator, a slight smile on his face. "Did you see him?"

"Yessir," came a voice from the speaker overhead. "We're checking it out."

"Everything clear to the top?"

"Yessir. The ninth floor is clean, sir."

Moments later Jack Canyon was inserting two keys in the door of number 902, his mind already going through the darkroom procedures in preparation for developing his newly acquired black and whites.

It was then that the lights went out for Jack Canyon.

Trayco's head jerked up as he heard the keys being inserted in the locks. He had his .45 in his hand and his back against the wall when he heard the thump of something hitting the floor on the other side of the door. Then there was silence. Precious seconds passed before Kenny's mind cleared sufficiently to catch hold of what had just happened. In an instant he grabbed the knob of the door and flung it open, forty-five clutched in both hands and stretched out before him. Jack's body lay in a heap on the floor, the hallway empty. Positioning himself against the wall, he used the forty-five to blow out the lights, then knelt by his friend and felt for a pulse. It was there, but weak. Pulling Jack by the coat collar, Trayco dragged him into the room and closed the door.

Grabbing the phone, he dialed a number and yelled orders. "Cobra! Man down! Close all exits! And get an ambulance in here!"

Slamming the phone down, Trayco jumped over the couch and yanked on the cord of the miniblinds, opening them fully. The street below was dark and empty. Rushing to the door, he checked both ways before running down the hall to the elevator and pushing the button.

Suddenly everything exploded, hitting with such force that it blew the elevator doors across the room and through a wall. Kenny was standing to one side and was missed by the full impact of the blast but was flung against the wall like a paper doll. As he slid to the floor, the lights began to blur and blood trickled onto his shirt. His last conscious thought was of Jack Canyon—and a curse for his own stupidity.

When Rolf Koln finished drying his hair, he put on a floor-length terry-cloth robe. As he strapped on his watch and placed his rings on the appropriate fingers, the alarm bell on his computer sounded through an overhead speaker. A message was coming through.

He brushed his teeth, rubbed his hair once more with the

towel, then put a comb through it before tightening his robe belt and leaving the bathroom. Moving to the end of the hall, he slid aside the false panel revealing the workroom door. He placed his hand on a screen on the wall, and the heavy steel door slid to the side, allowed him to enter, then closed again. The lights came on, dispelling what was left of the darkness.

After sitting down on the swivel chair, he pushed some buttons and the security console flashed on, the message typed neatly in capital letters.

SECURITY BREACH MONITORED AS PER YOUR ORDERS. SUBJECT DOWN. ALL OF SUBJECT'S EQUIP-MENT REMOVED AND NOW IN SAFEKEEPING. APPRO-PRIATE STEPS TAKEN AGAINST DISCOVERY. EXPLO-SION VERIFIES MORE THAN SUBJECT INVOLVED. ANY FURTHER ORDERS?

Koln smiled. The infrared cameras secreted atop his apartment complex had shown his security people pictures of the intruder in the decaying building across the street. He had ordered immediate elimination procedures.

Koln typed a quick response.

"Have medical contacts verify kills. Leave message on computer board one. I'll retrieve it tomorrow at my conve-nience and be in touch.

"By the way, I'll be out of town for a few days. Secure the building against any further intrusions. Confirm."

"Confirmed," came the response.

Koln pushed a button and the screen flipped off. He sat back in the chair, his brows furrowed (a habit when he was in deep thought). He had first noticed someone was watching him in London's Heathrow Airport. He wondered how long he had been under surveillance and by whom.

Koln had many enemies. In 1996 he had killed a number of uncooperative politicals in Italy. The Italian SIFAR intelli-gence organization had begun hunting him. Had they finally found out who he was?

Maybe. There were other possibilities, too. Every time he acted in his professional capacity he took a chance of discov-ery. That was why he paid for security. Had someone finally found something? Had he made a mistake?

He began pacing. Koln didn't make mistakes, but he had been involved a lot lately with SCORPION. It was evident that the organization had been breached by Daniels. Had the czar discovered him also?

Koln stopped in front of the window and stared into the darkness. His last five jobs had been for SCORPION. All of them were successful, but he had been forced to carry them out in less than ideal circumstances. He would have liked to have a new identity for each job, but had been forced to use the same two names for all five. That had been a mistake. If Daniels was onto SCORPION, he would have been watching for things like that.

Koln went to his chair and sat, his fingers pummeling the arm methodically. Jeremiah Daniels knew who he was. He could feel it in his bones. That made Daniels extremely dangerous.

After another half an hour, Koln leaned forward and typed the entrance codes to access SCORPION's system. Then:

> CODE RED. TOP SECRET
> EYES ONLY—DEFIANCE TO
> SCORPION.
>
> SUBJECT: JEREMIAH DANIELS—
> PERMISSION TO TERMINATE.

CHAPTER 6

8:00 A.M.—Federal Courthouse, Los Angeles, California

Mike sat next to the attorney, who would prosecute Tony D and waited, along with a sizeable crowd, for the judge to appear. She had hitched a ride with Jerry and Macklin aboard the Eagle, even though Jerry had been unhappy about her coming. She felt she had to be here for this one. Tony D was the big fish among those caught so far and she didn't want him getting off the hook on some technicality. She had spent the night going over the team's case with a fine-tooth comb and was pleased to find they were ready.

She looked at her watch. It was time. She glanced around the courtroom looking for Macklin and Jeremiah. They had turned DeGuillio over to hand-picked special agents hours ago. Where were they? Her attention caught on the far door where DeGuillio would come in; the bailiff stood there, waiting. He seemed nervous; probably was. There might be a killer in this crowd waiting for the moment the door opened and Tony D walked through it. Anyone near him would be in mortal danger.

Only a few knew it, but Tony wouldn't be brought into the court until after the judge entered and cleared the room. He didn't want a media circus, and neither did Mike. The defense had objected, but was overruled.

Mike glanced at Benson Wilder. Why would a man of his reputation take on a client like Tony DeGuillio? Wilder's firm was considered highly ethical. Tony D was scum to them. And yet, there sat Wilder. The Cosa Nostra must have a tentacle around the man's neck, thought Mike. A very strong tentacle.

Mike's eyes returned to the bailiff. He was wiping sweat off his forehead with a handkerchief, his eyes darting over the crowd, then becoming fixed in a distant corner. Mike couldn't help herself, and turned to see where he was looking. A pretty newswoman and a cameraman. Mike had seen both of them before when she had first entered the courtroom.

Everyone started to rise. Mike realized the judge was entering the courtroom and quickly stood, but kept watching the bailiff, who took a deep breath and dabbed the kerchief to his forehead again before shoving it into a rear pants' pocket. She glanced over her shoulder at the newswoman, who was still standing in the same spot. The cameraman had moved across the back of the room, his eye to the viewfinder of his camera, moving closer to the door through which DeGuillio would come. Nothing unusual.

The knock of the gavel on wood forced Mike's eyes to the front as the judge called the courtroom to order.

"Ladies and gentlemen, because of the danger the accused brings to this court, and because of the government's determination that his life could be in danger, I must ask that the courtroom be cleared."

The gallery of people erupted with belligerent questioning and conversation. The judge hammered with a gavel. "Order!

Order! Order in this courtroom! Bailiff, officers of the court, move these people out of here. *Now!*" He continued to hammer with the gavel until even the most reluctant began moving toward the double doors at the rear of the room.

Mike relaxed a little, and her attention returned to the bailiff. Although he had moved only a few steps from his original position, he was telling people to move along while two officers moved the audience through the double doors at the rear of the room. Mike saw the newswoman as she disappeared through the doors and into the hall. She looked for the tell-tale camera atop a shoulder but couldn't pick it out in the crowd. The cameraman was probably already out the door and in position for the newswoman's report on what was happening.

Finally the doors closed, the bailiff returned to his original position, and the judge banged with the gavel again. "Bring in the prisoner," he said.

The bailiff nervously nodded toward the two police officers, then moved toward the front of the court and away from the door where DeGuillio would appear.

"Coward," Mike thought as the side door opened.

It was then she saw the camera. Instantly she knew what was coming. "Down!" She screamed. "Down! It's a bomb!" She grabbed the attorney next to her and pulled him to the floor as the explosion blew the room apart. Shards of wood flew through the air and the windows blew out, clattering into the street below. Every door was blown outward from the concussion, and ceiling plaster crumbled into a pile, leaving thick dust everywhere. Mike lay still, momentarily stunned. Her head hurt and she felt the ooze of fluid across her legs. She sensed the chaos and panic around her and tried to get up, to get away. But something was holding her legs down, and she turned, only to find herself staring into the blank eyes of the young attorney she had tried to save. Someone grabbed the body and moved it aside, pulled her to her feet, and headed her toward the door. She tripped over wreckage, coughing at the dust that filled the air.

As she stumbled into the hallway she found the chaos to be even worse. People were screaming, running, and pummeling each other as they tried to escape from the building. Mike moved to the nearest wall and leaned against it, trying to catch her breath. Her eyes scanned, darting, searching, trying to find Jeremiah or Thomas Macklin.

Then she saw him. He stood out because he was moving into the crowd rather than with it. He was about six foot two, gray hair, with a moustache. He had on a long charcoal wool overcoat, and his hand was in his pocket. There was something about him—the nose, or the eyes? She had seen him somewhere before.

His hand moved from his pocket and dropped to his side. It held a revolver. The crowd had thinned out and he moved quickly toward the rear hallway—the hallway where DeGuillio must have been when the explosion struck.

Mike's eyes desperately searched for an officer, someone, anyone with a gun, but found no one. She had to act before it was too late. She fought her way back to the courtroom and through its wreckage toward the far exit.

When she reached the door, she realized she didn't have a weapon, and she bent over and picked up the severed leg of a heavy oak chair. Taking a deep breath, she plunged through the opening, the weapon in hand.

Tony lay on the floor, two guards covering his body. One had blood staining his shirt from top to bottom and was still partially conscious. The other was dead. Tony was yelling for help, moving—but barely—his body trapped under the dead weight of the two policemen.

Half a dozen other people were in the hall, stunned, their eyes blank with confusion. Mike saw a policeman at the far end doing his best to keep the crowd away, his arm covered with blood. Then she saw the gunman.

She walked toward him as he stopped and glanced past her toward Tony and the two mangled officers. She saw him lift the gun and slam it into the policeman's neck. As the policeman crumpled, Mike lunged, lifting her makeshift weapon and driving it downward as hard as she could. The blow crunched into the gunman's shoulder and he screamed with pain, dropping the gun. Mike lifted the oak leg for another blow, but he swung at her with his other arm and knocked her into the wall. She felt the pain of the blow and lost her breath. Gasping for air, she knew she had to do something when the gunman reached for his weapon. Striking out with her foot, she drove her spike-heeled shoe into his hand. He jerked away in pain and she kicked at the weapon, knocking it under the feet of fleeing people. He lunged for it, but it was too late.

Mike stood there, her back hunched, arms extended from

her side, one fist full of oak, the other doubled, her feet planted firmly on the floor, ready for the next round. A smile formed on the gunman's lips. Then he backed away and was gone.

Mike watched him disappear, then bent down and rolled the bleeding policeman over. Pressing her hand against his neck she checked for a pulse. It was there. She glanced down the hall as half a dozen policemen rushed through the front door and scrambled through the debris to where DeGuillio, now fully conscious, screamed and cursed, forcing himself from under the motionless bodies of those who had died or been badly injured saving him.

Mike stood and walked toward him, anger rising, pressing into her lungs. "Cuff him!" she said stiffly. "He still has a date with a judge."

CHAPTER 7

9:00 A.M.—Los Angeles, California

Jeremiah stepped into the elevator and punched at the button. His face was set in stone and his hazel eyes were dark with the cold hardness of determination. Everything was collapsing around his ears.

The doors closed and the elevator plummeted two stories into the earth before slamming to a halt. He punched the "door open" button hard with his knuckle.

The hall was empty except for two marines in full military garb, M-16As pointed at his chest. He flashed his identity badge as they approached him, and the shorter of the two checked it carefully. "The Colonel is waiting for you, sir. Last door on the right."

Jerry was already past him, his longish legs striding quickly to the steel door, his strong arms shoving it open. Macklin stood looking through a glass partition into a brightly lit hospital emergency room full of medical equipment, with nurses working feverishly over one patient and methodically over another. He turned from the window and faced Jerry.

"How bad?" Jerry asked.

"Canyon has a bullet in his head," Macklin responded. "It doesn't look good. Trayco was lucky. He was standing to the side of the elevator doors when the bomb exploded and the major impact missed him. Knocked out the walls in the shaft and blew the doors through a wall in the hallway. One of 'em broke Kenny's arm and put him in la-la land. Slight concussion. How's Mike?"

"Okay," said Jerry, shaking his head. "Four others were killed, a dozen injured seriously enough to go to the hospital. Two were trampled pretty good in the panic to get out of the building."

"Good thing Mike saw it coming. It could have been worse."

"Yeah."

"DeGuillio?" Macklin asked.

"Minor cuts and bruises. Two of the officers took the major force of the impact. One died. And Benson Wilder was killed."

"Tony's attorney!" exclaimed Macklin.

"His wife had a few problems. Sicily must have found out. The woman's mistakes cost her a good man."

"Any of our attorneys?"

"One. A wife and two kids." Jerry paused. "The judge had his eardrums blown out, along with just about everyone else, but he was strong enough to have Tony pulled into another courtroom and arraign him. They set a trial date as well. Mike said he was in full agreement on the use of our video setup from here on out."

"Then we take Tony back to Yellowstone," Macklin said.

"Today."

"We would have been there if this—" Macklin paused, then proceeded. "The question is, was nailing Jack and Kenny just luck or did Koln know where they were and decide to neutralize them?"

"Doesn't matter." Jerry sighed. "Either way he diverted our attention long enough to get a shot at Tony."

"Did the police find the cameraman?" Macklin asked.

"In an alley a block away. A bullet through his heart. Koln's work, I would guess."

"I sent a surveillance team to Koln's place as soon as I arrived at the safe house and got Trayco and Jack on their way here," Macklin said. "He was already gone."

Jerry took a deep breath. "I think Mike may have run into him at the courthouse."

Macklin's head jerked around.

Jerry shrugged. "She said it wasn't. He looked older, gray hair, wrinkles around the eyes." Jerry had a slight smile on his face. "Whoever he was, he pulled a gun. Mike hit him with a broken chair leg. Kept him from shooting Tony, but the guy got away in all the chaos."

"She's compromised him," Macklin said. "He won't want to take any chances. You'd better get her back to Yellowstone."

"She goes this afternoon."

Jerry watched the doctors, their gloves covered with Jack's blood. "Any chance of his regaining consciousness?"

"Not tonight," Macklin replied. "Not tomorrow. Maybe never."

"Did we cover our tracks?"

"They were brought here by special ambulance. Lucky for us Trayco had already called the emergency. He even had the building sealed off, but we didn't find anyone."

"Do we have any idea how they got in?"

"A chopper dropped somebody on the roof. He used ropes to come down the outside wall and entered a room on the same floor. We found an open window, and boot marks on the brick outside. Very quick, very efficient, very professional."

"How did he know which floor?"

Macklin shrugged. "The garage monitor shows a drunk came into the parking garage just after Jack did. He must have been watching the elevator lights."

"No sign of him, I suppose."

"None. The cameras show him leaving before the action started. Our people—"

"Should never have let anyone near that garage," Jerry said.

"The man at the garage entrance had no choice. We found him after everything was over. He's in the hospital with a concussion."

"What's the final casualty count in Israel and Florida, Jerry?" Macklin asked.

"Israel? One of ours, but Nabril could join him within the next twenty-four hours. Three of the enemy. In Florida, the pilot of the Cobra when it was hit by a ground-to-air missile. Three of theirs were injured. A couple are in jail."

"Any idea who the turncoats are?"

"In Israel they have a strong hunch it was an aide at the hospital. They haven't arrested him yet. He may be useful in giving out a little disinformation." Jerry shrugged again. "In Florida it was the FBI man, Match, and his partner. For twenty thousand."

"The enemy is us."

"We knew it would be. Can Kenny travel?"

Macklin glanced at Trayco, who was now conscious and fighting the doctors, refusing a plaster cast. "Do you think you could stop him?"

"I want him to take Tony D back in the Eagle."

"What about Alvarez?"

"Tight security. Gad replaced Match with a guy out of the Miami anti-terrorist squad, name of Buckles. I had him checked out. Alvarez will get to trial." He paused. "Can you go to Israel, take over for Nabril?"

"You want me to handle Boudia?"

"Yeah, you and Ruth are the only ones who knew that Nabril planned to get Boudia here incognito. I don't think Ruth should go back."

"All right, I'll take care of it."

Jerry looked deep into the eyes of his friend. "We lost this round, Tom. I have a hunch the Cosa Nostra knows more than we think they do. Maybe a *lot* more. I've talked to the head of the Justice Department. He's going to do everything he can to get these cases to court at the earliest possible date, but that will still be months, in the Alvarez case a full year."

Macklin laughed. "We won't survive that long, neither will our prisoners."

Jerry took a deep breath. "In the next sixteen hours a DEA task force working with state and local authorities will hit four of Lima's warehouses in the south. Tomorrow we'll hit another production facility. In southern Mexico this time. We escalate, Tom. We let them know that if they want war we've got the guts to take them on."

"We'll run out of targets before long," Macklin said.

"Jim Freeman's international task force connections uncovered enough to keep us busy into the next century. And there will always be predators waiting in the wings we'll have to deal with. People who will want to pick up the business and make millions. We'll have plenty of work." Jeremiah faced the window again.

"The politicians on the Cosa Nostra payroll will come out of the woodwork like rats to cheese."

"If I fear any part of the Sicilian Mafia, that's it. We have the knowledge and power to reduce this problem to a hundredth of its present proportions, but if the politicians get in the way we're dead in the water."

"Any word from the president?"

"It's started. A dozen congressmen called him this morning, but most of it's subtle arm-twisting. Some of it's honest concern. Innocent people died in that courthouse."

Jerry placed his hand against the glass as the doctors started pulling off their masks. A nurse took the oxygen mask off Jack's face and pulled the sheet up, covering him completely. Jeremiah's head dropped slightly, his breath catching in his chest. He forced himself to keep talking.

"I'm going to Washington. After the next raids the politicals will get ugly. It will be time to apply a little pressure of our own."

They watched in silence as the doctors pulled off their plastic gloves and gowns, tossing them in a canvas laundry bag near the door. The nurses began removing monitoring paraphernalia and I.V. needles from Jack's body.

Jerry faced Macklin, his eyes cold. "Be careful, Tom. They kill for fun."

Macklin was gone when the orderlies released the wheels on Jack Canyon's gurney and tried to remove it from the room. Kenny Trayco stopped them long enough to say goodbye. He and Jack Canyon had fought through the killing fields of Nam together. Jack had saved Trayco's life, and Kenny had returned the favor. They knew each other's thoughts like twins, felt each other's pain and deepest emotions. Jerry knew—for Trayco it was like having his heart ripped from his chest.

Kenny bent over and kissed the blood-covered forehead, then put the sheet in place and walked to a chair, where he sat down, his injured arm dangling unnoticed at his side.

Jerry removed his glasses and rubbed the socket around his glass eye. The fit hadn't been a good one, and it irritated sometimes. He used his handkerchief to wipe the moisture away as he took a small cellular phone from his pocket and quickly punched the numbers. There were a dozen clicks as the call was routed through a series of places that would make it untraceable. Dolph Stockman picked up the line at the other end. Jeremiah filled him in.

"I want you at full alert, Dolph. Anything suspicious, you get everyone out of there."

"Understood. When will Mike get here?"

"It depends on the weather, but she'll leave here within the hour. Trayco will bring DeGuillio as soon as he gets his center of gravity back." He looked through the window. Trayco was arguing with the doctor. He knocked the plaster bucket across the room and against a wall. No cast. "This evening at the latest."

Jerry hesitated. "Anything new on your end?"

"The DEA raids are set. If you think today was full of fireworks, wait until Sicily gets tonight's tallys."

"Good. I want pressure, Dolph. Unrelenting, hard pressure. We dismantle them a piece at a time until we break them."

"Macklin?"

"Tell Ruth he's going to Israel to replace Nabril."

"You'll visit LOGOS while you're in Washington?"

"Yeah. They say they have something interesting to show me." He paused. "Keep the home fires burning, Dolph. You're looking after just about everything dear to me." He paused again. "If something goes wrong, you find the boys. Make sure they're with their mom."

He hung up.

———————

Stockman put the scrambled telephone on its hook. Things were happening rapidly. Too rapidly. He spoke to Stone.

"What's the weather forecast for the next twelve hours?"

Stone pushed a button and the report was flashed on Stockman's screen. He read it quickly and his brow wrinkled. It was getting worse. The satellite picture showed an endless bank of thick white clouds trailing off into the Pacific. He pushed a button and read the details: up to two feet of snow; below freezing temperatures; winds up to thirty miles per hour; gusts to fifty. Maybe Mike and Trayco wouldn't be coming. But then, neither would the enemy.

He walked to a small window. The snow falling on the lake's cold, gray waters was thick. At least it would keep tourists out of the area. But just in case . . .

"Stone, have a severe weather warning put out for the lake through the Forest Service. I don't want any diehard fisherman wandering into our defense perimeter so that I have to blow him out of the water. No unexpected guests, Stone. Understood?" He started for the door. Ruth needed to be told.

12:21 P.M.—*John Wayne International Airport, Orange County, California*

Koln flipped the two Tylenol tablets into the back of his mouth and swallowed. Then he put the binoculars back to his eyes. The plane was moving to the end of the runway and was fifth in line. He was standing on the observation deck of John Wayne International Airport, where Michaelene Daniels had just boarded a plane. He smiled, moving his arm in a slightly circular motion, causing him to grimace. That woman swung a mean club. The bruise in his shoulder was deep, stiff, and painful. He glanced at his hand. The impression of her heel was emblazoned in red and blue where she had jabbed the point into his flesh.

Rolf Koln wouldn't soon forget Michaelene Daniels standing in the hallway, her dark eyes, wide stance, lifted club, and doubled up fist the picture of determination and daring. A lioness, that was Michaelene Daniels.

He focused the glasses on the tailwing and memorized the numbers. Another plane took off and the Lear moved up in line.

After the failed attempt to eliminate Tony D, Koln had left the courthouse and gone into the building across the street, where he had leased an office. Experience had taught him that police always looked for runners first and that if he became part of the landscape, they wouldn't see him.

While watching the chaos in the street below, Koln had altered his appearance and changed his clothes. The assassin had been a sharp, middle-aged businessman with dark black hair graying at the temples and metal-rimmed glasses. His new identity was much older.

While applying the heavy, gray eyebrows, he listened to the police scanner that was sitting on a nearby table keeping him informed of events taking place across the street.

After ambulances had cleared away the wounded and dead, a police van was brought in to pick up Tony. Koln had brought along a sniper's rifle, but he knew that to attempt the hit under those circumstances would be a serious miscalculation. He had watched as Tony was driven away under heavy guard. There would be another chance.

Then Mrs. Daniels had come out of the building. The scanner said she was being taken to a nearby hospital. It was there Koln had run into Jeremiah Daniels—literally.

Koln had confidence in his makeup abilities and had hobbled into the hospital only minutes behind Mrs. Daniels. He had never seen the damage one of his jobs had caused, never been close to the people who happened to be in the wrong place at the wrong time. As he stood near the door taking it all in, watching attempts at organizing the chaos *he* had created, Jeremiah Daniels had burst through the door and nearly knocked him to the floor.

Koln smiled at the memory. Everything had stopped around them as Daniels helped the old man regain his feet, then apologized while picking up the cane Koln was using and handing it to him. Their eyes had met and for the briefest of seconds Koln thought Daniels had recognized him, but the czar apologized again and was quickly hurried away by a policewoman who was waiting for him. The chaos had resumed.

Koln made a phone call. He was going to need help with this one. He then took a chair in the waiting room, where he could see who came and left through the emergency entrance doors. Ten minutes later a young lady dressed in a business suit strutted through the entrance. He signaled to her.

Koln considered it suicide to go after the Danielses in a public place. He had counted the uniforms around the emergency room when he came in, and he didn't like the odds. He would simply keep track of the Danielses for now.

Jeremiah Daniels left first. Koln nodded and the young woman followed Jerry. Her name was Claire John, and she was one of Koln's best field operatives. Claire wore clothing that made her inconspicuous, and although dark of skin with black hair, she had one of those faces that no one seemed to remember and that didn't stick out in a crowd.

Claire was a well-educated American Italian. Her position as a highly paid attorney was a good cover, allowing her to move about worldwide without being asked questions. Koln hired his own people. He investigated each thoroughly before putting them to work. Claire's past was impeccable. Her records declared she was the only daughter of Italian immigrants who came to America in 1948, just after World War II. According to her school records, she had a knack for learning from an early age and was highly competitive. Since Koln had come to know her, he found her not only competitive but also aggressive, the only woman who had ever worked for him who seemed to take to a gun as easily as she did to stylish clothes. Claire wanted it all: excitement, competition, thrills, and money. They worked well together and she had proven herself. She had a taste for the business and learned it thoroughly. Koln found himself physically attracted to her but resisted in the name of business. So far.

A few minutes later Mrs. Daniels was hustled off by two well-armed marines in an official vehicle. They had been foolish, taking no evasive action, but going directly to the airport.

Koln watched as the plane revved its engines, then launched itself down the runway. As it disappeared into the L.A. smog, someone tapped him on the shoulder.

"Mr. Sterling?"

Koln turned to face a young man in a white shirt and tie. He smiled. "Robert. Do you have what I asked for?"

Robert took the papers from his leather folder and handed them over. Koln glanced at them quickly then handed them back. Robert worked in the flight office and was responsible for the filing of flight plans submitted by private planes. "Thank you, Robert. How is your mother?"

"Much better, sir."

"Good. You're doing good work, Robert. I'll see that your account shows a bonus this month."

Robert smiled.

"Would you do me one other favor?"

"Certainly, sir." Robert wasn't about to turn down Alonzo Sterling. As a member of the board for United Airlines, Sterling could open doors for Robert Patchway.

"Call United, would you? Ask for a Ms. Walker. Have her book me reservations on our next flight to Salt Lake City."

"Yessir, consider it done."

"Thank you, Robert." They shook hands, and Patchway disappeared down the stairs. Koln marveled at how easily the boy had been taken in. Of course, Robert Patchway had never met the real Alonzo Sterling, so eight months ago, when Koln had presented himself as such, in order to "recruit" the young man for his purposes, he was easily convinced by Koln's picture-perfect appearance.

So far, Patchway had unwittingly helped Koln kill three men. Koln wondered if the boy could be tried as an accessory. The thought made him chuckle.

He walked to a public telephone and dialed a number in Jackson. He would have some friends waiting for Mrs. Daniels. He glanced at the departure screens overhead. His flight left in twenty minutes. He could be in Provo by three o'clock. It would be good to see Seriza again.

CHAPTER 8

1:00 P.M.—Provo, Utah

Seriza pushed the button on the remote, unlocking the door to her car and disarming the alarm. She never knew why her dad had insisted on such precautions, but expected it had something to do with his position in the government. She had quit kidding herself years ago about his profession. She knew he was involved in some sort of clandestine group like the CIA or the NSA, but she simply ignored it, preferring to believe he really did work for some regular corporation. She didn't see him that much, anyway.

After scraping the ice from the windshield, she seated herself in the driver's seat and started the engine.

Seriza's parents had divorced when she was young, about five years old as she remembered it. Her mother hadn't lived long enough to say much about the whys and wherefores, but her grandparents had. They were naturalized citizens of the United States from the tiny Arabian country of Oman. Her grandfather had been forced to flee the country when he opposed a relative in the government, a very powerful relative who became his enemy and sought his life. It was through an American CIA operation, she assumed one her father had headed, that Seriza's grandparents and their only daughter, age nineteen, had been able to escape with their lives, and with a substantial amount of their bank accounts.

Apparently Joseph Maxwell was smitten by Unnia Mabruk's beauty and began courting her. Of course, her parents were strongly opposed, holding fast to their Islamic customs, but Seriza's mother was in love and eloped with Joe Maxwell three months into the secretive courtship. Seriza's grandparents were devastated by their daughter's actions and disowned her.

Four years later Unnia Mabruk Maxwell divorced Joseph Maxwell. A few weeks later Unnia was dead, a fatality in one of Los Angeles's many freeway accidents.

Joseph Maxwell knew nothing about raising a child, so when his wife was killed and he received custody, he delivered Seriza to her grandparents, who raised her. She had never seen much of her father.

She turned right onto Center Street and headed for the branch office of Zion's Bank. The gray clouds were not producing any snow yet, although the radio said there was a big storm to the north of them, some of which they should get later in the day.

Seriza needed to deposit her check from work and go over her account with someone. She knew it was the same old mistake, but her account showed four thousand dollars too much, the exact amount her father always deposited—whether Seriza liked it or not—and the exact amount she always wired back to his bank in L.A.

It was a game they played. He felt the need to buy her love, and she felt the need to let him know it couldn't be bought.

As she sat across from the bank's supervisor of accounts and waited for the usual transaction to take place, Seriza felt the excitement mingled with distrust she always had when her father suddenly called or showed up on her doorstep. Joseph Maxwell had never been a *father,* at least not in the usual sense of that word—only a . . . what . . . ? She hadn't found the appropriate word yet, but thought *stranger* worked best. Their moments together were strained and filled with small talk, both of them anxious to get away. Yes, *stranger* fit very well. And yet she loved him because he was her father.

His job was partly responsible for their estrangement; her grandparents were another roadblock. They had never welcomed him, and when he had signed the guardianship papers, they had not allowed him much more than occasional visitation rights. For some reason that they had never shared with Seriza, they held their daughter's death against Joseph Maxwell. She had asked for an explanation, but they had been silent. Even her father refused to speak about it. His cold, detached look nearly freezing her solid whenever she mentioned it.

Calling her out of her deep thoughts, the supervisor of accounts apologized and said it wouldn't happen again; the checks would be sent along as she instructed and she shouldn't worry. Seriza smiled and left. As she stepped into the cold, gray day and got into her car, she reflected on something else that bothered her about her father. He frightened her.

She would never forget going out to dinner with him once in L.A. She had been flying to her grandparent's house on a semester break a year ago and had a stopover in L.A. She had called on a hunch, found him in town, and he had picked her up in his comfortable, luxury limousine.

As they entered the restaurant's parking lot, there had been a popping sound like gunfire. In an instant her father had her flat on the floor and had drawn an automatic weapon from some unseen place under the seat. As his driver brought the car to a sudden stop, her father had ejected himself from the vehicle with a cold, calculated killing instinct that had both amazed and alarmed her. Even though it had only been kids at a nearby apartment complex playing with firecrackers, Seriza had never forgotten the experience, and she had come to one terribly frightening conclusion. Her father had killed before.

Even now, remembering that experience sent chills down her spine, and she rubbed goose bumps away as she pulled the Pontiac into the student parking lot, passing through the rows looking for a spot to park. If she found one quickly, she could slip by the building in which Ahmad Tabriz had his next class and get dinner out of him. If not, she'd see him in the library at four o'clock. They had promised to study together again. She figured that she and her father could corner him then so the message could be delivered. If her father arrived in time.

Her father's revelation about Ahmad Tabriz hadn't surprised her. Seriza prided herself on what she called "people instincts," and she had known something wasn't true to form and that Ahmad had a secret.

Seriza smiled. She liked Ahmad, even though he was a year younger than she. In their evening together she had discovered a fun, mature, easy-to-talk-to, very intelligent person behind his outwardly quiet exterior. She felt comfortable in his presence—even safe. And *that* feeling she couldn't explain!

Seriza looked at her watch. Twenty minutes before she had to meet with her bishop about Relief Society business. Just enough time to find Ahmad.

She had only been Relief Society president since Sunday and there were hundreds of things to do. She was meeting to discuss names for the Spiritual Living teacher, the position she had loved more than any other. She had learned so much about the Church, which she had joined only eighteen months ago, and sharing what she had learned—it had been a wonderful time of growth in her life.

Her grandparents had been against her conversion from the start. They were Islamic, and for her to leave Islam for a Christian religion had shocked them beyond belief, even though she had never really worshipped as they had. The past eighteen months had been extremely stressful to their once close relationship. Perhaps that was why she had turned to her father more often.

She gathered her books from the back seat and shoved them into her cloth backpack, set the alarm on the car, and moved quickly down the sidewalk to find Ahmad. Seriza Maxwell had never felt this way about a man before, nor had she ever chased one. In fact, it was usually just the opposite. Seriza was beautiful, intelligent, and personable. She didn't have to knock boys down to get their attention. But most of the young men who came knocking at her door lacked something she seemed to see in Ahmad Tabriz (or was it Ahmad Daniels?). Something, she had decided, worth chasing.

1:27 P.M.—*Salt Lake City, Utah*

Joseph Maxwell and Rolf Koln had been created as two separate identities. The CIA had created Maxwell—Maxwell had created Rolf Koln. Along the way there had been plastic surgery, which had altered his hairline and his nose structure a little (he had explained it to Seriza and inquisitive friends as something needed after a nearly fatal car accident in Germany), and some adept manipulating of photographs and files in the real Rolf Koln's records in Germany and other places.

Joseph Maxwell and Koln had looked enough alike to be twins. That was why Maxwell had selected Koln as his new identity. It was important that Joseph Maxwell be able to be Koln and still be himself as well. Both identities were needed in order for Maxwell/Koln to be as effective as possible.

As a deep-cover CIA agent, Joseph Maxwell had access to United States government records and secrets that made him more effective as Rolf Koln. And because Maxwell was a protected American agent of the most delicate kind—an assassin—his photograph appeared in no newspapers, articles, or CIA reports anywhere in the world. It didn't even appear in his file in the CIA's record division.

In addition, the identity of Joseph Maxwell gave him the ability to plug into the CIA's clandestine operations apparatus and acquire passports, false identities, weapons, and information Koln needed to avoid detection while being a successful enforcer for SCORPION. The best of two worlds.

Of course, it was tricky business. In effect, he was a double agent, and that took a good deal of care. That was why Jeremiah Daniels was becoming an increasing threat to Koln personally. The man could discover the truth and ruin everything for him. That couldn't be allowed under any circumstances.

Koln smiled. Keeping up two identities—actually three, if he thought about how he had to act with his daughter—was taxing, to say the least. But he had worked hard at it, building two lives that were both very secretive, very private, but very real.

There had been times when he was tempted to drop the Maxwell identity, but that meant dropping his daughter as well. He wasn't ready to do that. Not yet.

When he arrived in Salt Lake, Koln went to a small house he owned there, removed the disguise, showered, shaved and microwaved a frozen TV dinner before making some calls. Mrs. Daniels hadn't arrived in Jackson. The weather had the airport closed intermittently and all flights had been detoured to Idaho Falls or Salt Lake City. The airport authorities told Koln's people they expected to be able to allow a few more incoming flights in the next few hours.

Claire John had left a message on Koln's machine in L.A. Daniels had left the private military hospital in Orange County, and headed straight for the airport. He was on his way to Washington, D.C., first class, non-stop, Delta. She had a ticket on the same flight. She would call again when she arrived in Washington.

His last call was to Pinedale, Wyoming. His people there had recruited Lance Madigan and would leave for the Gros Ventre Range within the hour.

Koln grabbed a topcoat from the closet and a pair of fur-lined leather gloves from the drawer. In the garage he chose the Lincoln instead of the restored 1965 Mustang his grandfather had left him. It was a convertible and in this kind of weather too cold.

As he backed the Lincoln out of the driveway he waved at a neighbor scraping ice off of her windshield. Mrs. McPheeters. She knew him as Denton Davis, international computer salesman, seldom home.

Koln drove down West Temple until he came to Fifth South, where he turned right and was soon entering south-bound traffic on the freeway. The road was wet and slushy from the heavy snow that was hitting the valley and traffic was moving slowly. Koln flipped in the *Phantom of the Opera* compact disc, then lifted the cellular phone from its resting place and dialed a number. The call was routed through Paris, Venice, Rome, and finally to a house in Sicily. While he waited, he removed a scrambling device from his briefcase and attached it.

"Hello." The voice was gruff and spoke Sicilian. Koln greeted in the same dialect then asked for Mr. Buscetti. While he waited, he began nervously tapping the steering wheel. Buscetti always made him nervous. Koln knew that with the snap of Buscetti's fingers half a dozen guns would be looking for Rolf Koln—and Rolf Koln would cease to exist.

"Hello, Koln."

Koln visualized Luciano Buscetti. He was six feet tall, weighed in at two hundred and fifty pounds, with black hair graying at the temples. Although he was solid, his face was dark and handsome. He usually wore a dark suit, even around his own house.

"Mr. Buscetti. . . ." Koln filled him in on the episode at the courthouse in L.A.

"Our luck has not been too good today," Buscetti said, and updated Koln on Alvarez and Boudia, then on what had happened in Miami and Israel. "Daniels's organization has Lima. Lima's family is trying to pick up the slack, but there seems to be some infighting."

"Daniels is smart," Koln said. "He has done a lot of planning and has good personnel. He's staying clear of the establishment. It won't be easy getting to Tony or the others."

Koln heard muffled voices in the background as Buscetti conversed with at least three other people. Then Buscetti spoke again.

"Your request for Daniels's termination has been granted, Mr. Koln. We will send the funds to the usual account. It will have ten million in it. We want Daniels, his wife, their family, and associates. Can you do that?"

Koln was silent. He had never killed children before.

"Mr. Koln? If this is beyond—"

"No. No, Luciano. I already have most of the family found. I thought you might want to use them . . . to pressure their father into early retirement."

"Retirement is not enough, Koln. It is apparent Mr. Daniels knows a great deal about our operation. He is very dangerous."

"But the family?"

"An example. We want to teach the government a lesson. The president must understand we don't allow interference in our affairs."

"Your usual methods aren't working?" Koln knew the Cosa Nostra had some very powerful purchases in Washington. People who could make the president's life miserable, perhaps forcing him to back off.

"Not yet. We'll keep applying pressure, but that could take too long. Because of James Freeman, Mr. Daniels has an extremely broad set of powers and he intends to use them. He has already cost us millions. He must be stopped, and the president must be warned against any further challenges to our business."

"I'll need help."

"You will be paid expenses in addition to the ten-million-dollar fee."

"I'll take care of it, Mr. Buscetti." Koln hung up. As he put the phone back on its perch, he hit the temperature control on the heater, resetting it for 78 degrees. He felt cold.

Koln parked the Lincoln a short distance from the apartment complex and let the engine idle. Buscetti's orders threw a new light on things. Seriza knew her father was looking for Daniels's son, alias Ahmad Tabriz. When the boy turned up dead, she'd ask her father questions he didn't want to answer.

He picked up the phone and dialed Seriza's number, his eyes trying to bore a hole through the apartment door as he heard the click of someone picking up the phone.

"Hello?"

"Hi."

"Dad? Where are you?"

The lie came easily. "In L.A. Sorry, but I can't make it. I have to leave for England in an hour."

Silence.

"What about the message?"

"Message?"

"The one to Ahmad. You said it was important. Do you want me to tell him anything?"

"Oh, no. I've made arrangements. Two men from my office will be there this evening." He paused. "He may have to leave, Seriza. His life is in danger. But don't say anything that might scare him away. Let my people take care of it. Okay?"

"Okay. When are you coming back?"

"I'm not sure. I'll call you." He hesitated, then hung up the phone. He sat there a few minutes staring at the apartment door. If this didn't work out well, if his hired help botched it . . . He'd make sure they didn't.

Koln shifted into drive and stepped on the gas. The honk of a horn shocked him, and he braked, jerking the wheels back toward the curb. A young man with a stocking cap pulled over his head, a pair of shiny ski glasses covering his eyes, driving a beat-up VW Rabbit swerved a little to miss the Lincoln. As he passed Koln, the boy threw him a smile while shaking his head. Koln shrugged and returned a forced smile as the Rabbit moved away. After checking traffic more carefully, Koln pulled into the street and drove away.

CHAPTER 9

3:00 P.M.—North of Ashton, Idaho

With his unbandaged arm Trayco grasped the Eagle's stick tightly against the constant pummeling of the wind. Even though the chopper's computer was doing the flying, keeping them from crashing into mountains or trees, he felt better if his hand followed the movement of the stick.

Trayco had only been flying choppers for six years and then usually only in good weather. This was making him sweat.

He had tried skirting the storm but hadn't been able to get around it. Then he had thought of going to Hill Air Force Base to their south, but had decided against it. The Cosa Nostra had agents there, too.

"How much longer are we going to be bounced around by this mess?" DeGuillio whined, a green hue to his face.

Trayco shrugged, then smiled as DeGuillio swore and put the barf bag back to his face.

Kenny glanced at the instrument panel as a red light flashed and an alarm beeped. Oil pressure was dropping. They were overheating. DeGuillio's head came out of the bag. "What the . . . ?"

Trayco's mouth felt dry as he glanced out the window. Ice was solidly packed against the black shell of the Eagle's fuselage. The blades must be covered with the stuff.

"I hope you're ready to meet your Maker," Trayco said, glancing over at a pale DeGuillio. "This weather . . ." He glanced out the side window toward the ground. It was nothing but a white sheet of flying snow with an occasional dark spot of trees. "We have no place to land."

DeGuillio only gulped, his mouth returning to his bag long enough for him to retch.

Trayco felt the shudder before he heard the cough in the motor. The bottom dropped out from under them and they began to fall, then the motor grabbed hold again and brought them up. Now Trayco *was* afraid, his eyes desperately searching for an opening in the storm, some sign of flat ground. He had to find something and quick. The cold was freezing up the Eagle's systems.

An overpowering gust of wind hit the side of the chopper and shoved it south as if it were just another snowflake. The computer guidance system adjusted and brought the Eagle back quickly. The wind struck again, making Trayco feel as if he were on a swing.

His stomach jumped into his throat when the wind punched them earthward. This time the computer didn't respond as quickly, and Trayco felt something hit the undercarriage. Trees! The system responded, driving them upward.

When the motor coughed again, Trayco was gasping for air, trying to shove his stomach back into place. He braced himself for impact. Twice he had gone down in choppers in Nam. Once on the way to action, once returning from it. He knew how bad it could be. Both times he alone had survived.

The alarms were sounding in his ears, the turbo coughing and sputtering as the wind drove them downward. Trayco reached for the landing gear then removed his hand. Better to have it up.

The computer fought to maintain control, but the motors wouldn't respond. Kenny saw the trees as the Eagle turbo shut down and the bird began to spin.

The heavy timber began splitting the large rotors into pieces as the belly of the transport lunged through the pines. The Eagle hit solid ground and bounced with a deafening crunch of metal. Trayco closed his eyes, fearful of the ball of fire he knew must follow if the tanks were compromised.

He felt the nose of the Eagle angle down, and the chopper began a slide down the precipitous side of the mountain. He felt the remaining blades catch on thick pine trees, snapping like toothpicks. He smelled smoke and saw flames shooting up at him from the console, forcing him to cover his face with his arms. A heavy tree limb banged against the bubble and thrust the metal and plexiglass back at them. He ducked, but the branch broke before the plastic and metal reached his face.

The fuselage skidded down the mountain like a huge sled, bounding over rocks, trees, and bushes that were sticking up through the thick layer of snow. He felt the cold wind blowing against his body and realized the front of the bubble was disintegrating.

Then he saw the river!

The Eagle took momentary flight again as it left the edge of a twenty-foot cliff and plummeted toward the cold waters. The sudden quiet stunned Trayco and seemed to put everything into slow motion. He saw the water come toward him, the nose of the bird dipping further forward to meet it. The impact drove his knees upward and he thought his backbone was going to snap. His head hit the back of the seat and rebounded into the remaining portion of the bubble. Stars flashed in his eyes and he felt himself slipping into unconsciousness. The smack of something wet and cold against his face and torso reawakened his senses and jerked him back from blackness. He tried to get his eyes to focus as the cold liquid came through the broken window and cascaded against his chest. The pain in his broken arm was excruciating! He had to fight it, keep it from knocking him out as the water rose over his chest and surrounded his neck. The hand of his good arm grabbed desperately at the latch on his harness. It wouldn't release. The water level rose above his mouth and nose; he struggled, trying to free himself, but to no avail.

Kenny Trayco realized he was going to drown.

Stone watched the chopper drop off the radar. Using the computer, he pinpointed the spot and immediately told Stockman. After verifying that the chopper was no longer visibly airborne, Stockman cursed. The storm had turned the skies over the command center into a black hole that had now taken its first victim. He could only wonder if there were any survivors.

"Give me a weather report, and let's keep our eyes and ears open," Stockman commanded. "The chopper's emergency system will send out a signal if they've crashed and we'll want to hone in on it."

Stockman didn't think the weather could get any worse, but the weather service, now frantically updating its information, said otherwise. Visibility was near zero, with a windchill factor of forty degrees below zero. The crash site was too far away for ground troops, roads were already closed, and the other choppers in Jackson were grounded because of the bad weather. Even if they could get to them by air, visibly locating the Eagle would be impossible, let alone finding a safe spot to land and rescue survivors—if there were any. At this point in time they could do nothing.

Stockman leaned forward, his fists planted firmly on the console, his eyes glued to the monitors. "Can you get pictures of the area via the satellite?"

"Coming in now, sir."

Stockman watched the monitor Stone pointed at. The satellite was the best there was, but looking through clouds this thick was beyond even its capability. It was a blur of white, gray, and brown. "Magnify, Mr. Stone."

The monitor zoomed in on a strand of silver, broken up by splotches of white. His eyes searched the visible terrain. Nothing.

"Must be under the clouds, sir," Stone said.

"Any way to clear these pictures up?"

"No, sir. Only when the clouds dissipate some—Sir?"

Stockman saw that Stone's eyes were fixed on the radar screen. "What is it, Mr. Stone?"

"The emergency beacon is sending a signal, sir."

Stockman knew what that meant. The emergency signal only came on when a chopper went down the hard way.

"Can you pinpoint the signal?" Stockman asked, moving to look over Stone's shoulder.

"It's strange, sir. It . . . it seems to be moving."

Trayco felt the cold water enter his throat and lungs, felt it numbing his entire body. He fought desperately to be free of the harness. The struggle sent precious air out of his lungs, and he felt himself begin to black out. Suddenly the harness released. He kicked himself free and through the broken bubble. While his legs were still dangling inside the pilot compartment, his head and shoulders broke clear of the water. He coughed and spat the water out of his lungs, gasping for air. When his lungs and mind cleared he remembered Tony was still under the water.

He filled his lungs with air and lowered himself down into the chopper. Releasing Tony's harness and grabbing him by the shirt with his good arm, Trayco yanked him free and through the hole in the bubble.

The cold river continued to drain his body of strength. They had to get to shore. With tremendous effort, he grabbed Tony by the collar and swam into the current. The chopper sank lower, hit bottom, and stopped, the current swirling around what remained of her rotor blade shaft.

He couldn't believe the cold or the stiffness of his body as he fought to pull a half-conscious DeGuillio through the water. He could only kick with his legs, the broken arm all but useless, the other gripping Tony. He fought off the natural urge to black out. The current tugged at his clothing, pulling him under and downstream. His legs cramped up and refused to work, and his grip loosened on Tony's shirt. He fought to hang on but the current wrestled DeGuillio from his grip and pulled him downstream. Kenny grabbed for the man's legs but missed. DeGuillio went under again. Kenny was driven into a protruding rock, then forced under by the current. When he came up, Tony was gone.

As Trayco bobbed in the waves of the current, gasping for air, he swam with his good arm, working to free himself from the grip of a cold death, until he couldn't swim anymore. Exhausted, he felt the current carry him quickly downstream, pummeling him into hidden rocks. He saw the rapids, then tumbled through them; the sudden thought of what was coming released additional adrenaline. With all the strength he could muster, he grabbed hold of the next rock he slammed against and hung on for dear life, forcing his head above water, gasping to fill his lungs with air.

The roar of the falls was like thunder in his ears and he wondered if they were big enough to crush him quickly, relieving his body from the life-sapping, freezing cold.

Desperately he looked for shore, first to his right, then left. He was fifty feet away from the left bank, seventy from the right. Miles, in his condition. Then he saw something. Someone. Who? DeGuillio?

He tried to focus, but his mind was blurry and turning dark, wanting to give up. He had seconds, minutes at most, before his brain completely shut down because of hypothermia.

Then he felt something hit him. Automatically his free but broken arm jerked toward it to push it aside. Pain shot to his brain, forcing him to grit his teeth.

A rope. He grabbed at it, holding it between the tips of his fingers.

Someone was yelling. Far away. He could barely hear them over the sound of the falls. What were they saying? The rope. Put the rope . . .

He couldn't. His muscles were frozen solid; they wouldn't move. Couldn't move. And the broken arm . . . he couldn't get the arm . . . he would have to let go with his good arm . . . he couldn't. The current would break him loose and shove him over the edge.

By pure will he forced his feet to search for a crack in the rock and jammed one of them in a hole, hoping it would hold him.

He took a deep breath and let go. The foot held him, but only for a second. Grabbing the rope with his good arm, he desperately tried to get it over his head as his body was swept quickly toward the precipice.

At the last second he swung his arm in a circular motion, wrapping the rope tightly around it. He felt the tug, felt it tighten, cutting into his coat and gripping his numbed flesh.

There was no pain. There was nothing. Darkness rolled over him. He fought to stay conscious but lost, his body at the mercy of a thin strand of rope and whoever controlled it.

Trayco felt the warmth of something soft and heavy against his bare skin and snuggled into it, the recollection of the icy water giving him a chill.

The icy water! The falls!

His body stiffened, eyes opening. He sprang to a sitting position. With his good hand he grabbed the blankets, ready to toss them aside, but someone grabbed his shoulders.

"I wouldn't do that! Your clothes are by the fire drying, and you'd embarrass us both."

Trayco's eyes focused on the woman sitting on the bedside. His mouth dropped open and he yanked the covers up to his chin as he plopped back on the mattress.

"My name is Kate—Kathryn Meadows." The woman smiled. "I'm with the Forest Service. My son and I were the ones who pulled you from the river."

The smile was a pretty one, a set of straight teeth between soft lips. It created dimples at the corners of her mouth just below tanned cheeks.

"The other . . . another man . . ."

Kate's brown eyes stopped smiling; she jerked her head to throw a curl of dark brown hair away from her eyes. "What's left of the helicopter is jammed against some rocks in the deeper portion of the channel about half a mile above the falls. Only the very top is visible. The man you were trying to save went over the falls. His chances aren't good, but my son is looking."

Trayco tried to sit up while keeping the blanket around him. "My clothes," he said firmly. "I need them. I have to find—" He suddenly realized how naked he really was. "Who . . . who undressed me?"

She smiled. "Your clothes are in by the fire. They won't be dry yet. You've only been out an hour." She walked to a closet, pulled some clothes from hangers, and tossed them on the bed. "Underwear is in the drawer, socks, too." She walked to the door and opened it. "If your man survived, Colt will find him. With that arm you won't be much good to us, but you're welcome to try."

Trayco glanced down at his rebandaged arm. He didn't feel much pain, just a hard, dull throb.

"With all you've been through, you'll be a little sluggish at best. Better let us handle—"

"The man I tried to save is dangerous, and he's a survivor. He'll kill your son if he gets the chance. I have to make sure that doesn't happen."

"Dangerous? But he couldn't have survived that fall." She faced Trayco, a look of concern wrinkling the darkly tanned skin around her eyes and mouth.

"Kate, right?" Trayco said. She nodded. "Well, Kate, I'll fill you in as soon as I get dressed. Was my .45 still on me when you pulled me out of the river?"

Kate nodded.

"Do you have any other weapons around here?"

She nodded. "Colt took one, a .30-30. I'll get the other one." She closed the door behind her.

Trayco joined her in two minutes. She couldn't help but smile at his appearance. Her son was big for his age but the broad shoulders of Kenny Trayco stretched the T-shirt to its very limits and the legs of his six-foot-four-inch frame stuck out the bottom of the jeans a good two inches. His slim, fit waist still pushed the buttons of the size 36 Levis almost to the point of bursting. He looked pale but determined. She could only imagine the pain he had caused himself when dressing.

"Are you all right?" she asked.

Trayco nodded. "A little dizzy, but I'm okay."

"Sorry about the fit. My son is a football player but not quite as big as you are." She tossed him a heavy parka of forest service green, then pointed at a pair of boots by the fireplace. "Those should fit. Size twelve. That's one part of the boy that is just about full grown."

Trayco slid his foot in the first one, the heavy wool sock filling up the half size difference. His fingers weren't bandaged and with some effort he was able to tighten and tie the laces.

Kate filled her pockets with 185-grain magnum cartridges, released the bolt on her 7mm rifle with scope, and shoved shells into the magazine. They'd stop a bull elk dead in his tracks at two hundred yards, but they were all she had. She only hoped she wouldn't have to use them.

Trayco caught his breath, gnashing his teeth against the pain his shoe-tying effort had caused, and watched Kate load the rifle; he was glad she knew how to handle a weapon. Then he stood and forced his arm into the parka. She saw his struggle and gave him a hand. After both arms were in, she pulled the front together and zipped it up, then buttoned the buttons. As she did up the top button their eyes met and held.

"Uhh . . . thanks," Kenny said. It wasn't often a woman made him blush. But then, it wasn't often he had much to do with women.

"You're welcome," she said, backing quickly away and reaching for his .45 laying on the table. "Here. Good as new." She started zipping her own coat, averting her eyes from his.

With one hand he released the magazine and checked it. It was damp. He wished he had time to clean it, but he didn't. "How long was I unconscious? How long has your boy been out looking for Tony?"

"An hour. Colt has been gone twenty, maybe thirty minutes."

Trayco snapped the magazine in place, put on the safety, and stuck the .45 in his coat pocket.

She threw him some gloves, walked to the door, and opened it. Trayco followed, the stiff wind hitting him full in the face as he shut it behind him. There was a good two feet of wet snow on the ground. Heavy stuff. The kind that looked as if it would hold your weight, but didn't, making it difficult to walk.

"Where are we?" he asked, as he came to Kate's side.

"Upper Falls on the Snake. This house was remodeled in 1993-94. A relic of the old days when people used it as a stopover on their way to the park; it had become pretty run-down. The state gave it to the Forest Service if we'd fix it up and use it. The Falls are a tourist attraction and my son and I are the caretakers. Have been for two years. Usually we go down to Rexburg in the winter, but we hadn't closed things down yet. The storm caught us by surprise."

Kate spoke against the wind, and pointed to some ramps. "Those go down to where we pulled you out of the river." Her gloved hand moved to their left. "Down that way is where Colt went." They tramped in that direction. Trayco could see a set of footprints largely filled in by the wind-blown snow.

A moment later they came to the edge of the canyon. Below, Trayco saw the cold waters of the Snake. It wasn't deep, lava boulders sticking through its surface creating eddies that would hold some fun for a fisherman. On their side was a good deal of shore, but it was rough. On the far side the canyon wall was sheer and steep. Solid rock. Tony D had no way out on that side.

"Careful," Kate said. "The trail down is slippery and steep even in the summer. I know it well, so just keep in my tracks."

They had labored half the distance to the canyon floor when Trayco noticed movement out of the corner of his eye, and glanced at a large buck as it moved deftly between boulders, picking its way up what seemed an impossible route.

Kate stopped, her eyes working their way over the ground from which the animal had come. "Something spooked it. It wouldn't leave shelter in weather like this unless—Look!"

Trayco's eyes focused on the spot where Kate was pointing. Two hundred yards further down the canyon a man lay in the snow, his coat and pants stripped from his body.

Trayco saw a flash of movement at the edge of a large snow-covered boulder and dived for Kate. The sharp crack of a rifle sounded as they hit the snow and began rolling down the steep trail. Trayco felt pain as his arm was hit by Kate's body and the ground. In the back of his mind he heard additional shots and was grateful for the trees and rocks surrounding them. With a thump, they smashed into a group of small pines and came to a stop. Trayco grabbed Kate by her coat and shoved her behind a boulder. In the place where she had been a puff of snow jumped, a bullet lodging in the ground beneath. Trayco dropped to the ground and belly-crawled to where Kate was catching her breath, her face red with anger.

"Colt! I've got to get to Colt!" she said, trying to get to her feet. Trayco grabbed at her clothing and pulled her down.

"Stay put! You'll be no good to the boy if Tony gets a clear shot at you!"

Kate's body relaxed a little, her hot breath turning the air white in quick short spurts. Trayco looked desperately up their back trail, his eyes searching for signs of the dropped rifle. Ten feet away he saw the barrel sticking out of the snow.

"We've got to get that rifle," he said, his eyes looking over the terrain for choices. "How much ammo did your son carry with him?"

"A box, then the magazine; probably twenty-five shells," Kate said as another bullet ricocheted off the boulder in front of them.

Trayco told her his plan. "I'll distract him. When the time is right, you go for the gun. Got it?"

"If he gets a good shot at you . . ."

"He won't. Besides, this parka you gave me is thick enough to stop any bullet." He forced a grin.

Crouching, Trayco withdrew the .45 and waited. At the crack of the rifle he lurched away from the rock and down the trail, firing his weapon in the general direction of Tony's hiding place. Even though he knew the bullets would never reach that far, the sound and the possibility would be a distraction to DeGuillio.

Scampering from tree to boulder, then tree again, Trayco kept on the move. He heard the distant sound of the rifle, then felt something crease his shoulder, the sharp sting making him flinch. His foot caught on the edge of a boulder and he toppled head over heels, rolling through the heavy snow. He bounced into a tree, grabbed for it with his good hand and hung on, his feet churning for a foothold in the wet snow.

The crack of a second rifle thundered in the canyon. Again . . . then again, giving him time to scramble for cover. From the shelter of a rock he looked up the trail, where Kate was injecting another shell into the retrieved rifle. Using the scope, she honed in on a distant spot and squeezed the trigger. Bang! Quickly she jerked on the bolt, reloaded, aimed, and fired. Trayco moved closer with each shot, finally reaching the boulder next to hers, gasping for air. Kate's face was set in concrete, a picture of concentration. With her next shot Trayco joined her, putting his hand on hers as she started squeezing off another shot.

"Relax. We'll need the ammo if I'm going to get behind him."

She glanced at him, surprised he was even there. Then her eyes cleared and her head dropped to her arm. Five seconds later she raised it again.

"What . . . what now?"

"Now—" He was cut off by the sound of DeGuillio's voice.

"This boy down here ain't dead, Trayco. But he will be if you don't come out of there and show yourself. Throw out your guns. Now!"

Kate looked at Trayco with frantic eyes.

Kenny knew they had no choice. He started to get up, .45 dangling from his index finger. "All right, Tony. I—"

DeGuillio stood and aimed his rifle. Trayco jumped for cover as he heard the distant report of the .30-30 and felt the bullet hit the snow near his ear. He heard the loud clap of Kate's weapon at the same moment he rolled for cover, another bullet from Tony passing through the loose sleeve of his parka.

Kate dropped the rifle in the snow and plunged toward where Trayco lay motionless in the snow. Grabbing him by the coat, she turned him over, fearful of what she'd see.

Kenny flashed a grin. "I'm okay. He missed."

She used her gloved hand to hit him on the shoulder as Kenny rolled over and pushed himself up. As Kate started to stand he pulled her down. "Maybe you missed, too."

Kate didn't smile. "I don't think so."

Trayco took the rifle and put the scope to his eye. Seeing that the lens was wet, he looked at Kate, his mouth open in dismay. She smiled.

"I've been hunting big game for years in weather worse than this." She shrugged.

He wiped the lens dry then put it back to his eye, searching for a sign of Tony. He was lying in the snow, his legs visible where they stuck out from behind the boulder. There wasn't any movement.

Trayco stood and offered Kate a hand. "Come on. It's clear. Let's go to Colt."

Colt had been hit over the head with a rock and had a concussion. Kate sewed up the gash in his scalp with a surgical skill most doctors would envy while Trayco took care of Tony D's body. The Mafia boss's skull hadn't had much of a chance against the 7mm Magnum.

He wrapped the body in a tarp that he found in a shed near the house then packed it in snow. It'd keep until spring, if necessary.

As he entered the house, Kate was warming her hands by the fire and turned to him, forcing a smile across her stressed but beautiful face.

"How's Colt?" Trayco asked, stamping his boots to clear them of snow.

She sat down on the raised hearth, letting the fire warm her back. Her elbows rested on her knees and her hands wrestled with one another. "His skull is cracked good. There may be some hemorrhaging; I can't tell without some x-rays."

"Has he regained consciousness at all?" Trayco asked.

She shook her head. "His vital signs are stable." She took a deep breath. "He needs a doctor, but in this weather . . ."

"What kind of car do you have?"

"Four-wheel-drive pickup, but this snow is too heavy even for it. And with this wind the roads between here and Ashton will be closed."

"Do you have a phone?" Kenny asked as he hung his parka on a hook near the door.

"No. No lines within miles. We took the radio equipment down last weekend when we were getting ready to close up." She ran her hand through her shoulder-length, curly brown hair.

"Nearest neighbor?" he asked, standing beside her warming his hands.

"Fifteen, twenty miles either way." She paused. "Did you take care of the body?"

He sat down. "Yeah. You okay?" he asked, blowing into his still chilly hands.

Tears began to trickle down her cheeks. "I . . . I shot . . ." She buried her face in her hands and began sobbing. Trayco put his arm around her shoulders and held her tight, wondering how to comfort her. He had never been good with women. They were soft and gentle. He was coarse and hard. He had dated very little in his life. When he had, it hadn't been serious. The very thought of a wife made him nervous—someone needing him, relying on him to be there.

And children.

Kentucky Trayco came from an environment in which large families were common, but few survived the day-to-day challenge of the streets. He had watched two of his brothers being hauled off to jail for selling drugs and a third killed by a policeman, who caught him trying to rob a neighbor's house to get enough money to support a two-hundred-dollar-a-day habit. His only sister still lived in L.A.'s inner city, refusing to leave, even when Trayco offered her a new life. She was hooked on booze. It wasn't only minorities who lost everything to the ghettos of the city of angels.

Kenny had only escaped because a judge gave him a choice: jail or the marines. He took the marines.

Kate snuffed her nose, stood and went to a nearby desk to retrieve a tissue. Trayco stayed put, rubbing his hands.

"Sorry," she said.

Trayco shrugged. "I understand. Killing isn't what we expect life to hand us."

She looked over at Kenny. "Who was he?"

He told her the whole story. Kate had earned it.

Her eyes were wide but dry. "DeGuillio was the only one who could tell you what you need to know to get to the top, wasn't he?"

Trayco shrugged. "One arrow in a quiver full of them. We have other ways." He stood, picked up a couple of logs, and added them to the fire. "Right now let's just worry about getting Colt to a doctor."

Kate went to the open bedroom door and looked inside. "There is a way."

Trayco looked up, waiting for her to continue. "We have a fly-fishing boat dry docked below Lower Falls. It'd be tough but we could get there by stretcher, then float to the Ashton bridge, and get some help."

"How far?" Trayco asked, his eyes turning to the fire.

"Down the trail we were ambushed on; once we get to the bottom it's probably a mile. The tough part will be getting him past the lower falls. We'll need ropes."

"Why not go around?"

"We'd have to go high, then cross a lava bed full of holes. We'd break a leg for sure."

Trayco walked to the door. It would be dark in another hour, maybe two. The storm wasn't letting up; if anything, it was getting worse. Help from Stockman, if it came at all, would be hours away.

"We should go in the morning at first light," he said. "Where do you keep ropes and stuff?"

"In the shed outside."

"I'll get 'em while you see to Colt." He put on his parka and left through the front door.

Kate went to the window and watched Kenny's powerful body trudge through the deepening carpet of wet, white stuff. He hadn't complained about the arm even though she knew the painkiller had worn off. He was tough.

She wondered about Kenny Trayco. Although he had told her everything about DeGuillio and the war to stop his organization, he had said very little about himself or his role. Who lived behind that granite square jaw, the aquiline nose, and those steel grey eyes that could be both cold and gentle at the same time?

Kenny Trayco made Kate Meadows tingle—a feeling she hadn't had for a man since the death of her husband. Having it again felt good.

―――――――

Trayco took a piece of bread and used it to slick up the remaining stew in the bottom of his bowl, then washed it down with a full glass of milk. Kate watched in awe. The man had consumed four big bowls of stew, half a loaf of bread, and three glasses of milk, not to mention a quarter block of cheese, three pickles, and a bunch of carrot and celery sticks.

Kenny saw the look. "You're a good cook." He smiled.

She returned the smile, picking up her dishes and heading to the sink. He joined her, carrying his dirty bowl and glass. While she ran some water, he finished cleaning up the table.

"Kentucky. An interesting name," she said.

"My mom's idea. It was her home state."

"I like it."

Kenny smiled. He handed her the towel. "I'd be glad to do these. Why don't you dry your hands and check on Colt."

She thanked him and moved toward the bedroom door. When she returned, Kenny was finished with the dishes and was stoking the fire. He threw on a couple more logs.

"How's the arm?" Kate asked, sitting on the couch.

"Thanks to the painkiller you had in that syringe it's bearable."

"I don't have much, but if you need more . . ."

"I'm fine."

It was silent. The crackle of the wood and the shadows of the flames dancing around the room were almost hypnotic.

"I can see why you love this place," Trayco said. "No phones, no busy city. Peaceful."

Kate slipped her shoes off her feet, then pulled her feet up under her. "I used to hate it."

Kentucky moved to the couch and sat down, turning sideways with one leg up, facing her, waiting for the story.

"I was a big-city girl from Seattle. Living in the forest was the farthest thing from my mind. I went to the University of Idaho at Moscow on a basketball scholarship and met Shane Meadows, a mountain man from a little town even further north near Lake Pend O'reille. He wanted to be Smokey Bear." She smiled.

"What happened to him?"

"He was killed about ten years ago. A head-on collision with a logging truck going too fast on a narrow road lined with pine trees. We were living in California at the time. Yosemite National Park."

"You didn't go back to Seattle?"

"Shane introduced me to a better life. I've never looked back."

"Never remarried?"

She shook her head. Their eyes met and held for a long moment. "What do people call you?" she asked.

"Friend or foe?" He smiled. "Trayco seems to be easier than Kentucky. Some call me Kenny."

"No one calls you Tray?"

He shook his head.

"Well, Tray, I'm debating whether to let you sleep in the house or make you bed down in the shed. I don't really know much about you. Maybe you should fill in a few blanks for me."

"There isn't much to know. I was a street kid raised by my mother in L.A. I was in fights more than I wasn't, refused to go to school, tough, king of the hill, stupid. A judge helped me face reality when he threatened to put me in jail; but he gave me an alternative. I joined the marines and went to Vietnam. They taught me how to kill people, then sent me home. A friend of mine took me in and found me work in Las Vegas, where, eventually, I started my own protection business. It's done okay."

"Never married?"

"Never found anyone who would say yes." He stood and went to the fireplace. One of the logs had rolled against the screen. Using the poker he flipped it back in place. He sat on the hearth, letting it warm his back. "I'm sorry about all this."

"Next time, crash somewhere else, will you?" she said, smiling. "Would you like some hot chocolate or something?"

"No thanks. How did you come to live here?"

"After I fell in love with nature I went back to school and studied to become a botanist. I was hired by the Forest Service two years before Shane was killed. After his burial I needed a change of scenery and came to the Targhee National Forest for it. I bought a house in Ashton and worked out of the field office there. When this came open I grabbed it."

His back was nearly on fire, so Trayco moved back to the couch. "You've fixed this place up nice."

Kate chuckled. "It isn't very many people that have a summer home with scenery like this one, furnished by the government." She paused. "Maybe you'd like to come back in the spring. It's beautiful."

"I'd like that."

Their eyes met again. This time Kate adjusted her position, moving close enough for Trayco to put his arm around her—and he did. She laid her head against his shoulder, her warmth making his side tingle. "Do you still have family in L.A.?"

"A sister. She's in a hospital. Drug rehab. My mom died a year ago. I had some brothers, but they're dead, or in jail. Nobody else."

"How did you get involved in this government mess?"

"Jeremiah Daniels is the one who kept me from making some serious mistakes when I returned from Nam. He's like a brother to me and, well, he asked." Tray paused. "But I have personal reasons, too. Drugs killed my brother, put two in jail, and made an addict out of my sister. When I go back to the inner city, where I lived as a kid, I wonder how I survived. How anyone can survive. Drugs are a big problem. When Jeremiah declared war on the people who created that kind of environment, that kind of pain, I signed up."

She looked up at him. For Kenny Trayco the world was black and white, good and bad. He had decided to be on the right side even though he'd been given every opportunity to do otherwise. She liked that.

She pressed herself against him lightly as she lifted her head toward his. Trayco felt the pressure and the movement and turned into her. Their lips touched lightly, his hand going to the back of her neck where it rubbed softly. Kate felt the hunger rise within her and pressed her mouth to his. Trayco's response generated more heat and they kissed each other passionately. As Kate pulled slowly away, she kissed his cheek, then laid her head on his shoulder, against his neck. The smell of her scented hair was heavy in his nostrils, the warmth of her making his heart pound inside his chest.

"I think I'll let you stay in this house," she said.

"Thanks. Where do I sleep?"

She patted the couch.

He laughed mischievously. "I'm not sure it's a good idea for us to stay under the same roof."

"Ummm. Didn't you say you owned a protection service?"

He nodded.

"What's your fee?"

"A thousand an hour."

"No special rates for people who save your life? Twice?"

"Okay, a hundred an hour. That will barely cover expenses."

"You're hired."

"What's my job?"

"You ask the obvious."

He looked into her eyes. "You ask the impossible."

He stood and helped her up. "But I know my job." He

pointed toward the bedroom. "See you in the morning." Smiling, she kissed him on the cheek, then moved away, closing the door behind her.

Trayco removed a handkerchief from his pocket and rubbed it across his forehead. He had never met anyone quite like Kate Meadows before. Never. He wondered if his heart could stand it.

CHAPTER 10

7:15 P.M.—Washington, D.C.

"The president will be detained a few minutes, Mr. Daniels," said the secretary. "Please, make yourself comfortable. Can I get you anything?"

Jeremiah flung his carry-on over a chair and seated himself. "How about a bulletproof vest. From the sounds of things, the hill is mounting an all-out attack."

The secretary smiled wanly. "I'm afraid they're using heavy artillery. A vest won't do much good. Can I get you a bomb shelter?"

"Thanks, but I get claustrophobia. Is there a phone . . . ?"

"On the table over there. It's scrambled." She closed the door behind her.

Jeremiah almost dialed Stockman, then hung up, wondering if it was safe even from the White House. He'd wait until he got to the safe house and LOGOS.

The last he had heard, everything was okay. Mike and Trayco were on their way back to the *ISSA*, Macklin was on a flight to Israel, and Gad was making arrangements to get Alvarez and Lima to safer ground. The only unknown was Koln. He had to trust that his people could handle the assassin.

He took a deep breath, pushed himself out of the chair, and went to the wet bar, pouring himself a glass of water, then adding the juice from half a dozen lemon slices. As he took the first sip the door opened and the president walked in. He had a guest with him.

"Jeremiah. Glad to see you are still in one piece," the president said.

"Mr. President. Senator Ridgeway." Jeremiah greeted them.

Cameron Cruise Ridgeway had replaced James Freeman as chairman of the Senate Committee on Intelligence. Jim had fought the replacement and Ridgeway had taken it personally. Jeremiah didn't expect a pleasant visit.

"Mr. Daniels." They shook hands. Round one.

"Be seated, gentlemen," the president invited. "Senator Ridgeway has some questions for you, Jerry. Tell him what you think you can."

Jeremiah sent an approving glance toward the president, thankful that Seth Adams hadn't sagged under this pressure.

Ridgeway leaned forward. "Just what are you trying to do, Mr. Daniels?"

"Sir?"

Ridgeway glanced down at Jeremiah's boots with disdain. "We don't live in the Old West anymore, Daniels. No vigilantes allowed."

"Vigilantes, sir? I don't understand."

"Then let me make it clear. So far you have circumvented every legitimate intelligence organization this country has in order to violate the sovereignty of several foreign countries, some of their citizens, not to mention the rights of a few of our own. You have broken the laws—"

"I beg your pardon, Senator, but you're wrong."

Ridgeway's face went as hard as a rock. "Listen, you—"

"No, you listen, Senator, and listen good. Everything I've instigated has been meticulously researched as to its legality, and the United States is well within its rights in that arena. We have extradition treaties with Colombia that specify we can use force to extricate known criminals within her borders without prior notice. That treaty was obtained in 1994. I'll see that you get a copy. Second, Israel went into Lebanon for Boudia. We didn't. They went after him because of his arms sales to terrorists who have declared themselves enemies to Israel. We are working out an extradition agreement with them. Would you like a copy of that as well? I'll see that you get one. Third, Mr. DeGuillio was caught in the act of murder, *and* we have a witness very close to Tony, who is willing to testify in court that he ordered the killing of James Freeman. A federal offense. I intend to get him to trial. That will be no small accomplishment when you consider the fact that those who really wanted Freeman dead and ordered Tony to have it done, now want Tony out of the way. They nearly accomplished it today. And Lima? He tried to kill Alvarez, again on someone's orders, and he got caught. He'll go to trial. Until then, I'll keep him where they can't get at either him or Alvarez."

Ridgeway had no place to go and decided on another track. Round two began. "The FBI is responsible—"

"Lima purchased the FBI in Miami," Jerry interrupted. "For twenty thousand dollars. They're in custody and you can have their fellow agents do anything they like with them, but it's apparent they can't be trusted to protect Alvarez—or Lima."

"But—"

"Senator," the president said, "Jeremiah has been given unlimited authority here. I told you that. I also told you why, but in case you missed it, let me repeat myself. I have proof that every major agency under your responsibility has been infiltrated by the enemy. In a word, *bought,* Senator. They have sold their souls for money. That is why evidence disappears from locked holding cages. That is why witnesses, promised protection, are suddenly found by their enemies and killed. That is why we can't get legislation passed to deal with the problem. That is why we're losing ground and the enemy is winning." The president leaned forward in emphasis. "And that is why James Freeman and other members of the international task force died. Insiders, Senator. People on the take." He rapped his knuckles on the desk top. "I intend to stop it!"

Ridgeway was trapped, but not finished. Round three. "I understand, Mr. President. I—all of us on the hill—want to bring the killers to their knees, but our agencies have been set up—"

"Jeremiah's position as drug czar is fully within the law. The powers granted him come either by legislation or through this office. Are you challenging those powers?"

"No, Mr. President. But—"

"Good, then we're finished here. Or do you have something further to say?"

Ridgeway stood, his jaw set. "Very well, Mr. President. I can see that talking to you will change nothing. I'll have to handle this another way."

"Yes, I supposed you would; but understand this, Senator: You'll be fighting me over an issue on which the public stands behind me. I'll fight you tooth and nail. I'll use public opinion and the media. Something I am very good at."

Ridgeway had a scowl on his face, his eyes those of a cornered weasel. "I'll eat you for lunch, Seth. And enjoy every minute of it." He strode to the door and left. The president collapsed into his chair. Round four would come another day.

"The big gun," Jeremiah said, forcing a smile.

"They've been in and out of here all day."

"Can you handle him?"

"For a while. Until he turns the tide of public opinion against me." He sighed. "Dollars to doughnuts says he's already booked himself on half a dozen news shows. He'll try to use his soft-soap sales style to make the public believe our intentions are good but that our methods stink."

"They do stink, but we've run out of choices."

"What are you doing in Washington, Jerry?"

"I thought you might need someone to bolster your waning spirits. I was wrong. Sorry for my misjudgment of you."

"No need to apologize; you're right. If you hadn't been sitting there, reminding me of my word to you, I'm not sure I would have leaned on him that way." He smiled. "I must say, though, it did feel good. I've never liked the man. Too much of a politician."

They laughed lightly.

"How are we doing?" the president asked.

"If everything goes well tonight, Senator Ridgeway will be knocking on your door a lot harder tomorrow morning." He told the president about the raids and the efforts in Mexico. "My team isn't doing these, but people I trust are. They were a little reluctant until they saw what we were able to do. Now the good ones want in."

"The Cosa Nostra is fighting back. It will get worse."

Jerry nodded lightly. "Don't wander, Mr. President. No flights to Camp David. No meandering about shopping for socks."

The president laughed. "Not to worry. Like most American males, I hate shopping." He took a breath. "Dolph informed me that Mike was almost killed at the courthouse."

"She's on safe ground now. She'll stay there until we're finished." Jeremiah stood. "I'm going to LOGOS. From what I'm told, we may have a lead on the money trail."

The president leaned forward. "If we could shut that off . . ."

"Yeah. A major coup. I'll be in touch."

Ridgeway settled himself in the back seat of the limo next to Claire John, grinding his teeth. "Intractable! Both of them!"

"Can you muster enough support to make the president back off?" she asked.

Ridgeway stuck a cigar in his mouth. Claire leaned against him, flipped open a cigarette lighter, and lit it. The senator puffed deeply, then spoke. "He has public support. They're outraged by what happened to the task force. The American people don't think much about the Mafia until they start killing good people. The people will wink at a lot of sinful crime, but not at that. It scares them out of their apathetic pants."

"It was necessary," Claire said, her fingers caressing his earlobe and neck. "Can you make him back off?"

"Yes, but I'll need time—and Jeremiah Daniels out of the way. He seems to be the backbone of this whole operation. With him gone, Seth Adams and everyone else would melt into oblivion."

"We're working on that," she said, smiling.

"You tell Luciano I expect something in return for all this."

She forced a pouty look. "You mean I'm not enough?"

"Lovely as you are, dear Claire, I have other needs."

"Such as?"

"The presidency of the United States."

She looked a little shocked, then a thin smile crossed her lips. "You'll need a wife."

He laughed. "I love you, Claire, but a background check of your past might give some starving reporter the Pulitzer Prize."

Claire laughed. "Yes, well, I doubt that. Even Rolf Koln doesn't know who I really am, and he did a pretty thorough check himself."

"Umm. Papa Buscetti is pretty good at putting out what people want to read."

"SCORPION has decided to bring everything back in the family, including enforcement. Someone needed to learn Koln's secrets so that his organization could be dealt with effectively. It was decided that I would do it."

"And how is Koln doing these days?"

She pouted again. "You know I can't discuss business." She smiled. "Having you in the White House would be nice. Did I tell you I went there once? I received the royal tour."

"You? When?"

"Two years ago, when the law firm I work with was negotiating with the government over a settlement for our clients. The government had knowingly dumped toxic waste materials into the aquifer at the Idaho National Engineering Laboratory. It got into the water supplies of several small towns. We met with the attorney general and the president, and settled for thirty million and a gag order. As a part of the celebration of coming to a meeting of the minds we had dinner with the president. The first lady showed me their personal quarters."

"Get me in there, dear girl, and I'll see that you visit often."

She smiled, taking off her shoes and getting to her knees, then leaning into him, kissing him hard. "Our association has been a mutually beneficial one, hasn't it, Cameron?"

He rubbed her lower back. "In more ways than one."

"We've paid you well?"

"My largest campaign contributor and the sole benefactor of my substantial Cayman Islands bank balance."

"Then earn it, dearest. My father doesn't feel like he's getting his money's worth when he really needs it. You're our contact here, the man we rely on in Washington to protect our interests." She paused. "We paid you nearly a million dollars last year, seven hundred and fifty thousand the year before, and we've asked very little, except that you deliver when you're needed." She sighed. "Deliver, Senator, or your season in Washington will come to an untimely end."

Ridgeway jerked his head around, a hard look of granite across his face. "Are you threatening me, Claire?"

She touched his lip with her index finger as she leaned into him, that pouty look on her lips again. "No, darling. I'm making you a promise. Sicily doesn't spend money for nothing. You deliver, or I have orders to see that you go to an early grave."

Her flesh was warm, but the look in her eyes was as cold as death. Cameron Ridgeway felt a sudden warmth that made him sweat. His mouth felt dry and his Adam's apple bobbed, a visible sign of the gut-wrenching tightness he felt in his stomach. His usual cool exterior was blown away to reveal a man afraid.

Her message delivered, Claire slipped off her knees and back into the seat, replaced her shoes, then pushed the intercom. "Charles, you can drop me off here. My own car has been following us." She took Ridgeway's hand and kissed it, easing the startled look on his face. "Don't worry, Cameron. I know you'll come through. In two days I'll meet you at your place. If everything goes well, I'll have a week off."

As she crossed over his lap to get to the door she leaned into him again, kissing him passionately. "'Bye."

Ridgeway closed the door behind her, then removed his handkerchief and wiped away the sweat on his forehead. Luciano Buscetti had a beautiful daughter. A woman with a passion for life and love that Ridgeway had found in few others and which she had used to trap him in her black widow's web. Like a mouse with a piece of steel sprung across his vitals, Cameron Ridgeway was painfully trapped.

He shoved the handkerchief back in his pocket with a shudder. He'd better lay the groundwork needed to force the president's hand in a major way or he would end up as dead as dead could get. He pushed the intercom. "To Senator Thurman's house, Charles," he said. "And please hurry." He shut off the intercom. "I've got a lot to do."

CHAPTER 11

11:00 P.M.—Provo, Utah

Seriza rolled over and checked the clock. She hadn't been able to sleep even though it had been several hours since Ahmad had returned her to her apartment after an afternoon of study and an evening of watching movies and eating a late dinner. They had talked a long time after the plates had been cleared away, and the manager had finally come to tell them nicely that if they didn't leave soon, they'd be locked in.

Ahmad told her at dinner he was leaving school. A family emergency. Seriza had to bite her tongue, knowing her father's men had given him the message somehow and were going to pick him up. It was important to her father that his involvement be kept a secret. She had honored his request, but it hadn't been easy.

She was going to miss Ahmad Tabriz. She tossed, trying to find a comfortable spot. How long would it be? Would she ever see him again? He had been so secretive about the future. What *was* the danger?

Seriza glanced at the red numbers on the face of her alarm clock again. Ahmad had only been gone half an hour; it seemed like ages.

She sat up and planted her feet on the floor. She wanted to see him before he left. Needed to see him. Ahmad had said they were picking him up at midnight. If she hurried . . .

Minutes later she was in the Grand Am and headed toward Ahmad's housing complex. When she arrived she pulled the Pontiac over and glanced up at the tower she knew Ahmad lived in. This was silly. He was on the fourth floor. The place had a curfew and didn't allow visitors after midnight. How was she going to get him to come down before her father's men arrived?

She rubbed frost off her window. Maybe a phone call. He did have a phone, and there was a phone booth in front of the Morris Center.

She saw headlights coming down the street. Two vehicles. One passed by, then pulled to the curb in front of the tower. The other went to the corner and turned toward the temple, pulling over with only its rear door in view. She rubbed the remaining fog away from the driver's side window and watched, curious.

The two doors opened on the vehicle. A man stepped out. She rubbed the window again, squinting through the icy surface. It was her father. What . . . ?

He seemed to be giving instructions, then walked to the second vehicle, opened the rear door, and disappeared inside. The car quickly pulled away.

Seriza's stomach churned. Something was wrong. She rolled the window down so she could see more clearly. A distant click drew her eyes to the man closest to her, and the streetlight glistened off a shiny object in his hand. A gun!

Another sound came from the tower and Seriza saw Ahmad step from the door and start down the walk, luggage in hand. Her mind worked frantically as she suddenly realized something was terribly wrong. Why would the man be checking his gun just as Ahmad appeared? Why had her father come? And what orders had he given? He was supposed to be gone. Could it be that her father hadn't been truthful with her? Was he after Ahmad for some other reason? Had she betrayed Ahmad?

She tried to shake her head free of the unpleasant thought but it refused to go away, old memories flooding her mind, overwhelming her senses. She had to do something.

She started the car and thrust it into gear, jamming on the gas feed. The Pontiac lurched away from the curb and she yanked the wheel hard and to the left, careening across the street and onto the sidewalk. She jerked the wheel and catapulted down the walk. She saw the startled men on her right, Ahmad on her left, his mouth dangling open. She slammed on the brakes. "Get in!" she yelled through the open window. Rashid hesitated, then grabbed the latch and threw himself and his luggage on the back seat as the Pontiac sprang away from the two running men. In the rearview mirror she saw one aim his pistol, the other grabbing his arm and thrusting it upward, yelling something at him. They ran for their car as Seriza steered hard to the left and pushed on the gas. The Grand Am squealed a little and darted up the street. She ran the red light and pushed harder on the gas.

"What are you doing?" Rashid demanded harshly as he climbed clumsily over the back of the front seat.

"Something's wrong!" she said, keeping her eyes on the road and the rearview mirror. "My father . . ." Seriza saw the headlights appear, the bigger car quickly gaining. She turned the wheel to the left and slid into a residential street, shifting into low and pushing on the gas again.

"Keep your eyes on the back window, so I can drive! We can discuss this later! Right now I'm busy." She swung the wheel quickly to the left, slamming Rashid against the door as the car whipped around a corner and down a slight incline, then went right, trying to use the smaller car's maneuverability to outdistance the larger car's power.

They came out across from the Marriott Center. She veered hard right, the car bolting down University Parkway.

"Any sign of them?" Seriza yelled over the high-pitched whine of the Pontiac's motor.

"Just now coming into the street!" Rashid said as they passed the Comfort Inn Motel and sped through the light on University Avenue. They had no chance of outdistancing their pursuers on a main street, and the big, powerful Lincoln was quickly breathing down their necks. As it came within feet of them, Seriza slammed on the brakes and jerked left into a car dealership. Switching off her lights, she drove the Pontiac quickly between rows of used cars. When they went over the curb at the far end, she turned the lights back on, the car plummeting down an embankment and onto a side road. Turning left, she lunged back onto the Parkway and hit the gas, going east. At the corner of University Avenue she turned the wheel right and slammed the gearshift into low. The rpms shot to nearly four thousand and Rashid thought the motor would fly into a million pieces. Seconds later she went left, bouncing Rashid's head off the side window as she went behind the deserted A&W Root beer stand. She turned off the lights and twisted the key in the ignition.

"Get down!" she said, pulling on Rashid's shirt. Seconds later they heard the powerful roar of the Lincoln's motor as it sped by and the screeching of tires as it turned and went west on 800 North.

Seriza was sweating, her breathing coming hard and fast. Her arms felt like lead as she tried to sit up. She tried to smile at Rashid but her eyes rolled in their sockets and she blacked out, collapsing on the seat.

When Seriza woke up she found herself in the passenger seat, a coat against the window and seat serving as her pillow. Rashid was driving with lights off down a sidestreet she didn't recognize.

"Where . . . where are we?" she asked, lifting her head and trying to shake away the cobwebs.

"I'm trying to get us back close to the towers. How do you feel?" Rashid asked, squinting into the darkness.

"Woozy, but I'll be all right in a minute." She laid her head against the headrest, remembering what had happened. "My father . . . he was there, but he wasn't supposed to be. He said . . ."

"Your father?"

"My dad's with the government or something. He called the other night and said he was coming here on business and he wanted to see me."

"What business?"

"He said . . . he said he knew your father and that he had a message for you."

Rashid didn't say anything. He *had* received a message but it was from Dolph Stockman. He should have checked it out, should have called. He felt stupid.

"My father called this afternoon just before you picked me up to study, and said he wasn't coming. He had to go to Europe. When I saw him . . . I felt something was wrong. They . . . they had guns."

"What guns?" Rashid's head jerked in her direction, eyes full of questions.

"One of the men was checking his gun. I saw it. The other man was in the shadows but held his arm to his side. I'm sure he had one, too."

Rashid gripped the wheel nervously while shrugging his shoulders.

As Rashid pulled the car into the parking area belonging to Wymount Terrace, the married student housing, she spoke. "What's going on, Ahmad?" She thrust her head back against the seat. "Who *are* you?"

He took a deep breath. "Rashid Daniels. My father is Jeremiah Daniels, the president's drug czar."

"My dad told me about your father. Why would they come after you with guns?"

"I don't know, Seriza. If I knew who your father was, who he worked for . . ."

"His name is Maxwell, Joseph Maxwell. I think he is with the CIA or something; he's never really said."

"What did he tell you—about me, I mean," Rashid asked.

"He said he was working with the president and that your life was in danger and he had to get a message to you from your dad."

Seriza looked hard at Rashid. "My father wasn't sent by your father, was he?"

"I don't think so. Dad said I should be careful unless contacted by members of his team or personal friends. He gave me names of people to trust. I thought the message I received was from one of them. I should have checked.

"Your dad could be just another agent doing his job. My father might know him, and even if he doesn't . . ." He hesitated. "My father has a lot of enemies, a lot of people who don't want him to accomplish what he's doing. Some of them work in the U.S. government like he does. Maybe your father is being used by someone in the CIA who is my father's enemy." Rashid told her about his grandfather and the drug wars. How enemies were found in lots of high places, and that was why they had to be so careful.

A heavy silence set in. Finally Seriza spoke again. "What are you going to do?"

Rashid opened the door. "First, get my wheels. They'll be looking for this car. Then I'm going to call someone and find out if that message was from my dad."

"I'll wait."

Rashid turned back again. "For what?"

"To see if you get your car. If you can't, you'll need this one." She smiled.

Rashid returned the smile. "Okay, but it shouldn't be a problem. You keep low until I get back."

"They'll be watching for you, Rashid."

"Maybe. But I think I can manage it." He smiled. "Be back in a jiff."

Seriza watched him disappear into some shrubs and didn't see him emerge. Ten minutes went by and she began to get nervous, glancing at her watch as a police car, lights flashing but with no siren, whizzed past the parking lot. It was headed for the towers.

She glanced at her watch again. Something was wrong—and the police car . . .

She moved to the driver's seat and started the engine.

Out of the corner of her eye she saw some movement, then the door was jerked open and someone had her by the arm. In a frightened reaction she yanked it away.

"It's me!" Rashid said in a loud whisper. "Slide over! Quickly!"

Seriza jammed the gearshift back into park and quickly moved across the console to the passenger seat, an excited relief making her heart bang against the inside of her rib cage. "Where on earth . . ."

"I couldn't get my car!" he said through tight lips. "The police are all over the place!" He reversed the gearshift and backed out. A moment later they were several blocks away.

Rashid hit his hands against the steering wheel in frustration. "Why the police?"

"I can get us a car," Seriza said. "I know someone."

He pulled over to the curb. *"Us?"*

"I'm going with you." She opened her own door and got out. Rashid sat there not sure what to do. Before he could think of a reason for telling her no, she was on the sidewalk motioning him to join her. He removed the keys, opened the door, pushed the power-lock switch, and got out.

"No. You—"

"At least until I can get you a car." She started walking, pulling on his coat sleeve. "It isn't far. The car isn't much, but it'll do."

Three blocks later Rashid stood by an old beat-up '55 Corvette while Seriza talked to some guy at the door of a nearby basement apartment. A guy she had been dating off and on since the first semester of her freshman year. Moments later she came back, keys in hand. She handed them to Rashid, then went around to the passenger side and hopped in. He stood motionless, unbelieving.

"This thing doesn't even have a top! We'll freeze to death."

"Blankets are in the trunk." She smiled. "One for each of us. And you're wearing a warm coat." She reached under the seat and pulled out something, tossing it to him. "Wool ski cap." She pulled one over her own head and ears.

Rashid did the same, got the blankets out of the trunk, then slid into the driver's seat, tossing the heaviest blanket to Seriza. "Does it even run?" he asked, laying the blanket across his legs.

"Just try it." She grinned mischievously.

He turned the key. It started immediately, the motor a soft and even rumble.

"Jared races it in the summer: 357 with dual carbs and fuel injection. It's very hot." She chuckled.

He shook his head disbelievingly. "Let's hope we can say the same for the heater." He put it in reverse and eased out of the driveway.

"Where to?" she asked, wrapping herself in the blanket and zipping her coat clear to the top.

"*You're* going back to your apartment," he said firmly. "I'll drop you off close enough so that you can walk."

She grabbed the keys, turning off the engine. The car coasted a few feet and stopped in the middle of the street. Rashid stared at her blankly.

"I'm going with you."

Exasperation showing in his face, Rashid tried to convince her to go home.

She only shook her head and smiled. "You may have already guessed, but I don't know my father very well." She hesitated. "I . . . I've never been able to trust him. I can't explain that, but that's the way it is. I'm not sure where he stands in all this. Until I get a better idea I'd rather not talk to him. I might say the wrong thing."

Rashid looked into the almond-shaped eyes and saw the confusion—and the fear. Seriza had seen the men with guns. If they were not from his father, they were the enemy, and she was a witness. Her father's enemies were the Cosa Nostra. They didn't like witnesses. "All right, but only because I'm not sure who we're dealing with. You saw them. That might endanger you."

"My father wouldn't—"

"Believe me, Seriza, your father might not have a choice." He stuck his hand out and she handed him the keys.

Rashid started the car and put it in gear.

As they moved down the street, he gave her a more detailed sketch of what Jeremiah Daniels was up to and why. Then he told her what he knew about the Cosa Nostra. Seriza's mouth was open slightly as she sat half turned in the seat taking it all in. When Rashid finished, they were pulling into a Chevron Quick Stop.

"I'm going to make a call," Rashid said. Seriza had a knot in her stomach. When Rashid returned, his face was ashen.

"Your father didn't send mine to warn you, did he?" Seriza said, reading the answer on his face.

Rashid started the car. "No. They don't know any Joseph Maxwell." He saw the disappointment in Seriza's face and went on quickly. "But they're checking. Dad went to Washington this morning. Possibly he sent him for reasons he hasn't told anyone else. They'll find out."

"Where are we going?" she asked quietly.

"My father planned for things like this. There is a safe house in Salt Lake. Someone will meet us there."

Seriza felt cold and huddled deeper into the blanket. There were things about her father she had never thought about very carefully that were now making frightening sense. The firecrackers, the sudden appearance of the gun. His obsession with privacy. An apartment, which she had only seen once, that was more like a fortress than a home. His travel. The refusal to talk about his work, things her grandparents had said in whispered tones.

She shook her head slightly. No, there was an explanation for all this. Her father wasn't a killer. He couldn't be. Although she didn't see him that much, when she did, he was happy, his eyes full of love and caring about her. A man who killed people couldn't love, couldn't feel, could he?

She tried to rub away the goose bumps that arose as she thought of her father.

"Are you all right?" Rashid asked.

"Wh . . . what?" Seriza responded. "Uh, yes, I'm fine." She forced a smile.

They were at the entrance to I-15, the Corvette heater worked well and the blankets trapped the heat around their legs and torso.

Rashid could see the confusion in her eyes. "There's got to be a logical explanation for all this, Seriza."

She smiled, nodding, grateful for his attempt, but the knot in her stomach didn't go away.

Koln put the phone back on the receiver. Nothing. The kids had disappeared.

Rashid Daniels would call his father. A search would be performed on Joseph Maxwell and the truth would slowly come out. Seriza would find out.

He slammed his fists against the steering wheel and cursed. He was cornered. If he backed off, Buscetti would send someone else and his daughter would be in the way. The assassin would be forced to kill her. If he stuck with it, he could save her life, but he would have to kill the boy. Seriza would hate him for the rest of her life.

But at least she would be alive.

As he pulled onto the freeway he tried to think as if he were Rashid Daniels. Where would Rashid Daniels go? He picked up the phone and dialed the condo in Jackson.

"Yeah."

"Koln. Anything happening?"

"Nothing. The airport is closed down but they hope to

open to get a few flights in and out within the next few hours. The roads are really bad. We still haven't gotten into one of the ranches, and won't. Not until this storm blows over."

"Watch the airport. Somebody has to come in there. I want them followed."

"It's covered. I've had a guy hanging around the sheriff's office, too. A local. He says a chopper went down north of us. Along the Snake in Idaho. An Eagle."

"A military chopper?"

"Yeah, like the two in the hangar at the airport."

Koln thought a minute. "Why would they go north?"

"In weather like this it's tough to come over the mountains. Dangerous. The local guy thinks the pilot was trying to come around them."

"Any word on who they are?"

"According to the report the sheriff got, it was a flight out of L.A. Two men." He hesitated for effect. "The flight plan was filed by Kentucky Trayco, Koln."

Koln smiled. "Well, well. The other one must be Tony DeGuillio."

"That's my guess."

"Any search-and-rescue team going in after them?"

"Not from here, but the sheriff in Fremont County, Idaho, has been contacted. They'll go in as soon as the weather breaks."

"Any chance of that happening any time soon?"

"Not according to the national weather bureau. I've got a hunch that if the crash didn't get them the cold and snow will."

Koln thought for a minute. "Doesn't Jimmy Townsend live over that way?"

"Yeah, in St. Anthony. Forty, fifty miles away from the crash site. You want me to contact him?"

"No, I'll take care of it. Have you heard anything on the other boy?"

"About half an hour ago. They called in by radio. The kid has taken them into some pretty rough country. Our people are out of their element. If it wasn't for Madigan, they'd be in big trouble." There was a pause. "They wonder if it's worth it."

"They aren't paid to wonder, are they, Colter," Koln said stiffly.

There was another pause. "The kid's good, Rolf. It will take some time." Another pause. "Daniels is smart. He's making us come after him on his turf. He and his family know this place like the back of their hands. We won't get them easily."

Koln thought a minute. Rashid Daniels would run for safety, too. "Rashid Daniels, the czar's other kid, is headed your way."

Colter laughed lightly. "What happened?"

"He'll have a girl with him. I don't want them harmed, do you understand me? You hold them until I get there."

There was a pause. "Yeah."

"I mean it, Colter. So much as touch a hair on either head until I arrive and I'll strip your hide off you an inch at a time."

"Relax, Koln. You're the boss, but she's a witness—"

"She's also my daughter!" Koln hung up. Colter would do as he was told because Colter had seen what Koln did to those who didn't, and because Colter knew of Koln's personal stake. Rashid and Seriza wouldn't be harmed.

Koln got a clear line while getting a phone number book from the day planner in his briefcase. As he passed the state prison at the point of the mountain, he dialed the number.

"Hello?"

"Hello, Jimmy. This is Koln."

There was a moment of hesitation as Townsend shook off the sleep. "Koln?"

"Would you like some work?"

"Maybe. This time of year I don't stray far. Stock to feed."

"Just up the road a chopper went down."

"Yeah, I heard. They're forming a search-and-rescue to go in the morning. They called and asked if I wanted in."

"Can you get me in and out before then?"

There was a pause. "Yeah."

"The usual fee. Same account?"

"That'll work. Where are you?"

"Salt Lake. I'll fly into Idaho Falls in a couple of hours, pick up a few things, and drive to St. Anthony before five o'clock tomorrow morning."

"I'll have someone meet you in front of the Maverick gas stop just as you get off the freeway." The phone clicked off.

Koln dialed his answering machine in L.A. There was still no message from Claire.

Rashid didn't like it. The safe house was being watched. It had to be the enemy. Stockman wouldn't be so obvious. His men would wait inside.

"How could they have found out?" Seriza asked, her eyes glued to the two men sitting in a black car up the street.

Rashid shrugged. No one was supposed to know. No one but those very close to Jeremiah Daniels. "I don't know if they're the enemy, Seriza."

"We can't take that chance, can we?"

"Nope."

"Maybe . . . maybe they have some way of intercepting your communications."

Rashid thought for a moment. All the messages were scrambled, but didn't both ends, both phones, have to have scramblers? Maybe. He couldn't remember.

"Let's go, Rashid. If they see us . . ."

Rashid put the Corvette in gear and backed into a drive-way. A few seconds later they were heading down Ninth South toward the city center. At Seventh East he turned south and pulled over to the curb.

"We're going to Wyoming." He faced her. "But we'll need a different car. One with a top."

She smiled. It hadn't been that bad. The heater was powerful and with the blankets holding the heat in she had been okay. "I appreciate the concern, but it's too dangerous, isn't it? Won't they be watching places like that? If we use our licenses . . . Maybe you should call your father's people again."

"I don't dare. You might be right about them intercepting the calls. I can't be sure." He looked away, then back again. "Are you sure you'll be all right? It'll be colder once we're in the mountains. The snow isn't coming down here, but we'll hit it before we get to Jackson, that's for sure."

She smiled again. "With intermittent rest stops and huge cups of hot chocolate I'll be fine." She nodded forward. "Come on, let's go. We're wasting time."

Rashid pulled the Corvette back in the street. A few minutes later they were eastbound on I-80 headed up the canyon toward Park City. On a good day it was a five-hour drive to Jackson. He glanced at his watch: one o'clock. If the weather would cooperate . . .

He turned on the radio to KSL. As the first flakes of snow started to fly over the front window and past their heads, the station gave a weather report: the center of the storm was north of Jackson but the Hole was getting its share; roads were clear to Afton, no blizzards; intermittent snow.

With a little luck they'd be in Jackson by sunup. Rashid breathed easier. There was safety in the Hole.

Day Four
November 16, 1997

CHAPTER 12

1:00 A.M.—Washington, D.C.

Danny Trevino heard the buzz of the security door and pushed for the button that would open it, then turned to see Jeremiah enter.

"Jerry."

"Danny. Where's Jan?" Jerry asked, as he removed his wool topcoat, the melted snow glistening in droplets on its charcoal-gray surface.

"Fixing sandwiches," Danny said, turning back to his computer. "LOGOS has something you should see." He punched several keys, cleared the screen, then pulled up a different program. Seconds later information flashed onto the gray field of the screen.

Jerry pulled up a straight-back chair and sat as close as Danny's wheelchair would allow. He started reading. His brow wrinkled.

Stockman had gone to full alert and the storm had the *ISSA* socked in. That was good. The thicker the clouds, the harder it would be for the Cosa Nostra to see the lake. It would be safe for now.

He read the report from Israel. Nabril was hanging on, even improving. Macklin would be there in less than two hours to bring Boudia back; and things were back on track in Miami. Gad was making arrangements to move Alvarez and Lima west to safer ground. From there the news became worse. Trayco's chopper had gone down. Jerry quickly read Stockman's report of the accident.

"Nothing from Trayco?" he asked Danny.

"Nothing. The Fremont County sheriff's office is sending in a search-and-rescue team as soon as the storm breaks. They're our best hope now."

Jeremiah leaned back in the chair, his brow deeply furrowed. "What else?"

"They tried to kidnap Rashid in Provo. He got away. Stockman sent him to a safe house in Salt Lake. He should have shown up hours ago but hasn't. We don't know where he is."

Danny reached for some papers and a photograph on his desk. "You'd better take a look at these."

"Who is she?"

"Your son's friend, Seriza Maxwell. She's with him."

Jeremiah smiled. "The boy has almost as good a taste in women as his old man."

"When Rashid didn't show up at the safe house, Stockman sent a couple of men to Provo. They talked to the girl's roommates." He handed Jeremiah another picture. "That's her with her father."

Jerry sat up straight. "Rolf Koln?"

"Or his twin. His name is Joseph Maxwell. I had LOGOS do a search on him." He took a deep breath. "Maxwell is a deep-cover operative for the CIA. An assassin."

"A double agent?"

"It looks that way. I contacted our man in the CIA. Years ago Maxwell was suspected of being involved in a plot with a renegade bunch inside the CIA to kill Gorbachev. Maxwell was the trigger man. Somehow his wife found out, took their daughter, and left him. When the thing went sour and was called off, Koln told one of the members that he was glad the assassination didn't happen because his wife had known about it, had left him, and now he could get her back. The woman was killed in a car accident a few days later. Maxwell blamed them. Four of the six original members of the plot are dead. Our contact says no one can prove it, but they think Maxwell wanted revenge and used his special talents to exact it."

"And yet he still works for the CIA?"

"Some people in the government would go to bed with the devil. They use him off and on. They say he's the best." Danny smiled. "The girl was raised by her grandparents. They were given some idea of what happened, but could never get the full story. *But,* once they had guardianship, the grandfather refused Maxwell full privileges. He hated Maxwell, probably believed the worst. It was only when the girl was old enough to make her own decisions that she started seeing her father more regularly."

"I'm confused, Danny. What has the girl got to do with this? How did she get involved?"

"Welcome to the club, Jeremiah. We'll find that out when we find these kids." Another pause. "Koln might have picked them up before they ever got out of Provo."

Jerry shook his head firmly. "We'd know. The Cosa Nostra would make sure of that."

"How? You're not exactly easy to contact."

"They'd kill him. Both of us know it. Make an example and try to scare us off. It'd probably work." Jerry paced. "What happened at the safe house?"

"What?"

"In Salt Lake. Were the men waiting inside or outside the house for Rashid?"

"Outside. They were afraid he'd get cold feet and wanted to be where they could watch for him, put him at ease."

"He probably thought they were the enemy. He has no place else to go but home."

"To Wyoming?"

"Yes. He's frightened. He'll try to get to people he feels safe with. I told him not to trust anyone outside family. He'll try to get to our place or Bob's ranch, then contact Stockman."

Because Jeremiah knew Bob and his family would be targets along with everyone else, he had tried to get his brother-in-law to take his family on an extended vacation. Bob had refused.

Bob was like that, stubborn, hardheaded, determined. He wasn't about to let someone push him around, no matter their size or numbers.

"Jeremiah," he had said, "you and Mike are set on changing the world by ridding it of riffraff. I think you're doing the right thing. But if I go off to Hawaii every time one of your enemies gets mad at you, I'd just as well move there." He had smiled and put his arm around Jerry's shoulder as they walked toward the ranch house. "Don't worry about any of us. We've survived your little escapades so far and we'll survive again." With that the subject had been closed.

"They can't get to the ranch. The road from Kelly is drifted with four feet of snow."

"Have you talked to Bob?"

"Nope. The highway department. The phone lines into the ranch are down, too."

Jerry paced again.

"Mike is in Idaho Falls," Danny said.

"What?" Jerry glanced at the clock on the watch. "She's had plenty of time to get to the *ISSA*."

"The weather has her grounded. She'll go to Jackson as soon as she can. She's okay."

Jerry sagged in the chair. He was exhausted. They were coming after him, trying to hit him where it hurt the most. He had to slow them down. He should never have let her go to L.A.

"Koln, or whatever his name is, where is he now?"

"We don't know."

The door between the operations room and the hall buzzed and Danny pushed the button. Jan Delling Trevino entered with a large tray stacked with sandwiches, hot soup, and cartons of milk. Jerry grinned at her, continually amazed at the change marriage to Danny had brought in her. A former high-paid, New York model, Jan had comfortably adjusted to the role of wife.

In former days Danny Trevino and Jan Delling had been outspoken enemies, having nothing good to say about each other. Now they were married and very happy. An event that Jeremiah, even after nearly eight years, still shook his head over and wondered about.

He had introduced them. Danny and Jeremiah were buddies from Nam, pilots of a Huey Transport helicopter. They had gone down and Jerry had been hurt. Danny had tried carrying him to safety but had become careless, tripping a mine. He had snatched Jerry out of the way, taking most of the blast. That was why he was in a wheelchair.

After Jeremiah's first wife had died, her sister, Jan, had come to Las Vegas, a broken model on her way out. She and Jerry had never gotten along very well because they had never tried. This time they tried and reached a state of warring friendship. Then Danny showed up for a visit.

Jeremiah had owned a big house. While he was out of the city on other things, Jan and Danny fought their way to love and ended up married. It suited them both.

"Jeremiah," Jan greeted him as she sat the tray down on a table, then moved to him and kissed him on the forehead.

He took her hand. "Jan, do you have enough for a third party?"

She nodded toward Danny. "The stallion broke tradition and let me know you were coming."

Danny laughed lightly. "I wondered if I should. I could have saved you the trouble of having to deal with her cooking."

Jan punched him on the shoulder, firmly. Danny winced, then rubbed the spot.

"Someday you'll learn, Danny," Jerry said, standing up to go for a sandwich. He handed Danny one as Jan picked up a cup of soup.

"Chicken noodle," Jan told them. "Good for colds, or so my mother used to say. Sorry if it isn't as hot as it should be. The kitchen in this place . . . well, in this section of town the facilities aren't top-notch."

Jerry smiled. The safe house was hidden beneath a tenement house in the poorest part of Spanish D.C. A man risked his life even coming into the area. Their enemies wouldn't look for them here.

Jerry's first wife, Liz, and Jan were opposites in more than just appearance. Jan was tall with a model's good looks, while Liz was shorter and constantly fighting to keep off weight. They had been different in outlook as well. Jan had been rebellious, anti-traditional. Liz had been just the opposite, a conformist who had gotten a medical degree in plastic surgery and was very traditional. When Liz died, though, Jan had changed.

"What's the latest?" she asked, shoving a spoonful of soup into her mouth.

Danny filled her in.

"What if Tony D is dead?" Danny asked. Jan cringed. All Jerry needed was another nail in his coffin. She was surprised at the response.

"It doesn't matter. They're after me now."

Jan smiled. "You've given them little choice, Jeremiah." Jan had never liked Jerry's placing himself and his family in this spot and she had let him know it. "They can't find out what you're up to and they're scared spitless." She smiled, softening the rebuke. Jan loved Jerry Daniels. Not romantically, but because of who he was, what he had meant to her sister, and for how he had helped change her own life. There were few men like Jeremiah in this world. If something happened to him it would leave a very large hole in a lot of lives.

"Good description." Jerry said, a smile creasing his lips. "After tonight it'll get worse."

"The raids?"

"Yeah. The enemy will not be very happy."

He took a small bite of his sandwich and chewed. "They're after my family because they have to make an example of us. They want to send a message to the president and anyone thinking about taking my job."

They all finished eating in silence.

Jerry threw his empty milk carton into the trash can. "You said you had something important. Let's see it."

Danny turned to the computer and punched several keys. A chart filled the screen. "You've seen this before. A configuration of what we think their organization is like. We don't know how many are at the top but we do know the rest." He pointed at a new block with a name in it. "Koln fits here. He's part of enforcement but an outsider, receiving his orders directly from the Super Commission. He has a lot of freedom, using people of his own choice."

Danny enlarged the lower section of the picture. "This is DeGuillio's group. We compiled it from records found in the raids on Boudia and Alvarez, and in DeGuillio's files given to us by his brother's son. It's interesting that the Cosa Nostra has gone outside, but our sources indicate it's being done on a trial basis. An attempt to distance the killing from the commission."

He pushed several keys and called up another picture. "More important are these."

"Account numbers?"

"They belong to Tony D, Boudia, and Alvarez. Half a dozen different banks, some American, some foreign. We decided to find out how far we could trace them back, see if we could find a common source. Thanks to Senator Freeman's previous work with foreign governments we were able to get the Swiss, London, and Toronto banks to cooperate. The ones in the Cayman Islands refused."

"We knew they would." Jerry confirmed. "Their economy would die on the vine without their banks, and the banks would go under without the money they get from drugs, arms dealers, and corrupt governments. What'd you find?"

Danny's index finger punched the "page down" key. "This."

Jerry was looking at a box chart, much like those used to illustrate a corporation's chain of command. At the bottom was a solid line of blocks with bank names printed in them. The line above had fewer, then the one above it had even fewer, until at the top there was only one.

"I couldn't get the two bottom rows on. Too many. But the top one is all that's important anyway."

"First International Bank of Germany?" Jerry said. "I don't know it."

"Low key, old money, unblemished record, very reputable. Nearly untouchable."

"Until now," Jan said. "Show him the numbers, Danny."

Danny hit the "page down" key again. "In 1989 FIBG was sound with accounts numbering in the thousands. Their business amounted to a modest ten billion dollars. This is a copy of their financial report." He hit the key again. "In December of 1989 several key members of the board of directors were changed and FIBG's president took out early retirement. A new man was hired."

"Nothing wrong with that."

"Nope, except that business doubled that year and several new policies were put into place. The board elected not to make their financial statement public and to take the same stance as the Cayman Islands banks with regard to client accounts. They were not to be discussed or divulged to any outside source, and accounts could be set up with cash deposits *without* names, addresses, etc."

"It was all done very discreetly," Jan added.

"But Germany's banking system doesn't allow . . ."

"They did in this case. The government official responsible for banking, some title I can't even pronounce, either looked the other way or is involved up to his blue eyes and blond hair."

Jerry sat back. "So the Cosa Nostra controls FIBG and uses it as its main funding source for at least the American drug trade."

"Yup." Danny confirmed. "But *not* its only source. The second row of banks, half a dozen in number, could be used if something went wrong at FIBG. Most of them are outside U.S. jurisdiction. Two are in the Caymans. If you shut down FIBG, it would hurt, but only for a few days. FIBG is only a money depot—a place where that which comes in changes directions in order to go out. On any given day I'd bet you half a billion dollars do the turnaround."

Jerry whistled. "That much? How did you come up with a figure like that?"

We know approximately what is going in," Jan said. "The street sales, as always, are strictly cash business. DeGuillio's family had twenty-five laundering agents spread in cities around the West. Their hired help picks up the money and takes it to a safe house, where it is separated, counted, and prepared for deposit. Then they would deposit the funds in one of the banks, brokerage firms, or savings and loans used to launder money. Via computer those funds were transferred on up the line."

"Eventually arriving at FIBG," Jerry said.

"By then it's completely clean, legitimate," Danny said. "Then it's transferred to front companies like pizza parlors, restaurants, real estate developers . . . The list is endless."

"As near as we can tell," Jan went on, "Tony's family gets forty percent of the cut—Sicily gets the rest. We suspect each American family is set up the same way."

"Sixty percent? Why? The families take all the risks. That's a mighty big cut for nothing."

"Maybe it's not for nothing." Danny handed him another paper. "That's from Alvarez's files. In 1989 Alvarez began having problems. He couldn't get the chemicals to process his cocaine, then the transportation he used to get the product to market went sour."

"Some of his planes blew up or disappeared before reaching their destinations," Jan said. "His associates were killed in the streets."

Jerry nodded. "Someone was after him."

"Things got worse," Danny went on. "That paper is a summary of how bad it was. In 1990 he was nearly ruined."

"A drug war?" Jerry asked.

Danny shook his head. "Not exactly. Boudia was having similar problems."

"As near as we can tell," Jan interjected, "most of the major producers were in the same boat."

"Sicily!" Jerry exclaimed.

"Do you remember the reference Jim Freeman made in his records to an Odessa meeting in 1991?"

"Yes, but he didn't say much. Only that he suspected the Cosa Nostra's Super Commission had held one and that a number of capi were suspected to be in attendance, but nothing was ever proven."

Danny shoved some more papers toward Jeremiah. "Phone receipts between April 15 to 20 in 1991. All three, Boudia, Alvarez, and DeGuillio made calls from Odessa to their homes."

Jerry took the receipts and scanned them.

"Huge payments showed up in these accounts a day after those meetings concluded," Jan said, "giving all three men, and more than likely many others, the funds to rebuild their businesses."

"It was then the elimination of belligerents began," Danny continued. "Cosa Nostra gained control."

"So that's how they did it," Jerry said, leaning back.

Jan spoke. "Each of the three men you picked up had accounts with money in them. The files you confiscated had access codes. We emptied their accounts and deposited the money into a Washington account. The DEA has begun confiscation of all other property suspected of being purchased with drug money. We expect another thirty-two million."

"And the total?" Jerry asked.

"Nearly eight billion dollars."

Jerry whistled and folded his arms across his chest, staring at the screen. "Can LOGOS or TITAN break into FIBG?"

Danny shook his head. "I tried. You have two chances to type in the proper access code. When you don't, it shuts you out—permanently."

"Permanently? How?"

"It reads your signal." Danny saw the quizzical look on Jerry's face. "Two years ago, computer experts found out that each computer sends out a particular electrical signature every time it transmits. Recent technology allows one computer to read the signal of another. When you hook into their system and request access, they identify your signature and file your identification in their memory. When you fail to access, they mark you as unfriendly, and automatically refuse access in the future."

"Neat."

"Very. We use it on LOGOS. It prevents computer hackers and thieves from playing around inside the system."

"Any chance we can close FIBG down?" Jan asked Jerry.

"Maybe. It depends on how much the Germans want to cooperate. Something like this will scandalize their banking system. Who's on the board of directors of FIBG?"

Danny thought a minute, hit some keys, and pulled up a

report from Standard and Poor's listing of banks. He read off the names, most of them German; one Canadian, an American, and one Englishman.

"What's the American's name?" Jerry asked.

"Bringhurst, William H."

"Find out who he is. Do a complete search on all of them: FBI, Interpol, everybody. Financial information, travel habits, the works. The Cosa Nostra is in there somewhere."

"Can do," Danny replied.

Jeremiah stood up and reached for his coat.

"Jerry, you look so tired," Jan said. "Get some sleep before . . ."

"I'll get some sleep later." As he opened the door, he turned and faced them. "You're the best. I love you both." He went through the door and started to close it, but came back. "When you talk to Mike again, tell her I love her; and tell Stockman to find the boys and get them aboard." He smiled and left.

Jan looked at her husband with pleading eyes. Danny could only shrug, then turn to his computer. He had never known how to tell Jeremiah Daniels what to do.

A few minutes later the building shook as a rented Pontiac Bonneville in the building's parking lot disintegrated. The police investigating the bombing would discover that the car had been leased to one Laurence Lightman. Mr. Lightman didn't survive; the charred remains slumped over the wheel attested to that.

And Mr. Lightman had no next of kin. In fact, in the first two hours after the explosion the investigating officer discovered, through police and FBI files, that Mr. Lightman didn't exist.

As they questioned people in the buildings surrounding the scene they didn't see the beautiful, former cover girl of *Vogue* magazine slip away without being noticed, her eyes filled with tears and her throat choked with gut-wrenching sobs. If they had, they might have discovered who Mr. Lightman really was.

Jan had driven a dozen blocks before she stopped shaking. She and Danny hadn't spoken, both dealing with what had happened. Danny was pale, sagging in his wheelchair.

"What do we do?" she said softly, choking back the tears.

"I . . . I don't know," Danny said. "I can't deal with it. It . . . it's impossible."

When Jan had returned from investigating the cause of the explosion in a total panic, screaming, tears running down her cheeks, he had been forced to shake her hard, bringing her to her senses enough to do what had to be done. Then he transferred all their records to a special file deep in the heart of TITAN, the country's mainframe computer, and emptied the system in the safe house. Then Jan pummeled the machinery with a sledgehammer until it was nothing but small pieces. They had planned for emergencies.

They drove a little further. Jan turned right into a full-service gas station. After giving instructions to the attendant, she sat back in the captain's chair, her head against the headrest and her eyes closed. Danny took her hand and kissed it gently. She squeezed his hand in response.

"We need to call Stockman," Jan whispered. "Mike . . . the kids . . . need to know."

There was silence; then Jan spoke again. "Everything will come apart. Everything Jerry tried to do . . ." She wiped her eyes with a tissue, and checked in the mirror to make sure her mascara hadn't run. The attendant knocked on the window. She rolled it down, took the clipboard and signed on the line. Removing her credit card from under the clasp, she handed the clipboard back and thanked him. Punching the button, she closed the window again.

She started the motor. Shifting into gear, she pulled into the street.

"It'll be all over the news tomorrow," Danny said.

"Only that a man named Lightman was blown up in a rental car. Nobody but us . . ."

"The enemy knows, Jan. They'll leak something to the press to let the president know he's losing and he'd better lay off."

Jan's mouth went dry with hate, and her stomach

wanted to heave. Then the tears started to flow again and she couldn't see the road clearly. She pulled to the curb and plunged the gearshift into park, sobs wracking her body and her head falling to the steering wheel.

Danny reached over and put his arm around his wife, trying to give her comfort while keeping his own emotions under control. He felt empty. How could they go on? Jeremiah had been the glue holding BOOMERANG together. Without him . . .

Jan pulled away. "We have to get to safe house two," she said, wiping away the tears with both hands. "We have to call the others." She put the van in gear and moved it into the street. "We can't let him die for nothing, Danny. We have to keep going."

"Jan, Sicily is winning, can't you see that? By getting to Jeremiah—"

She looked at him through flaming eyes. "No! We can still stop them! If we let them win, if we give up . . . We can't give up, Danny! We can't!"

Danny knew his wife. She was a fighter, determined, and headstrong. Now wasn't the time to argue. "All right! All right! We'll talk to the others. We'll see."

Jan took a deep breath. "FIBG. Somehow, someway we're going to get to that money. Hit them where they'll feel it the most."

"FIBG is untouchable," Danny reminded her. "They aren't going to open their doors to us and we can't break into their computers."

She glared at him again. "We will *find* a way, Danny."

"Okay!" he said, irritated. "We'll start with a search on the board, we'll keep looking for a crack in the armor!"

For a while all was silent. Jan turned off the freeway, her mind trying to deal with another problem. How to tell Michaelene her husband was dead.

———————

Claire John watched as the man strode quickly toward her, the red glow of the explosion in the next block illuminating the overcast sky. She switched on the key and pushed the automatic window button, extending an envelope. He took it, glanced inside, then shoved it in his pocket.

"He's dead?"

The man chuckled in a high-pitched voice. He leaned forward, and she could smell the stench of his garlic-covered breath. She moved away. "You ever see anyone survive an explosion like that?" He stood straight, jamming his hands in his pockets. "Get real, lady. You bought the best. I don't make mistakes." He turned and started away.

"You saw . . ."

He looked over his shoulder, then walked slowly back, an insipid smirk on his face. "You think my mama raised an idiot, don't you? Well, she didn't. I don't get close enough to *see* when I blow something up. It ain't safe." He smiled, showing yellowed teeth. "I went back. What was left of him was sitting in the front seat. Toast." He turned his back and started to walk away. It was his last mistake.

Claire pulled the silenced .22 from the side of the seat and fired. The hollow-point, soft-head bullet entered his skull. He was dead before he hit the ground. She stuck the pistol under the seat, opened the door, retrieved the money-stuffed envelope, then got back in the car.

When she was several blocks away she removed her leather gloves and threw them in the briefcase before picking up a portable cellular phone.

Punching in the numbers, she waited.

"Senator Ridgeway's residence."

"Tell the senator that Claire John is calling."

Half a minute later Ridgeway was on the line.

"Hello, darling," Claire said. "Just thought you'd like to know. That little problem you were so worried about is taken care of."

There was a pause. "You're sure? How . . . Never mind, I don't want to know."

"We'll also leak information that will make Jeremiah Daniels look like the biggest crook since Al Capone." She paused again. "Now it's your turn, Senator. We want the White House muzzled, controlled, stopped. If you succeed, we'll do our best to see that it becomes yours in the next election." She hung up, dialed, and waited for her call to be routed to a scrambled phone in Sicily.

"Bonjourno."

"Hello, Papa," she said in Sicilian.

"Ah, is that you, Maria?" Buscetti said.

"In the flesh, Papa. Daniels has been eliminated."

"Koln . . ."

"Koln told me to take care of it."

"You? That is dangerous, daughter. We have invested a great deal in your new identity. We have bigger things in mind . . ."

"There will be no connection to me, I've seen to that." She took a deep breath. "It had to be done. With Daniels as his backbone, the president had a very stiff resolve. We needed to make him more pliable."

There wasn't a response.

She continued. "Daniels was killed in the Spanish section of town. A story will be leaked to the press that he was there to buy drugs from Herrera Quintana's people out of Bogota. When we're finished, it will look like Daniels was using his office to get rid of competition, and that he intended to gain control of the drug trade in this country and use it for his own personal benefit."

There was a pause. "Daniels is squeaky clean, Maria. It will be hard to prove such a thing." There was a pause. "Has Quintana promised to leak information verifying your accusations?"

"I promised him we would double his business by allowing him to fill Alvarez's production quotas for the West Coast, along with his present responsibility for the northeast. He is more than happy to help."

"His word will be suspect."

"I have friends planting more evidence at Daniels's Washington residence, and we have deposited a large sum of money in his personal account. It will raise enough questions."

"And what will the president's response be?"

"If he defends Daniels he will commit political suicide. He knows that."

"He can replace Daniels. Someone else—"

"Senator Ridgeway will not allow confirmation of a new drug czar until a full investigation has taken place into the dead czar's actions. He and his friends will insist on a thorough unveiling of the whole affair before any further action is taken. By the time Congress is through with Seth Adams, the man will wish he had never become a politician."

"Ridgeway had better deliver, Maria."

"I've already told him that, Papa. You can depend on it."

There was a pause. "Daniels must have files, evidence, records; and his wife and friends still have Tony D, Boudia, and Alvarez. They have solid reputations and are still very dangerous to us."

"The senator will demand the records as a part of a congressional investigation. If they don't deliver them, they will be held in contempt. I will see that Ridgeway appoints my law firm as special counsel to the investigation. My boss will appoint me to oversee the paperwork and I will see that it is properly handled and that anything damaging to us is removed."

Another pause. "That is taking too much of a chance, Maria. If Mrs. Daniels uses her father's connections, she might be able to get around Ridgeway and prevent the senator from getting her files. Political battles are long and messy, and very indecisive. Too many things can go wrong. And I don't wish to jeopardize your position at the firm. It is where we want you. As we solidify our position and eliminate the American Mafia altogether, I want you where you can be our *consiglieri* over the entire operation. If your cover is blown, we must start again."

Claire knew her father's concerns. A good deal of money had been spent on her new identity and a good deal more would be spent in making her the firm's controlling partner. Bosk, Williams, and Tenet, one of the United States's most influential and powerful firms, would be hers someday, and Sicily's most powerful force in the legal world. It was worth protecting, but if Daniels wasn't stopped there would be no Sicilian takeover.

Luciano continued. "We must find Mrs. Daniels and the others and eliminate them and their records. We take no chances, it is the way we do business." He paused. "We still have a very strong message to send to Washington. We want no further meddling in our affairs."

"All right, Papa. What do you want me to do?"

"Make sure Koln is successful, but be careful. Do not endanger your position again."

"Very well, Papa. What is happening in Israel and Miami?"

"Hezbollah will take care of Boudia and Colonel Macklin. I think I have someone who will work things out for us in Miami as well. I will talk to him tonight." He paused. "You have given me honor. I am proud of you."

"The capo dei capi . . . Have you told him about our plans yet?"

"No, Maria. Now is not the time. Once we have you in place, and they see the brilliance of what you have done for the Cosa Nostra, they will have no choice but to agree. This is our proving ground, daughter. If we succeed in bringing the president's challenge to nothing, if we dispose of this threat, our future is assured." He paused. "The capo dei capi is getting old. No one will challenge my bid to replace him if we are successful." Another pause. "If we fail, both of us will lose our heads."

"I understand, Papa."

The phone clicked and went dead.

Claire tossed the phone toward the briefcase, then took a deep breath. At fifty-four her father was the youngest member of the Super Commission, but his family was powerful enough to gain responsibility for the American organization of the drug business. It could lead to ultimate power with the Cosa Nostra. Her father could become the single most important man in the underworld, and the richest. Maria Buscetti intended to be heir to that power. The first woman to lead the Cosa Nostra in its long history.

But if they failed—Maria knew the consequences. The Buscetti family, its power, and its very existence would cease to be. The other families would eliminate them with a violent and bloody purge, starting with her father and ending with Maria's youngest sister, the last of Luciano's seven daughters. In between, the Buscetti families, uncles, aunts, cousins, and soldati would all die as well. She would see that it didn't happen.

Luciano glanced at the clock on the wall. It was early morning in Israel. According to his contacts, Boudia wouldn't be alive at the end of the day, and Daniels's team would be dealt a second devastating blow: the death of Thomas Macklin.

Maria's direct involvement worried him and brought a feeling of regret. He had instituted the use of outside assassins after the Cosa Nostra had been hurt by traitors in its own ranks, losing billions of dollars and over four hundred good men, either to death or to prison. Soldati, it seemed, could no longer be trusted.

He put the plan into effect in the United States. It had worked well, enabling him to keep Sicily free and clear of suspicion of the assassinations that were necessary to eliminate uncooperative American family members. The Super Commission had seen its value and could say little.

But then he had contracted for the assassinations of James Freeman and members of the international task force. It had brought a lot of pressure and cost them millions in bribes to keep authorities at bay. The Super Commission had balked, telling him to bring enforcement back into the family. To do that he had to get rid of Koln's assassins.

Koln had been chosen for outside enforcement because he was the best in the business. Of the three hundred or more assassinations assigned to Koln, all were still unsolved by the police. Koln's team had never made a mistake and did exactly as they were asked. None inside the family had ever proven as effective. It saddened Buscetti to remove him.

But Buscetti was a realist. The Capo dei capi expected his orders followed. If Koln lived, Buscetti would die.

Getting rid of Koln had presented several problems. First, the man would not go down easily, and if the assassin discovered Buscetti had ordered his killing, Luciano would be Koln's next target. It must be done without Koln getting wind of it.

Second, in order to ascertain whether there were any other threats to the Cosa Nostra, Koln's organization must be monitored from the inside before its destruction. Who had Koln confided in? Who also must be dealt with? And who could be used in the future in a less significant manner?

That was why he had sent Maria to infiltrate Koln's organization. The information she could provide would be critical to the elimination of Koln. But it threatened her cover and the future of his plans. They must be very careful or everything would be lost.

Buscetti picked up the phone again, checked his memory for a number, then dialed.

"Yeah," answered a tired voice.

"How is the weather in Miami?" Buscetti asked.

There was a pause. "You're lucky. My associate is in the shower. We can talk."

"Can you do it?"

"Five million. I'll give you the account number."

Luciano wrote it down. "Swiss?"

"Close to home. I will call the bank in three hours. If the money is there, I will see that Alvarez and Lima are dead by sundown."

"It will be there." Buscetti hung up, mentally patting himself on the back. It had been a stroke of genius to do a background search on the Israelis working for Daniels. Buscetti had found a weakness—a man with extravagant tastes and a lot of debt. He would exploit it.

1:10 A.M.—Gros Ventre Range, Wyoming time

Raoul knew he was being followed. He could feel them coming for him, even in the cold darkness of the storm. It was evident they had a good tracker among them. Raoul had covered his trail as he had been taught, and was very careful to stay unheard, unseen, and downwind.

During the night, under cover of the heavy snowstorm, he had moved across Bacon Creek and climbed up the south side of Sunday Peak, hiding his horse and mule in a thick grove of trees and underbrush some hundred yards to the north and out of the wind. Two inches of fresh, windblown snow covered their tracks. The feed bags would keep them quiet.

Raoul removed his gloves, then took the infrared glasses from their case and placed them over his eyes, a soft cloud filling the air around his face as he breathed warm air into the mountain's frigid blackness. He knew the temperature was no more than ten degrees above freezing and was grateful he had prepared for cold weather.

Another three hours and it would be light enough to see, but he needed to do a little reconnaissance, lessening the odds he knew to be at least six to one. The infrared glasses would give him a distinct advantage, unless the enemy was prepared in the same manner. He doubted it, but he knew the value of caution.

The glasses were a lot like ski goggles and very unlike the unsophisticated ones used by soldiers and seen in movies. Those were heavy, not to mention ugly.

As his eyes adjusted, he checked his back trail; using wide-lens binoculars, he then scanned the valley below. He could see segments of the trail through thick timber, but saw no sign of his pursuers. As his eyes worked their way through the trees, he saw some movement. Focusing on the spot, he saw the antlers of a large bull elk, then its huge head and neck. A trophy. He'd remember where he'd seen it, but for now, the elk's presence in the valley was a good sign—his pursuers were somewhere else.

There were only two trails to where Raoul lay. The other crossed along the steep side of the hill opposite him, and it was in the open. He saw no sign of anyone on it. That meant they were working their way around the back side of Sunday Peak, trying to get ahead of him. Their tracker was good. If they succeeded, they could cut off his retreat into Fish Creek.

Without a sound, Raoul returned to his animals. Keeping the goggles in place, he slid the lever action .30-30 into its scabbard. Raoul was a bow hunter by nature. Ever since his father had first introduced him to a bow belonging to an Indian ancestor Raoul had loved the weapon, and he had practiced incessantly until it lost its spring. After that he built his own: a fiberglass model that could sink an arrow two inches deep into pine from a hundred and fifty feet. He used it to hunt because it was more of a challenge. But tonight he used the .30-30. The people who were after him were animals of a different kind and deserved no such respect. For now, the bow would remain tied to the mule's pack.

At his side he had holstered a Ruger Blackhawk, a .357 magnum revolver; a pistol that looked like the guns John Wayne used in old western movies—but with a larger bore and a bigger kick. On the other hip hung a club of wood, a stone fixed to the shaft with rawhide. An Indian friend, a distant relative of his father, who was part Shoshone, had given it to him. Next to it was Raoul's bowie knife, handmade after the old style: a bone handle, with a long, eight-inch blade, curved at the end. Its last two inches were sharpened on both sides. With it Raoul could have a bull elk gutted in less than five minutes.

He heard a noise as he was putting the feed bags on the pack mule. With his muscles tensed, his ears sought for the sound, the direction, the numbers. It took effort to keep his movements quiet, so as not to give away his knowledge to his enemy.

He heard the squishing of wet snow under a rubber sole.

He marked that sound at twenty-five to fifty feet away and behind him. Then there was the sound of fabric rubbing against a tree, to his left, near the same distance. They wouldn't be alone.

He made a slight sucking sound with his lips. The bay's ears stiffened and her head came up. She moved, placing her body behind Raoul.

In less time than it took to blink, Raoul had flipped a boot into a stirrup, laying his lithe body against the bay's side as she shot through the trees, the fleet-footed mule in tow.

He sensed the quick movement of someone hurling himself out of the horse's path, slamming into a tree, then hitting the ground. In the infrared goggles, he saw another man directly ahead raise up and position a rifle for firing. Raoul pulled on the rein and the bay leapt left, dodging trees, and jumping through underbrush. Raoul heard a rifle's report and the thud of lead as it hit the mule's backpack, but the bay plunged deeper into the protective underbrush. Raoul flipped himself up into the saddle, keeping low. Seconds later the two animals were plummeting down the steep side of the mountain, the bay's instincts avoiding one potentially catastrophic collision after another, the mule holding to the path provided for it.

Raoul drew the .30-30 from its scabbard as the horse's feet found the firm ground of the ravine floor and splashed into the water of a small creek. Raoul could hear shouts, and men and animals moving through the brush after him. Reining in the bay, he turned her the direction they had just come and put the rifle to his shoulder. The infrared goggles picked up an assailant's movements and Raoul watched as the man's horse stumbled and fell, rolling down the sharp embankment. His sights found another rider and Raoul pulled the trigger just as the horse lunged over a stand of thick brush. The bullet caught a hoof, the animal stumbling then falling head over heels on top of its rider. The rider struggled to his feet and moved a few feet, falling behind a fallen log and out of sight.

Raoul turned the bay and spurred her through the creek's cold water and up the far side of the ravine, her hooves digging through the foot of snow and into the soil beneath, thrusting Raoul away from his enemies. Raoul was cognizant of the sounds of shouting and cursing, but heard no weapons fired. The darkness and his night goggles gave him an advantage.

Raoul weaved his animals deftly through the trees. As the forest suddenly stopped and a meadow appeared, he drove his heels into the bay and she responded, the mule hard pressed to keep up. They sped across the open space and into the woods on the far side. He yanked on the reins and slid from the saddle, pulling the .30-30 from its scabbard. Going to the mule he removed the bow and arrows, then hit the bay on the rump and drove her deeper into the trees. She was well trained and would be ready when he needed her. An enemy bullet could bring her down if she was too close, and he couldn't afford such a handicap.

Raoul found cover behind a fallen log and waited. He had never killed a man before, and he had no intention of doing so now. But he would slow them down, make them think twice before they came stampeding across open ground. But if they did . . . if they tried to take him . . . He shook the thought away, his mind rejecting the reality of what he might be forced to do.

The first rider plunged into the open field. Raoul put an arrow into the bow and pulled back on the string, waiting. As the rider came within a hundred feet of his position, Raoul released his fingers. The arrow went through the man's leg, the razor sharp tips sticking through the back of his calf. The sudden pain made the man jerk on the horse's bridle, and the animal reared, throwing the rider into the snow. The shaft of the arrow snapped on impact but also jammed the arrow upward. The scream uttered from the man's lips was the sound of a wounded wildcat, full of pain and rage. He rolled in the snow, then tried to get to his feet and drag himself to cover. Raoul let him go.

The second rider exploded from the trees. Raoul picked up the .30-30 and fired in the air. The rider reined in, confused. Raoul took aim, then fired rapidly, kicking up snow around the horse. It lunged left, then right—unsure, frightened. Seconds later, horse and rider were racing back into the woods, afraid the next bullet would draw blood.

Raoul ejected the last empty shell and reloaded, then waited. No one else followed.

After a few more minutes he signaled to the bay and heard her quietly moving through the trees. Keeping close to the ground, he moved into the blackness of the forest and mounted. Moments later he had topped a ridge and was headed into Fish Creek Basin. He knew the enemy now—he knew their intent. They would want his hide for what he had done. It was time to lose himself in the mountains.

1:55 A.M.—Idaho Falls, Idaho

Michaelene watched through the small window as the Lear lifted off the snow-covered runway and into the clouds, the darkness engulfing them. She had been on the ground in Idaho Falls for nearly eight hours, waiting for a window of opportunity to get into Jackson. The window had finally come.

She had tried to sleep but couldn't. Mike could handle just about anything except waiting, especially when she was feeling so out of touch with everything, everyone. She hadn't dared contact Dolph. She had no scrambled phones and was fearful of giving away the ISSA's position. Jerry was in Washington, Trayco was probably back at Yellowstone by now. She found herself wishing she had gone with him.

She worried most about her family. The threat was so real.

Mike took a deep breath. She couldn't let shadows in the night scare her as if she were a schoolgirl. She would be of no use to anyone if she let fear take control or let it atrophy her ability to think clearly.

She glanced at her watch. They'd be in Jackson in less than twenty minutes. She looked out the window as the plane rose through the top of the storm clouds into the light of a full moon. The blanket of clouds below them looked like a feather bed, peaceful, inviting. The storm beneath was the worst they had experienced in years, especially this early in the winter.

She removed her seat belt, stood, and went forward to the Lear's cockpit. The two men glanced over their shoulders as she entered.

"Hi, Dutch, Cannon," she said, looking at each of them in turn. They nodded. "Any chance we won't be able to land in Jackson?"

"I just received a report. Jackson's got the runway cleared off but not for long. If we go in we stay."

"Get us on the ground. I'll decide what to do from there."

She straightened and went back to her seat. Ten minutes later she felt the nose of the Lear lower sharply, and she took one last look at the moon. To her right she could see the top of the tallest of the Tetons sticking through the clouds like the tip of a dark arrow through thick cotton. Then it disappeared, and the plane was being pummeled by ice and heavy winds. Mike's hands instinctively gripped the arm rests and her stomach churned. She peered out the window, looking for signs of airport lights, for an opening in the thick clouds. Her heart thumped as seconds seemed like minutes with nothing to be seen but endless darkness, the plane jumping and sliding in the sky, trying to find a thin thread of pavement somewhere below them.

The lights appeared suddenly and revealed the snow-covered stretch of runway, and she braced herself for landing. A gust of wind hit them, blowing the Lear a good fifty feet to the left, over a bank of snow that ran along the runway's edge. Mike caught her breath, but Dutch quickly adjusted and the plane swooped to the right in time for the wheels to hit the ribbon of ice-covered pavement.

Mike let out the air trapped in her lungs. *That* had been close. Of all the dangers her mind had rattling around in it, death by crashing into a snowbank hadn't been one of them.

Five minutes later, one gloved hand clutching her attaché case, the other shoved deep into a pocket, she entered the hangar where Jeremiah kept the choppers used to transport them north. Two men stood with their backs to her. It wasn't until she had taken half a dozen steps that she realized she didn't recognize either of them. She slowed her pace, at the same time noticing movement out of the corner of her eye. Her hand grasped the nickel-plated .45 in her pocket as she heard the door behind her open.

"Mrs. Daniels?" Dutch called out. "Do you want the Lear parked inside its hangar?" The man in the shadows to her left stopped where he was and the other two turned away.

Mike started moving toward Dutch, the hair on the back of her neck standing on end as she tried not to let on she knew that she—they—were in trouble. "Yes, out of the weather. And Dutch, will you give this . . ." She lifted the attaché case toward him while pulling the .45 out of her pocket. "Run!" she yelled.

Dutch bolted for the door as Mike fired toward the man

hidden in the shadows. The man ducked, giving her enough time to clear the doorway and run into the storm. Dutch had waited for her. Grabbing her arm, he pulled her behind a small tethered Cessna as the three assailants ran from the hangar, looking anxiously in every direction. Dutch lifted his own .45 and fired. One of the three went down, the other two lunged for the door and were quickly inside.

"I'll keep them pinned. You get out of here!" He saw the hesitation on Mike's face and yelled, "Now, Mrs. Daniels! Go!"

Mike ran toward the terminal, careful to stay behind parked airplanes and in the shadows, grateful she had changed into Levi's and warm, flat-heeled, insulated shoes. As she bolted through the terminal doors, she saw the other pilot coming toward her and quickly motioned him past her. "Dutch. Near the hangar! He needs your help."

Cannon glanced at the gun still gripped tightly in her hand, got the message, and was gone. Mike shoved the weapon in her pocket, and glanced around her, taking a deep breath. There were only a few people about and none but the pilot had noticed her.

With long strides she moved through the terminal, her mind racing, her eyes peeled for others who might be looking for her.

As she walked toward the front door, she saw a man standing a few feet away. He dropped his newspaper, shoved a hand into his ski coat pocket, and moved toward her.

Mike's heart caught in her throat, her eyes darting about, trying to find an escape. As he reached out for her, she lifted her attaché case and slammed it into his face. He was caught off balance and fell to the floor. Dashing past him, she burst through the exit, ran across the unloading zone away from the lighted front of the building, and into the parking lot, ducking behind a snow-covered car.

Catching her breath, she heard the man curse as he came outside, nursing a bloody nose and trying to find her. She kept low and ran behind the row of cars, stopping behind a Ford Explorer.

Peeking out from behind it, she saw him still on the sidewalk, his eyes frantic, his hand dabbing at his nose with a handkerchief. She looked through the Explorer's window. No keys. She needed transportation and quickly.

She moved from car to car, keeping one eye on the man

looking for her as he moved into the lot and began to search. Mike knew that if he kept coming the direction he was, he'd have her in his sights within minutes. She was quickly running out of cars.

Then she saw it—some sort of snow machine—parked near the end of the terminal that probably belonged to security or maintenance. If the key was there . . .

Mike kept low, moved behind the last car, then checked the location of her pursuer. She caught her breath. Standing only a hundred feet away, he had been joined by a second person. She ducked as they separated and moved one row closer, checking cars as they progressed in her general direction.

Watching him carefully, her eyes barely above the hood of a car, she waited for the right moment. One man was hidden from view by a Hertz rent-a-truck, the other was looking away from her direction. She bolted across the street, praying her pursuers wouldn't see her, praying she'd reach cover before they turned.

She got to the machine and threw herself on the snow behind it. After taking a second to catch her breath, Mike peered over its seat. Her two pursuers were still looking for her in the lot. She had made it without detection. She ducked, the cold snow against her hot cheek feeling good.

A moment later, keeping an occasional eye on the men across the street, Mike put the attaché case in a tool basket attached to the rear seat, then looked to see if the key was in the slot. It wasn't.

She ducked down, wondering what to do next. She remembered that Jeremiah had once shown her how to hotwire a snow machine when she had lost a key to one of theirs. He had told her, with a smile, that no one should be caught without such a skill, because one never knew when they would lose a key, did they—or in what kind of predicament they might find themselves. She had smiled at him and hadn't paid much attention. She hoped she could remember enough.

Unhooking the rubber latches, she lifted the hood just enough to see the wires. Out of one corner of her eye she could see the men moving in her general direction, but they were intently looking in the parking lot. As she found the wires she thought might be the ones she needed, she couldn't help but wonder what had happened to Dutch. She could only pray that both pilots were all right.

She tore the wires free but couldn't remember exactly what to do next . . . This one goes here? . . . no, here . . . that one . . .

"Hey! There she is!" one of the men yelled.

Mike's head jerked up as the men began running toward her. She touched some wires together and the engine turned over and caught. She grabbed hold of the handlebar throttle and pushed with one hand, letting the hood fall into place with the other. As the men bolted toward her, she hopped into the seat and throttled it. The machine's track spun on the icy surface of the sidewalk and slid to one side. She let off a little, let it adjust, then throttled it again just as one of the men lunged at her. She ducked and he missed, landing with a rib-cracking thud across the metal basket attached to the back seat. He bounced off with a scream as the machine hit a drift of snow at thirty miles an hour, and sailed through the air, landing ten feet further out in an open field. Glancing over her shoulder, she saw the second man flop atop the drift of snow and point his revolver in her direction. She jerked on the handlebars and dashed left behind a wall of equipment. Moments later she was racing down the main road away from the terminal.

No one was in pursuit.

3:46 A.M.—Washington, D.C.

Seth Adams put down the phone, his face the color and texture of pink-white stone. The president of NBC, who was a personal friend, had called to inform him of a news story the station had just received from one of its reporters. President Adams had listened as the story was unfolded for him. Not only had the Sicilians killed Jeremiah but they also were doing a first-rate job of character assassination.

"Can you keep it under wraps until the morning news?" the president asked.

"We might not be the only ones who have the story, Seth. It was an anonymous phone call. Keeping something like this a secret in Washington is asking the impossible." He sighed.

"I'm sorry, Seth, but this will break on the morning news. Everyone has it and it's too late to stop it. Sorry." With that he had hung up.

The president stood and began pacing, the legs of his silk pajamas slapping against his ankles. He had hoped to get some much-needed sleep for once. Not tonight. He looked at his watch: nearly 2:00 A.M.

Was it true? Could Jeremiah really be dead?

The phone rang.

"Yes?"

"Senator Ridgeway, sir."

"Put him through, Margery."

"Good evening, Seth," Ridgeway said.

"That depends on your point of view, Senator."

"A friend of mine in the city's police force says that Daniels has been killed. Is it true?"

"We don't know for sure. There will have to be an autopsy. Hopefully I'll have the report before the early news in the morning."

"If it is true, if Daniels is dead, what are you going to do?"

"I don't suppose I can count on any support from the hill."

"I tried to warn you, Mr. President. These high-handed methods . . . subverting proper channels . . . I might have been able to help you yesterday, but not now, not with the discovery that Daniels was using his office for personal advantage."

The president clenched his teeth. "Both of us know there's no truth to those stories, Senator, and for a man of your position to believe—"

"I'll reserve my judgment until after the hearings, Mr. President."

"Hearings?" Seth said angrily. "You're not serious!"

"Very serious, Mr. President. It's our duty. If Daniels was involved in the drug trade, that taints his entire operation. Others may be heavily involved. This could be a serious, serious scandal, Mr. President." He paused, relishing his victory. "One that may have reached the highest towers of government. The American people won't stand for a Congress that looks the other way while corruption eats at the very gut of their democracy. You said yourself that the people want this drug business stopped. We on the hill intend to represent their wishes—no matter who or what office may be involved.

"We'll be wanting all of Daniels's files and we'll call for a cessation of all operations under the control of his office. We'll expect full cooperation from your office, Mr. President."

"Politics as usual, eh, Ridgeway? I'll fight you, Senator, right down to the last drop of your blood."

Ridgeway laughed. "I'm not the one bleeding, Adams. You'd better give up on Daniels and try to save your own skin. Consider your other programs. The promises to the people about tax relief, job programs, the elimination of the deficit. We've gone through two full presidencies without answers. Three more years without any action on those items and we can kiss this country good-bye."

Ridgeway's voice became hard. "Move on, Mr. President, to business of a less volatile nature, business we on the hill can support you in."

"And if I don't?"

There was a deep sigh. "Daniels's reputation will be ruined and yours right along with it."

"A threat, Ridgeway?"

"Consider it an offer of help to a man about to drown." Another pause. "We live in critical times for our country. I wish only to keep a scandal from dividing a nation and destroying our—your—ability to accomplish things that are *really* important." He laughed again. "Have a good evening, Mr. President." He hung up.

The president went to the window and drew back the curtains, staring into the cold night. The city lights bouncing off the overcast sky gave an eerie look to everything. It gave him goose bumps and he closed the curtains, then began pacing. Ridgeway was a formidable foe. He had buried others who had opposed him; he would use this to the utmost advantage. It was no secret the man had his heart set on living in the White House. For the moment it looked like the good senator might get his wish.

The phone rang again.

He put the small cellular to his ear. "What is it, Margery?"

"Dolph Stockman, sir."

"Put him on."

"Mr. President?"

"Yes, Dolph."

"Sir, LOGOS just called." There was a strange shake in Stockman's voice, a quiver. "LOGOS said that Jeremiah . . ."

"We don't know for sure, Dolph. The body was burned beyond recognition. An autopsy will have to be performed. I'm trying to verify everything and get ready to defend what we've done. I can't make any promises. Everything may come apart like a straw boat in a heavy storm."

There was a long pause before Stockman spoke. "They almost got to Mike in Jackson. She's in hiding now and all right. We think they have one of Jeremiah's sons. He was supposed to go to a safe house in Salt Lake, but never showed up . . . Trayco . . . we're trying to get to him, but the weather isn't cooperating. If he survived . . . the weather . . ."

The president went weak in the knees and sat down. He rubbed his eyes with his fingers. What had he done? What had he gotten Jeremiah and his family into? Tears sprang to the corners of his eyes but he forced them back, trying to get control.

"Mr. President?"

"I . . ." the president cleared his throat. "I hear you, Dolph." He hesitated. "Can you get hold of Mike? Can you get her and the girls . . . the others . . . out of the country?"

"Yessir, but—"

"Do it, Dolph. Jeremiah . . . Michaelene has paid enough. Do your best to find the boy and Trayco, but get everyone else out of the country." He took a deep breath, leaning back in his chair, his shoulders slumped. "Enough is enough."

3:50 A.M.—Near Sunup—Israel

The well-hidden man atop the parts and equipment warehouse watched through binoculars as the ambulance, its lights flashing, moved toward a large hangar on the other side of the tarmac.

Mohamar Shariff was a member of Hezbollah, and the fourth member of the group who had tried, unsuccessfully, to assassinate Boudia at the hospital. It had been humiliating for him to report their failure, and a gift from Allah when he was given a second chance—a continued assignment to watch what was done with the Syrian drug and gun runner.

Mohamar had been told that an American named Macklin

would be coming to remove Boudia from Israel and that he was to use his contacts inside the hospital to let Hezbollah's leadership know when the Syrian would be moved.

Mohamar smiled to himself. The information hadn't been hard to come by. The same contact who had told him which room was Boudia's was still close to the situation, and still willing to give information for American dollars. When he had returned to his leaders, his information had been well received and he was promised full redemption from his former failure. But just to be sure, Mohamar had requested that he be allowed to do more. Leadership had consented. By the good graces of Allah his name would go down in history and his family be honored by his people forevermore. It was truly a great day in Mohamar's eternity.

Hezbollah had been busy with their contacts at Ben Gurion airport and had discovered that Macklin had ordered an Israeli-made Astra jet to be deposited in a hangar and made ready for a flight to the United States. It was to be a medically equipped jet with all the latest in lifesaving devices provided for its precious cargo, and it was to be ready on a moment's notice.

Hezbollah had even known the tailwing number. For that Mohamar was most grateful. He would not wish to waste a TOW missile—and his life—on the wrong target.

Mohamar put the binoculars to his eyes as the ambulance came to a halt in front of the hangar's huge doors, which were already opening to allow the vehicle entrance. He moved his gaze beyond the cascading light of the entrance to the sleek jet beyond. He could just make out the words and, although they were in Hebrew, read them to himself.

"IAI ASTRA." Then came the numbers. "Six . . . four . . . seven."

He smiled. Target confirmed.

The ambulance moved inside as another vehicle pulled up to the door. Mohamar turned a switch and the binoculars went to infrared, allowing him to see the men clearly in the darkness. One he recognized from his informant's description as the man who survived their attempt on Boudia's life. The other matched the description of the American, Thomas Macklin.

The doors began to close as the two men walked inside, the strand of light from the hangar becoming thinner and thinner until it disappeared. Mohamar put the binoculars aside and crawled on his hands and knees across the roof to an air vent. Reaching inside, he found the rope attached to his package and lifted it upward. The cloth bag containing two TOW missiles was soon in his hands. Moments later he had returned to his spot, opened the bag, removed the TOWs, and prepared them for firing. Laying them down, he took from his backpack a prayer rug. Stretching it out on the roof, he knelt down on it and began his last prayers. Mohamar was not deluding himself. He would not survive what he was about to do. Hezbollah had used all of its contacts to gain his entrance into the airport—but he was on his own to get out. He gave himself less than a ten-percent chance.

He heard the loud thump as the hangar doors began to open again. Quickly he rolled up his rug and put it carefully back in his backpack. Then he picked up the first TOW and put the night-vision sight to his eye. He had fired the TOW many times in training and a dozen times since. He had a steady hand and never missed.

The engines of the Astra went into a supersonic whine and the twin turbofan jet glided forward onto the tarmac. As it turned toward the runway, Mohamar squeezed the trigger.

The TOW leapt from its chute, and Shariff kept the sight steady. The TOW was the old wire-guided variety and had to be directed to the place the shooter wanted it to go. It takes a fearless man to stand straight long enough for a missile to cross the space between him and the target, especially when he knows that the flames and explosion of the TOW have given away his position.

The TOW plowed into the center of the jet's fuselage and exploded, blowing the sleek plane's aluminum-alloy skin into thin slivers of death. As a jet-fuel fireball erupted skyward, the back half of the fuselage separated from the front and collapsed onto the tarmac in flames.

Calmly Mohamar Shariff put down the still-smoking tube and picked up the second missile. Although he knew no one in the passenger section of the plane could have survived the blast, he was a careful man and wanted to be sure. The second missile was directed at the plane's blacked-out cockpit. Seconds later there was nothing but flame, smoke, and metal filling the air, the heat from the multiple explosions blackening the tarmac and hangar and knocking glass out of windows clear to the main terminal.

Mohamar lay the tube down and picked up his backpack

before taking one last look at his handiwork. There would be no survivors.

As he walked toward the ladder at the rear of the building, an IDF chopper came through the darkness, hovering overhead and shining its bright spotlight on him. He pulled a 9mm Makarov pistol from his belt and began firing.

4:00 A.M.—Miami, Florida

Detective Buckles watched as Gad shackled Alvarez, then Lima. He nervously turned the cigar over in his thin lips. He didn't like this plan of the Israeli's, didn't like it at all.

Gad put the two-way radio to his mouth. "All set. Everyone at their stations?" Each of his men reported in. They were ready.

Gad smiled at Buckles, who returned it with a scowl and a "humph!" Buckles took his policeman's .38 special from its holster and checked the cartridge cylinder, biting down hard on the stogey.

"If fools were millionaires, you'd be the richest man in town," he said, moving toward the door. "This will never work. Someone is bound to have found out." Gad only smiled.

Buckles and a dozen uniformed police surrounded Gad and his two prisoners in the hallway and moved quickly to the outside door. Gad found his heart beating hard and fast even though he had been through dozens of similar situations before. None had been, or would ever be, exactly like this one.

The outer door was shoved open, the cool night air and scent of Florida reaching Gad's nostrils. The street was deserted, not a soul in sight. So far, so good. A half dozen uniformed police surrounded him and his two prisoners, moving them down the steps toward the street. The black, unmarked Dodge swung around the far corner and moved toward them. Gad stood, impatiently waiting. It seemed that the vehicle was moving in slow motion, taking forever to get in front of him.

Finally the black Dodge arrived. He took a deep breath. The door flung open.

Buckles saw the gun appear, a silencer attached. He pulled his own revolver from its holster as the dull "crack-crack," of the pistol filled his ears. As Lima, then Alvarez, melted to the sidewalk, another pistol appeared through the front window and fired into the chest of the Israeli. Buckles aimed as the sedan door slammed shut and sped away. He fired, moving into the street and emptying his pistol. The Dodge banged into another vehicle and knocked it into an intersection, then regained direction, screeching around the corner to the right. It disappeared before Buckles could reload and get another shot. He pulled the two-way from the scabbard attached to his belt and barked orders. Seconds later blue and whites across the city were in pursuit of the assailants, and ambulances were directed to the scene.

The uniformed police gathered around the bodies and were using their weapons to keep a few shocked but curious spectators at bay. Buckles slipped between two of them and knelt by Gad. Gad's chest was splattered with red and his eyes were closed. He coughed lightly, then turned his head to one side and was motionless.

As Buckles dutifully checked Alvarez and Lima an ambulance came to the curb, and four medics came rushing over. Seconds later the three bodies were loaded on stretchers and the ambulance sirens screamed as they sped toward the hospital.

Buckles turned to his partner. "I want a complete blackout on this, Foster. Tell the uniforms that if one word of this leaks, I'll personally see that everyone of them lives to regret it."

Foster nodded, then reholstered his pistol. Everything had gone smoothly.

CHAPTER 13

6:00 A.M.—Upper Falls, Snake River

Kentucky was afraid they'd never make it. He looked back up the trail they had just come down, and wondered

how they had done it. Steep, twisting, slippery, they had tra-
versed the trail with a stretcher between them. Then there
was the snow. Overnight another eight inches had piled up.
It was to the top of his thigh now, almost to Kate's waist.

His arm was killing him. "How much farther?" he asked.

Kate was checking Colt's pulse. She stood and pointed
downriver. "A mile. Just around the outcropping. It'll be easier going from here on, at least until we get to the Falls."

Trayco adjusted the ropes he had around his shoulders
while Kate put the rifle back in place, the strap across her
chest.

Trayco didn't feel the cold wind anymore because he was
numb all over. He was used to the desert's heat, and this
cold seemed to go right through the parka and clear to the
bone.

"Ready?" he asked, forcing a smile.

She returned it, then bent down to pick up her end of the
stretcher. She amazed Trayco. Twice she had nearly fallen as
they came down the trail, and twice, through strength one
would never know existed from the look of her lithe body, she
had kept her balance while keeping the stretcher right-side
up.

They trudged through the deepening snow, made rough
by huge boulders from the broken-up lava flow. Several times
they fell, as their feet slipped on the uneven surfaces or sunk
into crevices between rocks, hidden by the thick layer of
white. It was slow going.

Finally they reached the top of the falls. Trayco pointed
toward a fairly even place and they laid the stretcher down.
He was in a lot of pain and felt nauseous. He had used the
end of one of the ropes to hold one side of the stretcher, leaving his broken arm free from the constant weight that made
him want to faint, but more times than he cared to count he
had needed to use the arm to balance the stretcher.

He dropped to the snow, catching his breath. Kate came
quickly to his side. "Are you all right, Tray?"

He forced a sarcastic grimace. "A little pain is good for
me . . . keeps the senses sharp."

"You look so pale. Stay put for a few minutes; I'll get
some water."

"Check Colt first, Kate."

"He's okay. He moved a minute ago." She moved to the
edge of the river, took a camper's cup from her pocket, and

scooped it full of water. When it crossed Trayco's lips he thought nothing could taste so good.

"Thanks, that hit the spot." He lay back on the snow. Kate took off her glove, leaned forward, and felt his forehead.

"You're running a fever!" she exclaimed. Unzipping his coat, she removed his arm from the sleeve. "It's inflamed, Tray," she said with a worried tone.

"Yeah, I know. I can feel the heat clear to the tips of my hair." He forced another halfhearted grin.

She leaned over him again, helping him get his arm back in the coat and zipping it closed against the cold. He was amazed how clear her green eyes were, how beautiful. His good arm went to her back and he pulled her closer to him. She didn't resist, her warm hand finding his cheek and rubbing it gently as she let her body ease against his.

As Trayco sat up, she started to remove a syringe full of painkiller from a small case in her pocket.

He touched her arm. "Later. I'm fine now. After we get out of here you can stick me with that thing. Right now I need my senses about me."

She put the cover on the syringe, and stuck it back into the small box, then placed it in her pocket.

"Let's take a look at what we have to do here," Trayco said.

She helped him up, and they walked to the edge of the falls. It was precarious, slippery, and cold. The rush of wind coming forcefully up the canyon below the falls whipped the icy water through the air around them. They covered their faces against the small, icy pellets shooting through the air.

She pointed to some pitons sticking out of the rocks. "We've been down here before. In the summer it's fun—we usually end up in the drink at the bottom. Cold, but refreshing."

"This time of year," Trayco said, "I think we'll skip the refreshing part, if you don't mind."

"Good looks, money, and smart, too." Kate laughed. "Can we get the stretcher . . . ?"

"We can get him down all right, but I'm going to have to go down first and cross over to that point with a rope. It's the only way to control the sway and direction of the stretcher."

She nodded. There wasn't any other way. They returned to the stretcher, and started preparing the rope, unaware that they were being watched from the top of both sides of the canyon wall.

Koln lowered the binoculars and handed them to Townsend. "Who is the woman?"

Townsend refocused the binoculars and took a look. "Kate Meadows. She's the caretaker of the government facilities at the falls. Your target must have found cover there for the night."

"What are they trying to do?"

Townsend handed the binoculars back. "Kate has a boat at the bottom of the falls. They can float down to the Ashton bridge and get help."

Koln looked at the stretcher. He couldn't tell (for all the blankets and parka hood), but it had to be DeGuillio.

He turned to Townsend. "How do we get down there in a hurry?"

Townsend chuckled lightly. "We don't. You watched them move along the river, and that was on a lot better ground than we have to cover. Try to get through that pile of snow-covered, icy, jagged rocks in a hurry and you'll break both your legs." He picked up the rifle and unzipped the sheath, removing a Redfield sniper's rifle. "Besides, that's Kate Meadows. She knows the lot of us," he said, pointing to the group behind them. "If she sees our faces, we will have to kill her. We don't intend to do that unless forced to." He injected a shell into the chamber and handed the gun to Koln. "Use this, and get it over with. It's cold out here and I've got chores." Townsend folded his arms, waiting.

Koln went to the edge of the hill. Lying flat in the snow, he lifted the rifle and peered through the scope. The falling snow was bothersome, and judging the wind at this distance would make this shot tricky at best.

He put the crosshairs on the unconscious man's head and started applying pressure to the trigger, but something hit the scope hard, driving it into his eye socket.

Koln dropped the rifle, and grabbed his face, cursing. Then he heard the distant crack of the rifle that had done the damage. Koln slammed his body into the snow trying to find cover.

He rolled away from the hill, wondering which direction to go to get away from a second bullet he knew was already on its way. "Townsend! I can't see! Get him, you fool! Someone shot . . ." Koln tried to get to his feet . . . to run . . .

Townsend tackled Koln and drove him back to the

ground. "Stay down, you idiot!" Townsend yelled, as a second bullet splattered in the snow beside them, then another. Townsend covered his head with an arm as more bullets made a circle around them. Whoever the gunman was, he was playing with them, and was obviously good enough to put a bullet through a head at any time. When the bullets stopped coming, Townsend started sliding back toward the trees. Reaching what he thought was a safe spot, he rolled Koln over and pulled his hands away from his face. Blood was everywhere, cascading from a deep, half-inch-long cut above his eyelid. The eye socket was filled with it, making it look as if the eye were badly damaged. As Townsend cleaned around the wound he saw how lucky Koln had been.

"You're a lucky stiff, Rolf!" Townsend pulled a hanky from his coat pocket and applied it to Koln's cut. "Did anyone see where those shots came from?" he asked the group, who were cowering behind snow machines and trees.

A tall, thin man with a blond mustache and beard was peering from behind an Arctic Cat 650 and pointed with his gloved hand. "There. On the other side of the canyon."

Townsend took a long look at the spot and thought he saw some movement. It was at least three hundred yards away atop a canyon wall that was nearly the same height as their own position. With the falling snow and stiff wind it was hard to see clearly. The man was a good shot, whoever he was!

Koln sat up and tried to look with his good eye, the blood-soaked handkerchief covering the other. "I want that . . . !"

The thud of lead implanting itself in the bark of the tree next to Koln's shoulder sent him rolling for cover again, the muffled crack of the distant rifle reaching his ears a second later. Townsend flung his body behind a fallen log.

"Jimmy, we can't let him keep us pinned down here! We've got to get to Trayco and DeGuillio before they get down that canyon wall!"

Townsend glanced at Koln from around the end of the log, not sure that Koln realized the gravity of the situation. "In case that blood spilling over your face hasn't made it clear, Koln, we're under fire here! We can't—"

Koln's face was covered with blood, his good eye full of hate. He yanked his arm toward Townsend's men and spoke through tight lips. "Tell those cowards to start shooting back, Townsend! Or is that"—his arm jerked toward the far side of the canyon—"someone you know as well?"

Townsend yelled the order. Rifles popped up and the men

began firing. Most of them carried good hunting weapons but none of them had the expertise of their opponent; their shots fell far short of the spot from which the enemy was firing. The response was immediate: well-aimed bullets ventilated the windshield and seat of one of the machines, forcing everyone to burrow into the snow and stay down.

"Who the devil is that guy?" Koln asked through clenched teeth.

"It doesn't matter who he is," Townsend grumbled. "He's giving Trayco enough time to get away. Come on, it's time to change scenery. I know a spot where we can pick off your friends down there without being sitting ducks." He pulled on Koln's coat sleeve. "Let's get to the machines."

When Kenny and Kate heard the shots, they grabbed the stretcher and frantically shoved it behind the outcropping and between large boulders. Trayco then realized the shots and bullets weren't intended for them. From his position, he could hear the rifle being fired above them. Then he saw the head of the rifleman, his gun pointed across their position to a distant spot on the opposite side. Kenny edged his way to a place where he could see better and looked upward. The wind-blown snow prevented him from seeing clearly, but he knew from the commotion that there were several people scrambling for cover on the canyon wall some distance above and east of them. He squinted through the snow-filled air, trying to figure out what was happening. Then those being fired on started shooting back.

A few moments later the air fell silent. He glanced back at Kate, who had the rifle and was using the scope to look things over.

"Who are they?" Trayco asked.

"I can't tell. Too much winter gear." She handed him the rifle. "The only one who is uncovered is hurt. I don't recognize him."

Trayco peered through the scope. Sitting on one of the snow machines was Rolf Koln!

"Killers, Kate. Cold-blooded killers. They won't let us out of here alive." He rolled on his side and looked up, wondering who was up there. Maybe Dolph had sent help. But would he have sent only one?

"Just one guy, wasn't there?" Trayco asked.

"That's all I saw. Where is he?"

"Gone."

They heard the distant sound of motors.

"They're leaving!" Kate said, joining him, and peering up the canyon wall. They watched as half a dozen machines headed into the trees, then disappeared.

"Or trying to get a better position."

Kate stood. "They could! A place . . . above us . . ." She moved down the river to a point just above the falls and clear of the outcropping. Trayco followed. "There," she pointed. "See the angle? They can fire at us if we try going down the wall, and the man up there can't see them." She glanced to where the friendly gunman had been.

Trayco was moving toward the ropes. "We have to get down quick. Without all the formalities."

Kate's mouth dropped open. "Tray! That's straight down. Colt . . . the stretcher."

"I'll carry Colt." He grabbed at the rope they had been tying to one end of the stretcher and started reeling it in.

"You can't be serious?"

"We have no choice, Kate. If they can pin us down, we'll either freeze to death or give them enough time to work their way down here. We can't go down that wall at night, and it will be suicide if they get up there. Our guardian angel won't be able to do much for us from up there." He nodded toward the place the gunman had deserted. "He gave us a little time; we'd better use it."

"Maybe he can find a place to shoot from further down the canyon. That seems to be his intent."

"It becomes too wide," Trayco pointed out. "It takes a marksman at three hundred yards. At five or six hundred . . ." Trayco shrugged. "He won't even be able to keep their heads down. He'd have to narrow the gap. The only way he can do that is to come down the canyon wall. Look at it. It's steeper than what we have to deal with."

Kate thought it through, her trained eye moving along the opposite canyon wall. Trayco was right. They had to move quickly. "All right," she agreed.

He cradled her head in his hand and looked into her eyes. "I'm sorry about all this. I—"

Kate kissed him to shut him up, and said, "I'll get Colt out of his blankets."

Trayco smiled and began preparing the ropes for rappelling. Minutes later he had the blue and white mountain-climbing rope dangling over the edge, twenty feet left of the cascading water of the falls.

Kate had worked out a timetable in her mind. She knew the trail the enemy had to take. It would only be a few minutes before they reached the spot she knew they wanted. She glanced upward and shivered. They'd never survive a barrage of bullets from there. Never.

"Let's go," Trayco said. "Help me get Colt up, then lash him to my back with that small rope."

Moments later Colt was fastened to Trayco in such a way that left Kenny's arms free. The boy had moaned during the ordeal and even opened his eyes for half a minute. But Kate and Trayco hadn't noticed. They were too busy tying him onto Trayco's back.

Trayco grinned. "Ladies first." But the smile left his face as he picked up the rifle and handed it to her. "Take this. You'll have to give us cover."

She quickly put the gun's strap over her shoulder and across her chest, then put the rope in the carabiner attached to her harness. Seconds later she disappeared over the edge.

Trayco spent the two minutes it took Kate to work her way to the bottom, watching her, then the cliff above. He figured the enemy should be in position any time.

Kate nearly fell as she neared the bottom. The rope was wet and slick from spray and she lost her grip, then caught herself before falling into the water below. Working her way a little further east, away from the water and jagged ice below, she pushed against the wall with her feet one last time and shoved away, dropping into the snow at the bottom. Unhooking her belt, she headed for a pile of rocks and trees, then disappeared. Good! Trayco thought, she's got decent cover.

He put his gloves on and grabbed the rope, hooked it into his own belt and carabiner and started down.

Soon after he started one of his feet slipped, and he had to use his broken arm to catch himself. Pain shot through his body like fire and he gritted his teeth, letting the arm hang loose again once his good one had a better hold. It was hard enough to rappel with two good hands. It took every ounce of physical strength to do it with one. He inched his way down, finding footholds, then pushing away and lowering himself.

He heard the crack of a gun and instinctively jerked toward the wall of the cliff, seeking protection under the overhang.

Kate returned the enemy's fire. The clifftop exploded with the rapid firing of weapons. He pushed away from the wall just enough to peer overhead. He couldn't see anything, the angle was wrong—but that meant they couldn't see him either. That also meant Kate was drawing all the deadly fire to herself. His stomach churned with anger. He had to get down, and fast.

Trayco glanced up and over his shoulder, hoping their friend, whoever he was, would be able to help. He saw nothing. He was on his own.

Taking a deep breath, Kentucky grabbed the rope behind him with the bad arm and gritted his teeth. He pushed away and let himself drop five feet. Then he pushed off again, this time going ten feet. He heard the ricochet, and knew the shot had come close to his head, but he pushed off again, revealing himself for a short period while he dropped.

Then he hesitated, hugging the rock wall. No sense in making it too easy for them by creating a pattern. Besides, he needed a minute to rest, afraid he was going to pass out from the pain, exertion, and the weight of the boy on his back.

It suddenly occurred to him that Kate had stopped firing. He looked desperately over his shoulder, but couldn't see her.

Panicked, he shoved himself away from the wall dangerously far, his entire body visible to enemy fire. He felt the rope snap, and he and Colt plunged the last twelve feet, landing in the icy snow with a painful thud. Trayco couldn't breathe, having had the wind knocked out of him by the weight of Colt's body as it smashed him into the heavy snow. He gasped for air while trying to get to his feet. His fingers and toes dug into the snow and propelled them to the safety of the cliff wall.

As he placed his chest against the rock and filled his lungs with air, he knew he'd made it. Unless Colt had taken a hit, they were still unhurt.

He unstrapped the boy and let him to the ground. Colt was moaning, his lungs heaving for air, the wind knocked out of them. His head was rolling from left to right and his face grimaced. He was coming to.

"Relax, Colt. We still have to get across open ground." As he spoke, Trayco unzipped Colt's coat and checked for blood. There wasn't any. He closed and zipped the coat. The boy was out again.

He turned to the spot where Kate had gone, but saw nothing. It was at least fifty feet across open ground to the spot, and he knew he'd never make it, but he had to try. Had to find . . .

He noticed something moving out of the corner of his eye and glanced across the river to the far canyon wall. The savior gunman had rigged a rope of his own and was quickly rappelling down the wall to the river bed. The enemy was concentrating on him, trying for a lucky shot. Their bullets were hitting low and they didn't seem to give the man on the rope a minute's worry.

Trayco decided to use the diversion and hoisted Colt onto his back, took a deep breath, and started across the open ground.

He was surprised that the snow held his weight. Then he realized the icy water that had been so miserable coming down the face of the wall was now his support, hardening the snow with its frozen cover. If he could just keep from slipping!

He zigzagged precariously on the icy surface, the bullets burying themselves in the crust behind and around him, making the hair stand up on the back of his neck. He felt as if he were on skates, out of control. Then he was into the pines and out of gun sight. He dropped Colt gently to the snow, his eyes searching for Kate. She lay in the snow next to a rock a few feet away, motionless, a spot of red in the snow by her head.

Trayco's heart sank as he crawled toward her. Grabbing her by the coat, he turned her quickly over. A bullet ricocheted off the rock, and another hit dangerously close to his legs as he tried to pull himself and Kate back in the trees.

The noise of gunfire came from across the river. Trayco turned and saw the stranger on the far side. He had reached the bottom and taken cover behind a large boulder. Trayco glanced up at the enemy and saw one of them fall to the ground, the rest ducking for cover. Kate moved, groaning.

"Come on, girl, hang in there," Trayco said. "Don't pass out on me now."

Ruth took a deep breath, placed her eye to the scope, and squeezed the trigger. The recoil shoved against her shoulder and the sharp crack of the SVD Dragunov reverberated across the canyon walls. In the scope's eye, a man dropped his gun, grabbed his leg, and fell to the ground. She injected another shell and fired again as the crowd at the top of the cliff jumped for cover.

The rescue operation had been a near disaster. When Dolph told her that Trayco's chopper had gone down and that they had no chance to get to him unless the storm let up, Ruth had offered an alternative.

A chopper could stand at least an hour of frigid weather before its blades iced over or the engines froze. That was plenty of time to get to the crash site. The problems were visibility and a wind that could drive the chopper into the narrow cliffs and canyons along the river. Attempting to get in close would be suicide.

So they didn't plan to get in close.

Another problem was acquiring a chopper. Mike had told them about the airport, so they were sure they couldn't get an Eagle from there. They had to come up with something else. Dolph was the one who did.

At four o'clock in the evening Ruth and two others had boarded the chopper Dolph was able to get in from West Yellowstone, and lifted up through the ceiling of the storm. Ten minutes later, using radar and the ISSA's satellite-generated pictures, Dolph had guided the pilot back through the clouds toward a field cut out of the forest by timber companies three miles west of the river.

That was when the trouble began.

The winds were gusting up to fifty miles an hour in the clouds, and the pilot wasn't able to keep the chopper on course. As they broke through the bottom of the white fluff they found themselves over a lodgepole pine forest with no place to land. Dolph instructed the pilot to abort immediately, and Ruth made a quick decision.

Punching the down button on the hook used for air-to-ground rescue, she grabbed the cable and swung herself out the side door. By the time the pilot realized what she was doing there was nothing to do but hold position as best he could until she hit ground.

She was lucky. The wind pummeled her into one tree after another, but her thick winter gear had cushioned the impact. Ten feet from the ground, however, her hands began slipping on the wet cable and she closed her eyes and let go, dropping into the snow below.

When she looked up the chopper was flying away.

Ruth had snowshoes attached to her back, and she quickly put them on. Finding her bearings, she headed through the forest, then took out her pocket radio and tried to get through to Stockman. She could hear his voice, knew he was cursing, but couldn't make out all the words because the storm was breaking up the transmission. She could only hope it would get better.

She hadn't realized how far they had been blown off course in those few minutes until the darkness collapsed around her and she still hadn't reached the canyon walls of the river. With the temperature drop and darkness she had no choice but to dig in for the night and get some rest. Finding a pine tree with limbs low to the ground, she dug a snow shelter, lined it with foil body blankets, and wrapped herself up in the sleeping bag slung to her back. Minutes later she was sound asleep.

The next morning she woke up before the sun rose and headed out, finding the canyon wall in less than half an hour. Walking north along the rim, she traveled another three miles before she saw someone struggling with a stretcher along the opposite side of the river. She used the Dragunov's scope and first focused in on Trayco. A minute later she saw Koln.

Her shot had meant to prevent Koln from killing Trayco. Now she had to help Kenny and those with him get away.

Ruth saw Trayco go to the person who had been firing a rifle. If only she could get across the river. But she couldn't—it was deep, too deep.

She saw the hump of snow next to the river, a dark green side protruding beneath it, and realized it was a boat. She fired another round, then yelled at Trayco.

"Get to the boat!" Trayco barely heard the "gunman" yell. It was a woman's voice. A familiar woman's voice. It was

Ruth Macklin! He stared at her from across the river, unbelieving. How on earth . . .

She was pointing at something. Kenny saw the wooden fly-fishing boat chained to a tree just a few yards away in a stand of trees, snow piled high on it. He ran to the spot, removed his .45, and blasted the combination lock. It fell open and he pulled the chain free. Hoisting the boat over and onto its bottom took all of his strength, and he fell in the snow, gasping for air. He had never been so tired, the strain and fatigue of the last twenty-four hours had taken its toll. But he had to get up, had to keep going. Everything depended on it.

He got to his knees, then to his feet, shoving the boat across the snow and into the water. Then he went for Kate.

He found her sitting up, eyes open, staring at the blood she had on her fingers after touching her wound. She gave Trayco a bewildered look. "What . . ."

The sharp crack of Ruth's rifle sounded in the canyon, and Kate's eyes filled with recollection.

"Colt . . ."

"There," Trayco said, pointing. "He's okay. Can you get to the boat?"

She nodded. He stood and pulled her to her feet, picking up the rifle. "Keep down!"

Kate put her hand to her head, wobbling a little, then moved. Trayco grabbed her, supporting her until she had hold of the boat's side. He boosted her in, placed the rifle beside her, and ran back for Colt.

Colt was breathing evenly, a slight flutter in his eyelids. Grabbing one of his arms, Trayco lifted the boy, trying to get him in position to hoist him onto a shoulder. Colt seemed to weigh more now, and it was all Kenny could do to hoist him over one shoulder and half stumble, half fall in the direction of the boat.

It seemed like an eternity of lifting, shoving, then pulling by Kate before Colt's body was over the edge and into the bottom of the tall wooden boat. Kenny knew the enemy was shooting. He could hear the claps of the shots reverberating off the canyon walls. To Trayco everything seemed to be moving in slow motion. Kate was pulling him, urging him over the edge, but the boat wasn't in the water. He knew he had to push it off the ice.

He placed his shoulder against the cold wood and shoved. The boat slid easily and he lost his balance, falling face down in the cold river. That woke him up.

He sprang for the boat, the frigid liquid seeping through his clothing and icing his flesh. Kate used what strength she had and pulled him inside.

"The oars!" Trayco yelled over the sound of the falls. "We have to get to the other side. Pick up Ruth." He grabbed an oar and stuck it in the oar lock, then did the same with the other.

Kate shot him a funny look, then glanced at the gunman across the river. The hood of the parka had been removed. It *was* a woman. "What the . . . Who . . . ?"

"Long story." Trayco started pulling on the oars. "Get the rifle. We'll be in the open any minute."

Kate picked up the gun and moved to the front seat, aiming the rifle at the cliffs above. She injected a shell into the chamber.

As they moved across the river the tops of the trees no longer blocked them from view and the enemy on the cliff began firing at them. Kate sighted and fired. Then did it again and again as Kenny strained into the oars.

Bullets embedded themselves in the wood frame of the boat as Ruth fired one more time at the people on the cliff, slung the rifle over her shoulder by its strap, and plunged through the shallow water toward the boat. The water deepened and was quickly up to her chest. Half swimming, half plunging through the cold liquid, Ruth slowly made her way to the boat. Kenny kept the vessel steady, allowing Ruth to grab its edge and hang on. Trayco dug the oars in deep and shifted their direction downstream. He strained into the oars, and the boat slipped quickly away from danger. Kate grabbed Ruth's arm and helped her over the edge and into the boat. The enemy was still firing, and Kenny dug the oars in again, the boat's keel skimming across the fast-moving waters.

"We're out of range," Ruth gasped, a smile crossing her face.

Kenny grinned back, letting go of the oars. "You, dear lady, are a sight for sore eyes."

They laughed as Kate watched them, mystified. Kenny saw the look.

"Kate Meadows, Ruth Macklin, our angel from heaven."

Ruth nodded at Kate, then glanced at Kenny, catching the glint in his eye. She looked at Kate. Just right for Kenny Trayco. "From heaven," Ruth qualified, "but no angel."

"I'm almost afraid to ask this, but where *did* you come from?" Trayco queried.

"Later." She glanced at Colt. "It looks like we both have a story to tell. Where's Tony?"

"Dead."

Kate slid into the bottom of the boat and put Colt's head in her lap. His eyes fluttered open, then closed again. There was a hint of a smile on his lips.

"How far to a doctor?" Trayco asked.

"An hour to Ashton bridge," Kate said. "And a half hour to the hospital if we get help right away."

Ruth took off her wet gloves and touched the wound on Kate's head; blood mixed with sweat and water was rolling down the side of Kate's face. "You've got a nasty cut," Ruth said. "How do you feel?"

"Dizzy, headache. My eyes aren't focusing very well."

"Probably a concussion." Trayco said. "Just relax; I'll get us down river." The cliffs above were disappearing in the snow and low clouds. "Can they catch us?" he asked Kate.

Kate shook her head. "Not unless they grow wings." She smiled. "They have to go the long way around. By the time they get to where the warm river comes into the Snake, we'll be halfway to the Ashton bridge. The only chance they have is beating us to that point."

"Can they get shots at us along the river?"

"No. Too many obstacles, too much distance."

Trayco picked up the Dragunov and handed it to Ruth. "Just in case." He grinned. "Where did you learn to shoot like that?"

"Israeli commando school. I'll get you in sometime."

Kenny laughed, then glanced over at Kate. Her chin rested against her chest, eyes closed, her breathing even. She was sound asleep.

"Pretty, even when she's asleep," Ruth said softly.

Trayco smiled. "Yeah, I know."

Koln, the handkerchief pressed tightly against his damaged eye, watched them disappear. "What are our chances of catching them?" he asked Townsend, who stood next to him.

"Zip. Our only chance is at the Ashton bridge on the main highway. No way we can get there in time to cut them off. You saw what the flatlands were like coming up here. The wind blows the white stuff . . ."

Koln swore, turned, and walked toward his snow machine. Townsend was right. It had been slow, the blinding snow like a heavy blanket. He had lost his bearings on several occasions and only Townsend's familiarity with the countryside saved them from wandering in the wrong direction.

He straddled his machine and pulled the cloth away from his eye. For the first time in his life Koln was worried. Sicily didn't like failure, and so far all Koln had done was fail. It was time to get ahead in the game.

He fired up the snow machine and turned it up the hill. He needed to get to Jackson.

8:00 A.M.—Gros Ventre Range, Wyoming

Raoul's white winter gear, purchased from a military surplus store, blended in with the two feet of snow surrounding him. Although encircled by leafless cottonwood and snow-covered scrub brush, along with the usual pine, Raoul could see in all directions.

The bay and the mule were well hidden in a thick stand of pine and brush some hundred feet to his left in a canyon that swept away to the east. Raoul's snowshoes lay buried under a thin layer of snow but were still strapped to his feet; his .30-30, scope now attached, was placed atop a dead and fallen tree for balance, and he used the high power of the lens to scan his back trail. The bow and a quiver of arrows were at his side.

He saw the movement and slowly let his body ease low to the ground. Seconds later, four riders cautiously left the band of trees on the far side of the meadow in front of and below Raoul.

One of them, a man in heavy winter gear fashioned after that of the old-time mountain men, slipped from his mount then knelt and checked the tracks Raoul had left. He stood, looking in the direction Raoul had gone, then his eyes began scanning the meadow and the expanse up the hill. Raoul, half buried in the snow, his white parka blending in perfectly, held his breath, knowing he was under the eye of a trained tracker and hunter. The slightest movement would give away his position. From under his frosty brow and white rabbit-skin cap Raoul's dark eyes peered into those of his enemy, locking on them over a distance of better than half a mile.

The hair on the back of his neck stood on end, the fear of discovery acid in his stomach. But the tracker's eyes moved beyond Raoul and along the crest of the hill. After a moment the mountain man spoke to the others, mounted, and began following Raoul's trail. Raoul began breathing again, while understanding that the tracker was a good one, was familiar with the mountains of the Gros Ventre, and would not be easily fooled.

The tracks Raoul had left would lead his enemies back into the pines and down a wide but gradually sloping canyon with a creek at its center. At the lower end, in thick under-brush, they would find Raoul's trail among those of a herd of elk that had come for water and then moved east over a hill and into a lower, sheltered canyon where snow was thinner and grass was more accessible.

When Raoul had followed the herd it had been a temptation to use his bow and drop one of the animals for fresh meat; it had been two days since he had felt the warmth of a fire and put a hot meal in his belly. But he resisted, knowing that his enemy, although some distance behind him, was his first priority. He had kept his distance so as not to alarm the herd and had crossed the meadow to a point where a creek meandered for a while and then flowed gently through a narrow but passable canyon.

He had urged the bay and mule into the cold water and kept them there for more than a mile before coming out on the far side. From there he climbed to a trail that took him back in the direction he had come, the ridge of the mountain being between him and the creek down which he had ridden.

Raoul had backtracked and hidden the horses before taking the position from which he had seen his enemies come into the meadow.

He had done all this for a reason. His enemies had proven to be better outdoorsmen than he had supposed, probably because of the tracker he had just seen, and with the snow making his tracks easy to follow he had not been able to disappear as easily as he wanted. He had to slow them down. In order to do so he was using every trick he had ever learned in the mountains, and a few he had made up.

He looked heavenward as he reached the animals. The snow continued to fall, but as he came out of the high country it was getting wetter. He was at seven thousand feet. The further he descended, the more difficult it became. Although deep at this altitude, the snow was still mostly powder, and the animals could get through it without much trouble. At six thousand he expected he would need to lead the animals and make a path for them. At five thousand it would be miserable and wet.

After sheathing his rifle, Raoul tied his snowshoes and bow on the mule and pulled half a dozen pieces of elk jerky from his food bag. He would need all the strength he could get for what lay ahead.

"So much as twitch, boy, and I'll blow a hole in your backside."

Raoul's heart sank, the sudden realization sending a chill through his veins. He had underestimated the tracker. Again.

———————

"Turn around," said the voice.

Raoul kept his hands in the air and pivoted. The stranger stood partly in the shadow of a stand of tall pines, but Raoul could make out the clothing he had seen across the meadow.

"You're good for a kid so young. What's your name?" The voice was deep, like the wind in the trees, but not harsh.

"Raoul Daniels."

"Jeremiah Daniels your pa?"

"He is."

"Yeah, I heard about you. Adopted Arab, been in the hills a lot. Good hunter and tracker, so I hear."

"Fair, but not good enough."

"You're up against the best." The man stepped toward Raoul. "Name's Madigan. Lance Madigan."

Raoul knew the name, and his eyes focused on the face. "Can't be. Lance Madigan wouldn't hunt down people for money." Raoul said it coldly.

The man smiled slightly. "I didn't know who you were. Those boys," he jerked his head in the direction behind him, "hired me out of Pinedale. Said there was a federal warrant for your arrest. Even had some papers—official like—said you killed a man. Fictitious name, of course." He paused. "When you came at us back there I got suspicious. Before your horse knocked me down I got a look at you. You didn't fit the profile I was given. This is the first chance I've had to find out for myself." He lowered the gun.

"Where are they?" Raoul asked, breathing more easily.

"On a wild goose chase. They think they have you cut off. I'm supposed to be driving you down to 'em. Willing to share that meat?"

Raoul smiled. He had forgotten the jerky in his hand. He tossed a piece to Madigan, now sure the hunter meant him no harm. After jerking off a piece and chewing on it, Madigan spoke again.

"I suppose you have a plan."

"A destination. A safe place northeast of here. I think I'll have help waiting."

"My horse is just over the hill. I believe I'll ride with you. Those boys are getting on my nerves." He started to retrace his steps then turned and faced Raoul. "The only ranch I know lies over that way is the Freeman place. That'd make Senator Freeman your grandpa."

"Yessir." Raoul said.

"Freeman did a lot to keep these mountains free for hunting." He turned and walked away, then turned back again. "The storm's played out. They have a chopper. Once they find out I've deserted 'em they'll call it in. We'll have to watch our trail, keep it in the trees. I think I know a way." He disappeared in the underbrush without a sound. Raoul knew he had found a much-needed friend.

8:00 A.M.—Hoback Junction, Wyoming

Rashid shoved the last piece of Twinkie in his mouth and threw the wrapper in the garbage. He stared into the thick falling snow with a scowl on his face. Ever since coming to Jackson he had loved winter. The quiet and peace of heavy snow seemed to slow life down to a bearable pace. Now all he wanted was for it to stop, while wondering if it ever would.

And Rashid was worried. A dozen times he had tried calling his Uncle Bob without success. The line was always busy. He had tried several of Bob and Charla's closest neighbors—nothing but a busy signal, a sure sign the lines were down.

Half a dozen times between Salt Lake and the spot on which he now stood Rashid had wondered if he should call Dolph Stockman. Each time he had resisted. But now . . .

Stockman, his mother and father—all of them—would be worried, thinking he had been taken. He had to do something.

Were his father's enemies able to intercept messages? Was this a good time to call? If he kept it short, just a few words, a clue to where he was. Didn't it take time to trace a call?

Rashid turned back to the woodburning stove where Seriza sat, shoes off and feet up on a chair. It had been a long and cold trip, but she had never complained.

They ran into snow at Big Piney, but it didn't get bad until Daniel. At Bondurant and the Hoback Canyon the roads were nearly closed, the moisture-laden snow piling up deep enough that the snowplows had difficulty in shoving it aside, the winds filling it in within an hour after it had been cleared. By the time they reached the junction at Hoback they were soaked, and chilled clear through. The temperatures were above freezing, but the movement allowed the wind to freeze their blankets solid and numb their faces.

Reluctantly he had pulled in at the market. He knew the first signs of potential frostbite, and they needed to thaw out. He also knew Ben Baedecker, the owner.

The junction at Hoback was on his way home from Jackson, and each day after school he would stop in at Ben's and get a candy bar. During his high school years they had had some pretty good talks. Ben was a transplant from the East; a man tired of the big city, but with a good mind for business. He sold his home and his stock portfolio and moved west. He had been in Hoback ever since.

Rashid considered Ben a cultured man. He knew art and science and listened to Beethoven and Bach along with John Williams, Narada, and Mannheim Steamroller; but most of all he was easy to talk to. Although Rashid loved Jeremiah Daniels and they had a good father-son relationship, Ben filled in blank spots; he was a friend of a different generation with whom Rashid felt comfortable.

"Are you sure about the roads, Ben?"

Baedecker smiled as he lowered his newspaper. "I'm sure. From here to the Park they're just like this. The turnoff to Kelly is closed, and you haven't got a chance of getting to your Uncle Bob's up Slide Canyon."

Rashid sat down as Ben put the paper in front of his face again. What should he do? He really had few options. He could stay here until the roads were cleaned—or he could go back up the Hoback and to his own home. The road would be closed from the highway up the canyon, but his father had solved that problem the first winter by building a garage near the main highway and putting snow machines there. When heavy snow came they could still get in and out. Rashid and his family had been doing it for years.

"We'll go back to the house," he said to no one in particular. "When the storm blows over we'll get to Uncle Bob's."

From there, he thought to himself, I can call Stockman. On Dad's scrambled phone setup. I'll keep it short. Between that and the scrambler we should be okay.

"Suit yourself," Ben said, putting the paper aside and reaching into his Levi's pocket. "But do the little lady a favor and take my pickup. I'll stick that Corvette in my garage. I ain't going anywhere in this weather."

Rashid thanked him. He wanted to confide in Ben as to what this was all about, but he decided against it—his dad's warning was sticking to the front of his mind. It could be dangerous for Ben. That was another reason not to phone now. If they intercepted it and traced the call to Ben, they'd come here. Ben wouldn't tell them anything. They'd kill him.

How he hated that "they"!

"Thanks, Ben. I'll leave it in the garage. We'll take the snow machines into the house. You can pick the truck up when the storm breaks if I don't get it back to you before then."

Seriza grasped her shoes and started putting them on, then had second thoughts. She glanced at her still steaming, soaked coat. Dropping the shoes on the floor, she walked to a row of snowmobile gear and selected an outfit, with matching gloves and boots. Moments later she had them on.

"There," she said. "That's better." She eyed Rashid. "How about you? What're you going to wear?"

He was amazed at how good she looked even in a thickly padded snow-machine suit. "What I have will do."

"Soaked!" She threw him a hat and coat. "Get some boots. Ben, how much does all this cost?"

Rashid tossed them back to her. "I don't want 'em", he said firmly. "Thanks anyway."

She looked at him with a tilt to her head. "A proud Arab," she said a little mockingly. "Isn't that sweet. You'll be a frozen one if you don't wear something warmer. Your jacket is soaked. On a snow machine you'd be a brick of ice before you covered a hundred yards. You can pay me back later." She threw the coat back to him.

He shrugged. The girl was so much like his mother that he felt he had no choice but to do as he was told, in spite of Ben's snickers.

Twenty minutes later they were in Ben's beat-up maroon and white Dodge four-wheel drive and headed back up the Hoback. Ben's truck wasn't a real looker, but it had a great heater and an even better stereo. Seriza flipped in a disc of light classical music and laid her head against the back of the seat. Moments later she was asleep.

Rashid had to stop several times to move the heavy snow off the edges of the windshield, where it gathered, the wipers being too weak to throw the heavy stuff off to the side. It took an hour to arrive at the garage, open it, and pull the pickup inside.

Seriza woke up and stretched as Rashid slipped out of the driver's seat and flipped on a light before lowering the garage door.

She joined him as he checked each machine's gas tank and oil.

"Have you ever ridden one of these?" he asked.

She shook her head. "But it doesn't look much different than a jet ski." She pointed. "That's the gas feed, the brake, the automatic starter, and the automatic shut-off cord I wrap around my wrist."

She mounted the light single-seat Indy 680 and turned on the key, then pushed the starter button. The '95 Indy was state of the art and, even though two years old, fired easily.

Rashid locked the pickup then went to a shelf and removed a helmet, tossing it to Seriza. Picking up his own, along with an automatic garage door opener that worked both here and at the house, he straddled his machine and put on his helmet and gloves. Then he fired up the new Honda 710, which had never been on snow before. Jerry had purchased the powerful two-seater for himself and Rashid's little sister, Shai. The Indy belonged to Rashid's mom.

Moments later they moved out of the garage and Rashid stopped for a moment and pushed the switch, bringing the door down. He then flipped the face mask of his helmet in place and pushed on the gas, quickly pulling alongside Seriza.

They glanced over at one another and in mock challenge Seriza throttled the Indy. They raced up the road between snow-laden pine, the thrill of the machines and open air making Rashid smile. It was good to be headed home.

In their exhilaration neither of them noticed the indentations of other tracks, visible only in spots because of the drifting snow. It would be a mistake Rashid would regret.

CHAPTER 14

Buscetti was sitting down to an early morning breakfast when one of his bodyguards brought him the phone. It was Koln.

"How are things in America?" Buscetti asked, stirring cream into his coffee.

"I'm not on a scrambled phone, Luciano."

"I got a call from one of your people," Buscetti said, waiting for a reaction. There wasn't any. "They tell me you're not doing so good." Buscetti added, "The trap you set in Jackson Hole failed—the she-fox got away."

Koln felt his stomach churn. Somebody in his organization was talking to Buscetti. Who was it? Who knew what had happened in Jackson besides he and Colter?

Koln kept his voice calm. "I'm going to Jackson. I'll take care of it."

"They tell me your hunt didn't go well either."

Koln felt the hair on the back of his neck tingle. Only Colter and Townsend knew that. Townsend because he had been there, Colter because Koln had called him immediately after getting back from Mesa Falls. They had exchanged bad news. Townsend hadn't been near a phone. It had to be Colter.

"This is a surprise to us, Mr. K." Buscetti said. "You seem unable to fulfill your contract."

Koln gritted his teeth. Colter was covering his own tail, trying to move up in the ranks. Rolf decided Mr. Colter would have to be taught a lesson. He took a deep breath and spoke firmly, forgetting the unscrambled lines.

"Daniels's people aren't some of your second-rate drug pushers and dealers. They're professionals gone to ground in country they know better than we do. That gives them an advantage that won't be easy to overcome. Don't expect a quick fix, Luciano."

There was a pause. "Koln." The voice was like ice and made Rolf shiver. "I and the others want no excuses. You have twelve hours to complete your task, then we'll hire someone else. And Koln—don't let your daughter's involvement cloud your judgment. Finish this business. No loose ends."

Koln heard the click and hung up his receiver, then glanced at his watch. It had been three hours since he had missed Trayco at the falls, one hour since parting from Townsend and his crew, and the storm was finally dissipating. The most recent weather report said clearing skies and decreasing winds. He'd be able to get to Jackson. He climbed into the idling Bronco, where it was warm.

Twelve hours. It wasn't much time. He had tried reaching Claire but had been unsuccessful, and there were no messages on his machine. Koln felt out of touch and it made him apprehensive. Where was Claire? What had she done about Daniels? Had she completed her assignment? He thought of calling Colter but decided against it. He shook his head lightly. Erick had betrayed him. Not that in his business betrayal was uncommon. If you didn't protect yourself, you could get killed. But he and Erick Colter went back a long way, and of all the men he had ever worked with, Rolf had come to trust Colter more than any other. Obviously, that trust had been a mistake.

He shifted into four-wheel drive and headed west through Ashton's snow-filled roads, dodging plow equipment. A good sign. Plows usually didn't work unless they could see a chance of catching up.

Turning left onto the main highway, he headed for St.

Anthony, his mind going over his conversation with Buscetti. The Sicilian was worried, and with good reason. The United States was Buscetti's territory, his responsibility. The American drug trade was by far the biggest moneymaker in the Sicilian Mafia's extensive holdings, and if they lost control of it they would lose, Koln figured, as much as fifty, maybe even sixty percent of their income. That would affect business worldwide. Buscetti's head was on the chopping block.

And that was why he had threatened Koln.

Koln didn't like threats from anyone—not even Buscetti—but this one carried weight. Buscetti knew about his daughter. He knew she was with Rashid Daniels. And Colter knew it, too.

And that was the biggest reason why Erick Colter wouldn't live to see another sunrise. It was one thing to betray Rolf Koln. That was business. But when Colter involved Koln's daughter, he stepped on sacred ground. So did Buscetti.

Koln knew the Cosa Nostra. If they caught up to Rashid Daniels, Seriza would be a witness to his murder. That would force them to eliminate her. Termination of Seriza would make Koln their enemy; they knew that. As long as Rolf was alive, the Super Commission knew they would have to be watchful. He would come for them. To them this would be unacceptable. They would kill Rolf Koln. He was now expendable.

The plow in front of Koln was only going thirty-five miles an hour, the snow flying from its curved blade piling high in the gutter. The wind blew the wet substance back toward the truck then over its back, splattering it on Koln's windshield. He flipped the wiper switch to high speed, trying to clean the muddy slush off. After a few minutes of following the plow, Koln's already frazzled nerves wore thin. He pulled the Bronco a little to the left, peering around the plow. He couldn't see very well, but it looked clear. Stepping lightly on the gas, he moved into the left lane and started to pass. The plow's wheels were throwing out a good deal of snow, and a pile of it slapped on Koln's windshield, blocking his view. Until the wiper could clean it off, he ducked down to look through a hole in the mess.

A huge truck came out of nowhere, and Koln jerked right on the steering wheel. The side of the Bronco banged slightly against the front of the plow as the ten-wheel truck hugged the outside of the left lane. They would have passed with an inch to spare if Koln hadn't overadjusted, causing the Bronco to slide. The Ford slammed into the back wheels of the ten-wheeler, causing the big truck to jackknife and head for the left gutter, plowing into the three feet of snow there. When the trailer hit the snow it stuck, then flipped the entire rig on its side. It hit with enough speed to drive it through the snow clear to the fence a hundred feet away, leaving a huge trench in its wake and piling snow over its cab until it was buried.

Koln's Bronco was knocked into a spin. As the plow braked, Koln's vehicle came into its path. The plow rammed into the side of the Bronco, which flipped over, somersaulting three times down the highway before landing on its top, and slamming into the deep snow piled in the right gutter.

Koln, thankful he had fastened his seatbelt, hung onto the steering wheel while watching the world flip and turn outside the Bronco's front window. He didn't feel any pain until his head crashed into the side glass and the steering wheel crushed into his chest. The front windshield was ripped away when the last crashing turn of the Bronco slammed it upside down into the snow-covered highway. The crushed metal of the roof cut into the snow as the Bronco burrowed into the gutter with enough force to carry it forty feet into the deep snow. Koln felt the icy snow piling in on top of him, crushing him against the seat and packing in around him. He felt it fill his ears and nose as it plowed over the back seat and filled it full.

The Bronco finally jerked to a stop. Koln knew he had to get free, but couldn't move, couldn't even breathe. He tried to suck air into his lungs but was choked by the snow filling his mouth and nostrils. He tried to move his lips to spit it out, but couldn't. The muscles in his neck tensed as he tried to shake his head free and nothing happened; the cold snow was so tightly packed around him that he couldn't even flinch. He was going to suffocate!

Panic set in. Every muscle in his body jerked to be free but couldn't move. He felt his chest muscles contract as his lungs fought for air but found none. The darkness seemed to thicken, his body jerked harder, fighting for life and freedom. He heard noises outside the vehicle as blackness enveloped him. He tried to scream, but felt his strength wane, his body weaken. He fought to get control, to conserve his breath until help could reach him. It was useless. There wasn't time! They would never get to him in time.

How could this be? he thought. Not now! Seriza! He strained against the crushing snow one more time, forcing his mind to fight the blackness overwhelming it!

Seriza! he screamed in his mind. Seriza!

He felt death enter his toes, then creep slowly up his legs toward his heart. From there it spread into his arms and shoulders. Then with one blinding flash it seared into the very center of his brain—and smothered it.

CHAPTER 15

12:02 P.M.—Madison Memorial Hospital, Rexburg, Idaho

Trayco and Ruth waited near the door. When the doctor came out Kenny quit leaning on the wall and took a step in the doctor's direction, and Ruth got up from the chair. The doctor flashed a quick smile.

"They're both fine," he said. "Kate's head has always been as hard as a rock, and her son is just like her." His brow turned up. "You, on the other hand, don't look so good. Come on. I want to have that arm x-rayed." He grabbed Kenny by the elbow of his good arm and started pulling him toward the x-ray room. "Kate told me that Madison Memorial should offer you our finest care."

Ruth followed, a smirk on her face. Trayco blushed.

As they turned the corner, a nurse came jogging down the hall. "Doctor!" she called. "Another emergency. An automobile accident. They're bringing him in now and you're needed."

The doctor glanced at Trayco, then at Ruth. "Don't let him leave here until we get that arm examined," he said, raising one eyebrow.

Ruth nodded.

"Go." Trayco said. "I'll be in with Kate."

The doctor called back as he moved down the hall. "Don't be long. She needs rest."

Kenny waved him on.

Ruth glanced at the clock on the wall: nearly 9:30 mountain standard time. "I'll call Stockman and find out if anything new has happened." She started down the hall to where she knew there was a pay phone. Trayco watched her go. Ruth Macklin was quite a woman. After all she'd been through in her life he wondered how she still managed the miraculous.

He headed in the same direction as the doctor. Kate hadn't been moved from the emergency room yet and he wanted to see her before they made the change. As he moved past the nurses' station he glanced toward the paramedics pushing an occupied gurney forcefully through the emergency entrance.

Kenny stopped and watched. The man on the gurney was giving them trouble, yelling and trying to free himself. His shirt was blood red and his face was lacerated in several places; a heavy, blood-soaked bandage was around his forehead. He seemed to be in a lot of pain but he still fought to be free. He slammed his foot into a paramedic's midsection and knocked him over a wheelchair that was standing idle near the door. The medic hit the floor with a crunch. Doctor Samuels grabbed the bleeding patient's arm and yelled for more help. Trayco rushed over and had a hold of the other arm in a couple of seconds. He felt the taut strength there and was forced to exert more pressure, bending the arm backward and twisting it. A nurse with a syringe in her hand approached quickly and was about to thrust it into the fleshy part of the patient's arm.

"No! Stop!" he yelled. He quit fighting, his eyes glued to Trayco. Kenny suddenly recognized him, and twisted harder on the arm. "Ahh!" cried the patient, in pain.

"Hello, Koln!" Trayco said, revenge in his eyes as he bent the arm further back. "Shoot yourself with your own gun?"

Koln wanted to yell, but bit his tongue. Trayco pulled harder. The doctor grabbed Trayco's shoulder. "Take it easy! This man has enough wrong with him without you breaking something else. Back off. Sit down over there until—"

"No!" Koln shouted. He looked at Kenny. "We have to talk!"

Trayco grinned a mean grin. "Something go wrong in your world, Rolf? Your recent failure put you out of the good graces of your friends?" He leaned over Koln, his face inches away from him. "I wouldn't give you the time of day, and if I did, it would be to tell you to take your last breath on this earth!" He gritted his teeth. "The man you killed in L.A. was like a brother to me, Koln. I'll see you in hell for what you did to him!" Trayco turned away from Koln in disgust.

"I can help you, Trayco," Koln said. "They're after Daniels's son. He . . . he's with my daughter."

Kenny stopped in his tracks, his shoulders slumping. He took a deep breath then turned to face Koln.

"Get us a room, please, Doc. A room where you can patch up this son of Lucifer. Then we'll talk." He glanced around him, suddenly aware of the panic he was causing. "And no police, Doctor. Not yet. Okay?"

Samuels eyed Trayco, then glanced at the nurse who held a phone in her hand, her finger above a button, a quizzical look on her face.

"Lives may depend on it, Doctor Samuels," Trayco explained. "I'll tell you the whole story while you start on Koln."

Samuels nodded at the nurse. She put the phone back on its hook. He took Trayco by the arm and followed the gurney. "You mean, there's more to this than what you've already told me?"

"Lots. Some of it you don't want to hear. Some of it I can't even tell you. But that man may be able to keep a lot of people alive."

———————

Kate opened her eyes when she heard the door open. Trayco looked rough and tired, but his blue eyes still held a glow that made her flesh tingle.

"Hi."

"Hello," she said.

"Anything you need?"

She moved her head lightly from right to left. "Unless you can get me released. I hate these places."

"I know what you mean. They've taken Colt to a private room. He's asleep now."

"Is he all right?"

"He'll be seeing double for a few weeks and will have to take it easy, but he'll be okay."

"A private room? . . ."

"On the house. My treat. Not exactly the suite at Caesar's Palace, but I did notice a hot tub across the way."

"The hospital's therapy room. I'll pass, thank you." She took his hand. "How is your arm?"

"Don't pull, it might fall off." He grinned.

She laughed, but it made her head ache so she stopped. Seconds of silence slipped by. Trayco noticed how long her fingers were, and how soft. He lifted them to his lips. She touched his cheek and the electricity between them pulled them together, their lips touching gently, then more firmly. Kate placed her hand behind his neck and held him there, feeling the warmth of his mouth and face against hers. Finally he pulled away, his hand caressing her cheek and snuggling against it.

"I have to go," he whispered.

She nodded. "When will I see you again?"

"Tomorrow. The doctor says I can take you out of here at four o'clock tomorrow afternoon. I intend to hold him to it. Colt will be at least a week. They want to keep an eye on him and make sure that blow to the head didn't do any permanent damage."

She nodded.

He leaned over and gently kissed her on the forehead, letting his lips linger. She pulled him close and kissed him with the passion and love she felt. "I think I'm in love with you," she said softly in his ear. "Do you mind?"

He laughed. "I wouldn't have it any other way." He started to pull away. She reluctantly let go of his hand. Smiling, he opened the door and slipped out, leaving her to snuggle into her quilts and fall fast asleep.

Trayco saw Ruth coming toward him as he came out of Kate's room. She was pale, her countenance crestfallen.

"What's wrong, Ruth?"

"Dolph . . . just . . . Kenny . . . Jeremiah is dead."

"What?" Kenny exclaimed in disbelief.

"Danny and Jan called Dolph." She told him what Jan said she saw.

Trayco was stunned, his head spinning. His knees felt like putty and he had to sit down.

"Danny and Jan? Are they okay?"

"Jan is beside herself; Danny's trying to hold it together at safe house two. He said they'd keep working on what Jeremiah had asked of them."

"They're sure about Jerry?"

She shook her head. "The president was supposed to receive an autopsy report early this morning and let Dolph know. There's been a holdup. The body was so badly burned that they can't identify it with the usual tests. It'll be another ten hours at least." She paused. "ABC broke the news this morning. It's all over Washington. Members of Congress are already hunting heads, calling for a complete investigation."

"Investigation?"

She told him about the accusations. "Huge sums of money have turned up in Jerry's personal account. Herrera Quintana swears Jeremiah came to him with a deal. It's a mess, Kenny. The whole thing is falling apart!"

"They *believe* Herrera?!"

"Not anyone who knows Jeremiah, but the establishment . . ."

"Yeah, the politicians. Jerry said they were the ones he feared the most in all this. I thought Quintana's place was raided last night."

"It was. He's in a federal prison in Texas. The DEA has him under heavy guard."

"The Cosa Nostra got to him," Trayco said.

"His knowing that Jeremiah is the reason he just lost his entire operation doesn't help, either."

"Dolph said we hit Sicily's operations in Miami hard," Ruth added. "Warehouses, production facilities, transportation. They will lose millions."

"We have to get the evidence to the president. We have to clear Jerry's name."

"There's more, Kenny. Dolph thinks the Cosa Nostra may have the boys, at least Rashid."

"Mike."

Ruth shook her head. "She hasn't been told. No one knows where she is." She told him about the airport. "She's hiding somewhere. As soon as she calls in she'll . . . she'll be told."

"The kids?"

"Dolph will get Mike onboard as quickly as he can so she can break—" Ruth started crying. Trayco stood and took her in his arms, the hot fire of anger in his belly.

After a few minutes she wiped away the tears.

"Koln says he can get us to Rashid."

"Koln?" Ruth asked, confused.

He pulled on her arm. "Come on." He quickly filled her in on the events in the emergency room.

"We have to act quickly, Ruth. If we're going to save the rest of Jerry's family, if we're going to salvage anything of what Jeremiah started, we have to work with Koln. He may be the only way to stop all this and save Jeremiah's family." He stopped outside the door.

"Where's Thomas?" he asked.

"He's in Israel, but Dolph hasn't heard from him since last night. He's worried, but Tom told him not to expect any contact for twelve hours. He said he would be strictly incognito for at least that long in order to get Boudia out safely."

"And Gad?"

"The last we heard, Gad was moving Lima and Alvarez west. No contact since yesterday evening."

"Probably too dangerous." He glanced at his watch, wondering if Tom and Gad knew about Jeremiah. "We'll have to begin on our own. Are you okay?"

She forced a smile, while dabbing at her eyes. "I'll be fine."

He paused. "Koln says his daughter is with Rashid."

"No wonder he's so willing to cooperate."

Trayco opened the door.

Koln's broken ribs had been wrapped and he was getting stitches in his forehead and a cut just above his eye. They waited until the doctor had removed the sanitary cloth from across Koln's face and bandaged the cuts. The nurses were quick to leave. The doctor removed his plastic gloves while filling everyone in on Koln's condition.

"One rib is badly broken. Pressure in the wrong spot could drive it through a lung. No exertion allowed." He eyed Trayco. "Keep your hands to yourself, Mr. Trayco. Even a love tap could kill him." He forced a smile, then closed the door as he left.

With effort and a good deal of pain, Koln sat up.

"All right, Koln. I'm only going to ask you this once. Who hired you?"

Koln glanced toward the two of them. The hate he saw in their eyes made his chest contract. He coughed violently. The pain was excruciating. When he stopped, he was able to speak.

"Sicily. The Cosa Nostra."

"Names."

Koln returned the glare. "No names. Not yet."

Trayco took his .45 out of his pocket and placed the tip of the barrel between Koln's eyes, released the safety, then drew back the hammer.

"No names, Trayco," Koln said evenly. "Not until my daughter is safe. Then I'll help you. That information is my only assurance that you'll do as I ask."

Trayco's finger tightened on the trigger. He wanted to kill Koln more than he had ever wanted to kill anyone. But he had others to consider. He eased off, pulled the gun away, and released the hammer. Putting the safety on, he stuck the weapon back in his pocket.

"We're listening."

"Erick Colter's men are after Rashid and my daughter. If they're in Jackson Hole, he'll find them. I'm pretty sure that's where the kids were headed, or do you know something I don't?"

"We don't know where they are. We haven't heard from him since yesterday," Ruth said.

"Who's Colter?" Trayco demanded.

"He used to work for me. He works for the Sicilians now."

"What's your daughter got to do with all this?" Ruth asked.

Koln told them about Provo. "It was a coincidence that Seriza ended up with Rashid. There wasn't anything I could do about it." He paused. "I told Colter to find them, but not to harm them. I threatened him. Apparently he didn't like it, and decided to pass the information on to Sicily. He's trying to replace me." Trayco could see that Erick Colter would pay for his treason.

"Because of Seriza's involvement," Koln continued, "I've become expendable."

"Why? She doesn't know anything, does she?"

Koln laughed lightly. "Trust me. Anyone within a mile of Daniels and his family are targets—loose ends. Unless I miss my guess, Rashid has told her enough to keep my inquisitive daughter happy. Any knowledge makes her dangerous. I know how they work. They won't take any chances."

"He's right, Ruth," Trayco said. "If they find the kids, they'll have to kill them both."

"Do you think they have found Rashid and your daughter?" Ruth asked.

"Maybe. Take me to Jackson. I'll ask Colter." He paused. "Where's Mrs. Daniels?"

"Not a chance," Trayco said.

"Is she safe?"

"Yeah, she's safe, and I intend to keep it that way."

"Good, that gives us some time. As long as she's out of reach, Colter probably won't harm the kids."

"Why not?" Ruth asked.

"Leverage, Mrs. Macklin. He'll use them to get to her."

"You could lead us into a trap."

Koln smiled. "Trust me."

"Not a chance of that happening either," Trayco said, without a smile.

"Look, both our interests are served if you let me help," Koln said. "Talk to Daniels. He's smart enough to use me. It's his family. Let him decide."

"You don't know?"

"Know what?"

"Jeremiah Daniels was killed in Washington by a car bomb yesterday."

Koln's eyes went to the floor. "Claire John."

"Who?"

"Claire John. One of my people. I gave her the order."

Ruth glanced at Trayco as he reached into his coat pocket and pulled out the .45. Koln braced himself, afraid he was about to experience death for the second time in six hours.

Chapter 16

12:20 p.m.—The Daniels Ranch Southwest of Bondurant, Wyoming

Rashid couldn't believe his own stupidity. He had been so enthralled with Seriza that he hadn't been paying attention when they got to his house. Before he knew it, several automatic rifles were pointed in their direction, and they were taken prisoner.

He glanced across the room at Seriza, who was sitting with her arms folded tightly. She was tense and Rashid understood why. Before they threw her into a windowless storage room for several hours, one of the men had said something crude to her. When she slapped his face, he had to be restrained by the other two. Rashid knew what she was thinking. He was thinking it as well. He had to get them free before anything else like that happened.

She cast him a quick but forced smile. During the night they had talked of escape. Rashid knew of a way. Hidden in a false panel in the wall of the living room was a gun. If they could get to it . . .

But now Rashid had his doubts. These men were killers: careful, methodical, unpredictable.

There were four of them. Two were packing equipment into packs, preparing to leave. One was adding a little wood to the fireplace, and the fourth, the man who had approached Seriza the night before, stood behind her, a semi-automatic pistol in one hand, and an evil grin on his smug, bearded face.

Ever since they had been brought up from the storage room, Rashid and Seriza hadn't been allowed near each other. That worried Rashid. In order for a gun to be any deterrent, he needed Seriza near him and out of their reach.

He stood, walked to the TV, and turned it on, watching the midday news with feigned interest as he adjusted the volume, then started toward Seriza. When he was within a foot of her the gunman waved his weapon, pointing at the other couch with an evil smile. "Not a chance, kid," he said.

Rashid hid his disappointment with a shrug, then moved to a chair, faking concentration on the television. The words he heard on the TV struck him like a blow in the belly.

The screen showed a burned-out car against the backdrop of a building with Spanish graffiti on the walls. The newswoman from the ABC Washington affiliate was giving the latest information on a previously unidentified victim.

"Although tests have not been completed on what remained of the body, our sources indicate that the man who leased the car was drug czar, Jeremiah Daniels. The president of the United States, in his weekly press conference early this morning, eluded the questions regarding Daniels, but was visibly upset. A few moments later he ended the press conference abruptly and left the podium. Sources in the White House indicate that he has received information verifying that Daniels was the victim. At this moment we have received no official response concerning the rumor, but we understand that something will be forthcoming within the next few hours. In the meantime, Senator Cameron Ridgeway has called for a complete investigation into Daniels's alleged misconduct."

The lead kidnapper punched the Off button. Rashid fought back tears and the overpowering desire to throw up, but it was a losing battle. He jumped up and ran the short distance to the guest bath, vomiting everything he had eaten in the last twenty-four hours. The man with the gun closed the door of the bathroom, leaving Rashid alone.

Seriza was pale and sitting quietly on the couch when Rashid came out fifteen minutes later. The assailants were busying themselves again. The television was still turned off. Seriza glanced at him; concern for him showed in her eyes, but her jaw remained set by the anger she felt against their captors.

She stood and embraced Rashid. "Are you all right?"

He forced a smile. "It's wrong, Seriza. That report has to be wrong."

The man seemingly in charge finished with his pack and stood. He looked Oriental but had no accent.

"Billy," he said to the man at the fireplace, "get their gear. We need to get down to the main road to meet the chopper they're sending for us. We're supposed to be there in thirty minutes. Things are happening at the other ranch and we need to get over there for another pickup."

"Why not just have the chopper come up here?" one of the others asked.

"We can't leave the snowmobiles behind, remember? Stacy will be at the garage with the Suburban and trailer. Besides, I don't like waiting here, especially now." He glanced at the TV. "Somebody might show up."

The man named Billy left the room, returning in a few minutes with Seriza's snowmobile suit and gear. He tossed them her way without a second look and left again.

Rashid didn't know any of the men but had seen at least one of them around town. He thought the man worked at the Flying J in the summer and at one of the ski hills during the winter. A person never knew who his enemies might be or from what walk of life they would suddenly emerge.

Billy tossed Rashid's gear to him. "Put it on."

A few minutes later they were all ready. Rashid pulled his gloves on, then grasped his helmet. He felt weak and upset, his mind focused on his father. He wasn't dead. He couldn't be. Rashid shook the thought off. If his father were dead, then these men were made from the same mold and he and Seriza were in serious trouble. He had to concentrate on getting free. Using his eyes he signaled for Seriza to move toward the wall where the gun was. She got the message, moving aside as one of the men picked up a weapon and slung it over his shoulder. She was close enough. Rashid wasn't. It didn't matter, if she could get the gun . . .

"Hey, you!" The one with the gun was waving it at Seriza. "Get over here!"

Seriza glanced at Rashid. Too dangerous. He motioned with his eyes and she moved toward the man with the gun.

"Downstairs," the leader motioned. The garage was in the basement. It now housed six snowmobiles with room for another half dozen.

Rashid took a deep breath and went to the stairs between two of the men. No chance now. It would have to be on the trail. He had seen the kidnapper's machines. None of them were as powerful as the 710, two were the same size as the Indy Seriza would be riding. His knowledge of the mountains would make the difference.

He straddled the 710 as one of the men pushed a button on the garage door opener. The fiberglass door lifted to reveal nearly two feet of snow. The air was cold and crisp; the wind had turned to only a breeze and the snow had stopped falling. It had frozen during the night. The wet snow would have a crust. Better for the snowmobiles.

The leader leaned over and put his face close to Rashid's while turning off the key on the 710. "You ride with the girl. That way we won't have any trouble keeping up with you." He smiled, showing a set of perfectly white teeth between Oriental-shaped lips.

Rashid stood and went to Seriza's machine. She started to slide back when the one called Billy stopped her. "You drive," he said. Rashid sat behind her, pulling on his helmet, controlling his frustration while the other men all chuckled.

Rashid was completely surprised when Seriza suddenly hit the gas! The Indy shot across the pavement and jumped onto the snow. Rashid glanced behind him, afraid of what he would see, but no one stood with a gun ready to fire. That was good, he thought, sweat already gathering inside his helmet. Orders were to bring them in alive. But if they caught up . . .

He didn't like to think about that. He saw them scramble for their machines, the leader being the first to catapult out of the opening. Rashid caught himself hoping they'd have enough sense to close the door behind them.

"Lean!" he yelled as Seriza whipped a left onto the road. She was already extending her body into the turn, anticipating what was needed. As the machine straightened out, she gave it full throttle. A second later they were moving down the road at over forty miles per hour. By the time they hit the rise of the hill they were going nearly sixty, but the enemy was already gaining.

"A hundred yards!" Rashid yelled. "A ravine that cuts into the mountain. A trail! Take it!" He glanced behind him, then positioned himself for the turn. Seriza jammed on the brakes and jerked the handlebars to the left. The machine came up on one ski and Rashid leaned as far out as possible in hopes it would come down quickly. It did. Seriza hit the gas as he fought to right himself and keep from toppling off the seat. It took all his strength to pull himself upright and yank his head out of the way just as she zipped between two trees, deftly guiding the machine along the trail. When they hit a stretch of straight path Rashid glanced behind. He could see only three pursuers. One must have bit the dust at the corner but would probably be scrambling to catch up.

"There's a creek up ahead!" Rashid shouted. "If you go left, there is a little rise. Hit it full bore and you will clear the water easily."

She did as he instructed, and the Indy leaped two feet beyond the far shore, the heavy snow making a hard landing and jerking them both forward. Seriza's helmet hit the windshield and cracked the plexiglass. Rashid grabbed for her and felt the stiffness of her adrenaline-filled body, the muscles taut and hard as she strained to control the heavy piece of machinery. He was amazed at her strength.

As they climbed the far hill, Rashid checked the pursuit. Two hit the creek at the same time. The one following in their path flew across as they had done and kept coming, the other hit the water but still nearly made it, the skis resting on the snow-covered shore while the track began sinking through broken ice. He was out of the picture. The third followed the first and was coming fast. Still no sign of the fourth.

"At the top of the ridge turn hard right!" he said. "I mean

hard! If you don't, we'll end up at the bottom of a steep ravine—a cliff!"

He felt her nod and realized he was hanging on tightly around her waist. He loosened his grip a little. "Sorry," he said softly. He thought he heard her laugh and say something in return but didn't have time to figure it out.

Seriza jerked the handlebars right and slammed on the brakes. Rashid had prepared himself by leaning, but the jolt of the brakes threw him off balance. When she hit the gas, he lost his handhold on the rear grip and tumbled off. As she hit the brakes, he jumped to his feet and started to run after her, but heard the roar of the other machines behind him and knew it was too late. He waved her on, yelling, "Go! Go!" She hesitated.

He turned around and faced the oncoming machines. Ripping his helmet from his head he threw it at the first rider and nailed him in the plexiglass visor, unseating him. The Yamaha came straight on. Rashid tried to jump out of its way but the front of the machine kicked him in the legs and threw him to one side. As the leader hit the top of the hill, he had to turn sharply to miss hitting the other man lying stunned in the snow. It gave Rashid enough time to regain his feet, run across the few yards of ground, and throw himself into the Oriental man, knocking him from his machine and into the snow. Rashid scrambled to his feet and began running. The Chinese-American drew a pistol from his pocket as Rashid glanced over his shoulder.

"Take another step, kid, and I'll kill you!"

Rashid stopped in his tracks, his eyes meeting those of Seriza some ten feet away. "Go!" he yelled. Seriza hesitated, glanced at the gun, then throttled the machine before it was too late. Rashid watched her disappear into the trees.

Taking a deep breath, he turned around. He had caused a lot of chaos. The leader was on one knee trying to catch his breath, his machine laying on its side, and his gun leveled at Rashid's chest. The other man lay in the snow, shaking his head and trying to force himself to his feet. His Yamaha had plunged over the edge of the cliff and was gone.

The Chinese-American spoke. "It's a good thing someone wants you alive."

Rashid's face remained impassive, his eyes cold and hard. Seriza had escaped. From here on out, anything he could do to mess up their plans would just be frosting on the cake.

Mike was coming around the last sweeping corner in the road leading to her house when she heard the snowmobile scream out of the garage. She jerked left on the handlebars of the Arctic Cat and slid to a stop in the deep shadows of half a dozen well-developed pine trees. As she shut off the engine the Indy zipped past her. It was Rashid and the girl! She was reaching for the key when she heard more machines blasting down the lane in her direction. Huddling behind the black Arctic Cat and remaining motionless, she watched as they sped past her. When they were out of sight she mounted the Cat and swept into the lane, desperate for an idea of what to do.

From a hundred yards back Mike saw the Indy take a sharp turn and knew where Rashid was headed. When one of the pursuers didn't make the corner she saw her chance to help. As he scrambled to his feet, she honed in on him, throttling the Cat. At the last second he turned, looked at her, and tried to jump out of the way. The Cat's hood hit him in the legs and he flew over her head, landing with a thud behind her. She slid to a halt, turned the machine around, and returned to the corner. The man lay stunned, but she could see his chest moving. She jumped from her machine and went to him, grabbed the key, and tossed it up the hill into deep snow. Then she remounted and looked up the path the others had used. She could just see one stuck in the creek. She turned the Cat and headed down the road, knowing where they had to come out.

She covered the mile in just over a minute and turned off the road, heading up the canyon. When she reached the spot below the ridge they would come down, she parked the snow machine in the trees and took the .45 out of her pocket. She could hear the sound of a machine coming her way and was hopeful that Rashid and the girl had lost their pursuers.

The Indy came over the rise and between some trees. It only had one rider—the girl.

She put the gun away and started the Cat. Before moving it into Seriza's path, Mike removed her helmet. She didn't want the girl to panic and run.

As the Indy reached a point fifty feet away, Mike slowly moved her machine out of the trees.

The girl lowered herself in the seat, ready to throttle again.

"Wait!" Mike yelled. "I'm Rashid's mother. Stop!"

The girl hesitated, looking through the plexiglass shield of her helmet with fear in her eyes. When she saw Mike's face, her body went limp and she began to sob.

Mike jumped from her machine and ran the few feet between them as Seriza let go of the handlebars and removed her helmet.

"I . . . Rashid . . . They caught him. He kept them . . ." She sobbed. "Oh, Mrs. Daniels. They have him, and it's all my fault."

Mike moved the Indy off the path and hid it in the trees, removing the key. The girl was in no shape to drive and they needed to get away quickly. The Cat was bigger and more powerful. Both of them could ride it without power loss.

Mike's heart ached. Rashid was trapped, and there wasn't a thing she could do about it. The kidnappers had weapons. She had seen semi-automatics along with handguns. All she would succeed in doing was getting them all trapped—or killed.

She put on her helmet as she heard engines back on the road. The enemy had stopped at the head of the canyon. At least some of them would be sent this way. They had to be.

Seconds seemed like hours. She needed to get away. There was still Raoul. But starting the engine would give away her position. She had to wait. If she heard machines coming up the canyon, she could go into the mountains, but with their weapons . . .

Seriza was under control now, and for that Mike was grateful. She seemed like a strong girl, but the chase had been a bit much. Mike understood.

The motors seemed to be moving away. She had disabled one of the four and the other was in the creek. Had they gotten it out? Were there three machines, or two moving toward the main road? She couldn't tell for sure, but she thought there were three. Had they gotten the one free of the water? Or had they hot-wired the one without a key?

She wanted to move but something made her hesitate. The quiet. It was too quiet. Were they gone? Or had they left someone at the head of the canyon, just waiting for her to start the Cat's motor and give their position away?

Long minutes passed and the other snowmobiles' noise diminished until it was nearly gone. She reached for the key, but Seriza grabbed her arm.

Between the branches of the tree in front of them, Mike saw a man walking up the path, a weapon in his hand. Carefully she removed the .45 from her pocket. He stood there looking up the canyon, his eyes following the track Mike's Cat had made. His stare seemed to catch at the spot where the two machines had come together, trying to figure out what had taken place, then his eyes moved further upward, following the track Seriza had made coming down. He hesitated. Mike raised the pistol and braced it with both hands on the grip, her eye moving to sight down the smooth barrel, sweat gathering on her brow. She couldn't let him get much closer.

Then she saw the other one.

"Hey! Come on! They're long gone! We'll miss the chopper! We got the kid! Come on!" The second man turned back, moving quickly downhill. The first glanced their way once more, his eyes focusing for a brief second on the trees in which they were hidden. Mike held her breath, her finger slipping to the safety and releasing it.

He turned and started to walk away. "All right, all right! I'm coming!"

Mike put the safety back on and let the air out of her lungs slowly. Seriza started breathing again, small billows of steam forming around her pretty face. After a moment Mike spoke.

"You're Seriza Maxwell. I've heard a little about what you've been up to the last few days. Thanks for saving my son's life in Provo."

"You're welcome," Seriza whispered, smiling. "How did you know where we were?"

"I called someone and found out Rashid had disappeared. I figured this might be the place to look. I was just coming up the road when I saw the two of you take off on the snowmobile."

Just then Mike heard the other snow machines start, then move down the road toward the highway. A few minutes later the sound was gone.

She removed her helmet and mussed her damp hair as she swung a leg over the seat in front of her and stood. Her legs felt cold and stiff, even though she was now dressed in her own dark blue snow-machine suit, acquired earlier from the garage.

"What about Rashid? We have to . . ."

Mike shook her head. "They have semi-automatic weapons. I have a .45 and one clip."

Seriza wondered if Mrs. Daniels had heard the news. She didn't act like it, but surely . . .

"It looks like someone decided to join you," Mike said. "Who were they?"

"Beats me. Maybe friends of my father," Seriza said stiffly.

"Ummm. Joseph Maxwell, CIA agent." Mike forced a smile. How did you tell a girl that her father's friends would kill her? You didn't. "I don't think they belonged to your dad . . . Come on. I think it's safe now. I have another son. We have to find him before they—"

Suddenly Seriza remembered. "They said something about a chopper and another ranch. They had a pickup at the other ranch."

Mike looked at the girl's frightened eyes and saw the reflection of her own in them. The kidnappers were going to Bob's place. Raoul must have gone there.

She took the Indy key from her pocket and handed it to Seriza. "We have to hurry. Are you okay?"

Seriza nodded.

As Mike lifted her helmet a sound stopped her cold. It was the distant thump-thump of chopper blades. The chopper would reach the other ranch before she could do anything. She scolded the phone company under her breath, then the storm. She had tried hundreds of times to call Bob's place, but the lines were down. Renting a four-wheel drive, she had even tried to drive in, only to be greeted by a road filled with four-foot drifts. She had comforted herself that no one else could get in either. At least not until the storm broke.

And the storm *had* broken.

She put on the helmet and jumped on the Cat. Minutes later they were in the basement of her own home. It had never felt so cold and lonely before. Fear sat in her stomach like cold oatmeal. She had lost. The boys were trapped.

She dialed a number, hoping the lines to Bob's house would finally ring through, that somehow the phone company had made the repairs.

Her heart sank as the sound of the continuous busy signal buzzed loudly in her ear.

Raoul watched through the window while he removed his coat and gloves. He could see the pursuers forcing their animals through the heavy snow about a half mile from the house. They didn't have much time.

"Uncle Bob must have been trapped in town," Raoul said.

"Uh-uh," Madigan said from near the back door. "Look."

Raoul moved to the door and stared through the window. Bob was coming quickly through the snow toward the house. As he got to the door, Raoul opened it and let him in. Bob grabbed his hand then hugged him. "Good to see you, kid." He glanced toward Madigan. "Lance," he said, "how did you—"

"Later, Bob. We've got company."

"I noticed." He moved to the side window. "Four of them. That shouldn't be hard."

"Where are Aunt Charla and the kids?" Raoul asked.

"In the barn keeping their heads down."

Madigan picked up his rifle and injected a shell. "I'll—"

"What's that?" Raoul asked, tilting his head to hear better.

Bob swore, his head lowering so he could see more sky from the window. "A chopper. They've got help coming in."

"Get your family in here, Bob," Lance suggested. "The log walls of this place—"

"Take a look." Bob pointed out the window.

Madigan moved to the window. The chopper was hovering above the pasture a hundred yards away. "An Eagle? Where did they get a chopper with missiles?"

Raoul looked, too, remembering the choppers his father had shown him in the hangar at the airport. The enemy had them now.

"Any suggestions?" Bob asked.

Raoul felt sick inside. He should have stayed in the

mountains, away from the ranch. Now Bob and the others were in danger.

"Yeah, I've got a suggestion," Raoul said, forcing a smile. "It's time we said uncle."

"Give up?" Madigan asked.

"If we do, they'll take us out of here quickly," Raoul said. "If we don't, they'll stay, and probably search the place."

"We can protect Charla and the kids by surrendering," Bob agreed.

Madigan leaned against the counter, staring at the chopper. It was landing. A man jumped out and was joined by the riders. They were gesturing toward the house.

"I see what you mean," Madigan conceded.

The man returned to the chopper and pulled someone out.

"Who's that?" Madigan asked.

Raoul and Bob both looked.

"My brother," Raoul said, disheartened. He glanced at Bob, then walked toward the door.

He should have stayed in the mountains.

As the last thump-thump sound disappeared into the storm, Charla released the catch on the hidden door and tried to lift it upward. It wouldn't budge.

"Randy, get over," she yelled. "Come on, boy, get over." She pushed upward as she tried to vocally entice the old workhorse to move off the heavy trapdoor. "Come on, Randy!" She felt the door give a little as the thud of hooves sounded on the wood. "That's it, boy, Get over." Finally she was able to lift the door.

Charla peered into the dim light. She could see Randy's large hooves and the slab-wood partition between stalls. She listened carefully.

"Mom, can you see anything?"

Charla glanced back at the twins, their frightened eyes catching a little of the light coming through the small opening of the door. "Shh, stay here," she whispered.

She lifted the door some more and slipped her lithe body free, Randy stamping his hooves and moving further away.

She let her hand run over his rump and withers as she moved toward the gate. Peering through the cracks, she did a quick once over. Nothing. But there were so many dark corners.

There were a dozen other horses in stalls on both sides of the main walkway that extended the length of the barn. Their pickup was parked in the middle at one end.

She waited, listening. The trapdoor lifted ever so slightly.

"Mom?" came the whisper.

She lifted up the door and let the boys out, putting a finger to her lips.

Bob, Charla, and the two boys had been in the barn feeding the stock when one of the boys had noticed two horsemen approaching the house. Bob had recognized Raoul's bay, but the other man had his rifle drawn and resting across his lap. Raoul looked as if he were a prisoner.

Seeing to his family first, Bob had hid the boys in the cellar made just for such an occasion, and let a little time pass before he and Charla went to check things out. Raoul and his apparent captor had gone in the house, their horses tied in the shelter of some trees near the bunkhouse.

Having taken his rifle from its perch behind the pickup seat, he was in the process of loading it and watching the house through a crack in the door, when he saw the other four riders. Convinced the man with Raoul wasn't the enemy and that the new riders were, Bob left the gun with Charla and ran for the house.

After Bob left, Charla moved to a perch in the hayloft, where she could see better, while she waited she heard the chopper.

Cocking her rifle, she opened the high loft door at the south end of the barn, and drew a bead on one of the riders as the chopper hovered over the south pasture, its missiles pointed menacingly at her home. She placed the scope on the pilot's forehead and released the safety.

But there had been no gunfight. When the chopper landed, a man jumped out and joined the riders. A minute later he had returned to the chopper, opened the door, and pulled Rashid into the open, putting a gun to his head. Moments later Bob and the others were walking out of the house with their hands on their heads.

Charla wanted to do something, but every avenue was closed. When the men had begun moving toward the outer buildings and searching them, she had returned to her two sons. When men had come into the barn, she had almost stopped breathing, only to start again when she had heard the barn door close as the searchers left.

Now the chopper was gone.

She pulled the wool collar of her jacket up around her neck and ears as she peered through a crack in the door facing the house. The four riders were inside. They had searched the place and apparently were satisfied that Bob had been alone.

Charla left the boys to watch, and went to the pickup. With the storm breaking, maybe she could get through on the CB. She had no luck. The pickup was used for hauling some of their prize stallions long distances for stud purposes and for sales, and the CB came in handy under those conditions. But here in the mountains it had never been very useful.

"Mom! One of the . . ." The boy started running toward her. "He's coming this way. With the horses!"

Charla shut the pickup door quietly and they started toward Randy's stall. Where was the other twin?

"James!" she whispered. "James, where are you?"

She heard a noise in the loft and saw the other boy as Jack started down the ladder into the hole. She waved frantically and James started to move across the piled-up hay, his eyes as big as silver dollars.

There was a noise at the door. Charla looked at Jack and told him to close the door. He hesitated. She signaled forcefully with her hand and the trapdoor went down. She closed Randy's gate while signaling to James to dig into the hay. As the door started to open she threw herself behind a stack of baled hay near the third stall in the row.

The man pushed on one of the large doors until he had opened it enough to bring in the horses two at a time. After closing the door, he began unsaddling the first horse. When he was finished, he took a cloth and rubbed her down, led her in the first stall, removed the bridle, and placed it on a nail on one of the beam supports.

Charla watched as he went through the same routine for each of the other three horses. When he was finished, he took a pitchfork and forked what little fresh hay there was on the floor into the feeding trough.

"Not enough," he said aloud. Glancing around, he saw

the bales of hay. Charla's breath caught in her lungs. If only she had the rifle, but she had left it in the seat of the pickup. She crouched lower, trying to burrow deeper into the small space between bales. If he—

"Well, looky here," he said. Charla glanced up at him, then started to stand as he reached for his pistol.

Thunk! A bale of hay crashed into his head and he went down. Charla scrambled for the gun as it hit the wooden floor, then pointed it at a spot between the man's closed eyes. He didn't move. She stood, keeping the gun in position while looking up at the loft. James stood there, his eyes wide and his face pale.

"Is he dead?" he asked.

"No, but you certainly knocked him out. Thanks."

The boy took a quick breath, then smiled.

Jack pushed up on the trapdoor, saw what was happening, and came out.

"Come on down, James," she said, pulling some twine from a nail. When he arrived by her side, she handed him the pistol. "Hold that while I tie this guy up." She stooped, found his hands and began wrapping them in the twine as he started coming to. Pulling a hanky from her pocket, she turned him over and jammed it in his mouth, then dragged him into an empty stall, where she tied his feet together. She was glad she had put the cloth in his mouth. What she could make out of his muffled words was not fit for her boys' ears. She wondered how long it would be before the others in the house became nervous and came looking.

James joined them. "Sorry, Mom."

Charla rubbed the back of his neck and smiled. "It's okay." She paused. "We have to leave. We'll use snowmobiles."

They ran toward the doors, opened one slightly, and peered out. Charla knew they couldn't be seen from the kitchen and hoped that was where the others were, feeding their faces on Freeman food.

She glanced at the equipment shed. Two hundred feet. "Did you leave the keys in the machines last time you used them?" she asked.

Jack looked sheepish. They had been told to bring the keys in the house. "Yes," he admitted. She smiled, glad for once that they had forgotten.

"All right. The two of you take your dad's; it's the fastest.

Jack, you drive, and stay close to me, understand?" They nodded, their eyes big. "We'll go to Kelly to Mr. Eames's house." They nodded again. They knew Eames. He worked on the ranch in the summer and was a good hand.

She took a deep breath, eyed the house, eyed the equipment shed, then eyed the house again.

She pushed open the door. "Go! Run!"

The boys ran as quickly as they could, the heavy snow grabbing at their boots and legs clear up to their knees. Charla was grateful Bob had been to the shed that morning and gassed the machines.

She glanced over her shoulder as she ran, watching the door, praying they wouldn't be seen. She stumbled, falling on her face in the snow. James stopped and helped her to her feet. She brushed the snow from her eyes with a gloved hand as she motioned him on, stumbling by his side.

Two men came running down the steps of the house, yelling and pointing. "Hurry!" she said to the boys, as she glanced over her shoulder. One of the men raised a gun and Charla felt sick, her stomach in her chest, her lungs unable to take in air. As James reached a machine and flipped on the key, Charla saw another man deflect the first man's gun just as he fired. She fell again, then stumbled toward her own machine. James hit the auto start on the big 650 and it erupted into a roar. The men were running now, the third coming down the steps. They were blocking the road.

Charla pulled the primer button and turned the key. The new Yamaha Stinger roared to life. She pushed on the throttle, letting it smooth out as her brain flashed across her options. Run for the hills or take them on? Either way they'd be sitting ducks. She looked at the boys; their faces were pale, eyes wide. "Just follow me," she instructed as she throttled the Stinger and it jumped from the cover of the shed. Whipping it to the right, she drove it directly toward the two men.

They stopped in their tracks, shocked looks crossing their faces as the Yamaha bore down on them. The man with the rifle dived to the left, the other to the right. Charla aimed the Yamaha at the third, who turned and ran. At the last second, she swerved slightly right and headed up the road, the boys close behind her.

Charla glanced over her shoulder. The men were scrambling to their feet, their hands wiping the snow from their faces. They stood helpless as the snowmobiles dashed up the lane and onto the main road. As they topped a hill and started down the far side, Charla took one last look at her house, wondering if she'd ever see it again.

Chapter 17

1:00 p.m.—Jackson, Wyoming

Claire John lit her cigarette and inhaled deeply. The news had been both good and bad when she arrived at the rented condo in Jackson two hours ago. According to Colter, Israel had been an explosive success, Boudia and Colonel Thomas Macklin having been eliminated along with half a dozen other support personnel.

And Colter's men had the czar's boys. Chong had been careless letting the girl and whoever aided her get away, but at least they had hostages—the key to flushing the rest of the enemy into the open.

She was still waiting to hear from Miami, but was sure the news would be good.

Daniels, however, had struck from the grave. Herrera Quintana's operation in Bogota was in the same boat as Alvarez's—a shambles—and Quintana was in a military prison in Texas. Lima's warehouses had been hit, and they had lost nearly twenty tons of high-grade cocaine to the feds, completely drying up their supplies in the southeast and severely hampering their ability to provide anything to the crippled West Coast.

Her only solace was that Daniels wouldn't be planning any further assaults on their business. She smiled. The man had come close. Very close. Even now it would take years to rebuild and resolidify their position. Already free-lancers were cropping up all over the place, and if SCORPION had to spend all their manpower on Daniels's team much longer, they would have to deal with complete anarchy.

Claire glanced at her watch. Where the devil was Koln? No one had heard from him for over four hours. What was he doing? She picked up the TV remote and punched the power button. A special report was being broadcast.

"Informed sources say that Daniels was using his office to eliminate competition in an effort to control the drug trade in this country. From his prison cell in Texas, Herrera Quintana has told ABC news that he had made a deal with Daniels in which Daniels had promised him, 'twenty tons of cocaine business in the western United States' on condition that Quintana help him eliminate competition. Quintana refused, and states that the raid last night on his compound in Bogota 'was Daniels's way of sending a message.'"

The screen showed Quintana being taken from a military vehicle by two soldiers and shoved toward the entrance of a holding facility. "The Colombian drug runner was further quoted as saying, and I quote, 'Daniels is dead because he got greedy.'"

The screen changed scenes back to the reporter. "Senator Cameron Ridgeway, commenting on the allegations against Daniels, said that the Senate would make every effort to find out if they were true, but that Mr. Daniels had an unsullied background and he found the allegations hard to believe."

Claire smiled. Ridgeway was the premier politician. He'd investigate Jeremiah Daniels, all right, but only so he could smear the president. When this was over Seth Adams would be destroyed, and Cameron Ridgeway would be the all-American boy who kept the country safe from corruption at the highest level.

When the anchorwoman came back on the screen, Claire John shut the TV off, then walked to the door of her bedroom and exited down the hall. They couldn't wait for Koln any longer. Now dressed in thermal underwear, jeans, wool shirt, and sweater, she was ready to get on with the business at hand.

Her fur-lined, rubber-soled boots squeaked as she crossed the marble foyer and walked into the living area, where Colter waited with Chong and two others. Claire John had a dark complexion with Sophia Loren good looks and a stunning figure that was seductive even when covered by a sweater. She smiled inwardly as the men all turned and stared. She walked to the bar and poured herself a glass of orange juice. Claire was used to such appraisals and used them to her advantage. There were few men around that could resist doing what she asked of them.

She gave them a smile, then sipped her drink. Colter had filled her in during their drive from the airport, but she still had several unanswered questions. Before she would get to them, she had a few things to say. She wanted no misunderstandings about who was in charge.

"We can't wait for Koln any longer," she stated. "It's apparent something's gone wrong and we need to get this business finished. There will be a twenty-percent bonus for everyone if we're out of here by morning." She smiled as each glanced at the others. Chong was the only one who didn't seem to accept the news with relish. Her previous tongue-lashing had damaged his ego.

"Koln won't like it," Chong said. "I don't like it."

"Let me handle Koln," Claire said.

"He won't like you taking over. You don't know what's going on here."

Erick Colter started to say something, but Claire lifted her hand and prevented him, her dark eyes glaring at Chong.

"Mr. Chong, I suggest you bite your tongue." She paused. "Next time I'll have it cut out."

Chong glanced at Colter, looking for support.

"I told you," Colter said, "SCORPION wants her in charge. You'd better do as you're told."

Chong felt the sweat gather on his forehead. He took a step and sat on a bar stool, downing his drink with a scowl.

"Where are the hostages?"

"Next condo, under heavy guard," Colter answered.

"I want them moved to a place that's inaccessible. Any suggestions?"

The four looked at one another. "There's a summer home, up Cache Creek a ways," said one of the local men. "Inaccessible this time of year, especially with the storm and all. We could take them up by chopper."

Claire gave him a smile that made him blush. "Excellent." She turned to Chong and spoke in a forgiving tone. "Move them there as soon as we're finished here."

"Anything from the pilot you captured at the airport?" she asked Colter.

Colter grinned like a kid who had lollipops for the whole class. "He says there is a yacht on Yellowstone Lake."

Claire smiled. "What does he say about defenses?"

"A single missile could sink it."

"I want it taken intact."

Colter had known she would want a plan of operation. He had one prepared. He cleared his throat, then began outlining his plan of attack. When he was finished, he could tell she was pleased.

"It will work. Do you have the equipment we need?"

"It arrived early this morning. I'll take care of it."

"Is Michaelene Daniels aboard the yacht?"

"I . . . I don't think so. She can't get in there without a chopper. We've been watching the private plane rental places and the airport. No flights have gone that way and all the roads are blocked by drifted snow. They won't open them again until spring."

She turned to Chong. "What about Koln's daughter and this mystery person who helped her get away?"

Chong looked away. Earlier Claire had berated him heavily for the way he had handled things in the canyon and ordered him to send men back. He had, reluctantly, swearing he'd bury Claire because of her humiliation of him. "Nothing. I sent two men. The tracks . . ."

Claire glared at Chong. "Colter. What about your man at the sheriff's office? Has the girl and her mysterious friend contacted the authorities?"

"No. He'll let us know if they do."

Claire was still drilling a hole in Chong's forehead with her stare.

"My . . ." Chong's mouth felt dry. "My men found some fresh tracks. They leave the house and go further into the hills. Two snowmobiles. We . . . my men are following . . ."

Claire's stare was filled with ice. "Did it occur to you that the second person might be Michaelene Daniels?"

Chong gulped. It had occurred to him. The man who had been knocked from his snowmobile had thought things through better after Chong had pistol whipped him out of anger and humiliation from Claire's tongue-lashing. "Yeah," he said, downing the last of the whiskey in his glass. "It occurred."

"Your incompetence astounds me, Chong, but I'm going to give you one last chance. You find that girl and whoever is with her, and you kill them."

She turned the cold stare on Colter. "By noon I want an assault team prepared for a briefing. We board that yacht no later than three o'clock this afternoon." She riveted her stare on Chong again. "Koln's daughter and her mystery helper

had better be dead and buried by then, or I'll kill you myself."
She turned back to Erick. "Until we know for sure that Mrs.
Daniels is either aboard the yacht or with Koln's daughter,
keep the hostages alive. After that, kill them."

She started toward the door, then turned back. "We
could blow that yacht to pieces and be done with it, but we
know that Daniels has evidence and records from our operation. They are probably on board, but I have to make sure of
that before we destroy it."

She turned and walked away.

Chong poured himself another whiskey and downed it,
anger making his temperature rise and his face turn red. "I'm
going to kill that woman," he said through clenched teeth.

Colter laughed at him. "Yeah, Chong, sure you are."

Chong jerked around and took a threatening step toward
Colter.

"Back off, Charlie," Colter said, filling his glass without
even turning toward Chong. "Or I'll kill you myself." He
turned. "Koln is out. That's SCORPION's decision. When Koln
shows up, there is a two hundred and fifty thousand dollar
reward for his body."

Chong stopped in his tracks. "What?"

"That's right, Chong. Koln crossed SCORPION. We're
under new leadership now."

"But why the woman? She ain't one of us. She hasn't
been around long enough to learn how we do things. She'll
get us all killed. You should . . ."

"It's just temporary—it's the way SCORPION wants it. If
you want to go against that, it's your funeral."

Colter was lying and knew it. He hadn't talked to SCOR-
PION. He and Claire had made the decision on their own.
Actually, Claire had decided. Colter had agreed when she
promised him Koln's job with less work and more pay for his
support. Claire was a driven woman, a beautiful one. Colter
felt there was more than money in his future with Claire
John.

"Use the Eagle we confiscated from Daniels's hangar, and
take the hostages up Cache Creek." He sipped his drink. "Do
you have contact with the men you sent back after Koln's
daughter?"

"Yeah." Chong looked away. "They followed the tracks
into the hills behind Daniels's ranch. I expect to hear from
them in the next hour."

"You'd better pray for good news."

Chong sat his glass on the counter, nodding toward the other two men in the room. It was time to leave.

"Get rid of the girl and whoever is with her," Colter said. "And, Chong, believe it when Claire tells you she'll kill you. She's better at it than anyone in this room."

Chong zipped up his ski coat and moved to the door. When it was shut behind him, Colter lifted the glass to his lips and downed the last of his drink. It was going to be a pleasure to kill Chong when this was finished. The man was an idiot.

———————

Koln pointed. "That's Chong."

Ruth and Trayco peered over the bank of snow where they were hidden and watched as three men walked from one condo to another. When the men disappeared from view, Ruth spoke.

"Which one do you think they're keeping the hostages in?"

"The one they just entered," Koln said. He was pale, the sharp pain in his chest constant, nearly unbearable.

"Are you all right?" Ruth asked.

"I'll make it."

"Are you sure?"

Koln nodded. Trayco eyed him, ignoring the outward signs. "Leave him be, Ruth. He's all right."

"But . . ."

"Leave him be," Trayco said firmly.

Ruth wanted to say something but bit her tongue. She felt the same disgust for Koln as Trayco did, but she had learned long ago that you couldn't let other people determine your own humanity.

"They're coming out," Koln said.

"How many?" Ruth asked.

"Ten. Maybe five or six with guns, the rest are hostages," Trayco said, the binoculars to his eyes.

"Is my daughter one of them?"

"I can't tell, Koln," Trayco said. "The parkas . . . and they have their backs to us."

"They're moving them to a safer place." Koln forced himself away from the ridge of piled-up snow, grabbing his chest as he stooped and moved toward their rented Suburban. "Come on. We'll have to follow."

The others joined him and were waiting with the engine running as Chong drove the panel van into the street and headed toward the main highway. Five minutes later they turned down a side road, went a mile and pulled over. Trayco turned the Suburban into a private drive with snow piled high to the side of the house, blocking their view but making it impossible for their presence to be detected. Ruth hopped from the vehicle and positioned herself to watch the van. They all heard the chopper coming.

Trayco and Koln joined her as the hostages were led from the van into the open field.

"One of our Eagles," Trayco noted, as the helicopter lowered itself into the field.

All but one man boarded the chopper, and the Eagle lifted off, swinging northeast toward Jackson. The single man started for the van.

"Ruth, when he gets to this spot, block the road with the Suburban. I'll do the rest. Koln, stay put."

Two minutes later Trayco had his .45 placed against the skull of the van's driver.

"Out," he ordered. "And keep your hands where I can see them."

Trayco opened the door.

"What do you want?" the man said, sliding from the seat.

Koln stepped into view. "Hello, Jackman."

Jackman's eyes widened.

"Surprised?" Koln asked.

"Yeah . . . uh . . . Colter . . ."

"You shouldn't trust Colter, Jackman. He'd sell his own mother for a nickel."

"How many hostages?" Trayco asked.

Jackman hesitated. Trayco released the safety and pulled back the hammer.

"Four," Jackman rushed to answer. "Daniels's boys, Bob Freeman, and a guy named Madigan."

"Where's my daughter?" Koln asked.

"I had nothing to do with that, Koln . . . I . . ."

"Where?" Koln said through clenched teeth.

"She . . . she got away. That's all I know. Honest! That's all."

"Where's Chong headed?" Koln asked, his expression never changing.

Jackman was visibly shaken and turning pale, his eyes dull with fear. "He'll kill me, Koln."

Koln's eyes were hard, his face a mask of death. He stepped forward and took Trayco's .45, shoving it under Jackman's chin hard enough to break the skin. "Don't push me, Jackman. I haven't killed anybody in the last twenty-four hours and I'm starting to miss it."

"Cache Creek," Jackman said, his chin shoved high, his eyes looking downward at Koln's trigger finger. "A place . . . up Cache Creek. He'll keep the hostages there until . . ." His voice trailed off, his eyes darting from one face to another.

Koln released his finger and handed Trayco the gun, then walked to the Suburban, opened the door, and slid in. The pain was nearly unbearable and he felt short of breath, exhausted, afraid he was about to pass out. Sitting down seemed to help.

Trayco put the gun in his pocket, turned Jackman around to face him, then swung with his good arm, his fist knocking Jackman's chin violently upward. The man collapsed and Trayco caught him over one shoulder, lifted him and tossed him in the back of the Suburban after Ruth opened the door.

"I'll tie him up," Trayco said. "You drive."

As she pulled back on the road, Ruth asked a question. "Do you know the place he's talking about?"

Koln shook his head.

Trayco climbed over the seats to the front, opened the jockey box, and pulled out a local map. "Here it is. Cache Creek. On the edge of Snow King ski resort."

"We have to contact the sheriff's office," Ruth said.

"Not yet," Koln said.

"But . . ."

"Colter told me he had a contact in the sheriff's department. Until we're finished with this, it's too risky."

"Can we get a chopper?" Koln asked Trayco.

"You're out of this, Koln. Your daughter's safe."

"Not by a long shot. She knows too much and can finger Chong. He has to kill her. We have to get to him first. I'm in until then."

They were all silent.

"You didn't answer my question. Can we get a chopper?"

"No. They have ours, and are probably watching the rental places." Trayco paused. "But I have an idea. Ruth, get to a phone. We have to call Stockman and find out where Charla Freeman is. She can get us to that cabin."

2:00 P.M.—Cache Creek

Chong paced the floor. His men still hadn't found the girl. Whoever was helping her knew the mountains and how to use them to the best advantage. At first the trail left by the two snowmobiles was easy to follow, the deep tracks leading his men deeper into the Hoback country behind Daniels's ranch. But then the trail had plummeted into a canyon that led to the main road, which had recently been cleaned out by snowplows. There they had lost the trail. They had searched for several miles in both directions but still hadn't come up with the direction the girl was taken by her partner. Chong could only wait.

"Stacy," he said to one of his men, "go to the shed and get some more wood for the fire. Billy, see if you can scrounge up some food."

"Planning to stay a while?" Bob Freeman asked from the couch, where he and the others sat shoulder to shoulder, their hands tied behind them. Chong only smiled, then lifted the two-way radio to his lips.

"Eagle, this is Chong. Where are you?"

"Overhead at about 11,000 feet. I'm getting low on fuel."

"What do you see?"

"Not much. Clouds are moving in. I could see the lift at the top of Snow King a few minutes ago, but not now."

Chong glanced out the window. "Yeah, it's starting to snow down here." He hesitated, thinking. "Go back to the airport and top off your tanks, but stay close to your radio." He lifted his finger from the send button.

"Roger," the Eagle's pilot answered. "It takes about five minutes. I'll be ready when you call."

Chong paced again, cursing the weather. If another storm hit they'd be trapped up here. He'd better let Colter know. He switched frequencies and pushed on the button to transmit, then thought better of it. He was in enough trouble as it was. If there were going to be more nails in his coffin, someone else was going to have to put them there.

The voice on the radio startled him. "Chong, this is Colter." Chong swore.

"Yeah."

"A change of plans. We're headed north in a couple of hours. What's your status?"

"We'll be busy. Better not plan on us."

"Roger."

The radio clicked off, and Chong took a deep breath. The key to saving his own neck was to get the girl. Given enough time, he'd accomplish it. He was glad not to have more pressures. He had four men with him. When the girl was found, he'd take two and leave two with the hostages. That should be enough, and still leave Colter plenty for the assault at Yellowstone.

Stacy was putting the last of his logs on the fireplace. It was getting warm, so Chong removed his parka, revealing his holstered Beretta.

Rashid glanced at it, wondering how long it would be before he'd be staring down its barrel and taking his last breath. He looked over at Raoul and the others. He knew that each was working just as hard as he was on their ropes, but that none of them had made much progress. Only his hands were free.

Mike threw another log on the flames, then stood back and watched it catch fire. Seriza was filling a bucket with snow so they could melt it and have drinking water and a little something to wash up with.

After calling Dolph from the house, they had grabbed a few food items, locked up, and headed for the line shack in Lightning Canyon. Few people knew about the place, and Mike knew they would be safe until Stockman could send a chopper for them.

Dolph had told her about Jeremiah. She hadn't accepted

it; she was convinced he had survived somehow and was alive, but in hiding. He just had to be. She knew she couldn't live without him.

During the trip to the cabin, however, hope had died as reality set in. Jeremiah wasn't one to leave her in the dark. If he were alive, somehow, someway, he would have let her know. Her mind knew it. It was her heart that struggled, refusing to let go of the thin strand of hope that kept her from falling off the edge of emotional collapse. A trip she couldn't afford to take right now.

She glanced at her watch. Another hour and they'd have transportation to the *ISSA*. Maybe Stockman had heard something new on Jeremiah. Maybe.

The storm was gone. There was only a slight breeze in the trees surrounding the shack and it was peaceful, the three feet of glistening snow muffling every sound around them.

She went to the window to look for Seriza. The girl stood on the covered porch, the bucket packed full of snow. Her eyes were riveted on an animal feeding no more than fifty feet away—a huge moose with horns that spanned six feet. It was a tranquil scene. If the world hadn't been disintegrating around her, Mike might have been able to enjoy it.

She returned to the fire, warming herself. Seriza came in and closed the door. Mike took the bucket from her and hung it on a hook inside the stone fireplace wall, the heat immediately beginning to melt the snow.

"Did you see him?" Seriza said with a smile.

"Yeah, he's a big one." Moving toward the small kitchen area, Mike asked, "Are you hungry?"

"Famished," Seriza said, following her.

"Breakfast okay?"

Seriza nodded. "Great!"

As they fixed some eggs, bacon, and hash browns on the propane stove, they talked. Mike explained everything to Seriza, then apologized that she ended up involved.

Seriza shrugged. "My father . . . he isn't really with the CIA, is he?"

"I don't know, Seriza. When the dust clears, maybe we can find out. Right now, we just trust the people we know are on our side, and try to stay out of the hands of the enemy. They have enough bargaining chips as it is."

Moments of silence passed. Seriza tried to fill them.

"I wish I knew Rashid was all right."

"He'll be okay. They all will." Mike forced a smile. She knew what was coming. The enemy intended to use her boys to blackmail her into the open and give up the substantial amount of evidence they had gleaned. She would have to fight them. The Cosa Nostra wasn't about to leave anyone alive, that was evident. She must fight for every minute of life now. She must fight to keep her family alive.

Seriza glanced at the guns leaning against the wall. They had brought them from a secret gun cabinet in the house. Mike saw her concern.

"Don't worry, we won't have to use them. A friend is sending someone for us before long, and we'll be in a safe place."

Seriza smiled wanly. "It's a very funny feeling to have people chasing you, wanting to hurt, even kill you."

Mike smiled as she added salt and pepper to the eggs.

They sat at the bar. "You've been through a lot haven't you," Seriza said, as she took a piece of bacon in her hand.

Mike laughed lightly. "Trouble hovers around the head of Jeremiah Daniels like clouds do around the Tetons. It comes and it goes." She smiled. "But either way the view is magnificent."

They ate for a minute without speaking. Seriza finished her first piece of bacon and picked up her fork before Mike spoke again.

"He's not dead, Seriza. Contrary to the news report."

"But how do you know?" Seriza asked. "Have you heard from him? Has the person you called from the house back there heard from him?"

Mike glanced at her, then placed her fork on the edge of her plate. "When I met Jeremiah, I fell head over heels in love with him. I've been falling ever since. He wouldn't dare leave me." She forced a smile.

Seriza tried to return it, hoping it didn't reflect the sorrow she felt for Rashid's mother. "Tell me about Rashid," she suggested.

"Rashid was a street kid fighting for his life and the life of his little sister against horrible odds in east Jerusalem. He was a man before he was ten, and Issa's first father. No one knows the things those two had to deal with—the hunger, the fear, the discouragement—and yet Rashid is the happiest, most carefree kid I know. Raoul is just like him." She paused. "And they both have minds of their own. We didn't want them to be by themselves during all this, but they wouldn't have it any other way. They're survivors: independent, hard-nosed, stubborn survivors. They fit very well in this family."

"Rashid loves you and his family. He speaks of Issa as if she were an angel."

"Issa can charm anyone. Especially the men in her life. And I don't know what I would do without her. She has never been sick a day in her life and has nursed all of us through colds, the flu, measles, mumps, broken bones, and a dozen other ailments."

Mike continued. "Issa missed the doll-playing stage of her life. She was with Rashid trying to survive on the streets. When Shai joined our family, she made up for lost time. They're best friends. You know how kids sit on the porch waiting for dad or mom to come home? Shai would make me take her to the bus stop to meet Issa. Winter or not. Of course, she still meets her daddy at the door, and her brothers, but Issa is special to her. To all of us."

"You have a neat family."

Mike laughed, pushing aside what was left of her breakfast. "You're getting a biased perspective, but I agree with you one hundred percent." She got up and started putting the dishes in the sink. Seriza went to the fireplace and removed the bucket of boiling snow water.

"Tell me about your family," Mike suggested as she started washing dishes. Seriza told her about her father and mother, her grandparents, her childhood, and missing her mom, her often strained relationship with her grandparents because of her father, and her doubts about her father really loving her.

"He loves you, Seriza, but some men have a hard time expressing it. My father was like that until after my mother became ill. The shock that he would be losing her woke him up to his negligence. The last months of their lives together were the best of their entire marriage. Sometimes . . . you have to lose someone, or at least be threatened with that loss, in order to understand how much that person means to you." Mike brushed a few tears aside before she could go on. "His leaving you with your grandparents was probably what he thought was best for you. I would guess it was a sacrifice for him. One that hurt very much."

"But why leave me? What was so important that he would do it?" Seriza asked, pain filling her voice.

"Men are career animals, or rather, some men are. They can't survive without work. It's their identity—the way they determine their worth to mankind. Without it they cease to exist as individuals. For some, that would be like death itself."

Seriza thought a moment. Her dad—his work—was it that important? Killing? In the back of her mind she had always suspected that was what he did for a living. A professional killer working for the government. But until Rashid had come along and forced her to confront those old bits of information, which she had accumulated in her childhood but had safely tucked away in the deep recesses of her mind, she had refused to believe them. What was her father? Good? Bad? Evil?

Seriza broke into tears, putting her face in her hands. Mike put her arms around the girl's shoulders, holding her close, letting her cry.

When her sobbing subsided, Seriza took the dish towel and dried her eyes. Mike took it and pointed toward the fireplace. "Would you put some more wood on. We still have a while before our ride comes."

Seriza poked at the remnants of logs and added a couple of new ones, then sat down, staring into the renewed flames. When Mike finished, she joined her.

"In my father's case, I hope you're wrong about men needing their work. He's a professional killer."

Mike turned toward Seriza, searching for a smile, something to show she was guessing. How could she know?

"You can't be sure of that."

"What happened with Rashid made me remember things from my younger years that I had forced from my mind."

"Such as?" Mike asked.

"Things my mother said to my father just before she took me and left—just before she was killed." She paused, her face sad with pain. "Over the last few days I have wondered if it was him who killed her."

Mike felt the hurt in Seriza's voice and wanted to say something but couldn't find the words. She stared into the fire, speechless, wishing the girl hadn't remembered her father's dark past. No child should have to be confronted with a father who killed human beings for a living. How could they ever have anything but sleepless nights?

"When I was . . . ten, I was allowed to spend a weekend

with my father. It was the last one I spent with him until I was nineteen. I had put it out of my head until yesterday when Rashid and I were driving here. During that visit, my father had to go out for an hour and I decided to be a big girl and clean up a little. In a closet in the living room I found a metal briefcase. Curiosity got the best of me, and I opened it. Inside was a gun. A rifle, in several parts, and some pictures of a man I had seen on television." She took a deep breath. "My father walked in on me then, took the briefcase from me, and put it away."

There was another pause while Seriza dealt with her feelings, which were now riding very close to the surface. "Two days later, after returning home, I was watching the news on television and saw that the man in the picture had been shot and killed by an unknown assassin. I started to cry. My grandfather asked me what the matter was and I told him. After that, he and my grandmother refused to let my father take me to his house again."

It was quiet for a few minutes and then Seriza spoke again. "It's funny what you force yourself to forget because you love someone. But I can't forget anymore. My father is a killer. He was sent to kidnap Rashid in order to get at your husband. He was hired to kill them. He's the one behind a lot of what is happening to your family right now. He's the one who took Rashid. He's the one who killed your husband."

The tears started to roll again. Mike moved to the arm of Seriza's chair and took her into her arms, comforting again. But what could she say without lying? Rolf Koln was a killer. One of the worst. She found it hard to believe that he could ever have given life to someone like Seriza.

"If . . . if Jeremiah is dead, your father didn't do it, Seriza. He wasn't in Washington." Mike knew it offered little comfort, but she had to try.

Mike heard the thump-thump of the chopper above the cabin. Seriza lifted her head from Mike's lap and looked toward the ceiling, listening, rubbing her eyes with the palms of her hands.

As Seriza stood, Mike spoke the only words she could find. "He loves you, Seriza. No matter what your father has done in his life, he could never stop loving you. Never."

Seriza wiped the last tear from her eye and forced a smile. Oh, how she wished it were true!

Chong's men watched as the chopper lifted off from the clearing outside the cabin and disappeared into a cloud bank hovering a few hundred feet overhead. They had found the girl's tracks two hours earlier and followed, but were too late.

One of them removed a radio from under his snowmobile seat and switched it on, pressing the send button.

"Storm One, this is Storm Two."

"Yeah, go ahead, Two."

"We found them, but they're gone. A well-armed Eagle chopper picked them up before we could get close enough."

No response.

"Storm One, do you read me?"

"I hear you, Dansy! Did you get a look at the person with the girl?"

"Yessir, a woman." He gave Chong a description.

"Where are you?" Chong asked.

"At the base of Hoback Peak, up Kilgore Creek about a mile."

"Get back to the main road. We'll meet you at the condo later, when we're finished up here."

Chong switched frequencies and called Colter, telling him about the Eagle picking up the girl. "Mrs. Daniels is with her," he said.

"Are you sure?"

"My men saw her, Colter. Track that chopper and you'll find everything you're looking for."

"Okay. We'll let you know. Stay there, Chong. You'll have to dispose of the hostages once we're finished up north." The radio clicked off.

Chong removed his Beretta and checked the clip. Another few hours and he'd be headed back to his ranch in another part of Wyoming, two hundred and fifty thousand dollars richer. He had his eye on half a dozen quarter horse champions. Now he'd be able to add one, maybe two, to his stables. Something to look forward to.

Chapter 18

Claire watched the chopper's radar screen. The Eagle with Michaelene Daniels aboard was nearly to Yellowstone Lake. It was time to go.

They had two Eagles of their own: choppers they had confiscated from Daniels's own hangar, well-armed, well-manned. Aboard each of these missile-laden Eagles was an assault team made up of six men, all well-trained and well-armed mercenaries whom Colter had used before. All with a penchant for violence and a lust for money.

"All right, Colter," she said into her headset, looking out the chopper's bubble toward the other Eagle. "Let's go."

Colter gave a thumbs up sign. "Roger. We're right behind you."

The pilot of Claire's command chopper pulled back on the stick and the Eagle jumped into the air. Claire had timed it so that Michaelene Daniels would have time to get on board the yacht. She wanted her there when the assault team boarded. That way everything could be finished at once.

She spoke to the pilot. "Keep us low; below radar."

He nodded.

She glanced at her watch: 3:12. If everything went well, she'd be in L.A. for dinner.

Ever since Koln's disappearance she had been apprehensive. In talking with her father, she had discovered the content of his last conversation with Koln. The threat was obvious and one Koln wouldn't take lightly. Rolf Koln was an extremely intelligent man. Coupled with an apparent talent for killing, it made him extremely dangerous.

But she couldn't worry about Koln. She'd deal with him when—and if—he ever showed up. For now she must concentrate on Mrs. Daniels. Her father had told her the details about Israel and Miami. All they had left was her responsibility at Yellowstone Lake.

She hadn't told her father about Koln's disappearance. He would have turned everything over to Colter. She refused to allow that. There was too much at stake, and now that she had control anyway, she felt she'd better keep it. Although she didn't consider Chong a threat at the moment, he could become one. By taking charge and proving herself now, she would be in a better position to eliminate the rest of Koln's team in the future.

Then there was the Super Commission. By her establishing herself as a resourceful leader with total control of the American business, they would be forced to accept her as an equal: an essential element to her future and the future of her father's family.

The choppers flew at fifty feet above snow-laden treetops. Clouds hung over the thick pine forests, but at a height that allowed visibility for miles. It was a beautiful, tranquil scene. Their flight to the lake would be a speedy but pleasant one.

3:15 P.M.—Snow King Mountain, Jackson, Wyoming

Trayco flipped the two Tylenol pills into the back of his mouth and swallowed. By the time they reached the cabin he expected the two red and yellowish capsules to take the edge off the pain in his arm. He slid his skis back and forth. The snow was sticky, but the newly waxed surfaces slid freely.

Koln leaned between his poles catching his breath. He wasn't sure how he was going to make it. The last few hours since leaving the hospital had given him time to think. His life was over. Whether it was ended by execution in a federal penitentiary or by a Cosa Nostra soldati didn't matter, he was finished. All that was important now was Seriza—and what she would think and remember of him.

Trayco had found out that Mrs. Daniels was with Seriza and that they were on their way to a place of safety. Trayco had guaranteed that Seriza would be protected, and Trayco was the best at protection. Koln couldn't ask for more.

Kenny Trayco had been lenient. In fact, Koln marveled at the man's restraint. Twice Koln had earned a bullet from Trayco. Twice Trayco had resisted.

Rolf Koln and Kentucky Trayco had made a deal. Trayco would care for Koln's daughter, and Koln would help free Jeremiah's family—even if it cost him his life. Koln felt like he had made a good bargain and had thrown in Luciano Buscetti as frosting.

He slung the Uzi's leather strap over his head, unzipped his jacket, and tucked the Uzi inside to keep it from pummeling him on the trip down. He carried half a dozen extra clips in the pack on his back.

Ruth slung the M-16A Plus over her shoulder using the strap. The Plus was the newest improvement on America's most noted combat automatic and the one she found best fitted to her needs. It carried a dual clip of nearly fifty rounds of ammo and, unlike the old model, seldom overheated.

Charla adjusted her goggles and glanced at the others. Each nodded. They were ready.

Charla knew her task. She had worked the back slopes of the Snow King resort since she was a child and knew every nook and cranny there. As a former Olympic hopeful for the American women's team (until she had nearly been killed in a skiing accident during a downhill race), Charla was the most skilled skier among them. She was to lead the others down the slopes and into position above the Hostetler cabin, nearly a mile below and to the north of their present position. As the only cabin inaccessible during the winter, Hostetler's place fit the bill described by the man Koln called Jackman.

It hadn't taken Trayco long to locate Charla. She was with friends in Kelly, but had called the number Jeremiah had made them memorize in case of an emergency. She had told Stockman where she was. It had been torture waiting for word about Bob, especially when Stockman told her about what was going on. Jeremiah's project seemed to be a mass of chaos and failure, its members fighting for mere survival. Now she was helping in that fight because it had become her own. She wanted her husband around long enough to help raise the twins.

She nodded to the others, then dropped over the nearly vertical cornice and plummeted across the short snow field and toward the trees, the others following in her tracks. Her eyes searched for the trail she knew was there, the trail that would get them through the thick stand of pine and to the snow field beyond. She saw the trailhead and veered sharply left, letting her momentum carry her into what looked like solid forest. She worked her way through the trees and down the sharp vertical slope, knowing that if she fell, the crash would slam her into unforgiving wood. She wanted to glance over her shoulder to see if the others were following, but she didn't dare. The slightest wrong move now could be a deadly one.

At the edge of the trees she veered sharply right and cascaded over another cornice, sailing through the air and to the field of white below. Charla hit the deep snow and sunk out of sight, then exploded out of the powder and began zigzagging across the second snow field. Now she could look for the others. She turned uphill and stopped. Trayco was only a few yards behind her and came to a halt just below her position. Ruth was just coming over the last cornice but came off it at the wrong angle. When she hit, she somersaulted several times, then, miraculously, came down with her skis still attached and kept coming. Charla found herself admiring the woman's tremendous athletic ability.

Koln hit the last cornice and caught a ski. There was no chance of recovery, and he slammed into the powder below, somersaulting, and rolling toward them, finally coming to a halt twenty feet away but buried by the snow. Quickly they sidestepped to his position, and pulled him free. He clenched his teeth and moaned with pain as Trayco tried to help him stand. Kenny let him lie in the snow to catch his breath. After a minute Kenny extended a hand again and helped him up.

"You won't make it through another fall like that, Koln," Ruth said. "We'd better go ahead. You can . . ."

"No. I . . . I'm all right—or at least no worse." He jammed his hands into the ski poles Trayco and Charla had retrieved and let them help him replace a ski that had fallen off. Moments later they were on their way again.

Charla took the second stand of trees more carefully. They were getting close to the Hostetler place and she didn't want to get careless. It had been at least ten years since she had skied this part of the mountain. It was off limits to normal ski traffic and had no lifts back to the top. If you skied it, you had to ski all the way down to Jackson. When she was younger, she had done it more times than she cared to remember.

She came to a stop behind a thick stand of pines, the others right behind her. They removed their skis and flopped themselves in the snow, their white clothing blending well with the snow around them. Crawling forward, they positioned themselves on an overlook created by a stand of boulders jutting out from the mountainside. The cabin stood in a grove of sparse cottonwood and pine trees two hundred feet below them.

Trayco removed the binoculars from his backpack and

scanned the cabin. There was some movement on the porch. A man with an Uzi. He moved the binoculars to look at the window of the cabin. It was an older cabin, the window a large, single-plate glass encased in dozens of twelve-inch by twelve-inch sections. He could see the four hostages sitting on the couch. Only one man was watching them. Trayco noted that except for one or two trees, the path from their position to the cabin was clear.

He signaled for them to back away, out of sight.

"It's like Charla said. Ruth, I'll give you and Koln ten minutes to work your way around to the bottom side of the cabin. There should be a door into the basement. Right, Charla?" She nodded. He glanced at his watch. "At exactly 12:30 I'll start down. Charla will follow once we've secured the place. Agreed?" They nodded, then moved back to their equipment. Moments later Ruth and Koln had attached military-issue snowshoes to their feet and disappeared into a thick stand of trees to the left. Trayco put his skis back on and worked his way to the overlook. Charla followed. He handed her his .45.

"Just in case," he said. They watched the house for several minutes, waiting. Trayco pulled the parka away from his watch: 12:30. Time to go.

3:27 P.M.—Yellowstone Lake

Stockman stared at the radar. There *had* been a blip; he was sure of it. He watched and waited for another one. Nothing. Was it his imagination? Probably. Minutes earlier Michaelene's chopper had landed on the promontory. He had been paranoid ever since, wondering if she had been followed.

The door opened behind him and Issa came in, a tray of sandwiches and drinks in hand.

"How are things topside?" Stockman asked. "Is Shai okay?"

"Fine," Issa said. "Is Mom coming?"

Stockman smiled. Issa had held up well. Even after being told that her father might be dead.

She had come to Stockman in tears during the night because of a bad dream, a dream about her father. Stockman had been forced to tell her what had happened. They had spent two more hours helping each other face the reality before dropping off to sleep; she on the couch, him in the chair across from her, his .45 in his hand. He wasn't about to let anything happen to anyone else in Jeremiah's family.

"Sir, there it is again," Stone said.

Stockman glared over Stone's shoulder.

"It was closer. I think we've got company."

Stockman stood. "All right, Mr. Stone. Let's be ready. Once they come out of those mountains, they can't evade the radar anymore. Get a position on them." He turned to Issa. "Go upstairs, Issa, and take care of Shai." He hesitated. "There . . . there is a gun in your parent's bedroom, in the closet."

"Dad's .30-30. I know how to use it."

"I wish I had someone to spare to go with you," Stockman said.

"I'll be all right," Issa said, forcing a smile. She placed the tray on a table and went to the door, her heart pounding. "Warn Mom."

Stockman nodded, then turned to the business at hand.

Mike heard the choppers as she and Seriza moved away from the Eagle and toward the Glastron tied at the end of the dock. The wind was still too strong across the lake to try boarding the *ISSA* directly from the chopper, so they had elected to take the boat.

Her heart was in her stomach, and a helpless, frightened feeling clung to her stomach as she quickly hopped aboard the Glastron, opened the jockey box, and removed a pair of binoculars. She was scanning the low-hanging clouds to the south as the Eagles exploded into view and swung over the lake toward the *ISSA*.

Mike threw the binoculars down and jumped from the boat, running past Seriza toward the Eagle. The pilot already had the blades turning, ready to lift off, when Mike jumped through the open door. Two seconds later they were in pursuit of the other choppers. As she placed the headset over her ears, Mike glanced out the door and saw Seriza standing on the dock, stunned. She waved her toward the Glastron. Seriza saw the signal and moved.

Mike spoke to the pilot. "Patch me into the Glastron, Jimmy. Then prepare your missiles. I don't want those choppers anywhere near the *ISSA*."

———————

Seriza watched the direction the chopper was going as she ran to the Glastron and turned on the key. Where was the radio? Mike would try to reach her by radio.

She saw it and flipped on the switch, immediately hearing Mike's voice. "Get to cover, Seriza. Do you hear me? Get out of the boat and find a place to hide. Now!"

Seriza frantically tried to figure out how the radio worked. Grabbing the mike, she pushed the lever on the side. "I . . . I hear you. Do you hear me?" It sounded so foolish.

"Yes. Seriza, do as I tell you. Find cover!"

Seriza hung up the mike and stared into the distance. The chopper was moving quickly away. She glanced at the key, then at the chopper, and decided what she must do.

Turning the key, she made the Glastron's motor rumble to life. She had driven boats before. Lots of them. This one was a piece of cake. Moving forward, she untied the rope, then did the same in the rear. Seating herself, she moved the gas feed forward. When she was away from the dock, she gave it full throttle. The sleek boat rumbled deep in its belly, then leapt forward with power she had never felt before. It made her adrenaline flow. She looked around her but could see little through the light mist hanging on the water. Which way! As the boat bounced through the waves, she started reading the buttons on the dash. She pushed the one marked "Radar."

A panel on the dash slid aside, revealing the screen. She pushed the power button and saw the display. There were four blips on it. One was stationary; that was the *ISSA*. She figured out that the arrow at the bottom of the screen represented the Glastron, and she turned the wheel, adjusting to a collision course for the *ISSA*. She'd be there in less than five minutes.

Stockman saw it all on radar. "All right, Cantera," he said to the steersman, "get us under way. Stone, use a zigzag pattern and make it difficult for them to catch us. I think they intend to board. I'm going on deck to prepare a little surprise for them. You have command." He closed the door behind him.

Stone watched the radar as the two leading choppers separated. Jimmy's Eagle would be forced to make a decision, but at least the *ISSA* would only have to deal with the one Jimmy didn't chase.

But Jimmy didn't follow either Eagle. Instead he moved toward the *ISSA*, placing himself between it and the choppers. Then Stone saw the other dot.

The Glastron had left the dock.

Mike saw the enemy choppers separate, but ordered Jimmy toward the *ISSA*. The enemy Eagles immediately turned and headed after the yacht, but kept their distance, avoiding confrontation but forcing the *ISSA* toward the east shore. Soon the yacht would run out of water. Mike had to do something. "Jimmy," she said into her headset, "challenge one of them."

Jimmy turned the stick and the Eagle sprang east across the *ISSA*'s bow. Mike grabbed the handles of the fifty-caliber machine-gun hanging in the doorway and tried to figure out how it operated. She pulled on the lever then aimed the thing into the water and fired. The gun barked and nearly jerked itself out of her hands. It worked.

Jimmy positioned the chopper twenty feet above the water and zigzagged, trying to keep the enemy from getting a missile lock with their computers, while still working out a way to get them locked on his. He saw the other Eagle turn into him and knew he and Mike were about to be fired at. He yanked on the stick and sent the chopper toward shore. The other Eagle fired from a mile away as Jimmy swept over the treetops. At the last minute he jerked the stick backwards and to the left, and sent his Eagle on a hard turn, up and away from the missile's trajectory. The missile flew by them and exploded into the trees and mountains beyond.

Mike hung onto the gun, trying to maintain her balance. She felt the chopper seemingly go out from under her feet, and lost her grip. Only the harness that she had secured around her waist and torso kept her from being thrown through the open door and to her death. Sweat poured down her face even though a cold, freezing breeze filled the chamber.

"Are you all right, Mike?"

"Yeah, Jimmy. I'm okay. Are they still coming?"

"Yes ma'am, but I'm going to swing hard right and come back at them at an altitude about twenty feet higher than the other chopper. You'll have a good shot with that fifty-caliber."

"Got it," she said, taking a deep breath and bracing herself. "What about the other chopper?" she asked.

"It's hovering," Jimmy said. They're unloading a raft. A boarding party."

"How far away from the *ISSA*?" Mike asked frantically.

"Half a mile. We can't get to them in time."

Mike's heart froze.

Stockman saw the chopper hover and the raft plummet into the lake's cold waters. With the binoculars he counted six men in thermal wet suits as they jumped into the water and climbed into the raft. He readied the hand-held TOW missile and braced himself as the chopper dipped its nose and flew towards them. In order for the smaller raft to catch the *ISSA*, the chopper had to disable the yacht. Stockman could see that was their intent. He wasn't about to let it happen without a fight. Out of the corner of his eye he saw the east shore getting closer, then felt the *ISSA* change directions as Cantera did a sweeping turn away from the raft. The chopper kept coming.

The Eagle would have to get close to maximize its shot. Stockman waited, knowing the TOW had limited capacity.

The chopper hovered, ready to fire.

Stockman pushed the TOW's button.

The missile thrust itself from the chute on Stockman's

shoulder and swept away from the *ISSA*. He held the sights on the chopper, hoping that the TOW would get there before the Eagle launched one of its own. As the TOW slammed into the Eagle, Stockman saw a streak of fire explode in his direction. At first he thought it was just part of a fireball created by his TOW's collision and destruction of the Eagle, but then he felt the impact as a Hellfire missile hit the stern of the *ISSA*. The shock made the huge yacht shudder, but it didn't explode. Stockman picked himself up from the deck and ran down the side of the yacht as it slowed, its huge engines quiet. As he reached the back of the vessel he saw that the back end was damaged and that fire was raging from the yacht's motor compartment. Grabbing an extinguisher, he began spraying the flames, fearful that the fire would reach the fuel tanks. Stone appeared out of nowhere with another extinguisher and they were quickly able to quell the flames.

Each glanced at the other, breathing hard, trying to catch their breath. Stone pointed.

"Look!"

Stockman saw them. The assault team was only a few hundred yards away, their weapons ready to fire.

Mike pulled the trigger as Jimmy swept over the oncoming chopper. The pilot veered away but the fifty-caliber bullets caught him in the engine. Black smoke and oil vomited from the machine and it began to cough and sputter. Jimmy swung in for the kill just as the raft was shoved from the door and six swimmers in wet suits and bags full of gear jumped for their lives. Mike pulled the trigger as Jimmy came alongside the chopper. As Mike's bullets ripped through the enemy Eagle's skin the motor shut down and the chopper hit the water without exploding. In seconds it sank out of sight, the pilot swimming in the frigid water.

"Swing around, Jimmy. We have to stop that raft. We—"

Their own motor began coughing and Mike realized Jimmy was trying desperately to keep them out of the lake. She saw the black cloud that trailed behind them and knew it was just a matter of seconds. She grabbed a life jacket and pushed the automatic release on the harness.

"Jimmy?"

"Go, Mike," he said, pulling on the stick and trying to get the Eagle to hover. "Go! It's your only chance."

Mike grabbed an inflatable life raft from the inside of the chopper and jumped. Her body hit the water at an angle that peeled the raft from her hands. The icy fluid took her breath away and she sank like a rock, her heavy winter clothes dragging her down. Grabbing the release on the life jacket, she felt it fill with air and pull her to the top. Coughing and sputtering, she looked around desperately, trying to locate the raft. There it was, just a few yards away filled with air, bobbing, waiting for her.

She started to swim, knowing she only had moments before hypothermia would start draining her of strength and will. She flinched instinctively when she heard the explosion. Glancing over her shoulder, she watched as Jimmy's Eagle hit the water.

Seriza saw the helicopter explode, then the missile hit the back of the *ISSA*, bringing it to a stop. The assault team in the raft was gaining quickly on the *ISSA*. She veered to the right and pushed the throttle as far as it would go. The Glastron slammed against the wakes, becoming airborne every third one and sending chills of fear up Seriza's spine as she imagined the boat flipping over.

The Glastron bore down on the raft, Seriza's heart thumping so hard it was making her teeth chatter.

One of the men on the raft pointed in her direction and aimed his rifle. Seriza jerked the wheel left then right as the gun spat flame at her. A hole appeared in the windscreen, then another. She ducked lower, but kept the boat at full throttle and pointed at the man with the gun.

At the last second the raft veered right, but the Glastron's hull crashed into its motor with a teeth-grinding crunch, then drove over and past the raft as men sprang into the water and away from the Glastron, out of harm's way. A hundred feet further on, Seriza swung the wheel hard and pulled back on the throttle, bringing the boat quickly around for another run.

Then she saw Mike.

The small, yellow raft was floating in the water, Mike lying flat on her back, exhausted, cold. Seriza spun the wheel and quickly moved alongside.

"Grab hold!" she yelled, while extending an arm.

Mike lifted herself up, took Seriza's offered hand, and thrust herself toward the Glastron. Seriza grabbed Mike's soaked coat and used all her strength to pull her on board. As Mike lay limp in the bottom of the boat, Seriza thrust the throttle forward and swung the boat around and toward the *ISSA.*

The yacht sat dead in the water, its deck empty. Seriza's eyes scanned the water's surface. The assault raft was gone, but the enemy had reached the *ISSA* and were swimming toward the docking ladder. She couldn't stop them from getting aboard.

Trayco positioned himself to go, gave Charla one last smile, then turned and jumped onto the steep slope leading to the house. The waxed skis quickly picked up speed and he plummeted toward the cabin, his body lowered into a crouch. As the man on the porch caught sight of him and turned to fire, Trayco pulled the trigger of the Uzi and sprayed the porch. The man flung himself over the railing and into the deep snow below. Trayco crouched even lower, making himself a human cannonball. As he hit the small bank of snow twenty feet away from the window, he put his head between his knees and became airborne, praying that his coat was thick enough and the glass dull enough not to cause any permanent injury.

Rashid heard the gunfire and looked up. He saw the white apparition plummeting toward them down the steep slope and knew what was intended. As Chong turned to face the window, Rashid launched himself into the man's back and knocked him to the floor, the window erupting at the same time and filling the room with a million pieces of glass and wood. The human cannonball on skis hit the wood floor, his boots releasing from their skis. He was thrust forward and did several somersaults before crashing into the couch where Rashid had been.

Chong began to scramble forward, looking for his weapon. Rashid grabbed the kidnapper's shirt and pulled frantically with both hands, holding him back. He heard gunfire in the distance but was occupied with grabbing Chong's hand as it reached for the weapon. Chong cursed and rolled right, throwing Rashid off balance and against the wall. Rashid scrambled to his feet and thrust himself on top of the gun as Chong grabbed for it. Something hit him in the back of the head, causing a sudden wave of darkness and nausea to wash over him. The strength left his body and he felt the gun being ripped out from underneath him as he blacked out.

<hr />

Ruth and Koln had approached the back door only to find it blocked by a thick bank of snow. Koln glanced at his watch and knew Trayco would be on his way before they could ever dig their way through. Climbing a drift to the first level he peered over the railing on it to find one of Chong's men facing him, gun aimed. Koln let himself slide down the drift as the bullets ripped the wood railing, barely missing him. He heard a crash of glass in the cabin, then a solid thump on the floor and knew Trayco was in the house. As Ruth ran around front and fired upward, Koln lowered his shoulder and thrust himself through a lower-floor window. The pain from the exertion was excruciating, but it grew worse when his body hit a solid object on the other side of the glass. He forced himself to scramble to his feet, only to find another of Chong's men on the floor, searching for a weapon. Using the butt of his gun, Koln knocked the man out cold.

Koln couldn't catch his breath, and he felt the blackness start to envelop him, a sharp, knife-like pain in his chest, the taste of blood in his mouth. He struggled to a door and forced himself up the stairs he found there. Something was wrong—the pain—inside, the burning in his lungs. He felt weak. Unable to pick his feet up, he tripped on a step and fell. Grabbing the rail, he pulled himself upward. He could hear voices on the other side of the door, but had no time for caution. He rammed himself against it, the doorstop shattered, and he fell headlong into the room. Chong stood there with a gun in his hand. In a blink of an eye Koln aimed his Uzi and fired.

Chong spun around from the impact of the bullets and crashed against the outer door. It gave way, and he fell backwards on the porch, gasping for air. Trayco came to his feet quickly and removed the gun from Chong's hand as the latter's eyes fixed themselves on the roof overhead. Chong was dead.

Ruth took the stairs from the basement two at a time and found Koln sprawled on the floor, his Uzi still in his hand. She knelt and took a pulse. He was still alive. Rolling him over, she unzipped his coat and felt for blood. There wasn't any.

Koln coughed. The blood gurgled, then appeared at the corners of his mouth. The rib had finally punctured his lung.

"We need a doctor," she said to Trayco as he reentered the house and went to Rashid's side.

"Yeah." He turned the young man over just as Rashid started to regain consciousness.

Ruth saw the others on the couch and went to them, quickly untying Bob, who untied the others. She returned to Koln's side.

"Chong had a radio," Bob said. "I'll call Harry Mason's chopper service. He can be up here in ten minutes."

Ruth looked up, nodding.

Koln coughed again. "Tell . . . tell Seriza . . ." The cough stopped him, the blood was thick and red, filling his lungs quickly. "Tell her . . ."

"I know, Koln; I'll tell her. Relax. We'll get you to a doctor."

Koln smiled, then closed his eyes against the pain.

Raoul saw Charla on the porch undoing her skis and pointed her out to Bob. Bob walked through the door and took her in his arms.

"What the devil are you doing here?" he asked.

"Guide service. Everyone okay?"

"Yup," he said, looking over his shoulder. "We're okay." He reached down and took the radio off Chong's body and tossed it to Madigan, giving him a frequency and call sign. "Call Mason."

Just then it occurred to Bob that two of the kidnappers were unaccounted for.

Billy Peoples had seen Chong break through the door and fall dead. It suddenly became clear to him that he had best get clear of the premises.

Earlier, while gathering wood for the fire, Haze had rummaged around in the shed looking for something valuable. He found a closet full of ski equipment. When Chong had gone down, he and Peoples had sneaked inside and each found a pair that fit.

Now it was quiet. Too quiet. Haze cracked the door a little and saw the woman taking her skis off on the front porch. He quickly closed the door.

"It's over, Billy. We've got to get out of here."

Peoples nodded.

Haze threw the door open and thrust his skis into the snow. Jamming his poles in, he pushed off and headed downhill toward the snow-drifted road, Peoples right behind him.

Both were good skiers but not great skiers, and when they hit the first thick drift, Peoples caught a ski and knocked himself into Haze. Both fell and rolled a short distance before righting themselves again. Scrambling to get reoriented, Haze looked up toward the house only to see a body hurling in his direction and catching him in the head and shoulders.

Peoples hesitated a moment, then shoved off with his poles and plummeted down the hill away from Haze and the opponent battling in the snow.

Raoul had seen Bob go over the rail and quickly came out of the house to see what was going on. When he saw the man escaping on skis, he grabbed Ruth's M-16A Plus and went to the railing. Using the redwood top rail to steady his hand, he judged for distance and wind, then fired. The bullet hit the ski on the left and shattered it. Peoples somersaulted, then slammed into a tree at the side of the road. He didn't get up.

"Nice shot," Madigan said, taking the rifle. "You bring 'em down, you retrieve 'em. And don't be long. The boy might freeze to death knocked cold in the snow like that."

He walked a short distance to the other end of the porch where Bob was finishing up with Haze. "Need some help?"

Bob looked up with a grin. "Not unless you want to skin him."

Madigan grinned back. "Not a bad idea. Good market for varmint skins this time of year. Bring him on up here."

Ruth stayed by Koln. Trayco joined her, kneeling on one knee. "Koln," he said.

Koln's eyes fluttered, then opened.

"Thanks," Trayco said.

"Your promise. Take . . . take care . . . of my daughter, Tray." His eyes closed, then fell open, glazed. Rolf Koln was dead.

Claire had seen the Glastron sink the raft, her men struggling for survival in the frigid waters. She waved at them to swim toward the *ISSA* even as she throttled her own raft in that direction.

Fifty-five seconds later two of her men were throwing grappling hooks over the railing and climbing the twenty feet to the deck. She opened her bag and pulled out two smoke bombs. Pulling the levers, she threw them on board, giving her men a chance to board unseen. The first reached the top before the screen had become thick enough. A shot was fired and he fell wounded into the icy water. One of the others reached for him to pull him into the raft.

"Leave him!" she said through clenched teeth. "Go! Now!"

Quickly her men climbed the ropes, fanned out on the rear deck, and began moving through the smoke. Stone fired shots from the roof of the bridge and knocked two men down. Incoming fire shattered the fiberglass windscreen and forced him down. Quickly he went down the ladder and took up a position facing the front of the boat where swimmers were boarding. He fired and the first one fell. He fired again as another poked his head above the deck, then quickly ducked. An automatic was stuck above the deck and aimed in his direction. He threw himself into a doorway and inside as bullets ripped into the thin wall where he had stood.

Stockman was waiting in a small locker storage area. When he heard one of the men come near the door, he swung it open, hitting the man smack in the face and knocking him to the deck, unconscious. As Stockman started to step out of hiding to fire, a bullet passed through the door and hit him in the arm, knocking his gun from his grip. He watched it clatter across the deck and slide over the edge. With pain shooting through his elbow, he ducked and ran for the yacht's main door into the living area. He felt the whiz of bullets around him but scrambled through the side door into the cabin and threw himself toward the gun cabinet. Grabbing another weapon, he quickly positioned himself behind the couch and readied the semi-automatic for firing. He heard a noise in the hallway and pointed the weapon with his good arm. It was Stone.

Stone saw the man at the other door and fired while moving across the living area. The man ducked, then raised up again and fired his weapon through the broken glass of the door. Stockman nailed him. "Come on," Stockman said. "Let's get out of here. Too much window!" Stumbling toward the hall, Stockman trained his weapon on the door, then the windows. They were quickly down the steps and into the command center.

"Where're the kids?" he asked.

"I couldn't find them!" Stone replied. "I looked everywhere I could think of."

"Me, too," Stockman said, grimacing with the pain in his arm as Stone wrapped it tightly. "At least the enemy will have a hard time of it as well. Where's Cantera?"

"Down the hall. If they come this way, we'll have them in a crossfire."

"Good," Stockman said as he stood. "Hold down the fort. I'm going after the kids. They've got to be in their parent's quarters."

"I was there, Dolph; they—"

Stockman was already gone.

Issa had never been so frightened. Her father had made their hiding place by building a false wall next to the closet. Only she and her parents ever knew about it, and her father had told her that if someone ever came on board, that was the place she was to take Shai—and stay.

The sweat poured off her face. It was so hot in the tiny space.

"Issa, how much longer do we have to stay in here. It's so hot! I need a drink!"

"I know, Shai, but, please, whisper. We have to stay here until Mom comes. We have to . . ."

She heard the sound in the room outside their secret compartment and put her hand gently on Shai's mouth. Issa's breath caught in her throat as the noise got closer and closer.

Then it went away. She started breathing again.

Her hand touched the warm steel of the rifle next to her. It was loaded. If she needed it . . .

She shook off the thought. Even though she knew how to use guns, she also knew she could never shoot anyone.

"Issa?"

"Shai, please . . ."

"I have to use the bathroom," Shai said, mournfully. "I . . . I can't help it. If I don't go right away . . . Please, Issa, I've got to go."

Issa didn't know what to do. She put her ear to the panel and listened. Nothing. Maybe it would be all right. Just long enough for Shai . . . and she needed to go, too. She listened again. It was quiet.

"All right, but you have to hurry. Right into Mom and Dad's bathroom, then right back here, okay?"

Shai nodded in the darkness. Issa listened one last time then shoved outward on the panel. It slipped aside. Issa's eyes started to adjust as Shai got up.

A woman stood in front of them, gun in hand, a smile on her lips.

Mike forced herself to her feet and balanced her freezing body against the back of the seat. She could see men boarding the *ISSA*. One fell, then another. One of them put his gun over the edge of the deck and she saw Stone dive for the door. After a moment's hesitation, the enemy moved quickly onto the deck and began moving toward the cabin.

"Go!" Mike barked. Seriza throttled the boat enough to move them through the water without a lot of noise. Mike opened the gun compartment and removed an Uzi, a .45, and extra clips. She handed the pistol to Seriza as the girl deftly swung the craft alongside the *ISSA*.

"I can't . . ."

"This is the safety," Mike instructed. "This is how you change the clip. These people will kill us, Seriza. That is their intention. My children are in there. They'll kill them, too."

Mike started up the steps of the rope ladder as Seriza pointed the gun past her, sweat forming in large beads on her forehead. If someone appeared . . . if she had to shoot . . .

Mike reached the top and peered over. One man near the door, his back turned to her. She forced her cold, chattering body to go forward across the deck. Her wet shoes squeaked and the man turned just as she drove her Uzi toward the back of his head. She caught him in the face; he crumpled. As Seriza appeared, Mike rolled the man over the edge and into the lake. She signaled for Seriza to pull up the ladder.

Mike moved to a porthole and sneaked a glance inside. Seriza joined her.

"Put your weapons on the deck." The voice was to their left. Mike felt Seriza's body go rigid.

"Now!" Colter said. "Or I'll kill you."

"You're going to kill us anyway," Mike said, her finger tightening on the Uzi's trigger. She turned to face the gunman, bringing the gun up slowly, challenging him.

"Don't press your luck, Mrs. Daniels. I'll shoot the girl in the legs first."

Mike tried to keep her face impassive but was sure she was failing. She had never felt such hate before. Her whole body shook with it, her mind burning to kill the man where he stood, to wipe out the evil that had come into her life, taken her husband, and threatened her family.

"You don't have a chance this way," Colter said evenly. "Even if you kill me, I'll get both of you. How are you going to save your kids then?"

With a great deal of effort, Mike forced her grip on the Uzi to loosen, and let it drop.

"Now, you," Colter said, looking at Seriza's pale face.

"You work for my father," Seriza said through tightly drawn lips. "I remember meeting you, at a restaurant a few months ago when I was in L.A."

"Yeah, I used to."

Seriza felt weak. The revelation overwhelmed her. Now she knew—no doubts, no more need to wonder—her father was the cause of all this wickedness. All of it!

She felt her knees buckle, felt Mike grab her arm and steady her, help her along, cognizant that they were moving toward the cabin door but unable to see through the water in her eyes and the blackness in her mind. She felt herself being lowered on a couch, heard voices around her as if it were a bad dream. She took deep breaths, trying to pull herself together. Mike didn't need this. She had to help, couldn't let herself be a hindrance. She grabbed the back of the couch and forced herself upward. Mike put an arm on her chest and gently pushed her back. Seriza didn't resist. She needed a minute more. She needed to make the blackness go away.

"Where are my girls and the others that were on this ship?" Mike asked.

"My men are doing battle with a couple guys on the lower deck. Now that we have you, we'll convince them to give it up."

"Your girls are right here." The voice was a woman's, and Mike turned herself in the direction from which it came. Shai and Issa stood at the door to Mike's personal quarters, pale and scared. The woman held a gun.

Mike stood and signaled to the girls to join her. Issa glanced at the woman, who nodded. Mike scooped Shai into one arm and put the other around Issa's shoulder, her eyes fixed, glaring at the woman with the weapon.

"Colter," the woman nodded toward the doorway, "Tell Mrs. Daniels's men that we have her and the children." Colter left through the hallway as the woman motioned with the gun. "Sit down."

Seriza forced herself upward, making room on the couch for the children. Mike sat Shai in Issa's lap but remained standing.

"What do you want?" Mike asked the woman.

"Your records, the evidence, that sort of thing. And Tony DeGuillio."

"Tony's dead."

"When?"

Mike didn't reply to the question.

Claire pointed her weapon at Issa. "When?"

"Two days ago." Mike told what she knew of the story at the Falls.

"Well, then, except for the evidence and your records, we have a clean sweep." Claire smiled. "We've beaten you, Mrs. Daniels."

Mike glared but didn't respond, her fists opening and closing at her sides, her adrenaline building, waiting. Waiting to crush the life out of the woman two steps away.

Dolph had seen the man take Mike and the girl inside, and he cursed softly under his breath. He had to come up with something! Quick! After a moment's thought, he climbed the ladder to the crow's nest and removed the mike to the onboard intercom. Stone was in the command center and Cantera would be in the bedroom at the end of the hall. He hit the buttons and spoke. Both responded immediately. Dolph could hear their guns firing intermittently as he told them the bad news.

"They'll try to force you out," Stockman said. "You have to give me some time."

"It's getting awfully hot down here, Commander," Stone said.

"How many of the enemy are down?" Stockman asked.

There was a moment's hesitation. "Four," Cantera replied.

"There are at least a half dozen more," Stockman said, adjusting his position, the pain in his arm nearly unbearable. "Can you give me five minutes?"

"Yessir," came the reply.

"All right, I'll try to give you a hand." He hung up the mike, unsure of just what he had meant. The only way to their position without coming into the direct line of fire was through the living area. At present it was occupied.

He got to his knees, his head spinning. He felt nauseated. There was a thick, dark spot on the rug where he had lain. He was losing more blood than he thought. Grabbing hold of something, he pulled himself into a crouch and went to the ladder. He checked the decks. No one. He started down, his foot missed a rung, and he slipped, letting go of the gun in order to catch himself. It flew out and away from his reach, cleared the edge of the ship's main deck, and fell into the water below. He was grateful it hadn't hit the deck.

He lowered himself down and moved to where he could peer into the main cabin through the small porthole near the kitchen. A woman in a wet suit held a gun on Mike and the girls but seemed to be alone. His mind focused intently on a way to get inside undetected. He glanced at his watch. Three minutes left.

He noticed a movement to his left. He turned and swung with his good arm as a man in a wet suit grabbed him, another man pinning his arm to the side of the ship and clamping a hand over his mouth.

"Quiet!" said the familiar voice.

Stockman smiled as the hand was removed from his mouth. He had never been so glad to see anyone in his entire life.

"Where are the records?" asked the woman, pulling the hood of the wet suit backward and shaking out her hair.

"Safe from the likes of you."

Claire sighed, the gun dropping to her side in exasperation. "Mrs. Daniels, you don't seem to understand the situation here. I'll kill your kids and Koln's daughter while you watch." She paused. "Then I'll kill you. It's as—"

Mike saw her opening and took it, crossing the short distance in a split second and tackling the woman, knocking the gun free and sending it skidding across the carpet. As they rolled over, grabbing at each other, Issa jumped from the couch and ran for the weapon. Mike came out on top and drove her fist into the woman's face, once then twice. Claire knocked Mike aside and scrambled to get the upper hand, her lip cut and blood flowing down her chin. Issa scurried around the chair and aimed the pistol.

"Stop!" Issa yelled.

Claire looked up and saw the weapon. Her face turned hard and she tightened her grip on Mike's clothing. She stared at Issa, daring her. Then her eyes darted toward a movement at the door.

Mike's heart fell into her stomach as she saw a man's wet-suited legs out of the corner of her eye. They stepped forward toward Issa, then past her. A hand reached for the woman, grabbing her arm and yanking her upward. "You heard the lady," Jeremiah said, flinging Claire toward a chair.

"Daddy!" Shai squealed, jumping from the couch, her face aglow. She wrapped her arm around Jerry's leg. He put down his weapon and took her in his arms, kissing her on the cheeks.

Mike scrambled to her feet, her mouth open, too stunned for words. Issa dropped her weapon and flung her arms around Jeremiah's waist as Dolph and Thomas Macklin pointed their weapons at a shocked Claire John, floundering on the couch. Mike's eyes darted from one face to the other, her heart swelling inside her chest, the tears seeping into the corners of her eyes.

"What . . . ? How . . . ?"

"A long story, sweetheart." He put Shai on the floor and raised his weapon at Claire, nodding at Macklin, who immediately headed for the hallway, Stockman on his heels. "Come on!" Jeremiah said. "We're getting off this tub. Get the kids to the Glastron. Seriza," he smiled, "you're as pretty as your picture."

Seriza stood, unable to speak. "My father didn't . . ."

"No, he didn't." Jerry's eyes looked sad. "Go. We'll talk when we're away from here."

Mike led the way, and the four were soon hustling down the ladder into the Glastron.

"But . . . you're dead," Claire said, her mouth open. "I . . . the explosion, the body . . . in Washington."

"A near miss."

"But who was in the car?"

"A thief. A stupid kid who thought he could make a few fast bucks selling the Bonneville for profit. I was coming from the building when I saw him duck down to hot-wire the car. I tried to sneak up on him." He touched a dark bruise on his forehead. "The explosion knocked me over two cars and gave me this and a few other cuts and bruises, as well as scorching my hair and setting my wool topcoat on fire. I was a bit disoriented, but managed to get away. A lady who had come out of her apartment building to see what happened helped me."

"But the president—" Gunfire erupted on the lower deck, then it was silent.

"Thinks I'm dead. So does everyone else. They think a lot of people are dead who aren't. That's the way I want it for now."

Claire stared as Colter was shoved up the hallway and into the living area, Macklin behind him. Three others followed. With Dolph, Cantera, and Stone shoving guns forcefully into their backs.

"Tie their hands," Jerry instructed. "Hers, too. We'll take the woman with us. The U.S. Air Force is sending a chopper after the others. Cantera, you and Stone take them back to Hill Air Force base and keep them under lock and key. No one is to know who they are or what has happened here. The dead are to be put in the cooler until you hear from me. Next of kin aren't to be notified until then. Understood?"

Stone and Cantera nodded.

Macklin finished tying Claire then helped her up. When Claire recognized him, she went pale. "But you . . . Israel . . . "

"Another miss," Jeremiah said. "We knew who the Hezbollah informer was at the hospital. We fed him some incorrect information. The plane was empty, operated by remote control. A ruse that allowed Tom to get Boudia out of Israel on an army transport."

"Then the Israeli in Miami . . ."

"Captain Akitsa may have problems, but one thing he isn't is a traitor. When he was contacted, they used it to set up their own disappearance. They're safe. All of them."

Claire's usual tanned face was pale pink, her eyes murderously hard. "I want an attorney."

"In time."

"Now! My rights—"

"Sorry, the phones here are out of order. Get her aboard the Glastron, Tom."

Dolph had fallen in a chair, exhausted.

"You okay?" Jeremiah asked.

Stockman forced a smile. "I figure I've got less than a pint of the red stuff left, but I'll make it. What now?"

"Macklin and I will mine the *ISSA*. As soon as everyone is

away, we'll sink her by remote control." He paused. "When you get to Hill Air Force base notify the press that the *ISSA* went down with all on board. Give them a list of names." He smiled. "I want the rest of you to join us beyond the grave. It isn't half bad."

Two Days Later
November 18, 1997

CHAPTER 19

10:00 P.M.—Palermo, Sicily

Luciano Buscetti stared into the fireplace. The Super Commission had been pleased with his report, but he was empty. Maria had disappeared, probably a fatality aboard the yacht Daniels had been using as his hiding place; and Luciano was filled with grief.

Information on what had happened had been slow in coming. With Maria and Colter out of the picture, his eyes and ears had been removed, and he was forced to be satisfied with news gleaned from remaining sources: paid informants in the government and the news media. But, gradually, he had understood the full picture and presented it to the Commission.

Daniels's forces had been destroyed, witnesses eliminated, evidence apparently destroyed in the blaze aboard the yacht on Yellowstone Lake. The president's office had been silent and there had been no replacement for Daniels. In fact, the president had been in seclusion at Camp David since the car bombing and had said little about anything, his presidency disintegrating under the pressure of a congressional clamor led by Cameron Ridgeway.

And Ridgeway had been a stellar performer. Using the media as a hammer, the senator had nailed Jeremiah Daniels to the wall and was getting ready, via hearings, to do the same to the president. The office of drug czar would be disbanded and its powers shredded.

Buscetti smiled. There was nothing quite like a power-hungry politician on the scent of blood. Especially when the politician saw himself as the next president of the United States as Ridgeway did. And, in fact, it was bound to happen. Public opinion polls regarding the handling of the drug problem were already dropping as the press rattled on about destroying Jeremiah Daniels and about the president's "high-handed, dictatorial methods of running the administrative branch of government." A direct quote from the anchor-woman on CNN.

But Buscetti was still uneasy. Daniels had made a lot of progress. The second wave of raids on storage and production facilities, the night Claire had called and announced Daniels's death, had been devastating to their organization. There was anarchy in the ranks and a lot of people were branching out on their own, reducing profits to a bare trickle. Another blow could put the Sicilian organization on its knees and create a chaotic war of blood among those trying to take over the remnants of the Sicilian business. If the takeover was successful, it would be years before drug sales ever reached their present zenith, and even longer before Sicily could gain control again. The Super Commission would not be happy with such news. The American market had been sixty-eight percent of present volume and moving higher. It was also providing the finances for them to move deeper into the Russian market, a major step before getting a solid foothold in the Baltic and Eastern Europe, where gangs and self-proclaimed Mafia organizations were so unorganized that they were pitiful in their accomplishments. So much potential. So much relying on his American operation.

He snuffed out his cigarette in the ashtray. Another week would tell the story. He had already made calls setting up new leadership to replace Lima, Alvarez, Boudia, DeGuillio, and Quintana, among a half dozen others, but there was a lot of discontent. The infighting would go on well into the next decade. In a few days' time he would visit the United States himself and do what he could to get things back to normal. It would take a lot of time, and it would be dangerous. The American families were not happy with the way things had gone and saw it as Sicily's fault. He would have to be careful, but he had no choice. If they showed fear now, they would lose everything. And it was what the capo dei capi would expect.

Now that Daniels was out of the picture, they could make new contracts in Colombia and Syria. Shipping lanes were being worked out and renegotiated. It was going to cost them billions, but in three months Buscetti figured they would be headed in the right direction.

Daniels had created a lot of chaos and caused untold damage to their operation. Thank goodness Daniels was gone!

Buscetti took a deep breath. There was a silver lining in all this. By their making Daniels, his family, and his organization an example, the United States government would have a hard time finding a replacement. Men like Jeremiah Daniels were few and far between anymore, especially in Washington. Most politicians didn't have the guts to buck special interest groups, let alone the worldwide drug trade. By eliminating Daniels, Buscetti couldn't help but feel they had also eliminated any future governmental interference, and if Ridgeway rode this wave into the oval office, their troubles were over. Of course, if further lessons needed teaching, it would be done, but for now he could see a potential for even greater power than before. By the end of Ridgeway's second term, they would be so solid that nothing could remove them. He must make sure the Super Commission understood the benefits of such a silver lining.

But had it been worth the loss of his own daughter?

He shook his head in an attempt to dislodge the grief festering in his heart like a huge sore. She had made him proud. Few men in the brotherhood could claim such a child. She had accomplished more than anyone could have dreamed possible; she had performed miracles.

He looked at the picture resting on the table next to him. He and Maria at her last visit, sitting atop the rock wall behind the house, wine glasses raised in salute. It was that day, three years ago, that she had left for America.

He glanced at his watch. An hour. The members of the commission would be coming for another meeting. He must shower and prepare himself.

He stood and walked toward the entry and the stairs beyond, turning the light off as he left the room.

The shadows created by the dancing flames in the fireplace glinted off the patio window as it opened gently, allowing the entrance of a man completely dressed in black, a silenced Beretta in his right hand. Moving to the chair just vacated by Buscetti, he lifted it, then attached a small microphone. Drawing several others from a black pouch hanging at his belt, he placed them at critical places around the room, then disappeared through the door as quietly as he had come.

Don Guiseppe Leggio was the last member of the Super Commission to enter Luciano Buscetti's spacious den. Buscetti closed the door behind him. Sitting on the couch were Tomaso Alberti and Cesare Marsala. Standing warming themselves by the fireplace were the brothers Michael and Joseph Ciaculli.

The man Buscetti feared most sat in the straight-backed leather chair on the left, his fat jowls folded around a smelly Havana cigar. Leonardo Greco had started as an assassin and worked his way up the ladder, his weapon opening many doors. No one was feared as much as Leonardo. His heart was ice, his spirit possessed by the devil himself. Buscetti hated to be in his presence and upon leaving it always crossed himself, fearful the man's evil would overtake and destroy him. Leonardo was the capo dei capi.

Buscetti, like the others, was dressed in a dark business suit, white shirt, and tie. His black shoes glistened from the reflected light of the overhead chandelier. Without wasting time, he began his report, watching the eyes of the others, waiting for some sign of approval or disapproval, but he saw none. He felt the sweat trickle down his side.

When he was finished, Leggio spoke. "You will meet the deadline for reorganization?"

"Yes. I will go to the United States in a few days' time. I will see to the entire operation."

"The cost?" asked Joseph Ciaculli.

"I don't know. But we will have to pull supplies from our European operations to meet demand and make people happy. We have to show them we can still deliver or they will go elsewhere. Everything is in disarray. It is nearly as bad as when we first began to organize things in America. We must start from scratch in some places." Buscetti shrugged.

"Will anyone else challenge us?" Leggio asked. "Will the government reorganize?"

Buscetti told them about Ridgeway and the silver lining. "If we choose to throw support behind the senator, we will control the administrative branch for at least eight years. Nothing will touch us after that."

Everyone waited for Leonardo Greco to speak. He rolled his cigar to the opposite corner of his mouth then removed it. "You have salvaged much Luciano, for that we are grateful. But we must replace you. We have no choice."

Buscetti's mouth dropped open, but he quickly closed it, trying to keep his eyes and expression impassive.

"None of this could be helped," Buscetti said evenly, sweat collecting on his forehead.

"You are wrong," Leonardo said. "James Freeman should never have been allowed to go as far as he did. Daniels should have been dealt with before his first month in office was finished. You knew his talents, his determination. You let it get out of control." He puffed on his cigar. "You broke other rules. Trying to establish your daughter in leadership without consulting with us was a grave mistake. She can never be accepted by us. She is a woman. You abused your powers, Luciano. You desire to fill my shoes by consolidating your family as leaders in the American part of our business. It disturbs me; it disturbs us all. I feel you cannot be trusted. Your greed must be punished; however, we wish also to reward you for salvaging the American operations. For that we will allow the rest of your family to live, but they are to be exiled from Sicily. If any of them show signs of disagreeing with this decree, all of them will be punished without mercy. You will tell them this."

Buscetti's eyes went to the floor as Greco walked past him toward the entrance. "How long do I have?"

"You have two days to get your affairs in order," Greco said, opening the door and walking into the entry. The others followed.

Buscetti sank in his chair as their bodyguards joined them at the front door, escorting them to their cars. The capo dei capi had spoken. Luciano Buscetti was a dead man.

Macklin punched the key on the recorder and rewound the tape.

"Would you like to hear it again?" Jeremiah asked Claire John.

"No. That's enough."

Colter had been easy to get to, telling Jeremiah and the others who Claire was and about her Sicilian father. With Koln's testimony to Trayco, Jeremiah had enough to make arrangements to fly himself, Macklin, Trayco, Gad, and other trained commandos to the island of Malta. They had brought Maria Buscetti along.

"What do you want?" Maria asked, running her fingers through her hair.

"I want a detailed report of the operation from top to bottom—names, places, contacts," said Jeremiah.

"In return?" Maria queried, her voice filled with tired sarcasm. "You're going to save myself and my father, right?" She laughed loudly. "No deal. I know what those men are capable of, Daniels. You can't keep us safe."

"You're forgetting something Maria," Jeremiah said, leaning forward across the table. "You're dead. I'm dead. Everyone in this room is dead. We'll stay that way until those men are prosecuted. You can stay that way for the rest of your life if you like. And we'll see that your father dies a similar death as well. Then he can make the choice with you."

Maria didn't answer, her mind reeling with the decision she must make.

"What about the rest of my family?"

"You heard Greco. They'll be safe for now. Once this is over we'll help them disappear. They can join you under new identities."

"You'll let *me* walk free along with my father and my family?"

Jeremiah smiled. "Not exactly, but you will be alive."

"In a prison I suppose."

"Minimum security. Because you'll both plead guilty, you will be sentenced privately. No press. No outsiders. Your sentences will be adjusted for your cooperation." He smiled. "You recently deposited five million in a bank account in Zurich. We'll spend some of it to make your accommodations acceptable. You'll both serve your sentence, then we'll free you. But understand that once you're out, if you step out of line, we'll notify your enemies of your whereabouts and you'll be on your own."

"How do I know you won't do that anyway?"

Macklin spoke. "You have our word, Ms. Buscetti. What more do you want?"

Maria leaned back in the kitchen chair. "Yes, what better guarantee do I have," she said sarcastically.

"Look, lady," Trayco said from where he stood against the wall. "We're going to go in there and get your papa, deal or no deal. We're going to put him on trial and let him take his chances. With what we have on him he'll be imprisoned. But he'll still be a target, and your Cosa Nostra friends don't like loose ends. We both know it."

"And if you don't agree," Trayco continued, "we put you on public trial as well. We have you cold, Maria. Murder, attempted murder. Colter is ready to testify and so are two of the others. You're another loose end." He paused. "Now! An answer if you please. I don't have all day."

Maria ran her hand through her hair again. She was exhausted. She knew she really had no choice. "All right. Get a tape recorder. I'll trust you, Daniels. But this identity thing works both ways. You break your word to me and I'll tell your enemies you're alive, and that your family is as well." She smiled. "Like you said, they don't allow loose ends."

Day Seven
November 19, 1997

CHAPTER 20

10:00 A.M.—*Washington, D.C.*

Mike watched as the two judges finished reading Maria Buscetti's fifty-page affidavit. Judge Carmine Corleone, a Sicilian by birth, finished first, laid it aside and stared into space, deep in thought. He was a portly, sixty-year-old man, and a survivor of wave after wave of Sicilian recriminations over the years. Twice he had been wounded in what should have been fatal shootings; he had even lost his wife to the death squads of the Cosa Nostra. His only child, a daughter, was in hiding under a new identity. For the past five years Corleone had been a marked man, going nowhere without protection from his six trusted bodyguards, who had also lost family members to the Sicilian Mafia; he was grateful for each day he lived, knowing it might be his last. Mike and Jeremiah had been in touch with Corleone since Jim Freeman had been killed. Carmine and Jim had worked closely before Jim's murder.

Judge Alfred Whitehead lowered the papers. As the judge responsible for trying cases brought to the United States, he would be the American Carmine Corleone. A widower with no children, he was a man of tremendous integrity and a hate for the Mafia and what it was doing to the world. Mike respected him like no other on the bench of the federal judiciary.

"You have them," Whitehead said with a slight smile. He sat half slumped in the chair behind his desk, the sleeves of his white shirt rolled up, his tie loosened.

"Yessir, we think so."

"Two loopholes," Corleone said with a soft Sicilian accent.

"She can't testify," Mike said. "I know that makes it difficult, but what she has given us has opened new avenues. We'll have plenty of witnesses when the day comes and tons of physical evidence." She paused. "Once we have Luciano, we'll have our prize witness. What you read in that affidavit will be nothing compared to what Papa Buscetti can give us. We won't need his daughter."

"But will he act as witness?"

"We think so. His daughter's life will be at stake; so will the lives of the rest of his family, not to mention his own. They gave him two days to take care of his affairs. But we won't be assured of his testimony until he's under our protection."

Corleone smiled; Whitehead leaned forward. "Two days?"

"Yessir, but there is only one left."

"And he knows it's coming?"

"He knows."

"But how can he sit idly by and—"

"Because he has been promised that the remainder of his family will not be harmed," Corleone said.

"And he believes that?" Whitehead asked, leaning back in his chair, incredulous.

"In the family, Alfred, your word is everything. It can get you killed, but it can also give you safety. They will not harm his family. He is a brother. They have given their word." He shrugged. "That is the way it has always been."

Mike stood and walked to the window. "I need those warrants, gentlemen. You've seen the evidence and read Ms. Buscetti's statement. To finish this we need to start rounding up the opposition, starting with Luciano Buscetti."

Corleone leaned forward, removing a pen from his suit coat pocket. Shuffling through the papers, he found the ones needed and signed them. Whitehead watched, then extended his hand for Corleone's pen.

"A historic moment, Carmine." He signed his stack of warrants then handed the pen back to Corleone. "Gold plate that pen and put it in a prominent place. It may have just changed history."

Corleone sat back in the chair, a broad smile covering his face. For the first time in years he felt there was a chance that the stigma of bloodshed and horror brought upon the country of his birth by men like Greco and Buscetti would be removed. He looked forward to sitting on the bench for their trials. He looked forward to it very much.

Whitehead handed Mike the last warrant. "That's a big one. You'd better get your hands on him quickly."

"Yessir." Mike smiled. "It will be a pleasure."

Danny grabbed another handful of iron bar and moved his wheelchair quickly down the hallway, Jan at his side. Two uniformed police officers accompanied them.

When they came to the door of Ridgeway's office, Jan took the warrant from her purse and waved it at her husband. "You do the honors."

"No, you. I insist." He grinned back, positioning himself to open the door for his wife.

"You twist my arm."

Jan and Danny had continued their search into FIBG and found Ridgeway buried deep, but clearly visible to the trained eye. The man had received money from FIBG on numerous occasions and had had several million stashed in the Caymans. It wasn't there anymore.

Then there was the testimony of Maria Buscetti. She had nailed his coffin so tight he'd never get out.

"May I help you?" the secretary asked.

Jan went past her toward Ridgeway's door. "Nope, but I'd start looking for a new job. Your boss is going to retire."

"But . . ." One of the policeman helped the secretary sit down, then joined them at the door. Jan opened the door. Ridgeway sat in his chair, feet propped up on his desk. The feet came down when he saw the uniforms.

Jan walked to the desk and handed him the warrant. "A gift from Jeremiah Daniels."

The cigar tipped off the end of Ridgeway's lip and fell on the desk. Danny spoke to the policemen. "You know where to take him. And don't forget to read him his rights."

They moved around the desk and took Ridgeway by the arm. He still hadn't been able to speak.

"Goodbye, Senator," Danny said. "Oh, by the way, the president says to tell you, he's called a cessation of the investigation of Jeremiah Daniels. New evidence. Have a good day." Danny waved as Ridgeway glanced back over his shoulder with an anxious look on his face, then disappeared into the outer office.

Jan bent over and kissed Danny. The war was almost over.

Day Eight
November 20, 1997

CHAPTER 21

8:30 P.M.—Palermo, Sicily

Luciano Buscetti drank the last of the wine, savoring the taste. It had been a good last meal. He glanced around the dining room. The chairs that were usually filled with his family were empty, the room quiet enough to hear a pin drop. He had put his family on a plane that morning. He glanced at his watch. By now they would be making a new home for themselves in the suburbs of Venice. A new life he had purchased with his own.

He stood and took the dishes to the kitchen. The cook was already gone along with the rest of the house help. Only his personal bodyguard remained, and he would be dismissed at ten minutes to nine. Buscetti's home would be taken by young Joseph Galante, his replacement in the Super Commission. Young, exuberant, competitive, that was Joseph Galante. He had already proven himself valuable to the Cosa Nostra by doubling profits in the European market over the last year.

Galante was well educated, smooth, and ruthless. A man with no soul. The kind of man the Cosa Nostra needed these days, it seemed, what with so much killing to be done.

It was rumored that Galante had set up his own acid chambers, patterned after the ones used in Palermo years ago, in which he tortured errant members of competing organizations. After severely torturing his enemies for information, he would kill them by slowly lowering them into a vat of acid. Twenty minutes later everything except the victim's jewelry would be gone. No evidence. The Cosa Nostra had changed in some ways, but in others it was just as violent as it had ever been. Possibly more so.

Luciano wondered if Galante had been given the contract on him. Or would one of the Super Commission do the job himself? He shrugged. It made no difference. Dead was dead.

Buscetti placed each of the washed and dried dishes neatly in their places before shutting off the light and going to the entry. Opening the door he found his last remaining bodyguard standing on the porch, ever vigilant. Buscetti handed him an envelope with his pay enclosed, then sent him on his way. The guard didn't question Buscetti's dismissal. The rumor of the change in power hadn't been wasted on the man's intelligence. He knew when to disappear.

Buscetti watched as the man vanished into the night, glad that it hadn't been his bodyguard the capo dei capi had given the order to. He had liked Salvatore Provenzano. He was a good boy—a good bodyguard.

He closed the door and returned to the den. There was a chill in the night air and he thought about starting a fire, then reconsidered. It would be a waste of time and good wood.

He looked at the clock on the mantel: 8:52 P.M. He sat in the chair that over the years had given him so much comfort. A good place to die.

Kentucky lay next to Macklin in the heavy shrubs a short distance from the front of the house, their black clothes and soot-covered faces blending in perfectly with the dark surroundings. Each of them wore a headset with mike for communication and had weapons with silencers.

Jeremiah and Gad were moving to the rear of the house and would contact Macklin as soon as they had gained entrance. Unsure of just how things were going to happen, the team had decided to take every precaution by having someone within shooting distance of Luciano Buscetti. At this point in time it wouldn't do to let the Cosa Nostra do away with the government's potentially star witness.

"Red One, this is Red Two. We are inside. Anything new from the hidden microphones?"

Two other members sat in a van half a mile from Buscetti's house and were monitoring what was happening inside, using the same mikes planted there two nights previously when the leadership had given Buscetti the bad news.

"Nothing," Macklin replied.

Trayco tapped Macklin on the shoulder. There was a car turning into the head of the lane at the bottom of the winding drive. A man got out of the passenger side and slipped a card into the automatic gate opener. The heavy steel swung inward.

"We have company. We're going to move in closer so we can deliver the package."

"Roger, Red One."

Trayco and Macklin waited for the car to pass their position, then followed, grateful for the cover Buscetti's personal forest gave them. They watched from twenty feet away as four men got out of the car and went up the steps. They didn't knock.

"Four," Trayco said into his mike.

"Roger," came the reply from Jeremiah. "We're down the back stairs in the kitchen."

Trayco pressed his headset closer to his ear, listening to the translation of the conversation between Buscetti and his killers, grateful that Akitsa understood the language. Macklin pointed to the car and started to move closer. Trayco removed his backpack, took out several items, then followed.

"He says hello," Akitsa said. "They return it. He offers them wine. They are grateful. Good grief, this sounds like best friends getting ready to go out for a fine meal and good entertainment!"

"Never mind the commentary," Jeremiah said.

"Just small talk now. Uh, here we go. The one called Galante says he's sorry but it's the Commission's wish that he take care of business. Buscetti says he understands, no hard feelings. Can you believe this?" There was a pause.

"Uh-oh," Akitsa continued. "Someone took out a gun. Buscetti says it isn't needed. Galante apologizes but it's only a precaution. Buscetti asks them what they want him to do. Go to the car. They'll take him to the warehouse." There was a pause. "They're coming out!"

Trayco glanced at the door as he shoved the box under the front seat of the car where it couldn't be seen, then quickly slapped a mike in the space between the floor and the back seat. Macklin was shutting the hood as quietly as he could; Trayco did the same with the rear car door. They disappeared into some shrubs just as the door of the house opened.

Buscetti and his associates walked down the steps and got into the vehicle. As they pulled around the circular drive, Trayco and Macklin dashed for the wall and were over it before the car stopped at the gate. They followed the car containing Buscetti on heavy-duty motorcycles with heavily muffled exhausts.

Jeremiah and Gad removed the microphones from the den, exited the house, and met the van at the main gate. Using the directions given by Trayco, they were soon gaining ground.

The route was direct; Galante's car was moving through the outskirts of Palermo and into her warehouse district. As near as Akitsa could tell, Buscetti knew where he was going and asked only that they be sure he was dead before they destroyed his remains. "There is fear in this man's voice, Kenny," Akitsa commented. "He knows what's coming."

"Yeah. Judge Corleone told me about Galante. He boils people in acid when he's finished with them. Some are dead, some aren't."

"Let's hope this works," Jeremiah said. "Nobody deserves a death like that one."

"They're nearly there," Akitsa said. "Push the button, Trayco."

Trayco took a remote from his pocket and pushed the button on it. Inside the Sicilian's car a clear gas exited from the container and entered the lungs of the five men. There was no immediate effect, but none was intended. Five minutes from the moment the gas entered the lungs all five would become disoriented and lose their memories and their physical strength—much as with a serious hangover from an all-night drunk. If they hadn't killed Buscetti by then, Jeremiah's team would be home free.

Buscetti felt the sweat trickle down the side of his face. Despite his resignation to his inevitable death, he felt the panic start to rise in his gut and the fear gnaw at his brain. He knew Galante. The man played at torture. Had Leonardo Greco given him permission for such a thing? He took a handkerchief from his pocket and wiped his forehead.

The car came to a stop in front of the warehouse. Galante's men opened the doors and pulled Buscetti out and toward the warehouse door. Buscetti knew what the inside of the place was like, knew the position of the acid vat, the ropes and chains used to lower victims to their annihilation. He felt the fear weaken his knees and make him nauseated. The men at his side each took an arm and lifted him toward the door, then through it. He tried to regain his feet, to keep himself together, and to face the inevitable with some dignity.

He was placed next to the vat. He felt strangely dizzy; his head began to spin, making him unsure of where he was, yet he was still cognizant that his hands were being tied and that a heavy rope was placed around his feet. His heart pounded against the front of his chest until he thought it would explode. His head hit the floor as his feet were pulled toward the ceiling. He screamed, struggled, and cursed Galante as he spun around on the end of his lifeline. The acrid smell of the acid was strong in his nostrils as he felt himself being lowered toward the stained, rancid liquid. His eyes were open, he knew they were, and yet it was dark. His strength was gone, but he jerked one last time before the darkness overpowered him.

Trayco lunged for the rope as Galante lost consciousness and let go of it. Macklin grabbed higher on the thick rope and yanked as Buscetti's head neared the vat, burning the hair that flowed downward from the unconscious man's head.

Jeremiah checked the other unconscious men as Trayco and Macklin swung Buscetti back to solid ground and released the ropes. Gad removed the man's watch, shirt, pants, shoes, and socks and tossed them in the vat, then flung Buscetti over his shoulder and headed for the door. Jeremiah poured a sack of beef bones into the water and watched the boiling stuff do its job. Trayco positioned the rope back in Galante's hands, then helped Macklin set the other two in chairs. He checked his watch.

"Thirty seconds. Let's go."

Jeremiah checked the scene for any last-minute details, then followed the others from the building. Trayco and Macklin hopped aboard their motorcycles and disappeared into the night. The others followed in the van.

Akitsa asked a question as Buscetti started to come around. "Won't those guys know they've been unconscious?"

"The disorientation has screwed up their ability to make sense of anything, to remember. As they come out of the stupor, reorientation will take place and they'll think they were just feeling a little sick. Hopefully the evidence we've left will convince them it was just temporary—something they ate. Without Buscetti's body, they won't have much of an alternative."

"Galante isn't about to go back to Greco and tell him he failed, especially without a body," Gad said. "He'll never be sure exactly what happened, but it would be suicide to make an issue of it."

Buscetti moaned. Jeremiah crouched beside him, put his arms behind his back and handcuffed him. After that he helped him sit with his back to the paneled side of the van. Buscetti was dazed and disoriented, unable to place any of the faces that hovered around him. He shook his head, then closed his eyes.

"A dream," he said. "I . . . I had a bad dream."

"Yeah," Jeremiah said. "Let's hope it only gets better from here on out." Then he read him his rights.

One Year Later
November 20, 1998

CHAPTER 22

10:00 A.M.—Northwest of Las Vegas, Nevada

The president watched as the chopper cleared the distant mountain, then swung down to the valley floor, skipping across the hot desert as it raced toward them. Minutes later it hovered, then settled to the earth, its blades immediately beginning to slow, its passengers disembarking.

The woman, her hair a dark brown and cut in a page-boy style, wore dark glasses and a stunning white dress of light, airy material.

The president hardly recognized the man who followed her. His brown hair was now blond, the graying sides gone, as were the prescription glasses. His charcoal suit was set off by the usual red tie and well-shined cowboy boots. As he stepped from the chopper he put on sunglasses. He turned and took the hand of a young girl, lifting her from the chopper as another tall, handsome man jumped to the tarmac. Between the two of them, they helped two other ladies down from the chopper's door. Then they all moved across the tarmac to join the president.

The woman extended a hand. The president shook it happily. "Michaelene, you look wonderful." He glanced at Jeremiah. "And you! The blond hair . . ."

Jerry glanced at Issa. "My daughter's choice. She said no one would be looking for Jeremiah Daniels under a California haircut."

The president leaned down and took Shai's hand. "Glad you could come, young lady. I hope you enjoyed the trip."

"It was fun," Shai said, her eyes wide. "Are . . . are you really the president?"

"I am." He pointed toward his limo driver. "If you don't believe me, ask him."

Shai smiled then moved toward the driver, who was opening the front limo door on the passenger side. "Is he?" she asked as she seated herself.

The driver smiled, looking in the direction of the others. "At least until the election two years from now," he said with a smile. He looked at Shai. "You select the music for our trip will you? There are some CDs in the case between the seats." Shai started looking.

Meanwhile, the president reached for Raoul's hand. "It's good to see you, Raoul. I hope your glorious mountains are still as beautiful as ever."

"They are, sir," Raoul said, shaking the extended hand. "Are you still planning to hunt with us in the fall?"

"Only a world war would keep me away." He grinned. "Come on. Let's get out of this heat." They moved to the limo and were quickly seated in its comfortable facing seats.

"Mommy," said Shai, looking over the back of the front seat while putting on a set of headphones. "They have my favorite music!" She settled into the front seat as the driver put the limo in gear and moved toward the exit between two other vehicles carrying the president's Secret Service contingent.

"Nice to see you, Seth," Michaelene said sincerely.

"You're looking tanned and well, Mike. And beautiful. If you weren't married . . ."

"She is," Jerry said, fielding the grins from the three young people sitting opposite them. "As married as any woman I know. How are things in Washington, Mr. President?"

"Good. Not great, but good."

The car pulled onto the main highway and moved southeast toward Las Vegas.

"This is a great day, Jerry," the president said.

"Yes. A red letter one," Jeremiah responded.

"How are the others? Trayco, the Macklins . . ."

"Safe, and happy," Mike said. "They're meeting us here."

"Kenny has a new wife," Jerry said.

"And the Macklins have a new baby," chimed in Issa. "A boy. They adopted him last month."

"That's wonderful," the president said sincerely.

"Yes," Mike agreed, looking at her children. "It is."

"Trayco married the woman he met in the middle of all the ruckus," Raoul added. "The one who saved him at the Falls."

"Kate Meadows?" the president asked. "They were married a month after you dropped out of sight, weren't they?"

"Yeah. They've been living in England."

Mike laughed lightly. "In a castle, if you can believe it."

"A castle?"

"Yup," Jerry said. "Kenny said Kate thought he was her knight in shining armor so . . ."

"He bought a castle." The president laughed.

"It's been a good hiding place," Jerry said. "We visited them a couple of times. They're very happy but tired of the hiding."

"All of them are meeting us, I assume?" the president asked.

"Yes, they wouldn't miss it."

"Any problems in your new quarters?"

"None," Jeremiah said. "After a year of city hopping, it's been a nice change of pace. Almost like home." He smiled.

"You were raised there, weren't you?" the president asked.

Jeremiah nodded. The Lee Creek safe house in the north end of Teton Valley belonged to a good friend who taught at Ricks College and was within a year of retirement. Secluded and peaceful, it was very much like their home in Jackson.

"We're looking forward to going home," Mike said, reading her husband's thoughts.

The president glanced at Seriza. "How have you been, young lady?"

She smiled. "Good."

"You've been in the Ukraine?"

Seriza glanced at Raoul. "Yes, Raoul and I have been working with the Peace Corps, teaching English."

Raoul responded to the president's quizzical look. "It was a good way to disappear while she waits for Rashid to get back from his mission, and I was there on mine. I wanted to see the people again. No better time than when you're being hunted." He glanced at Seriza. "Now she speaks the language better than I do."

"I'm going back for another year," Seriza said.

"And you?" the president asked, looking at Raoul.

"Back to the ranch. Dad has a thousand head of cattle coming in this week. We'll be busy."

"Where is Rashid?" the president asked.

"In Romania," Mike said proudly. "He's doing fine."

"Under an assumed name, I take it."

Jeremiah smiled. "Nope, but where he is even the Cosa Nostra couldn't get to him. A little village high in the mountains." Jerry laughed. "He loves it."

There was a long pause.

"The *New York Times* . . . Buscetti took the stand in Sicily?" Mike asked.

"When he found out Galante had been instructed to kill him slowly, he burst a blood vessel. Of course, seeing his daughter alive and knowing her future depended on his compliance with your proposal did him a world of good as well."

"I'll bet," Jeremiah said. "Will Greco and the others get the death penalty?"

"The people are demanding it. Your evidence, Buscetti's testimony—highly damaging."

"Any word on Galante?"

"He's never been found. It's suspected he was the last to die in that acid pool you saved Buscetti from. There is a lot of shuffling going on in Palermo. With the Super Commission in prison and the police rounding up their soldiers, a few entrepreneurs are trying to start something for themselves. The government is adamant about stopping them."

The president looked at Seriza. "Have you seen your grandparents since your father's body was returned to L.A. for burial?"

Seriza looked out the window. "Yes. I told them everything." She smiled. "They helped me take care of the burial. He's next to my mother." Her work in the Ukraine had given her time to deal with her father's past . . . and with his future. She had arrived at a level of peace for which she was grateful. The nightmares had gone away and good feelings had replaced the confusion of whether she could hate or love Joseph Maxwell.

The president leaned forward. "After having a long talk with your grandparents, I had my director at the CIA do a full investigation into your mother's death. There were five men involved. Only one was still living." Seth Adams leaned back in his seat. "I know this isn't much consolation, but he'll be tried next month. The evidence is solid. He'll go to prison."

Seriza smiled. It didn't matter anymore.

"Alvarez, Lima, the others?" Mike asked.

"They go to trial next week. They won't see the light of day for a long time. With the use of their files, the DEA has dismantled their organizations. We'll be prosecuting for the next two years. Under the new laws, passed after my revelations before the special session of Congress, most of them will never get parole." He sighed. "We're a long way from finished. But we're organizing internationally again. That will help. Eventually we'll get there. Even the hardliners, whose economies are being dealt a horrific blow by the lack of illicit drug traffic, are coming around as other nations pitch in economic aid for the development of new crops and markets."

"Progress will be slow; it may even go backward from time to time, Seth. We'll always have the battle."

"True, but it sure feels good to be moving forward again."

"What about the addicts that aren't getting supplied anymore?" Mike asked, as the Las Vegas skyline came into view.

"Rehab centers and hospitals are deluged, of course. The problem was out of control, the sickness an epidemic. The cure will cost the American taxpayer millions."

"The price of a drug-free society," Mike said. "Let's hope it's a temporary cost."

"Crime?" Jeremiah asked.

"The cost of a fix has soared so people either get help or get money. Crime is up, especially robbery."

"Low-cost drugs did have their good side, didn't they," Jeremiah replied.

"Just a different face on the crime," the president responded. "Addiction in this country was our worst sickness. From it, AIDS and other sexually transmitted diseases were raging out of control. Thousands were dying and continue to die from it. Even worse, the age of the hardened addict had fallen from late teens into midteens, even preteens. And more were becoming addicted. Another generation like that and our society would have been a complacent, maladjusted bunch of coke heads unable to work a job or feed themselves. The welfare rolls would have grown, medical problems would have soared, more infectious diseases would have evolved."

"We still have a long way to go," Mike said.

"I'm not sure we'll ever be a totally drug-free nation again, but we've definitely made a big step in the right direction." He paused. "By the way, Europe and the other countries have learned a lesson from our sad experience here. They're taking a very hard look at what you've shown them about the Cosa Nostra and its worldwide organization. They've begun an eradication program, and are working very hard internationally to bring pressure on drug-producing countries to solve their problems. Financial aid from France, Germany, and a dozen others has been forthcoming as an honest attempt to help those countries make a new direction for themselves."

"Issa," the president changed the subject. "You've grown up."

Issa smiled. With her fifteenth birthday just a month away she had matured—physically and emotionally. Even though she was not Mike's flesh-and-blood daughter, they looked very much like each other, right down to the page-boy haircut.

"You'd better watch her carefully, Jeremiah. The boys at Jackson High . . ."

Jeremiah lifted his eyebrows. He was discovering that raising a teenage daughter whose interest in boys was quickly flowering was not as easy as raising boys. "Yes, I know."

"What happened to Ridgeway?" Raoul asked.

The president's brow furrowed. "The federal grand jury indicted him on the Buscetti testimonies. He'll be imprisoned. Even the sharpest attorneys can't help him. In fact, several firms have refused to take his case. The sad part is the numbers of others he's bringing down with him. By the time his trial is over I suspect we'll have a couple dozen congressmen in serious trouble. Every branch of government was affected. It's been a game of dominoes—one falls and the rest tumble after him. I won't promise that we'll be rid of corruption in Washington—you'd have to close us down to accomplish that—but we're definitely ridding the ship of a few of the rats."

As they entered the outskirts of Las Vegas, Mike remarked at how much the city had grown since she and Jerry had met there years ago. They drove past the Meadows Mall, then turned right on the I-15 freeway and went to the Sahara exit. Shortly thereafter they were parked at the back entrance to Jerry's old office building.

"You're sure you want to do this?" the president asked.

Jerry glanced at Mike, then the others. "We're sure."

"And Trayco and Macklin?"

"Sure. We all believe that in order to show that the Cosa Nostra can be beaten we have to go public."

"You're issuing a direct challenge. They'll send more men after you."

"Yes, they might," Mike said. "But hiding isn't our forte, Seth."

"No, I don't suppose it is. Well, all right. We have tight security. The press was notified, but were told it was just another political stump by the president for his economic reforms. You're going to shock the pants off some people. What with all the rumors that have been going around."

Ever since Jeremiah had blown up the *ISSA* the winds of journalism had been rife with rumors about what had really happened. Most of the enemy soldiers on the lake that day had been given reduced sentences for keeping their mouths shut about who had survived and who hadn't, but the rumors still persisted. Now the rumors would come to a screeching halt.

"Give us a moment?" Jerry asked.

"Sure. I have a couple of senators I need to talk to." The president opened the door, then turned back. "I thank you all, for your country as well as for myself. What you did . . . well, I've come to feel for your sacrifice." He looked at Seriza. "Your father's life . . ." He hesitated. "What he did at the end . . . It made up for a lot of things." He looked at Mike and Jeremiah. "Your lives will never be the same." He leaned over and kissed Mike on the cheek, then shook Jerry's hand. "My door is always open to you. This country will never forget."

He stepped into the heat and closed the door. They watched as he was surrounded by security guards.

"He's insisted on giving us some of those."

"No, thanks," Raoul said.

"For a while."

"Okay, a month," Issa said, smiling.

"Four," Jeremiah responded.

"Two," Raoul said.

"Three," Jeremiah countered.

"That's all, not a day longer?" Mike verified.

"Not a day."

He looked at each of them. "I love you all."

They smiled. Shai was kneeling on the front seat now, the headset removed. Raoul caught her as she slipped over the back of the seat and into his lap. Then she sat between her parents.

Jerry kissed her on the forehead. "You go with Raoul. Mom and I need a minute." He looked at Raoul, who got the message and opened the door, letting Seriza and Issa out, and taking Shai by the hand.

"We'll see you in a few minutes," Jerry said. "Find Kentucky and the Macklins. Let them know we're here."

Raoul nodded and closed the door. They were immediately surrounded by Secret Service men and women.

"It'll be okay, won't it?" Jerry asked. "The kids' lives . . ."

"Yet they did not fear death;" Mike responded, "and they did think more upon the liberty of their fathers than they did upon their lives; yea, they had been taught by their mothers, that if they did not doubt, God would deliver them."

"That's what you were doing up last night?"

"A little soul-searching. I'm afraid—not for myself, but for them. They would never be happy hiding for the rest of their lives, and yet I know the brutality of the Cosa Nostra."

Jeremiah smiled. "I talked to Luciano Buscetti."

Mike waited.

"He told me there were no guarantees, but that he didn't think they would harm the kids."

"Why not?"

"They live in fear of retaliation themselves. They have children and grandchildren of their own. Buscetti says they know I can reach them."

"But you wouldn't."

"He says they don't know that." Jeremiah smiled. "Buscetti and I have reached a mutual understanding. We'll do our best to protect each other from a common enemy. Through his people he is spreading the word that my family is off limits, that I 'can reach right down into the very depths of their lives and rip out their hearts.' His words, not mine."

"It's the only language they understand, isn't it?"

"Yes, and I'm not sure that I wouldn't go after them if they harmed any of the kids. No, actually, I'm sure I would. I hope they believe Buscetti's rumor." He took a deep breath. "It's time to go in."

"Jan and Danny?"

"The only ones not really known to anyone. I told them under no terms were they to show their faces around this place today."

"They'll be here."

"Yeah. Jan wouldn't miss the fun, and Danny would want to be with her."

They were both silent.

"I'll be glad to get back to the ranch and a normal life," Jerry said.

"Me, too." She leaned toward him, pulling his chin toward her, then kissed him gently on the lips. "I love you, Jeremiah."

"And I, you, Mrs. Daniels." He paused, relishing the warmth and love that passed between them and made him tingle.

"Come on," he whispered. "Let's get it over with before we chicken out."

Mike pulled back on his arm as he reached for the door. "Kiss me."

He smiled. "Again?"

She poked him in the ribs, hard.

"Uhh. My pleasure." They kissed gently.

"Thank you."

"You're welcome. Anytime, actually. Want another?"

"Not for the kiss, but for being the man you are. Thank you for . . . for fighting for us."

He reached for the door handle, his eyes catching a view of his children as they stood in the window beside his friends; then he looked over at his beautiful wife. "Some things are worth fighting for."

They got out of the car and started up the walk arm in arm. The children met them at the door and the press collapsed around them. The flashbulbs stunned their eyes, the questions made it a circus.

After a year of bored seclusion, life for the Daniels family had returned to normal.